MOON WARS

PAUL BELLOW

Published by Level Up in the United Kingdom in 2021

Cover illustration by Sippakorn Upama
Cover by Claire Wood

ISBN: 978-1-83919-353-8

www.levelup.pub

AUTHOR NOTE

I'd like to thank Conor Kostick and everyone else who helped make *Moon Wars* a reality. As a fan of LitRPG books and RTS games, writing this novel was a labor of love. You can occasionally find me on the battlefield playing matchmaker in Zero-K, a free RTS available on Steam. If you check it out, tell them Paul "The Lobster" Bellow sent you. I hope you enjoy reading this book as much as I enjoyed writing it.

– Paul Bellow

CHAPTER 1

Eyes glued to a glowing computer screen, I blocked out the sounds of loud music and laughter at the party going on elsewhere in the house I shared with six other students. My body tensed as the game music changed in front of me. Using my mouse, I selected a group of knights to prepare my final assault on my opponent's weakest flank.

While the *Age of Empires II* tournament I'd signed up for wasn't official, I had followers on the forums I didn't want to disappoint with my performance on the battlefield. WarTurn007 had almost beat me, but a bit of good micro on a hill a few minutes earlier had given me a window of opportunity I planned on using to my advantage.

"Come on," I muttered, my mind darting over the half-dozen data points I was trying to follow on the screen.

Hunched over in my chair, wrapped up in the game, a female voice barking orders over my shoulder startled me.

"You forgot to defend your left treeline! He's coming for you! You need that wood. Don't fall for it."

"The party's outside, not in here," I said, not turning around to acknowledge her despite my curiosity.

1

"I know," the mysterious woman said, not leaving.

Once again, I turned my entire focus to the game. The worst part was that she was right. Whoever she was, she knew a thing or two about real time strategy games. I rerouted half my knights to the other side of the map, knowing they would be too late to stop me from taking massive damage to my economy.

"Ring the Town Center bell!"

"Give me a minute!" I shot back, disliking my backseat player yet still thoroughly intrigued.

"You need to get some villagers on stone now if you want to finish this game."

"Do you want to play for me?" I quipped.

"Scoot over."

I sighed as she pulled up a nearby chair. My *D&D* group usually met in my bedroom at Hudson House, so I had quite a few spare seats available.

She pointed to the screen, brushing against my arm. "Your right flank!"

I couldn't help noticing her long, thin fingers and lack of nail polish. Who was this woman and why had she burst into my room? I pushed the questions aside as I tried to get back into the game and salvage what I could. Losing to WarTurn007 was even less of an option with someone in my room watching me play.

"There you go," she said, after I'd made a flurry of quick decisions. "You're not half bad."

"Let's see how you play with someone dictating orders from the sidelines."

She stayed silent as I regrouped my growing mass of Hun knights. Thanks to having taken her earlier advice about stone, I had just enough of the resource to plop a castle outside the weakest part of WarTurn007's outer defenses. The height of the hill and a few trebs would help me break through his Persian walls and do some damage inside his main base.

"Who are you, anyway?" I asked; the game had turned in my favor and I could probably play this out from here, relying on my automatic responses to WarTurn007's efforts.

"Haley," she said. "You're Alex, right? Tom said you were in here playing some war game, so I thought I'd see what is keeping you so busy when there's a rager going on outside."

I nodded, still focusing on the screen. "Tom's parties aren't really my thing."

"Mine either, but it's the weekend and we're in college. Not to mention the world ending because of Y-two-K."

I snorted and craned my neck to steal a glance at her: long, curving red hair; green eyes; sharp cheekbones, the whole face somewhat equine. Pretty, though. "Oh, wait, you're in my English two-o-two class, aren't you?"

"Yeah," she said. "You're the weird, quiet one that's always late, right? Now I know why."

Silently, I continued my assault on WarTurn007's base, waiting for him to surrender. The 'gg' was inevitable at this point.

"Just teasing." She lightly bumped her shoulder into my arm. "Loosen up. You need a drink. Come join the rest of the party."

"I'm fine, thanks…"

We both grew quiet as the game music lowered its intensity near the end of my siege. I still had a sizable force of knights with more on the way. My castle drop had denied him his last bit of gold, making it even more difficult for him.

"Incoming gg," Haley said.

"One would think…"

Right after the words came out of my mouth, the two letters appeared on the left-hand side of the screen: 'good game' typically meant you knew you had been bested, a sign of surrender. A few seconds later, another message flashed on the screen, signaling that he had resigned and forfeited the game.

"Yeah!" I sat up, full of adrenaline as I quit and entered the lobby.

A few congratulatory messages scrolled by.

"Alex-fortytwo, huh? Imaginative name."

"I like to keep it simple," I replied, still staring straight ahead.

"Now that I know, maybe we'll meet on the battlefield."

"Yeah…" I finally swiveled around to face her, meeting for the first time the full force of her green eyes. "You play a lot?"

"Too much for my own good." She smiled, the glow of the computer monitor giving silver highlights to her red hair.

Her beauty intimidated me a bit, but I felt drawn to her type: her forthright and brash character was so different than mine.

"I usually play *Total Annihilation* more often than *Age of Empires*, but this crazy WarTurn-o-o-seven guy has been trash talking in chat for over a week now. I had to teach him a lesson."

"That you did…" Her face scrunched up. "What's going on with your computer? Maybe this Y-two-k thing is real."

I turned around. The game lobby had disappeared, replaced with a simple command line interface straight out of the *War Games* movie.

"That's weird…" I moved my mouse, not seeing a cursor.

Letters appeared.

QUE: Hello…

"Answer him," Haley said, nudging me on the shoulder.

I typed out 'hello' in response.

"Did Tom put you up to this or something?" I asked her; it didn't make sense that the machine was acting up. But I hadn't seen her touch it.

"What? No…"

Both of us became entranced with the tiny glowing letters that continued to appear.

QUE: Nice game. Would you like to play something a bit more complicated?

ALEX42: Who is this?

QUE: I'm just a human guy, with a game he wants you to try.

"Interesting," Haley said. "Just a human guy? That's an odd thing to say."

"Does he always speak in rhyme? That would be pretty lame."

Haley chuckled, a lovely, genuine sound I wanted to hear again.

QUE: Are you still there? Did I lose you?

ALEX42: I'm still here. I don't play 'games' from strangers on the internet. How did you hack my computer?

5

QUE: No worries. I'll find someone else if you're not brave enough.

"This guy is manipulative," Haley noted. "But you're not the type to be drawn in by challenges to your manliness, right?"

I sighed, not enjoying having to formulate a response to her question and the guy on screen at the same time. After a moment, I leaned back over the keyboard.

ALEX42: What's the game?

QUE: Ah, your interest is piqued! I see I made a good choice. After watching your last AoE2 game, I wasn't so sure.

"Damn," Haley snorted.

"Everyone's gotta be a trash talker…"

ALEX42: Funny. What's the game?

QUE: Straight to the point. I like you even more. The game is called *Moon Wars*, and there's nothing else like it available on the market. My employer is looking for people to beta test the game before we go live. Would you like a copy?

ALEX42: Sorry, I don't accept software from strangers…

QUE: I'll mail you a copy on a new computer, so you don't have to worry. Is that okay?

ALEX42: A new computer… Is this, like, a scam to find out my address? Are you some player I've annoyed?

QUE: Not at all. I have your address. Alex Carter at Hudson House in Athens, Ohio, correct?

"How the hell does he know my address?"

"That's definitely weird," Haley added.

ALEX42: Who are you? How do you have my address?

QUE: No worries. Gotta go. Computer is on its way. Power is goi…

The black screen flickered, replaced by the *Age of Empires II* lobby.

"Whoa," Haley said. "That just happened, right?"

"I'm not sure. Glad you were here to see it too."

After scooting back, I swiveled around to face her again.

"It's probably that guy you just beat messing with you," she said.

"Yeah, but how would he know my address?"

"Maybe you gave it out online? Or he's bluffing, trying to scare you."

"I may occasionally need a bit of game advice, but I'm not stupid."

"Touché." She grinned, tossing her hair back. "Well, he implied he's been following you for some time. He also said he'd send a computer. If he's for real, then maybe he's got access to AoE registrations or something."

I leaned back and crossed my arms over my chest. "I don't like it. Not at all."

Haley looked somber too, then caught my eye with an indecipherable expression. "What are you going to do now?"

What was I going to do? A part of me had settled in for a night of gaming. That part was unsettled now, both by Haley and the evident insecurity of my personal details on the ever-expanding world wide web.

Evidently seeing my hesitation, Haley stood up. "I should be going. Sorry to burst in on you…"

"No, no, not at all," I found myself wishing she wouldn't leave. "That tip about stone was spot on."

7

That brought a warm smile from her. "We should totally battle sometime."

"Yeah." I got to my feet. "Soon."

"I'll see you in class tomorrow. Don't stay up too late."

"Yeah, for sure."

Haley turned and headed for my bedroom door. While the music from the party outside had died down a bit, I knew people would be partying until well after midnight. I watched as she paused outside the door, turned, and closed it behind her.

Did any of that just happen? I sat down in my computer chair and leaned back, hands behind my head. The sleeves of my black and red flannel shirt scooted down my thin arms as I stared at the glowing star stickers on my ceiling. *Haley's Comet.* I grinned, making a note to never drop the bad pun in her presence.

I returned to the lobby to find one more game before calling it a night. Thoughts of Haley and Que floated to the back of my mind for processing. Taking out WarTurn007 wouldn't stop other challengers from coming at me. As one of the top hundred players around the world, I constantly had to defend my title.

Worry about my grades and the end of the world could wait; once more, I was drawn into the addictive gameplay of *Age of Empires II*. One more short game turned into two long ones, but it was the weekend, and I was young. I eventually crawled into bed long after the party had died down. Sleep came quickly.

CHAPTER 2

When Monday inevitably rolled around, I found myself sleep deprived and not ready to face the new week. I still managed to drag myself out of bed, sling my backpack over my shoulder, and take off toward campus. Ohio University hadn't been my first choice, but as far as Midwestern schools went, it wasn't the worst. I stopped in the *MT Mug* for some coffee before heading to my first class, English 202.

As I waited in line to pay for my dark Kenya brew, I wondered if Haley would speak to me in the light of day and around other people. Why had she really come into my room over the weekend? I'd given it some thought in between games, but I still had no answers. The most appealing thought was that she was checking me out as potential boyfriend material. Most people failed to understand me. I sometimes felt like the version of myself I saw in my head was vastly different than how others perceived me.

"Is that all?"

"Huh?" I glanced up, startled out of my thoughts.

"Just the coffee?"

"Oh, yeah," I said, smiling.

The bored barista rang up the order. After paying, I slipped out of the queue and made my way across campus. *Que. What an odd name for someone to have online*, I thought, suddenly remembering the strange takeover on my computer Friday night.

At nearly the same time, my cell phone rang. I stopped on the sidewalk and dug it out of my pocket, flipping it open and glancing at the name Tom.

"Yeah?" I asked after lifting it to my ear. "I'm on my way to class. What's up?"

"There's a guy here with a package, bro. You need to come sign for it."

"Like I said, I'm on my way to class. What is it?"

"Guy won't say, and he claims he's not coming back if you don't sign for it right now, bro."

I sighed. "Tell him I'm on my way."

After flipping my phone shut and disconnecting the call, I took a large swig of the quickly-cooling coffee before turning around and heading back toward Hudson House. Late in the semester with more than a few skipped lectures already, I couldn't afford to ditch again, but the package intrigued me. Had the mysterious Que actually sent me a new computer? Or was someone playing an elaborate joke on me? I needed to know.

Tom had left by the time I arrived at Hudson House. An annoyed man who looked as old and as aggressive as my father stood on the porch of the dilapidated house. I sped up my pace as I approached him. "Sorry, I was on my way to class."

"Does it look like I care?" the delivery guy asked.

I glanced past him at the wooden crate sitting on the porch.

"Sign here, kid. I've wasted enough time here already."

I grabbed the clipboard he shoved in front of me and scribbled my name near the bottom as I continued checking out the crate.

"What is it?" I asked.

I glanced up when nobody replied and saw the guy heading toward his running truck on the street. *How the hell am I supposed to get this inside?* I stared back at the wood crate. Why hadn't Que sent it in cardboard like a sane person? As I stood and wondered, my phone rang again. I took it out and flipped it open, not recognizing the name attached to the text message.

Where are you? Class is starting.

Another message came in as I struggled for a witty reply.

This is Haley, btw.

I sighed and began pecking out letters with my thumb.

Package came. Think it's from that Que guy. Gonna check it out. Take notes for me?

Will do, she replied. Then a moment later: I'll come over after class. Gotta go.

I smiled as I stared down at the piece of plastic in my hand. Text messaging had come such a long way in a short period of time. We'd had audio phone calls forever, but text messages directly to a handheld communication device opened up a strange new world. I sometimes wondered how it would affect society, but in that moment, all I could think about was what might be in the crate. Well, not quite all. Haley was coming over.

11

After walking onto the rickety porch, hoping it didn't all cave in, I touched the crate with my left foot to get a better grasp of its weight before I bent down to lift the delivery. The wooden box didn't budge. *Great.* Everyone at Hudson House would either be at class or too hungover from the weekend to offer any help. I bent down and firmly placed my hands on the rough wood, hoping I didn't get a splinter. With a heave and a ho, I pushed the crate to the front door.

Inch by grueling inch, I got closer to my destination. Luckily, I had one of the better rooms on the first floor. My second year living at Hudson House came with a few minor perks. A lot of students fled as soon as they could, but being in school on a small writing scholarship, I stuck around because it was the cheapest option so close to campus.

Once I got the crate into the living room, I used the long, red rug in front of the door to pull it toward the back of the old house. Boards creaked under me as I neared my room at the end of the hall. *Come on. Just a little bit further.* I stopped and stripped off my flannel shirt, not wanting to get it all sweaty. After a quick break, I continued my simple yet unforgiving mission. When I got the crate into my room, I glanced down, suddenly realizing I didn't have a way to open it. I examined the nails pressed into the wood. Someone had gone to a lot of trouble to package whatever sat before me.

I retrieved a crowbar from the shed out back and got to work prying the top off the crate. While great at video games and anything computer related, when it came to real-world stuff like opening crates, I struggled a bit. Then again, who else would be able to open something so ridiculous? It was almost the twenty-first century! With a final burst of energy, the last nail loosened, and I popped the top off. The scent of hay hit my nostrils. *Packing hay? I guess if you're going old school, go all the way.*

After moving the dead grass aside, I saw what looked to be a computer from at least four or five years ago. That a stranger on the internet had sent me anything at all still intrigued me. I reached in and grabbed the hefty twelve-inch monitor.

Piece-by-piece, I set up the computer equipment on my *D&D* table. Game night was a few days away, and I didn't want to bother taking apart my main computer for more space. I fiddled with all the old connectors and power cables a bit longer then finally sat down in a swivel chair at the edge of the card table.

"Here goes nothing," I muttered, hitting the power switch.

I half expected something bad to happen, but the monitor instantly came to life. Granted, all I saw was a black screen with a blinking monochrome cursor.

QUE:

I stared at the blinking cursor a moment.

QUE: You got the package!

I sat back in my chair, almost toppling over. Was it a script? I didn't have the computer hooked up to a phone line yet.

ALEX42: Is this like an Eliza clone or something?

ALEX42: Very funny. Where's the game?

QUE: No, not Eliza. This is real time. I'm using the power line to send you data.

ALEX42: I don't know a lot about networking, but I know that's not possible.

QUE: Not to you in your time period, perhaps, but it's entirely possible.

I took a deep breath while staring at the flickering screen. This was one hell of a practical joke. I waited for Que to make the next move.

QUE: Do you want to play the game?

ALEX42: Sure. What's it like? An RTS?

QUE: Sort of. You'll see once you play.

QUE: Starting game...

The screen flashed bright white momentarily before the most amazing graphics I'd seen on any game appeared. Several pods of some sort rushed through space, heading toward a desolate moon. The camera followed them closely, the hunk of cratered rock looming larger. I sat forward, hunched over and entranced at the cinematics. How had he done this on such an old computer?

One after another, the pods plowed into the surface of the moon, throwing up clouds of dust. When it settled, I could barely make out twelve glowing lights scattered around the face of the moon. The cinematics ended and the character creation screen popped up. Well, what I thought might be a character creation screen. I stared at a digital copy of myself on the screen. How had they...? A notification window popped up in the upper left.

QUE: Nice, huh? I'll let you get started and play a few games. We're tracking your score, but no pressure, kid!

As the chat window faded from view, I grabbed my mouse with my right hand. My 3D doppelganger climbed into a spaceship on the screen. When would the RTS stuff show up? My character was depicted as piloting the solo craft toward the moon displayed in the cutscene. Were they ever going to give me control?

The moment the thought entered my mind, the screen flashed red as the ship veered off course. I frantically clicked the mouse, trying to right myself. After a few tense moments, I had the ship once again on a straight course toward the dusty planetoid. The closer I got, the more prominent the green-blue planet behind it became.

While it didn't look like Earth it could have easily been my home planet's twin. Despite the apparent age of the computer Que had sent me, the graphics on the screen were unlike anything I'd seen before, including some of the graphics workhorses the university owned. If *Moon Wars* had any sort of gameplay, the developers would have a hit on their hands.

"Approaching Moon #4524-A. Prepare for landing..."

The real world floated away as I hunched over even further, intent to find out what would happen after my character landed. Would I start collecting resources and building like most RTS games? I smirked at the thought of traipsing across the barren moonscape to collect dust or something. Everything else about the game pointed to something deeper, however.

After my ship landed on the moon, kicking up a cloud of dust that hadn't been disturbed in who-knew-how-long, I noticed a nearby beacon similar to one from the beginning of the game. A planet in the distance also caught my attention. Before I could process all the information, a HUD appeared before me with glowing green text.

"Moon Wars Simulation #9873983-A commencing. Please select your character..."

"Character?" I muttered as a standard creation screen appeared.

Wasn't this supposed to be an RTS? I occasionally played an RPG to switch it up, but I didn't want to get sucked into something like *Baldur's Gate* so close to the semester ending. My grades were awful enough already and skipping another day wouldn't help any. Even so, I found myself unable to peel my eyes away from the glowing monitor.

Please Choose Your Character Class:

Soldier Bonus: Combat **Penalties:** Diplomacy, Production
Scientist Bonus: Research **Penalties:** Diplomacy, Healing
Engineer Bonus: Production **Penalties:** Combat, Diplomacy
Diplomat Bonus: Diplomacy **Penalties:** Research, Production
Medic Bonus: Healing **Penalties:** Combat, Diplomacy

"That's really odd..."

I went for the type of play that most appealed to me: Soldier. The following screens allowed me to customize the skills available to me. I wasn't sure how any of them would help me command a large army, but I went along with the game and made choices that seemed most likely to help me should I end up in charge of an RTS-style operation. I had 100 skill points to distribute. As a soldier, I went for mostly combat skills to start.

Combat Skills	Base	Bonus	Added	Total
Unarmed Melee	25	50	0	75
Light Melee Weapons	25	50	10	85
Heavy Melee Weapons	25	50	0	75
Ranged Light Weapons	25	50	25	100
Ranged Heavy Weapons	25	50	25	100
Thrown Weapons	25	50	10	85
Demolitions	25	50	10	85
Survival Techniques	25	50	10	85
Recon	25	50	0	75
Stealth	25	50	10	85

I didn't spend too much time agonizing over the skill points as it was my first time playing the game. Once I had a better idea of how it all worked, I could tweak my character better. With a deep breath, I hit the start button.

Game Commencing!

I expected a shift to the battlefield or something, but I remained in my synthetic pilot's seat, staring out a viewscreen. Maybe I should look for a gun on the ship? I scanned the rows of buttons, dials, and knobs, not seeing anything that might be a fire button. As I hesitated, the hatch above me slid open.

The lack of air on the moon hit me instantly, along with the fact that I didn't have a space suit of any sort on. As I struggled to breathe, the world around me slipped into darkness as if it had been sucked up by a black hole. When I could see again, I found myself still in the pilot's seat, once again approaching the moon.

"Approaching Moon #4524-A. Prepare for landing..."

17

Had I died on my very first attempt? I scanned the screen, searching for a space suit. When I finally found the key command to raise a protective helmet of translucent energy around my head, the game announced the new start.

"Moon Wars Simulation #9873983-B commencing. Please select your character..."

I sighed and clicked through most of the same choices, but I did make some changes. This time, I put a few points into non-combat skills like hacking electronics.

Combat Skills	Base	Bonus	Added	Total
Ranged Light Weapons	25	50	25	100
Ranged Heavy Weapons	25	50	15	90
Thrown Weapons	25	50	15	90
Demolitions	25	50	5	80
Research Skills	Base	Bonus	Added	Total
Chemistry	25	0	5	30
Mathematics	25	0	5	30
Healing Skills	Base	Bonus	Added	Total
Minor First Aid	25	0	10	35
General Skills	Base	Bonus	Added	Total
Acrobatics	25	0	5	30
Hack electronics	10	0	15	25

When the hatch popped open this time, the energy helmet protected me from the cold vastness of empty space. I climbed out of the cramped cockpit and onto the lunar surface.

"Alright, let's see what this is all about…"

I pulled up a list of all the moonbases.

Moonbase 1	Light Vehicles	Wheeled or tracked machines.
Moonbase 2	Heavy Vehicles	Tanks.
Moonbase 3	Small Mechs	Bipedal death machines < 10'
Moonbase 4	Large Mechs	Bipedal death machines > 10'
Moonbase 5	Air	Unlock air units. Everyone always chooses this one to be able to attack earth on the ground.
Moonbase 6	Sea	Unlock factory for sea units.
Moonbase 7	Infantry	Infantry units
Moonbase 8	Research	Research boost
Moonbase 9	Engineering	Increased production
Moonbase 10	Combat	Combat bonuses
Moonbase 11	Diplomacy	Diplomatic bonuses
Moonbase 12	Medical	Medical bonuses

Did these tie to an RTS battle later? Why hadn't Que given me more information? Maybe figuring the game out was part of his marketing test? I'd figure it out. No problem.

CHAPTER 3

Four hours and six other characters later, I still hadn't made very much progress. While I'd managed to reach one of the ancient beacons on the moon, automated defense systems had taken me out when I got too close. Leaning back in my chair, fingers interlocked behind my head, I wondered what other strategy to try.

"New computer?" Haley asked from the doorway.

I lowered my hands and sat up, feeling sheepish. "Que sent it to me with that *Moon Wars* game. I'm not getting very far yet."

"Because you obviously suck at RTS games."

She smiled and crossed the room, pulling up a chair beside me.

"That's the thing. It's not strictly an RTS game, but it's not really your typical RPG either. After playing all afternoon, I can't even get into the first level."

"Mrs. Crossland wasn't happy that you weren't in class again." She spoke without real concern, all the while intently staring at the screen.

I sighed. "Yeah, I should've gone, but I was curious about this package. The delivery guy said it was now or never."

"Can I try?" she asked.

"Sure…"

While Haley took over the mouse, I explained my difficulties. "I thought it had to do with the soldier class I was picking, but no matter what character I start with, I can't get into any of the moon-bases."

"Show me. Let's start from the beginning."

I went through all my beginning moves for game #9873983-I. Would I run out of tries if I reached Z? "Okay, this is where I've been having problems."

"Look over there." She pointed to the screen. "On the horizon."

"Oh, wow, I hadn't noticed that before," I admitted. "Let's investigate."

I navigated my avatar toward a dark grey rock formation on the horizon.

"Do you have a weapon or any other equipment?"

"No..." I stopped myself. "Actually, I don't think I checked. There's so many commands in this game."

"Did you try I for inventory?"

"Yes, I tried I for inventory...Oh, wait, I had caps lock on. It's working now."

"Aren't you glad I'm around?"

While I was hesitant to mention it aloud, it was true: I was happy she had come over. "I've got a blaster pistol. That's better than nothing!"

"Something's coming toward you!"

I scanned the screen, seeing several red blobs heading toward my character. "No, you don't," I said, equipping my newly found blaster. "Die!"

I fired a few shots in quick succession, still unsure of what I was facing.

"Red robots of death!" Haley leaned forward, her leg brushing against mine.

"Dead robots of death," I corrected as I continued firing.

"You're running low on ammo, be careful."

"I see the warning too."

After a flurry of mouse clicks and some deft maneuvering, I disabled all three approaching droids.

```
Combat is Over!
+100
You have 100 xp
You have reached level 1 soldier!
+0 Skill Points
+2 Health Points
You need 100 xp to reach level 2.
```

Haley rubbed her hands together. "Loot their bodies."

"Give me a minute…" I moved my character closer to the red remains scattered across the moon's surface. "Oh, look! More ammo!"

```
You receive the following items!
1) Red Power Core (Half Charge)
2) Red Power Core (Full Charge)
3) Quantum glasses (Targeting)
4) Fluxen Capacitor
5) Red Air Tank
```

```
6) Medical Kit (Half Charge)
7) Red Power Core (Full Charge) x2
8) Red Power Barrel
```

"Interesting," Haley said. "You should use it all as soon as you can."

"No," I said.

"Why not?"

"The parts can be used to improve equipment now, but the more we have at the end of the RPG portion of the game, the better commander bot we will be able to build. From what I've learned so far, the level you reach in the RPG portion also determines how many Mech Points you can use to construct your commander bot."

"Commander bot?"

I nodded. "Yeah, there's supposedly a big RTS battle at the end of the game, and you create the main commander robot using parts you collected during the RPG section with limits based on the level you reach in the RPG portion plus ten levels."

"Oh, that's cool."

I smiled. "Right? I've not made it that far yet."

"We'll get there," she said. "I vote to keep most of the equipment for later. We've got a basic weapon and more ammo now."

"I agree. With this extra ammo, I should be able to make my way to the first beacon and into the first moonbase finally."

"Maybe that's it."

"What?" I turned to look at her.

"Have you been trying to get into the same moonbase every game?"

"Yeah…"

"Maybe there's others? Like in the cut scene?"

"Possibly. I don't see why they wouldn't be as well protected."

"Levels. I bet you were trying to clear a later level early."

"You know, that could be it. Let's keep going toward the horizon."

I walked my character in the direction the red robots had come from. Sure enough, I soon reached a second beacon. From what little I had gathered, they had been shot onto the moon as a means to establish a beachhead. Some sort of AI set-up underground moonbases at each location to defend against an eventual attack from the planet. That would be the RTS portion of the game.

"Would be nice if they had some instructions. Are you sure—"

"Yes, I double-checked for a help screen. The graphics on this are great, but they really need to work on their narrative design and user interface."

"Watch out!"

I followed Haley's pointing finger and saw another wave of red robots emerge from the new moonbase. All seven rushed toward me. I let loose another string of energy bolts, taking out three of them. The other four surrounded me, taking no time at all to drain my health. Before I could run away to heal up, a final blast of electricity hit my character and killed him. The screen faded to black once again.

"Dammit!" I push my chair back, fed up with the so-called game.

"Are you hungry?" Haley asked.

I turned to her and nodded. "Yeah, I kinda skipped lunch."

"Let's go to Alberto's and grab a pizza." She stood, staring down at me.

"Okay, sure..." Normally, I would have freaked out at the idea of sitting in the busiest pizza place on campus with a beautiful woman, worried about what I might say to her, but Haley was easy to be with. She gave me no cause to get anxious.

"Come on." She tossed her head, her brilliant red bangs swaying.

I stood and followed her outside.

At our impromptu dinner, we discussed possible strategies for *Moon Wars*. Haley had more RPG experience than me and had some good ideas. I really wanted to see if the game ever transitioned into real-time strategy mechanics, but I was content spending time with Haley. I half-expected her to excuse herself after we ate, but she insisted on coming back to Hudson House with me.

****

Two hours later, we finally managed to enter the first moonbase. We quickly learned from a high-quality cut-scene that it was one of twelve on the moon. Moreover, the transition to an RTS was further explained by the same sequence. There was a countdown. Every base I managed to clear and all the skill-ups and buffs I'd

25

acquired counted in my favor when the RTS phase began at the end of the countdown. I only had so much time to clear the moonbases while concentrating on my character's level to ensure I could eventually make a decent commander bot.

"Red Robots!" By now Haley was evidently even more intensely involved in the game than me. There was a real urgency in her voice.

I leaned forward, clicking madly to shoot down the wave of drones we'd both come to hate. After I dispatched them and looted their bodies (four strips of polycarbon sheet, whatever that was, some iron fragments and two memory chips), I moved the avatar to a ramp leading down to the second level of the moonbase.

"That's one level down," I said and took a deep breath. "Ready to go deeper?"

She smiled. "Let's do this."

We both hunched forward, engrossed by the actions of my avatar on the screen. My heart beat faster as I approached what would hopefully be the last room in the vast, underground complex. While the game wasn't strictly an RTS, I found myself intrigued by the notion that the level my RPG character obtained and the moonbases I cleared would both have an effect on the eventual battle.

"Hold up," Haley said. "Go back a bit."

"Where? Here?"

I maneuvered my character, retracing several steps along a stark, metal corridor.

"Yeah, on the right. The wall. Doesn't that look odd?"

"Oh, I see it now."

I walked closer to get a better view of the odd flicker on a small portion of the wall. An interactive notification popped up on the screen. I turned to Haley. "Could be a trap? Especially this close to the end."

"Don't chicken out now. I want to clear this level before I leave."

"Yeah, it's getting late. We can play again tomorrow."

"Are you nuts?" she exclaimed then grinned. "There's no way you would stop playing if I left."

Glad that she was willing to stay longer, I turned back to the screen. "You're right. Let's see what's behind this wall."

With a click of the mouse, my character reached out and pressed the small spot on the wall. An aggressive chirping sound blasted out of the computer's speakers. I whipped my avatar around. A small robot with antennae emerged from the left of the screen. The robotic creature made its way across the screen, stopping only to sniff the air and examine something on the ground.

I could not see this object, and the robot disappeared back into the wall. Soon another robot entered the screen, this one with large red and blue eyes, and a rotating antenna. It walked across the screen, then dropped to the floor. It stayed there, wide eyes fixed on me as if staring directly at me. It kept its eyes fixed on me for a few moments before approaching menacingly.

"Ugh," I sighed. "Here we go again."

"Wait, try that whistle we found a while back."

"The whistle?" I kept shooting my blaster pistol at the oncoming robots while dodging to the left and right, desperately backing off in the direction of the last junction: I could get some cover there. "What whistle?"

"The whistle we found in that orange room, remember?"

"Oh, yeah. Well, I'm kind of in the heat of battle right now..."

Haley leaned over me, her thin arm snaking underneath mine. I kept my eyes glued to the screen as she tapped a few buttons on the keyboard.

"There," she said as the whistle popped into an equipment slot. "Press X!"

I quit firing the blaster pistol and pressed the X key repeatedly. As my character raised the molded metal to his mouth and blew, the robots all came to a halt.

"What the...? How did you know?" I turned to Haley.

She was grinning from ear to ear. "Just a hunch based on how they looked."

"Damn good hunch." I turned back to the monitor. "What now?"

"Whatever you do, don't blow the whistle again. I bet it's an on-off switch of some sort."

"The wall's opening," I said.

As we both watched, a panel in the wall slid open, revealing a room unlike any of the others we'd come across.

"The bridge or command room?" Haley asked.

I nodded, liking her assessment. "Yeah, I think so."

"Okay, let's think about this a moment. It seems too easy."

"Right?" I hesitated in the hallway, my character looking in. "This game is something else. I almost feel like I'm there in the base."

"Yeah, it's the most immersive game I've ever seen." She glanced at an old watch on her wrist. "I can't believe how late it's gotten."

"Are you hungry? I could whip you up some eggs or something."

"No, it's fine, I will go after we finish exploring this room. I just have to know if this is actually done; if we've finally cleared one of the moonbases. Can't believe there's twelve of them."

"I'll get through them all eventually."

"What about the timer?"

"The timer?"

"On the top of the screen." She pointed.

"How did I miss that before?"

"I figured you'd seen it, so I didn't say anything. Sorry."

"No, this is on me. When did the countdown start?"

"When I first noticed it, it read forty-six hours, and we'd been playing a couple of hours at least."

"Well, the timer has forty-four hours left now. If we clear this base soon, that's four hours per base, almost exactly right for a twelve-base game."

"Let's make sure we finish here first."

"Yeah... Here goes nothing."

I clicked the mouse to make my character move forward. Once again, a strange sense of vertigo washed over my body. It was like my brain actually thought I was inside the game. The sensation settled down as I got caught up in the moment. I surveyed the room on the other side of the wall, and it was almost a shock when Haley spoke and I was reminded I was just playing a game.

"Lots of command terminals," she muttered, "I bet it's the control room."

"Here's hoping…" I walked toward the largest screen near the center of the room. "Can we access the system, maybe?"

"Just don't set off any other alarms."

"Hey, you told me to press the wall."

"Do you always do what women tell you?"

"Just the special ones," I shot back, not turning to face her.

"Noted."

"Okay, here goes nothing…" I pressed E on my keyboard to interact with the terminal. Instantly, my computer screen—the one Que had sent me, as well as perhaps the one I was looking at in the game—flashed a brilliant white, blinding me temporarily.

"That was bright," Haley said.

"Oh, look. It's an operating system of some sort."

"Congratulations on clearing the first moonbase," a robotic voice intoned. "You have unlocked its resources."

Still blinking away afterimages, I read from a report on the base. "It looks like we're in Moon Base Three which specializes in small mechs. Control of this base will be helpful for the final battle, I bet."

"Something feels off," Haley said. "This was almost too easy at the end."

"Don't jinx it," I teased.

She yawned next to me. I pulled back from the screen as she stood and stretched.

"Nice session, but I should get going. Don't stay up too late play-ing."

"I'll try…"

"Call me tomorrow, okay? I got your number from Tommy, by the way. Hope you don't mind."

"Not at all." Our eyes locked a moment. "We should do this again sometime."

"For sure. I want to see if we can get all twelve moonbases cleared before the timer counts down."

"Can't believe I missed that."

"There's so much going on in that game." She raised her right hand. "Talk to you later."

"Yeah, laters…"

I watched as she crossed the room and left, closing the door be-hind her with a final wave. After she left, I turned back to the com-puter screen. A few months earlier, I would've stayed up all night playing, but I wanted to get some rest. Then too, there was Haley. I was in serious danger of being smitten. For I found that despite how interesting the game was, I preferred to lie on my bed, turning my thoughts to her than to play it. It seemed that she liked me. There had been moments of real intimacy during our combined ef-forts to beat the game. Should I let myself believe that? Ask her out even?

There were a lot of girls in school that I had half-daydreamed about. About what it would be like to date them. Imagining us to-gether, eating out, or at parties, or the cinema. None of these scenarios had ever disturbed my thoughts as much as Haley did, because I always knew they were groundless. Picturing Haley with me as my girlfriend was impossible. My arm around her as we walked up to school? Hand in hand leaving a restaurant? No. But working together as a team, a smart team, in *Moon Wars*. That I could imagine.

CHAPTER 4

I awoke the next morning with every intention of going to class, but fragments of a dream caused me to sit down in front of Que's odd computer. I panned around the control room of Moon Base Three, looking for a clue we might've missed the night before. In my dream, Haley and I had somehow been transported to the game world. Together, we'd found a hidden panel in the control room. As I scanned the area, noting all the advanced computer terminals with very few controls, I began to think I was crazy. Then I saw it.

Across the room, a tiny section of a wall glimmered in the light. Breakfast and my education could wait. I walked my character toward the odd flickering on the smooth, white wall. The closer I got, the more I realized it might actually be something. Had my dream led me to a breakthrough in *Moon Wars*? I briefly thought about Haley, but she brought about thoughts of classes and the real world. While it didn't have a lot of great world building, *Moon Wars* had me intrigued. I stopped and stared at the imperfection on the otherwise smooth wall.

Whistle in my left hand and blaster in my right hand, I reached up with my left to press the spot on the wall. Half expecting another alarm bell to go off, the lack of any immediate consequence surprised me. Then I noticed the timer on the upper left-hand corner of the screen. It had been counting down all night. Only thirty-four hours remained on the clock. Did the game designers really except someone to play two days straight without a break to win the stupid game? Perhaps they did. The idea of participating in a marathon session intrigued me. Haley and classes could wait.

Beating an unreleased video game might not have been important to many, but my mother's constant insistence that gaming would lead to me being a failure in life spurred me on. Video games had taught me quite a few lessons over the years, including that of not giving up too easily. With only thirty-four hours to go, I raced to the kitchen to grab a bowl of cereal, a banana, and a double-sized mug of coffee.

When I got back to my room, I closed the door behind me with my foot. Another lesson video games had taught me was that if things were getting more difficult it usually meant you were on the right path. I stepped over a pile of dirty t-shirts next to my unmade bed and made my way to the card table with Que's computer on it. I briefly wondered if I should try to contact him again, but I decided on beating his silly game first. At that point, I would thank him for the computer and hope he didn't get weird.

Bowl in one hand, spoon in another, I slurped up my *Honey-Nut Cheerios* as I turned my focus to the game. In my absence, the flickering section on the wall had grown: it was an irregular line, about a meter long and lengthening downwards, like someone was on the other side of the wall, running their finger downwards and leaving a trail I could see. Wait a minute. Was this someone trying to spell something?

As I watched, I grew more convinced that a pattern was forming. Slowly though. The game had an option to speed up time, which happened when you rested to restore your health, but I didn't want to waste too much time, especially with only one of twelve moonbases conquered. Still, I couldn't leave without understanding this pattern more. Maybe I'd found another hidden feature? I set my avatar to rest. The countdown timer went faster.

The strange mark on the walls also sped up. Was that an H? When a second letter began forming, I knew I was onto something. An E. Now an L. And a P. HELP? Nothing new appeared, so I stood up, which had the effect of restoring the timer to its normal pace. All the while, I was staring at the scrawled message on the wall. How odd. I wondered if Haley would have an idea. My flip phone sat on the end table next to my bed, but I resisted the urge to get it. She would likely lecture me for skipping class again. Even if she was a gamer and had the same interests as me, she took college a lot more seriously than I did. Over the last couple of days, I'd come to admire that about her.

I set the half-finished bowl of soggy oat rings on the table and peeled open the banana as I stared at the cryptic scrawling on the wall. Had a programmer of the game snuck it in as an Easter egg, or had I discovered a side quest that would help me more easily beat the rest of the moonbases? While I'd wanted to dive into the RTS battle right away at first, the more I played the RPG element of the game, the more it hooked me.

For one thing, the game world was amazingly detailed. Maybe it was because my imagination really connected to the game, but it all felt completely real. The other thing I liked was the fact that it was an RPG that led to an RTS battle at the end. One of the coolest things so far was determining what moonbases to clear in order to build the best commander mech for the final portion of the game. While I hadn't reached that far yet, I was beginning to see how closely the RPG part tied to the rest of the game.

I noticed the obvious Fibonacci sequence in the skill point bumps for each level gained in the RPG section of the game. This made me think that getting the highest-level character possible in the amount of time allotted would give me the best chance of winning the RTS battle if I ever made it that far. It was almost too obvious, though. I still wasn't sure if that was the best way to beat the game or not. *Moon Wars* was turning out to be more involved than it appeared at first glance.

For the moment, I was still alive after capturing one base and had to keep moving forward. With less than thirty hours remaining, I felt a tiny pressure in the back of my mind that kept building as the timer ticked down. I knew the game designers were just messing with the players to create tension (and maybe addiction), but I couldn't help but get sucked deeper into the world they had created. Thoughts of school, friends, and even Haley took a backseat to more pressing matters. Namely, how to clear the next moonbase in less time. Could I maybe find a map to the locations of the other bases? Or should I track down the HELP clue? I tossed the banana peel into the bowl of milk then stretched.

That peculiar HELP message hadn't been easy to uncover, so I decided to pursue that lead rather than just going for the next moonbase right away. I scoured every inch of the control room and every other area in the sprawling underground moonbase. For the most part, everything looked shiny, bright, and brand new despite it having been buried on the moon for hundreds of years.

After entering an air shaft, I found a disturbingly messy chamber mid-way down to the level beneath the control room. The moment my character emerged and turned on a hover-light, I knew I was onto something.

You found me.
The words had been scrawled on the wall opposite me.

A computer terminal, eerily similar to the one Que had sent me and that I was now using sat on a stainless-steel table. I moved closer, hoping I could interact with it. I could. And it set my heart beating fast to see the familiar prompt pop up. Leaning forward, I stared at the QUE> prompt on the screen-within-a-screen. This was so meta. I wished Haley was here. Not wanting to interrupt this adventure, however, I pressed on without her. Curious, I typed 'ls', a standard Unix command to list the directory. To my surprise, it worked.

I soon had a better sense of the operating system embedded within the game. A few random text files had been scattered over the system. It didn't take me long to figure out that the guy sending the messages was named Haruto; I used that information to grep everything I could access. Only twelve text files came up, but some of them were quite long. I opened the largest first, wanting to see what it contained. My stomach growled as I scrolled down, mutinying, but I wasn't distracted. What was I looking at? Complex schematics. Plans? For what?

Numerous ideas floated through my mind as I walked like a zombie to the kitchen for a peanut butter sandwich or two to shut my stomach up. Were the plans part of the game or something else? I needed to find out what following the instructions would build. That would probably give me a clue or two about how it fit into the context of the game. *Moon Wars* was turning out to be a bit more complex than I thought at first. And I hadn't even reached the RTS portion of the game.

After slicing a banana and peppering the peanut butter with thin bits, I capped the sandwiches with another piece of bread and grabbed a couple of paper towels to serve as a plate. On the way back to my room, I resisted the urge to send Haley a text message. I didn't want to appear too pushy. Nor did I want her to try to talk me out of marathoning the last twenty odd hours of the game, either. Back in my bedroom, I shut the door and sat at my makeshift desk.

Between bites of my pb&j sandwich, I scrolled further down through the largest file I had found. From what I could gather, the goal of the machine outlined by the schematics was to digitize a person's mind, enabling it to be uploaded to a digital network. What an interesting twist. Was it something to do with how the game transitioned from RPG to RTS? I ate and dove deeper into the documents that described the mechanics of the strange machine. Hours passed quickly as I jotted notes and made simple diagrams to try to understand Haruto's contraption and how it might tie into *Moon Wars*. The game was deeper than *Baldur's Gate*.

****

A knock at my door later that evening startled me. Several cans of Mountain Dew sat scattered across the table along with my bowl of cereal and rotting banana peel from that morning. I had neglected to take a shower too. Quickly sniffing my left pit, the stinkier of the two, I scrambled around for a clean t-shirt.

"Hold on," I said.

"Are you naked or something?" Haley asked then giggled.

I threw on a cleaner shirt then walked over to the door and opened it.

"Hey," I said, out of breath.

She cocked her head. "What were you doing?"

"Gaming."

"A gamer 'til the end," she teased.

"Funny. Really, though, I've made some progress on *Moon Wars*."

"You missed class—"

"I know, I know," I interrupted. "Come check this out, though."

She followed as I walked back over to the computer. My eyes went to the countdown timer first. I had less than a day left to finish all the other moonbases or at least figure out what Haruto was up to inside the game.

We sat down.

39

"Did you clear all the moonbases or something?" Haley asked.

"No, I found a hidden room," I said. "And a working computer."

"What? A computer inside the game? That's so meta."

"I know, right? Check this out."

She leaned forward as I scrolled down to one of the better visualizations of the blueprints and schematics I'd found. "What is it?"

"I'm not sure yet," I said. "The plans say it's for a machine to transfer a single consciousness to a digital realm. I think it's real, not part of the game."

"Uh huh," she said, sounding unconvinced.

"Seriously, look at this…" I opened another of the text files I'd found. "Some guy Haruto apparently got suckered into digitizing his mind and entering a digital universe to play a game. He got trapped, and—"

"Let me interrupt you this time," she said. "That sounds a bit far-fetched. It's likely part of the marketing campaign for the game. Think about it for a minute. You get this fancy new computer in the mail for free and the game. It's all connected, I think. They probably expect you to build a website or something and promote their game for them."

"I would if I had the time, this game is sweet."

"So, did you read all of this Haruto guy's messages?" she asked.

I shook my head, opening another one at random. "Not yet."

"Don't worry about class, by the way. I covered for you."

"Oh?"

She nodded as I turned to face her.

"Thanks," I said. "Despite my recent behavior, that actually means a lot. My scholarship is in jeopardy if I fail a single class. At the moment, I'm slipping in everything; not by much though, I should be able to turn it around."

"You don't have to convince me."

She smiled and reached up to tuck a lock of her red hair behind her ear. We stared at each other awkwardly a moment before both turning back to the screen.

"I'm going to take these to the kitchen." She grabbed my bowl from earlier that morning. "It's kinda grossing me out."

"No, no, I got it. I've been distracted with the game, and..."

I stood and grabbed the bowl, our fingers brushing against each other. She took her hand away. I lifted what remained of my morning meal, adding a few empty soda cans too. "Be right back."

After a momentary smile, Haley's attention turned to the computer screen, while I ferried the dirty dishes and trash down the narrow hall to the kitchen. That was good of her: not to pester me about classes. And Haley seemed at least as interested as me in the game, she understood why it was worth skipping a few lectures to explore it.

Que popped into my thoughts. I wondered if he had designed the game himself.

After dumping the empty cans and banana peel into the garbage, I emptied the last of the milk out of the bowl and rinsed it out before setting it in the sink. The other guys in Hudson House weren't the type to complain about a single dirty bowl. I rushed back upstairs, taking the steps two at a time. When I reached my door, I saw Haley hunched over the keyboard, typing furiously.

"Hey, I found something," she said, motioning me over.

I took her old seat, glancing at the screen. "What is it?"

"Haruto's file names."

"A bunch of numbers. What about them?"

"Not just any numbers. Coordinates. Check this out." She copied one of the twelve file names then opened the game map. "I'll just drop this number in, chop it up, and... voila!"

"Oh, wow. It's another moonbase." I grinned. "Well done."

"Thanks. It kept bugging me that there were twelve files. Why not put all the info in one file, you know?"

"Yeah." I kept nodding. "We don't have a lot of time left to get to all of them."

"No, WE don't." She turned briefly and smiled.

"I've got to get to the RTS battle at least once, Haley."

"Oh, I know. I was hinting that I might stick around if you don't mind."

"Not at all. I think we can get through at least half of the moonbases before the timer runs out. Are you ready for a marathon?"

"We can order a pizza later tonight. Do you want to drive?"

I cocked my head to the left. "Drive?"

"The character. Do you want to control the character again?"

"Oh, no. You're doing great. I could use a break."

"Bet that Que guy didn't think we'd team up to beat his silly game."

"If he's even a guy. Could be a woman."

"True, true…" She turned back to the screen.

"I've been wondering if I should forget the other moonbases and try to figure out more about Haruto."

"Don't you think the coordinates are the payoff?"

"Maybe, but it's almost too small, you know?"

"I say we go to the next moonbase. We can look for other clues he might have left."

"Agreed. Let's get moving."

We gamed late into the evening.

****

Very early the next morning, as cardinals chirped outside my bedroom window, I yawned, unable to resist any longer.

"Don't do that," Haley said, then copied me.

"I don't think I can keep going," I admitted.

"Yeah, I've not stayed up this late since trying to beat *The Legend of Zelda: A Link to the Past*."

"Loved that game, but I never beat it."

"There's some great stuff at the end."

"Would love for you to tell me about it sometime."

She stretched and yawned again. I stole a glance, concerned when I saw her brow furrow and her eyes narrow. She pointed at the screen. "What's happening?"

I turned and saw the game fading from the screen.

"Noooooo…."

A black, blank screen faced us. Then the almost forgotten Que cursor appeared. I breathed a sigh of relief then could hear the righteous anger in my voice: "Que better not be playing with us."

Furiously, I began to type.

ALEX42: Que? Is that you? We were doing well.

QUE: I had to cut it short. There's not much time.

ALEX42: I know. The timer was running out.

QUE: No, not the game timer. This is much bigger, I'm afraid.

ALEX42: Whatever. It wasn't cool to stop our game. We were close.

QUE: Oh, you were, were you? Don't you want to know more about Haruto and how you might help him?

Haley nudged me with her elbow. "Tell him yes."

I turned to her then back to the screen, typing the whole time.

ALEX42: Tell us more about Haruto, please. We're tired and don't have much time either.

QUE: Okay, hold on a second, let me just activate this code, and...

The screen flickered again, and the monochrome text was replaced by a hyper-realistic 3D representation of a man standing in a medieval village. His attire fit the time period of the scene, but a woman walking by stared at him in surprise as he spoke to us.

"Can you hear me? I had to cut access to my sight to enhance my broadcasting, and I'm afraid I can't tell if you're still there in front of the computer."

"Whoa…" Haley stood, raising her arms in the air. "This is too weird. Are you playing some kind of joke on me? Because this isn't funny."

"No, I swear," I said.

"I can hear you two," Que noted.

A man in shiny armor riding a horse strode by.

"Look, this isn't funny," I said, mimicking Haley's concerns. "How are you simulating real-time conversation?"

"I'm not simulating anything, kiddo. This is me. I'm digitized. The plans you found in the game are real, and I'm giving them to you so you can digitize yourself and save humanity."

"Wait... how do you know we found plans?" Haley asked.

She took her seat beside me once more, leaning forward.

"I've been watching you play," Que said. "Not many players find Haruto's clue or the location of all twelve moonbases."

"Hah! You said 'or.' That means there's something more to Haruto's message? Is a real person in trouble?"

Que frowned, averting his eyes. "I'm afraid so, my boy." He glanced up. "Unless you two can help him."

"Present your papers, digital denizen!" the man in armor yelled.

Que twisted to the left, the color draining from his face.

"I've got to go," he yelled in an urgent tone. "You've got the plans. Use them!"

The screen faded to black. No matter what I did, neither the game nor Que came back. Haley yawned again, bringing me back to reality.

"What did he mean by plans?" Haley asked.

I shrugged. "No idea, but this is all so weird."

"Yeah..." She nodded, her voice drifting off.

"I mean, it's not like you can really digitize a person," she continued.

"Right?" I shook my head.

"This is all some sort of elaborate prank. I better not find out you're behind it."

"And I better not find out you're the one playing a trick on me," I countered.

We stared at each other a moment.

"This is all just too weird," I repeated.

"We should take the plans to Professor Lambert," she said. "He can tell us if this is a machine that can be built or if it's just gibberish."

The science department professor had a reputation for being eccentric, but if anyone in the science department would know anything about the weird diagrams and instructions we'd received, it would be him.

"Good idea," I said. "He'll be able to tell us if this machine is real or just some elaborate prank for whatever reason."

"We should both sleep first," she said.

"Yeah, yeah, the sheets are clean, I promise…" Halfway through, I realized she hadn't meant that we sleep together. "I mean… you know…"

Green eyes smiling, Haley leaned forward and hugged me. "Call me later this afternoon when you wake up. We'll go see him together." She pulled back, still staring into my eyes. The intensity of her gaze mesmerized me more than my lack of sleep.

"Yeah, I've got your number, I'll call you."

"Or text. It's almost the twenty-first century, you know." With that, she raised a hand in farewell.

After she had closed the door, I glanced back at the computer Que had sent me. Since the screen was still lifeless, I collapsed on my bed. Sleep came quickly with dreams of moons and Haley flooding my synapses. I didn't mind at all.

CHAPTER 5

Thunderous bass shook me awake later that evening. Usually, I would have been upset by the other residents being so rude as to blast their music through the house, but thoughts of Haley and meeting Professor Lambert had me excited to get up. While I hadn't had a full eight hours of sleep, I felt energized and ready to save the world.

After crawling out of bed, I walked to the computer Que had sent me. The hard drive and monitor lights were still on, but the screen was blank. All the important files had been transferred to my laptop, so I didn't have to worry if it stayed shut down. I grabbed a clean towel and left my room, heading for a quick shower.

As warm water ran over my body, I wondered if Professor Lambert would be interested in the plans and schematics we had found buried inside the game or call us crazy. If half the rumors about him were true, he was the perfect person to check it out the possibility of digital transference. My thoughts returned to Haley. I adjusted the water a bit colder then rinsed off a final time before getting out.

A few people I didn't know were standing around in the kitchen, bobbing their heads to the music blaring from the living room downstairs. I paid them no attention as I grabbed a couple granola bars to eat on the way to pick up Haley. She had texted me while I was in the shower, asking me to meet her at her apartment.

She only lived a few streets over, but the trip to the science department on campus would take a bit longer. I gobbled the granola bar down as I walked to her apartment, saving the second for later that evening if I started getting hungry. The whole *Moon Wars* game and Que's cryptic message intrigued me so much. I hurried down the uneven sidewalk, tall sycamore trees to my right.

Their leaves had started to fall. With Halloween on the way, the semester was quickly coming to a close. I pushed thoughts of failing my classes out of my head. All I needed to do was pass. I also knew I had a problem with getting addicted to video games until I could finally beat them. Would the same happen with *Moon Wars*? I had to buckle down and study enough to not lose my scholarship.

As I neared Haley's apartment, I slowed, stuffing the granola bar wrapper in the front left pocket of my faded jeans. My right hand held my laptop. While not the most powerful system, the bulky machine made it easier for me to keep track of all my classes and assignments. I took a deep breath as her house came into view.

She stood on the stoop where she had been sitting and waiting.

I smiled as she walked over. "Nice bar."

"Huh?" She stopped in front of me on the sidewalk.

A clump of leaves blew by us, landing in the nearby street.

"Your granola bar." I pulled the wrapper out of my pocket. "The oatmeal raisin ones are the best."

"No way. Team chocolate-covered all the way." She smiled. "I overslept...or didn't sleep long enough. One of the two. Professor

Lambert fit me into his schedule after I emailed the files from *Moon Wars* to him, so we should get going."

"Yeah..."

"I like your sticker, by the way?"

This time, I was probably the one displaying a furrowed brow in confusion.

"It's the *Last Starfighter* logo, isn't it?" she asked.

"Oh!" I lifted my laptop. "Yeah, it's one of my favorite movies."

We walked north toward campus, the makeup of the trees shifting from ancient sycamores to newer birch trees. The smell of burning leaves wafted through the air, brought to us by a brisk breeze.

"It's going to be a bad winter," I said as we reached the Quad.

"Don't say that. I'm stuck here over break. Although... maybe this *Moon Wars* will turn into a huge game, and we'll have something to do."

I nodded, playing cool at the idea of us hanging out over winter break. Rubbing her hands together, Haley then slipped them into the pockets of the maroon sweatshirt she had on. We continued down the main path between the four quadrants of buildings. The science building was one of the oldest on campus.

"He said he'd leave the back door open for us," Haley said.

She slowed down as we reached the front of the three-story brick building that looked like something from the 1950s Soviet Union. "Come on..."

Brushing her bangs to the side—copper under the pale sun— Haley led the way around the building, following a cement path on the side of the building. A few bikes had been tied up to a railing near the east entrance which we passed on our way to the back.

"I've not been to this building since my freshman year," I noted.

"Professor Lambert is friends with my dad," she said. "They get their pot from the same guy."

"Oh… That's why you're stuck here over the holidays. Your father works here? And they smoke pot?"

"The cat's out of the bag. Can you guess who he is?"

"No idea."

She turned and flashed a smile as we rounded the corner to the back of the building. "Guess!"

"Again, no idea."

"He teaches English."

I gulped. "Your last name is Henderson?"

She stopped at the rear entrance to the science building and nodded, making direct eye contact. "You better not ask me to have him pass you."

"I'd never…"

"Just kidding. Settle down."

I breathed a sigh of relief. "He's a good teacher."

"Yeah, but it's weird being in his class. That's why I don't tell a lot of people."

I nodded as she stepped toward the door, grabbing the huge, brass handle. She stepped inside with me close behind. Clinical black and white tiles stretched down the barren hall with nondescript doors on either side.

"He's in the basement," she said. "Come on."

"Do you know where you're going?"

"I spent a lot of time exploring campus as a child."

"That must've been fun."

"It was… okay. Anyway, let's hurry. We're almost late and I hate being late."

"Noted."

I increased my pace to keep up with her as she scurried down one long hallway after another, eventually reaching a set of steel stairs behind a door with a "No Entry" sign with black letters and a neon-yellow background. This Haley flung open as if she owned the entire college. I followed her down the stairs, wincing every time the rusty metal creaked in the slightest.

At the bottom of the stairs, she continued down a less ornate concrete hall. The familiar, pungent scent of marijuana got stronger the deeper we delved into the basement. While I didn't smoke myself, the halls of Hudson House were frequently filled with the smell of fresh weed.

"Is Professor Lambert growing pot down here or something?" I asked.

She stopped and turned, leaning close. "No, but be quiet about that, okay?"

I raised my hands defensively and nodded.

"Somebody else is growing, but I don't want to out them, okay? The less you ask…"

"That's perfectly fine with me."

She nodded then turned and continued down the desolate, grey hall. Flickering fluorescent lights overhead gave the building some strange cyberpunk vibe. The smell of weed faded, replaced by a terrible smell, a cross between burning rubber and manure. I plugged my nose, not caring if I sounded funny when talking.

"What's that smell?" I asked.

Haley turned and laughed when she saw me.

"You didn't grow up on the farm, did you?"

I shook my head. "City boy all the way."

"The professor is testing some new kind of micro-fertilizer."

"Now I see why the other guy—or lady—is growing pot down here."

"Come on. I hate being late."

I double-stepped to keep up with her as we reached the end of a hall and a double set of grey, steel doors. Another neon-yellow sign forbade entry once again. Haley pushed the left side open, completely ignoring the sign.

Led Zeppelin? I followed her in, amazed at how much louder the music sounded inside the room. Was he dampening the sound somehow? Haley raised a hand as a man in a white lab-coat glanced up from across the immense room. Different equipment sat on the tables scattered throughout the area. Some of them held beakers with various experiments going on while others had haphazard piles of electronic chips and circuit boards. One had a half-assembled robot hand repeatedly raising the middle finger.

"Haley!" Professor Lambert called out as he hopped off the stool.

The table in front of him contained piles of manure in no seeming order.

"You're right on time," he said. "I like that about you."

"How are your experiments going?" she asked.

Standing beside Haley, I was in no rush to introduce myself and I stood quietly, observing them.

"Good, good. How's your father? I haven't heard from him in a while."

"Busy with finals coming up, but good otherwise. Thanks for taking the time to meet with us."

Professor Lambert turned to me. "And who might you be?"

"I'm Alex," I said, quickly adding. "Haley's friend."

"Uh huh," he said, nodding with a knowing grin.

Haley giggled then saved me from my embarrassment. "Did you get the files? We're not sure what they do exactly."

"I'm not either," Professor Lambert said.

Turning back to Haley, he stroked his unkempt white beard. His hair looked like he'd slept in his laboratory the last few nights.

"Your machine intrigues me," he said. "Where did you get it?"

This time, Haley waited for me, so I obliged. "Some guy that said he could transport information over electrical wires, so he's probably not very trustworthy."

"I see, I see," Professor Lambert said in a distracted voice. "Go on."

"That's about it," I said.

"Someone online sent Alex a game called *Moon Wars*, and we found the plans inside the game," Haley added.

The old man's eyes widened even further apart, his bushy eyebrows on the move. "Very interesting. I saw some references to the gravitational pull of the moon in the plans you sent, but I have to admit I'm confused as to what this device might do."

"Que said it was for the digitization of the human mind," I said. "Crazy, right?"

"Perhaps not," Professor Lambert said then peered off in the distance. "You know..."

His voice drifted off. I turned to Haley. She smiled.

"It might not be crazy," Lambert said finally.

"Oh?" I asked, intrigued.

"Can you help us build the machine?" Haley asked.

Professor Lambert looked off into the distance again, stroking his beard.

"If not, it's okay," I said after a few moments.

"No, no, I'll help you build the machine," he said. "I started gathering supplies and parts before you two arrived, in fact. Right now, I'm just trying to remember if I ordered a pizza for dinner or not. If I'm going to be here all night, I'll need to eat."

"I've got a granola bar." I pulled the extra one out of my pocket.

"Nice and warm from leg friction, just how he likes it, I bet," Haley teased.

"That does sound good." Professor Lambert accepted the oatmeal and raisin granola bar and ripped open the packaging. "I must say, I prefer the chocolate-covered type."

Haley turned to me and grinned but didn't say anything.

"What can you tell us about the machine?" I asked.

"Not much yet, I'm afraid." The professor took another nibble. "I'm intrigued by the depth and breadth of the information in that document you sent, Comet."

Haley rolled her eyes then looked away.

"Comet?"

"It's her nickname," Professor Lambert said. "She loves it, right dear?"

Haley smiled politely and nodded, not making a fuss. "You didn't send him all twelve?" she asked.

"I combined them all into one file," I said. "Figured he didn't need the moonbase coordinates."

Professor Lambert's left Woolly Bear caterpillar eyebrow raised. "A base on the moon? What? Tell me more."

"From the game," Haley explained.

"These plans are from a game?"

I wondered how often Professor Lambert smoked pot.

"Yes, we told you," Haley said in a patient voice.

I really liked the way Haley had the measure of the much older man. Her maturity was impressive. Well, that and that she enjoyed playing games. I couldn't wait to play against her competitively once we figured out the strange Que mystery.

"How long will it take to build?" Haley asked.

I glanced at Professor Lambert as the question dragged me out of my thoughts.

"No idea," he admitted honestly. "Should be a week or two at least. I'm not sure if I have enough power to actually run tests."

"Well, we'll leave you to it unless you have any other questions for us."

"No, no, I just needed to make sure you weren't playing a joke on an old man."

"I'd never do that to you," Haley said, frowning at the very idea.

"Let me get to work." Professor Lambert popped the last of the granola bar into his mouth, chewing away. "I'll call you if I make any breakthroughs."

"Thanks again." I pivoted, ready to leave the creepy basement.

"No, no, thank you, dear child. I've not been so excited about a project in a while. Even if the machine doesn't work or we can't build it, I'm sure I'll learn a lot."

"Good. Call me soon." Haley gave the professor an encouraging smile, then took my hand in hers and strode away. I prayed my palm didn't start sweating heavily as we walked back toward the hallway at the other side of the room. She squeezed my hand tightly twice then let go.

"That went better than I thought it would," she said.

"Holding hands?"

"No, silly. Professor Lambert."

"Oh, yeah…" I let my voice drift off.

"Want to grab something to eat?" she asked.

"Yeah," I answered. "Name the place. My treat."

"Such a gentleman. How about Alberto's?"

"More pizza?"

"Are you complaining?"

"Nope."

She swerved to the left, bumping against me before running down the long hall, her footsteps echoing.

"Hey, wait up," I called after her, taking chase.

CHAPTER 6

The night continued at Alberto's pizza just south of campus. Known as *The Village*, a few blocks of shops and restaurants catering to the students served as a perfect place to meet up and get away from campus while not straying too far. Haley headed straight for a booth in the very back of the restaurant. I followed her, feeling as happy as I'd been since coming to college.

She sat on one side of the table with me on the other: the tall, black leather benches basically blocking the rest of the restaurant from view. I gently put my laptop, one of my most prized possessions, on the rough wooden top of the table. Scents of garlic, dough, and cigarette smoke filtered through the air. She reached forward and touched my *Last Starfighter* sticker.

"Why's it your favorite movie?" she asked.

"I'm not sure that's a story for our first date," I said, chuckling nervously.

"Oh, we're on a date now, are we?" she teased.

"No, I just meant…"

"Relax, it's a date to me too." She smiled, putting me at ease. "I'm just making conversation. You don't have to talk about it if you don't want."

"No, it's just that nobody usually even notices the sticker, but it means a lot to me. I saw it at the theater when it first came out."

"Wow. You must have been what... four?"

I nodded. "Yeah, I don't really remember it..." I paused, then caught her eye. "Not long after taking me to see it, my father took off."

"Oh, I'm sorry. I didn't know..."

"Don't worry about it. He left fifteen years ago, and I haven't heard from him since. Apparently, my mother said I was enamored with the movie, wouldn't stop talking about it. She eventually got her hands on a used VCR and a bootleg copy of the movie. I think some of it had to do with me sharing the same name as the main character in the movie, but it was also helpful to remember my father in a good light, you know?"

She smiled. "Yeah, I can see it."

A bored, blonde waitress walked up, chewing gum. "What can I get you two?" she asked.

I glanced over at Haley. "The usual?"

"We have a usual now, huh?"

The waitress sighed as I stared dreamily at Haley.

"We'll have a medium pepperoni and mushroom with extra cheese," I said. "And a pitcher of Coke."

"Can we make it a diet?" Haley asked.

"Sure," I said. "Not that you need to diet."

"Oh, geez," the waitress said then slipped away.

Haley and I laughed, both of us enjoying the cynical waitress and how lame my comment must have sounded to her.

"I wonder if the digital uploading machine has a name," she wondered.

"The moon-i-nator, maybe?"

She giggled as the waitress returned with a pitcher of Diet Coke and two frosted glasses. I moved my laptop to the windowsill just in case as she set everything on the table.

"Your food will be here shortly, lovebirds."

Haley rolled her eyes. "She's just jealous. Back to more serious matters, though, what happens if this machine is real?"

"The men in black show up?"

"I really hope they make a sequel to that movie."

"Yeah, me too…"

We both grew quiet. Skirting around the implications of a machine that could digitize a person's consciousness, we kept bringing up unrelated topics. The gravity of the situation weighed down on both of us, however, casting a serious tone over our first date.

"Tell me something about you," I said to break the silence.

"Like what? I like long walks on the beach?"

"Very funny." I pointed to her wrist. "What about that watch? It's old, but it seems special to you."

She glanced down at it a moment, fidgeting with the metal band. "My grandfather gave it to me right before he passed."

"I'm sorry. We're both digging too deep for a first date."

"No, it's okay." She made eye contact. I got lost in the green depths of her gaze. "He passed a few years ago. I still miss him, but it gets easier, you know?"

I nodded. The waitress arrived with our steaming hot pizza on a flimsy aluminum tray. She plopped it on the center of the table, almost knocking over the pitcher of Diet Coke. I cast a side-glance at my laptop to make sure it was still safe. Two plates and silverware wrapped in napkins followed. After setting them on the table, the waitress wandered away without even addressing us.

"They're lucky the food here is so good," Haley said.

"Right?" I motioned for her to take the first slice. "Go ahead."

She pulled a tasty triangle away from the circle and moved it quickly to her white porcelain plate. I followed suit, waiting for the slice to cool enough to eat safely. She broke into her silverware and started cutting off a bite right away.

"Don't even make fun of me right now." She raised a small nibble to her mouth.

I grinned but didn't say anything, enjoying the look of satisfaction spreading over her face. We spent the next ten minutes joking, laughing, and eating the best pizza in the Midwest. I teased her about eating three slices when I'd only eaten two. She rolled her eyes again in that adorable and not at all annoying way.

When the waitress came by with the bill, I snatched it off the table like it was a million-dollar lottery ticket. "I've got it."

"Thanks," Haley said.

As I pulled out my wallet, Haley's phone rang. She picked it up. "Hello?" Pause. "Oh, no." Pause. "Are you sure?" Pause. "Okay, we're on our way."

I scooted over to the edge of the bench and stood. "What's up?"

"The feds have the science building surrounded."

"What? The men in black? Already? Do you think Professor Lambert told someone?"

A hundred questions flew around my mind.

Haley stood and shrugged. "I don't know, but we should go check it out."

"Yeah. I'll get the bill. Meet you outside?"

She nodded, then put on her maroon sweatshirt. After paying the tab, I walked out the front door. With the sun set, the night air had become even cooler. Together, we headed toward the quad. Red and blue lights flashed across the surrounding buildings as we approached. How many people had they brought? Haley slipped an arm around my waist as we watched from a safe distance, thinking of what to do. "Wait here," she said.

I watched as she walked away without further explanation. She stopped at a nearby campus police car on the outer perimeter the feds had formed around the building. My heart raced as she talked with a man in uniform. A moment later, she returned, her shoulders relaxed a bit more than when she'd left.

"What did he say?" I asked.

"They're not here for Professor Lambert. Seems someone else had an illegal magic mushroom operation in the basement."

I shook my head. "This university..."

"Cheap for a reason." She smiled.

"That was brave going to talk to the cop, even if he's campus security."

"I'm a journalism major, remember? Tom and I have talked a lot over the last year. He's my best source for what's happening with local law enforcement."

"That's right." I stared past her at the men and women marching out of the building with strange glass cases in their arms. "We still can't get in to check on Lambert. Can you reach him on the phone again?"

"Do you think it's safe?"

I nodded, curious whether he was still in the building or not.

Haley pulled out her phone and flipped it open. After pressing a few buttons, she held it to her ear. I took a deep breath. While I avoided breaking the law, authority figures still made me anxious. Perhaps it had something to do with my absentee father who had been a security guard at the local mall the few years of my life he lived with us. "Hey, it's Haley. Are you okay?"

I turned my focus to her and the call.

"That's good." Pause. "How long?" Sigh. "Okay. Will do. Thank you."

She lowered the phone then flipped it shut before putting it back into the left pocket of her loose-fitting sweatshirt.

"What did he say?" I asked.

"He left for his private laboratory off campus."

"Do you know where? We should go talk to him. I want to know more."

"Me too, but he wouldn't give me the address yet. Said he needs time to work on the plans and build the Quantum Uniformitarianism Entanglement machine."

"So, it has a name?" I paused. "Oh, wait. The Q-U-E machine?"

"Yeah." She nodded. "This is getting strange, Alex."

"Us meeting or everything else?"

"All of it." She put her hand on my forearm. "Meeting you and this stranger sending us plans for a machine that can digitize people like in *TRON*."

I smiled, loving how she casually dropped fitting pop culture into any conversation. My mirth faded quickly as the flashing red and blue lights all simultaneously stopped. I took a deep breath, watching as the black sedans left one after another. The local campus cops left soon after.

Haley's hand moved from my arm to my waist. She pressed the side of her head against my chest. I stroked her back as I desperately fought to process all the information coming at me. Between raging hormones and the mysterious QUE machine, I couldn't handle much more without losing my cool. She squeezed me tighter briefly before letting go.

"We should go," she said. "It's cold."

"Did he say how long it would take to build the machine?"

She shook her head, arm still around my waist. We both stayed silent on the walk to her apartment. She stopped at her front door and turned to me.

"Is it too soon for you to have dinner with my father and I?" she asked.

"No, not at all." I stared into her eyes, a brand-new universe to explore.

"Careful." She grinned. "You only know my father in the classroom."

"Is he different outside of the classroom?"

"He's protective of me."

I wanted to be protective of her too. Before the moment passed, I leaned forward and gave her a peck on the cheek. She wrapped her arms around me and kissed me properly. Time lost all meaning for a moment. She pulled away first, her cheeks flush, her eyes twinkling. "Does tomorrow night work for you?" she asked.

I nodded. "Yeah. My only plans involve waiting for Professor Lambert."

"Don't forget your classes," she said in a serious tone.

"Yeah, I should concentrate on them a bit more…"

"I'll help you study."

Visions of "study sessions" turning sensual flashed through my mind, which, it seemed, she could already read. "Okay, Romeo. Settle down. I meant study for real. You can't get kicked out of school right after we meet each other."

Haley leaned forward and kissed me on the lips again: light and lasting. "Call you tomorrow." She pulled away and turned.

Fragments of sonnets that I'd forgotten I'd ever read danced in my head. There had to be phrases to match the depths of my feelings. But I found the words hard to get out. I wasn't practiced in this. We hadn't known each other for very long, but we connected on so many levels. "Goodnight, Haley…" was all I could manage.

After Haley had slipped inside, I turned and trotted toward the sidewalk like a teenaged boy who had just received his first kiss.

66

Conflicting emotions swirled through my synapses as I pondered a possible future with Haley. The walk back to Hudson House went by quickly.

CHAPTER 7

I awoke the next morning to the sound of my phone buzzing. The text from Haley was short, but it made me smile. She was on her way over to help me pull my grades up. Later that night, we would have dinner at her father's house. I stretched then got out of bed before lazily going through my morning routine.

Half an hour later, while waiting in my room for Haley to arrive, I cycled the power on Que's computer one more time. It fired up, the green monochrome QUE> prompt glowing, calling to me. After sitting down, I typed a quick message.

ALEX42: Hello? Que?

QUE: There you are! Where have you been?

ALEX42: The computer's not been working.

QUE: Have you built the machine yet?

ALEX42: No, but someone's working on it.

QUE: I keep forgotten your species isn't very advanced.

ALEX42: Hey, no need to diss earthlings.

QUE: You don't understand. Time is short! I need you!

The parallels between what was happening to me and the *Last Starfighter* movie weren't lost on me. As Haley had pointed out, things were getting surreal.

QUE: Are you there?

ALEX42: I'm here. We're working on it.

QUE: Hurry!

The screen flickered then went black again. I sat back and sighed, resting the back of my head in my hands. Haley walked in, removing her backpack and setting it down. I glanced over as she walked toward me. "Did you get it working again?"

"For a moment. Que said to hurry up with the machine."

"It's out of our control right now."

"Yeah…"

"What's not out of our control is your grades." She crossed her arms over her chest and stared down at me.

"Yes, ma'am," I teased in a semi-mocking voice.

She rolled her eyes then pulled up a chair.

"What are you failing?"

My smile faded. "Everything, I think."

"Alex!"

I loved hearing my name come out of her mouth, even if she was mad.

"Have you reached out to any of the professors yet?"

"No," I admitted, lowering my head.

"Okay, we'll start there. Most professors will give you extra work to make up what you've missed. Not all of them, but maybe we'll get lucky."

"Thanks for the help," I said, glancing up to get lost in her eyes.

"Not a problem. Thanks for taking me on this *Moon Wars* adventure. It's nice to break the monotony of reality sometimes."

"Yeah, exactly…"

Over the next hour, she helped me craft intelligent, apologetic (yet not whiny) messages to send to each of my professors, asking for help in getting my grades up. At the end of our session, she stood up, smiling like a proud carpenter who just finished her best table ever. I joined her, stretching, then rolling my head around.

"Are you still on for dinner tonight?" she asked.

I straightened my gaze and nodded. "Ready as I'll ever be. Around six?"

"Yeah." She nodded. "I've got to go, but call me later if anything comes up, okay? Otherwise meet me at my apartment around five thirty or so."

"Sounds like a plan."

Haley grabbed her white jacket before slipping it on. "Talk to you later…"

She stepped forward and hugged me briefly before turning to leave.

I returned to my laptop, checking to see if any of the professors had emailed me back. Putting together a real-life plan to get out of my scholastic mess brought me comfort. My gaze wandered to Que's computer. Should I try it again? One more time? I hit the power button. To my delight, the loading screen for the game returned.

I pushed my laptop aside and scooted over to the desktop. The old mechanical keyboard made a clickety-clack sound when I typed, bringing back memories of my childhood: of hours spent learning how to make computers do things. All of that had ended up with me chasing a computer science degree to become a video game developer. Such memories dissipated like fog once the sun came out as *Moon Wars* once again entranced me. Just one more moonbase, I kept thinking.

****

Hours later, my cell phone buzzed. After getting my latest character to a safe enough spot, I grabbed the phone and saw Haley's name in block letters. Crap! I stood, frantically glancing around the room for clean clothes. How had I let time get away from me? I flipped my phone open and tapped to read her message. "Where are you?" No angry all-caps or exclamation points.

"Lost track of time. On my way," I replied.

It was 5.41. Only a few minutes after the time I was supposed to meet Haley, which meant we still had time to get to her father's house. After throwing on my last clean checkered flannel, I rushed out of my room. My *Moon Wars* character would likely die, but Haley meant so much more to me than the game. Before I reached the stairs at the end of the hall, my phone buzzed again. I kept walking as I dug it out. "Don't bother. I'm downstairs. Can I come up?"

At the end of the hallway, I bounded down the stairs.

"Haley?" I asked when I reached the bottom.

"Over here," she said from the foyer on the other side of the living room.

I walked past three leather couches forming a C (one of them with only bits of ratty duct-tape holding the black leather together). Haley poked her head into the room.

"Hey," I said, reaching her. "Sorry, I…"

"Got caught up in the game, right?" She smiled. "It's okay. Dad cancelled anyway. I was going to tell you when you came over to get me, so we could go out, but you never showed, so…"

Her voice trailed off.

"When I fired up Que's computer and saw the game had returned, I got wrapped up in it."

"How far did you get?"

"Level three medic this time, and I cleared two moonbases again. With permadeath and no save-slot, it's been hard to get too far."

"It's definitely a hard-core game. Did you just die or something?"

"No, I dropped it to come and see you."

"Aww." She smiled. "Can I help you play?"

I nodded then turned and motioned with a toss of my head for her to follow. "You've got a unique way of looking at things. Maybe you can help me get past this third moonbase."

"What if we're not supposed to conquer all twelve of them?" she asked as we walked across the living room, both side-stepping to avoid empty cans or red plastic cups.

"I just want to get to the RTS battle. That part of the game should be a lot easier to handle."

We reached the stairs, climbing the broad steps side by side.

"The whole concept of the game fascinates me. I hope Que doesn't mind me reviewing it once we beat the stupid thing," she said. "I wonder when they'll release it to the public."

At the top of the stairs, I stopped. "I'm more curious about the plans for the machine we found inside the game."

"We don't even know if the machine is real. I've been thinking about it more. Between all the weed Professor Lambert has smoked over the years and other little things, there's a good chance he could be wrong. I'm starting to think the secret plans might just be some marketing scheme."

"Drink your Ovaltine…"

"Huh?" She tilted her head.

"*A Christmas Story*. The movie?"

"Oh!" She smiled. "Loved that movie. And yeah, like that…"

"We'll see if Professor Lambert can turn it into reality. The implications of such a machine would be too huge. I don't think there's a way it could actually be real."

She rubbed her hands together. "Maybe we'll find more clues inside the game."

I smiled then resumed the walk to my bedroom with her by my side.

****

Over the next week, in between taking care of my academic obligations (I had obtained several positive responses and was determined to make the most of them), Haley and I delved deeper into *Moon*

73

Wars. Que hadn't contacted us again. Professor Lambert hadn't either. We dove into the hybrid game, coming up with a plan to have a forty-eight-hour marathon to actually finish a complete run through. I glanced over at Haley as she sat on the edge of my bed, looking down at the phone in her hands.

"There," she said then looked up and smiled. "All set."

"Great. Neither of us have anything to do for the next forty-eight hours."

She raised a finger. "Except eating and sleeping."

"Well, yeah. Like you said, we'll take shifts. That way, at least one of us is playing at all times."

"I don't know how they think they'll sell this game without a save or even a pause feature."

"That's what has me thinking it's not just a game," I said.

She rolled her eyes while standing at the same time.

"No, really," I said as she walked over to the cardboard table with Que's computer. "Think about it. Why would some big gaming company choose a random gamer like me?"

"Oh, I've thought about it." She sat down in an older swivel chair next to mine. "I think your theory that we'll get a big Drink Your Ovaltine message at the end is more likely. Or maybe it's a government study on crazy teens and their video games."

I grinned. While we had only known each other less than a couple of weeks, we had grown close over that short period of time. Something clicked between us.

"Let's do this..." She clapped her palms together then rubbed them.

I turned to the computer and clicked the New Game button. Maybe we would actually get through an entire game. Even if we didn't, spending two entire days with Haley would be fun. This time through, I paid closer attention to the character creation options available. The five base classes could learn any skills, but they each had some skill sets that came more easily to them, while others were more difficult to learn. Any non-class skills cost two skill point to move up one while main-class skills could be spent one for one. I was sure choosing the right character class was key in winning the RPG portion of the game and making it all the way to the RTS part at the end.

"What are we playing?" Haley asked.

"I went with the soldier the last two games, but I'm not sure if I want to mix it up."

"Stick with soldier," she said. "We can brute force our way through."

"Yeah, that's usually the easiest method for any game."

"I still can't believe they think people will play this game two days straight."

"Yeah, who would be *that* crazy?"

She laughed as I clicked to create a soldier character.

Before spawning, I stared at the long screen of skills, concentrating on the combat skills first because of my bonus.

Combat Skills	Base	Bonus	Added	Total
Unarmed Melee	25	50	0	75
Light Melee Weapons	25	50	0	75

75

Heavy Melee Weapons	25	50	0	75
Ranged Light Weapons	25	50	0	75
Ranged Heavy Weapons	25	50	0	75
Thrown Weapons	25	50	0	75
Demolitions	25	50	0	75
Survival Techniques	25	50	0	75
Recon	25	50	0	75
Stealth	25	50	0	75

Unarmed and melee weapons hadn't been that much of a focus in my first two attempts at beating *Moon Wars*, so I instead concentrated on ranged weapons.

"One hundred points to assign…" I mumbled.

"Save some for the other disciplines," Haley said.

I nodded, clicking up proficiency in Ranged Light Weapons to 100%, leaving me seventy-five points to distribute. After discussing the best strategy with Haley, we came up with a decent list of starting skills. Knowing more about what we would face beforehand definitely helped make the process easier. I hadn't once used the production skills, for example. I figured they might have something to do with the RTS portion of the game, but I needed to get that far.

"How's this look?" I asked.

Combat Skills	Base	Bonus	Added	Total
Ranged Light Weapons	25	50	25	100
Ranged Heavy Weapons	25	50	5	100
Thrown Weapons	25	50	5	80

Demolitions	25	50	5	80
Research Skills	Base	Bonus	Added	Total
Chemistry	0	0	25	25
Mathematics	0	0	5	5
Healing Skills	Base	Bonus	Added	Total
Minor First Aid	0	0	25	25
General Skills	Base	Bonus	Added	Total
Acrobatics	0	0	5	5

Haley nodded as she stared at the screen with me. "Not bad. The chemistry should help. Do you think we need more? Mixing all the elements we found last time worked out well."

"Only having a hundred skill points to add at the start is tough, but we'll get more along the way. I think the combat skills are more important in the beginning."

"The progression level is so weird," she said.

"Yeah, I think the Fibonacci sequence is a clue that using skill points are super important."

She bobbed her head back and forth slowly. "I'm not convinced, but let's play. This game is way too long with no save feature."

I pressed the button to finalize our character build. The same cinematic as before played on the screen. We both watched closely. I'd seen it before, but I looked at it with different eyes, looking for new clues. A lot of our additional skills would start at the baseline minimum or 25% or 0% depending on their main skill type. While the game loaded, I called up the XP needed for the first ten levels.

	Soldier	
	xp needed	skills points
Level 1	100	1
Level 2	200	1
Level 3	400	2
Level 4	800	3
Level 5	1600	5
Level 6	3200	8
Level 7	6400	13
Level 8	12800	21
Level 9	25600	34
Level 10	51200	55

The numbers went up all the way to Level 50 with an obscene number of skill points once you got past level ten. Even playing the full forty-eight hours, I didn't see how we could possibly reach higher than that level before the timer ran out. Time would tell. If nothing else, playing was allowing me to spend more time with Haley.

****

"On your left!"

"Got it," Haley replied then yawned.

She moved our character to the left and took out the last of the level three red rover robots in our fourth moonbase. We had already captured moonbase 1, 2, and 8, unlocking light vehicles, heavy vehicles, and research for the later RTS battle. At least I hoped that was the last of the mundane robots. We had been playing just over twenty-four hours in shifts, and it showed: two pizza boxes sat stacked on one another, surrounded by a sea of soda cans.

"I'm so tired," she admitted.

"Me too." I kept my eyes on the screen. "You can quit if you want."

"And let you take all the glory? No way."

I smiled, enjoying the time we were spending together. "We're not going to get through all twelve moonbases. I don't see how anyone can beat this game in one go over two days."

"Me either. This is the craziest game ever."

"Well, it's definitely not easy."

Haley yawned again. "I'm going to rest my eyes a bit."

"Sure, go ahead. The sheets are all clean."

"Thanks. Wake me up if anything big happens."

I nodded, sliding into her seat after she got up.

While Haley slept in my bed behind me, I resisted the urge to turn around. The game made it easier by drawing me into the tactical situations and strategic choices. We had found Haruto's secret message again. Interestingly, while the locations of the twelve moonbases had changed when we started a new game, so had his vectors describing them. If he had dynamically encoded his Easter egg into the game, I was even more impressed.

After opening the file with all the moonbases laid out, I wondered which I should try to conquer next. Haley and I had decided to start with moonbase one (light vehicles), then moonbase two (heavy vehicles), and next moonbase eight (research). Should I go for more units or other bonuses for the big RTS battle? I glanced over my shoulder to see if Haley was still awake to advise me. Her eyes were closed, her breathing steady.

I turned back to the game. We'd been able to clear three moonbases in half the time allotted to us, so I figured we could do at least three more. Would that even be enough to get to the RTS battle? I assumed that when the timer ran down the RTS would start. But maybe that was wrong, maybe you had to trigger the RTS. If so, it surely couldn't be that you had to clear all twelve bases? That was impossible.

Should I go for more unit production or something else? I decided to head toward moonbase seven to pick up infantry units, the backbone of any decent army. After punching the coordinates into the interactive map, I moved my character toward the nearest exit.

On the long, slow walk, I found myself fascinated with the amount of detail in the game. While I was controlling a third-person character, I found my mind slipping into the scene in a first-person way. It was hard to describe and probably had something to do with the lack of sleep. The game had a strange hypnotic quality. I trudged forward, laser rifle in my hands, ready for anything that might pop up.

Both the layouts and the robots we had encountered in each of the moonbases so far had been differently themed in a way that was loosely tied to the nature of the factory. The light vehicles moonbase had been filled with tracked robots and mini-tanks of all sorts. I wondered about sea vehicles and the many other moonbases we had to clear. Would they all have a distinct theme? I hoped so. Red rovers were getting old. The difficulty level of each moonbase seemed to be increasing with each one we cleared. I just wanted to finally reach the RTS battle at the end and create my mech commander.

"Time to grind," I whispered as Haley slept behind me.

****

Six hours later, a minute after releasing some pent-up gas as quietly as possible, I felt Haley's hands on my shoulders.

"You're up," I said in a voice I hoped didn't sound too startled. "Hope I wasn't gaming too loud."

"No, your gaming was quiet…" She paused, rubbing my shoulders. "Something else woke me."

I lowered my head in embarrassment.

"Don't worry." She chuckled as she sat down next to me. "I grew up with three brothers, so it's nothing I haven't heard before. Besides, it just means we've made it to that next crucial step in our relationship."

I glanced up and turned toward her. "The farting stage, huh?"

"You're so cute when you're embarrassed." She stood and stretched. "Want some coffee, or are you going to try to sleep?"

"Want me to get it?"

"No, I need to hit the bathroom and freshen up. I'll be back."

She turned and walked toward the door. While I waited for her to return, I focused again on the game. Even after so many hours of playing, we had only cleared four of the moonbases. I wondered if anyone had beaten them all before the RTS stuff started. I clicked on the stats screen to see where we'd gotten.

Class: Soldier

Level: 7

Experience: 9,800

Moon Bases Cleared: 4

I also took a look at where we'd added the 33 skill points we'd received.

Combat Skills	Base	Bonus	Added	Total
Ranged Light Weapons	25	50	25	100%
Ranged Heavy Weapons	25	50	15	90%
Thrown Weapons	25	50	15	90%
Demolitions	25	50	5	80%
Research Skills	Base	Bonus	Added	Total
Chemistry	25	0	38	63
Mathematics	25	0	5	30
Healing Skills	Base	Bonus	Added	Total
Minor First Aid	25	0	45	70%
General Skills	Base	Bonus	Added	Total
Acrobatics	25	0	5	30%
Hack electronics	10	0	0	10%

We felt underpowered for a level seven character, but the skill points were based on the Fibonacci sequence and would increase exponentially as we crept up to level ten and above.

"You used all our skill points, I see," Haley said behind me.

I glanced up, feeling sheepish. "Sorry, you were sleeping on our last level up."

"No worries. We really don't have many points to play with yet."

"Yeah, I tried to make us better at what we're already using: combat and healing. You can pick the next upgrades if you want."

"Sounds good to me."

I stood. She took my seat.

"Did you save us some parts for our commander bot at the end?"

"Yeah, pretty much everything. I don't have instructions to build anything cool yet, so…"

"Great. You go get some sleep," she said. "I'll be okay."

"Maybe I'll just rest my eyes a bit."

She chuckled but didn't say anything. I walked over to my bed and plopped down. Sleep overtook me right away as I stopped fighting to keep my eyes open. The game appeared in my dreams.

****

"No!"

I sat up in bed, alarmed at Haley's outburst.

"Everything okay?" I bounded out of bed and over to her side. "What happened? Are we dead?"

"No, not dead, but close. This last boss in moonbase 10 is tough."

"Interesting," I said as I stood behind her and peered over her shoulder.

"What?" she asked.

"You went for the combat bonuses moonbase. That's the one I wanted to go after next."

She smiled then turned back to the screen. "Great minds think alike. Now, how can we defeat this boss? Any ideas?"

"You ran into it this high up in the structure?"

"No, I retreated just before it killed me. You pumping points into medical skills saved us. I'm three floors above where I encountered him. The robot's scanners can penetrate a lot farther than the last ones we fought. I don't think he'll come up here to chase us, but we've got to take him out."

"Okay…" I sat down next to her, leaning forward. "At least we're still alive."

"So close to leveling up too," she said. "This has been a tough moonbase."

I glanced up at the timer. "Only eleven hours left…"

"Yeah, that timer's getting on my nerves. I don't think anyone can beat this game."

"All I want to do is get to the RTS section. Maybe we should just try to stay alive until the timer runs out and not level up anymore."

"I've spent so much time on this moonbase, though."

"Yeah, I hear you…"

My voice trailed off as I wondered what to do.

"What's our inventory like? Have you found anything new?"

"Oh, yes!" she exclaimed, clicking a button. "Check this out."

I stared at the screen and saw the list of our items.

"Something called a trans-dimensional storage box. Basically, it's a bag of holding! Even better, we finally have enough robot parts to build a decent commander mech if we ever get that far. I wanted to wait until you got up and get your input. Should we use the robot parts now or save them? I've found the Forge and the Assembler in this moonbase, so we can build pretty much anything."

"The only problem is that we didn't put any skill points into building robots."

"Yeah, but we should at least give it a try. Might be the only way out of this."

I nodded. "Okay, let's see what we can do."

After navigating to the room with the Forge, Haley melted down the parts to base metals. The Assembler was in the same room, so she selected all the raw resources we had collected and hit the 'build' button. A new screen popped up with a list of simple robots we could construct with the pieces we had in storage. This was the most fearsome boss we had faced so far, and I really wanted to beat it so it didn't slow down our progress. We had little time left.

"That one…" I pointed a finger at the screen. "Jammer-bot A-o-one."

Haley nodded, the mouse pointer hovering over the selection of bots we could build. "I like it. We could jam the boss's radar and maybe sneak up on him."

"Let's do it."

"Give me a minute." She clicked to build the bot. "I wonder how long it takes."

The game answered her by throwing up another timer.

"One-and-a-half-hours?" She sighed.

"Maybe we should cancel it."

"It's greyed out," she said.

"There has to be another way to take care of this boss."

"If you have ideas, I'm listening."

"Have you tried sneaking up to him?"

She nodded. "Yes. A few times. His sensors are too good."

"We need to dampen them then."

"The Jammer-bot would work, but it takes so long to build."

I took a deep breath, slowly letting the air back out. "Waiting might cost us getting another moonbase cleared or at the very least additional xp to level up our character before the RTS portion of the game. I wonder how much our success here counts toward that final battle."

"Me too, but we've got to worry about what's right in front of us."

"I've got it!"

She turned toward me. "What?"

"Can I?" I nodded toward the mouse.

We swapped seats. Back in control of our shared character, I opened the trans-dimensional box.

"You think there's something we can use in there? There's way too much stuff to go through in time. We've been collecting a lot of stuff."

"Not if we get a bit of help. Watch this…"

I clicked the bubble to use our mathematics skill. When asked how I wanted to apply my knowledge, I typed in a single directive, "Create search script."

"Ooh," Haley said, sounding impressed.

"We'll see."

I anxiously watched a reverse progress bar filling on the screen as the computer applied my skill to the task I had given it.

"Yes!" I pumped my fist in the air as a green success bubble popped up.

"Will it work, though?"

"Easy enough to find out."

I clicked on the new subroutine I'd created. A search box appeared. I typed in the word jammer and hit the enter key. Ding. Another green bubble announced two matches in the trans-dimensional container. I scanned the list. Gun Jammer. No. That wouldn't work. The second hit caught my interest. Low-yield EM jammer. I clicked to get more information on the item.

Low-Yield EM Jammer:
Weight: 100kg
Power Source: Nuclear
Range: 0 to ten meters

> Details: Activating this item will send out a quick pulse af-
> fecting a five-hundred-foot radius. Upon detonation, the
> entire radius will become contaminated. Additionally,
> your trans-dimensional storage will be eradicated, caus-
> ing a chain explosion that may destroy you and the rest
> of your equipment.
>
> Use Item? [YES/No]

"No!" Haley cried.

I cancelled the screen. "So frustrating to be so close yet so far away."

"Hold on a minute," she said. "This game has been about synergy so far, right?"

I craned my neck and nodded. "Yeah. Why?"

"Do we have anything to protect us from the effects of the LYEM Jammer?"

"Lie-um Jammer? What?"

"L-Y—Low-Yield EM..."

"Oh, I get it. Let me see." I called up my search subroutine and paused. "What should we search for next?"

"Beam me up!"

"Huh?"

"A transporter," she said. "What if we transported the LYEM Jammer to the final boss? It should be far away enough from us that it doesn't affect our storage."

"Let's see..."

I typed "transporter" into the search box. Nothing.

"Having a magic box with everything we needed would be too easy," Haley said.

I smiled, loving her positive attitude. "Yeah, but maybe there's another way we can deliver the jammer to the lowest level to take out the boss."

"Oh, you've got an idea?"

"No, not yet, but there has to be something we can do."

"The timer's running out. We shouldn't dwell on it too long. Maybe we should try to brute force our way to the boss to take it out."

"No, I don't think it'll work."

"That storage room one level up!" Haley exclaimed.

I tilted my head to the left. "Huh?"

"Come on. I'll show you."

Haley led me to what appeared to be a normal storage room.

"I don't get it," I said.

"Here." She walked over to the area that separated the rows of shelves and pointed at the wall. "Waste Disposal Unit."

"Yeah, but that goes to an incinerator on the bottom level. We've run into them before. The final boss won't be anywhere near the incinerator."

"Think about it," she insisted. "What do you do if something gets stopped in the waste removal process?"

"Oh, I see it. If the incinerator gets jammed, they must reroute the waste and store it somewhere until they can send a maintenance team to fix it."

"Exactly! What would the maintenance team do when they arrived?"

"They usually use a remote emitter to move the waste around the moonbase."

"Right, which means they'd have to beam the waste close to the incinerator and hopefully close enough to the boss robot."

I smiled. "And if they did that, the LYEM jammer would get beamed with it. I see what you're saying. I think you're on to something."

"We just have to disable the waste disposal system," she said.

"Stand back." I raised my level 2 laser rifle and shot at the control panel, sending up a shower of sparks.

"Oh no," Haley said. "I just thought of something."

"What?"

"If the worker bots arrive, they likely won't transfer a known weapon."

"We'll have to set it on a timer and put it in the trans-dimensional box," I said.

"But we'll lose it!"

"It's that or we're stuck here and have to start all over..."

"No, I don't want to start over."

I set the timer on the LYEM jammer—thirty minutes—and then put it inside the trans-dimensional box.

Haley and I then both hid, waiting for the maintenance bots to arrive. They did several minutes later, scanning the box then teleporting it away. I glanced at the timer I had started in the upper right corner of my HUD.

"We've got twenty minutes," I said. "We should make our way down to the last level…slowly."

She nodded, and I walked our character down to the lowest level.

"The scanner's deactivated!" Haley cried a few minutes later.

She leaned forward and put her hand on my thigh.

I smiled, staring at the screen as I directed our character to the nearest lift. As we descended to the final level, I hoped the boss would still be disabled.

"Wait," Haley said. "We should go slow and be careful."

"No, we need to hurry," I countered.

"That's not been smart in the past."

"No, but we don't know if this boss will wake up somehow. I want to clear the moonbase and be done with it."

"Something's not right. I've got a bad feeling."

"Okay, Haley Solo," I teased, grinning and turning.

"Alex, watch out!"

Her wide eyes told me everything I needed to know. In the time it took me to swing my head back toward the screen, a swarm of tiny robots covered our body in the game, extinguishing our life.

"Noooo…" I moaned.

Haley sighed but said nothing.

"I'm sorry."

"You should've listened to me," she snapped.

"I'm running on little sleep," I shot back.

She stood, frowning and shaking her head.

"I should go."

"Yeah, maybe you should…"

No sooner had the words escaped my mouth, I regretted uttering them. She pursed her lips together, nodded, then silently turned and walked toward the door.

"Haley, wait…" I stood.

"We're both tired, Alex. I'll talk to you later."

As she left, I turned to the main menu of *Moon Wars*, still loving and hating it at the same time. Why make a stupid game you had to play forty-eight hours straight? I took a deep breath, frowning as I realized Haley and I might have had our first fight. On the bright side, it hadn't been over anything too important. I would give her some space, wait for her to reach out. While waiting, I had plenty of school work to catch up on to make sure I passed. I would push Haley and *Moon Wars* out of my mind and concentrate on leveling up my real-world life.

CHAPTER 8

The next day, Haley reached out to me via email, inviting me to dinner with her and her father. I almost declined, nervous about meeting her father, but I couldn't resist spending more time with her outside of playing *Moon Wars*. As I walked toward his house in a fancy neighborhood north of campus, I wondered how Lambert was doing with creating the machine we'd found buried in the game. Que hadn't contacted us in a while either. In some ways, it felt like the weird stuff had been nothing more than a crazy dream.

When I reached the address she'd given me, I stopped at the end of the short, brick paved driveway, studying the house. Haley had never said her parents were rich, but I'd always wondered because of the way she carried herself and acted occasionally. After a deep breath to calm my nerves and popping a breath mint into my mouth, I walked to the elaborate porch connected to the front of the red brick house. A light over the doorway flickered on as I stepped up and stopped at the front door. I ran a hand through my hair before ringing the bell.

The heavy oak door opened almost immediately. Haley stood in a foyer, light from a chandelier overhead cascading over her body. I forgot about our silly fight the night before as I smiled. She motioned me in with a nod of her head, her bright red curls swinging and her eyes sparkling.

"You're early," she said.

I paused. "Sorry. Do you want me to come back?"

"No, silly. Dad's not home yet. It'll give us time to talk."

"Okay." I stepped in.

She closed the door behind me as I glanced around. Beyond the foyer, a grand room with a fireplace and wooden walls greeted me.

"Come on..." She took my hand in hers. "We'll go to my old room."

Excitedly, I followed her, not caring what was in store for us. Just spending time with her made life feel more meaningful. She led me up a flight of stairs and down a hallway. At the end of it, a room full of pink, posters, and sports trophies met us. She stopped just inside the room and turned before throwing her arms around me and planting her lips on mine. We shared the intimate moment until we heard her father's voice downstairs.

"Haley? Is that you?"

She pulled back, grinning. "Come on."

I followed her back downstairs. Her father, a man I'd only ever looked upon as a teacher, loosened his tie. "You're early."

"No, you're late," Haley insisted.

"Am I?" Her father checked his watch. "I guess I am."

"Which means you don't have dinner ready, right?"

"No, but we can order a pizza. You like Alberto's, right?"

Haley nodded. Tom Henderson, her father, trained his sights on me.

"Hello, sir," I said, holding out my hand. "Nice to meet you."

"You don't look like a kid who would flunk out of college," he said, putting his hands on his hips. "Do you have a job?"

"I'm here on scholarship, but I help people with computer stuff occasionally."

"Leave him alone, Dad," Haley moaned. "I'll call in the pizza while you two get to know each other. Are the coupons in the usual spot?"

"On the fridge like they always are," Mr. Henderson said

He didn't take his disapproving eyes off me.

I smiled nervously as Haley left the room.

"So…" the older man began. He crossed his arms over his chest.

"So," I parroted nervously.

"How did you two meet?"

"At a party, kind of…"

He tilted his head. "Go on."

"I live in Hudson House, and my roommates were having a party. She barged in while I was playing a game and helped me win."

Mr. Henderson smiled. "That's my Haley. You mind if I have a drink?"

"No, sir," I said.

He unfurled his arms then walked across the dining room to a cabinet full of liquor bottles. After pulling one out along with a glass, he poured himself a few fingers worth of whiskey. He lifted the glass to his mouth, draining it before pouring another.

"To be honest…" He sat down at the head of the table. "You look more promising than the last three guys she's dated put together."

I graciously grinned at his joke as I pulled out a chair and sat, leaving one empty seat between us. "She's great."

"That she is." He took another sip then set the glass down. "What are you goals in life?"

"Graduate, get a job… be a games tester for Ensemble Studios. You know, the usual, sir."

He chuckled as Haley walked back into the room.

"You two seem to be getting along. The pizza is on the way." As Haley sat down between her father and me, her phone rang. She pulled it out of her front jeans pocket and flipped it open.

"It's Lambert." She turned to me before accepting the call. "Hello?"

She nodded. "Okay. We'll come soon. Text me the address."

"Andy Lambert?" Mr. Henderson asked.

Haley nodded and sighed. "Yes, but it's not what you think."

"What did he say?" I asked.

"It's almost ready. We need to go see him."

"You can't leave," her father said. "You just got here. Andy lives ten miles from campus."

"We'll stay for dinner. Can I borrow your car?"

Mr. Henderson shook his head. "It's in the shop. Didn't I tell you?"

"No." She frowned and turned to me. "Do you have a car?"

I shook my head. "No, it's easier to walk to campus with the parking situation."

"Don't remind me," Mr. Henderson groaned.

He stood and poured himself a third drink.

"What about Tom?" Haley asked.

My roommate loved his light blue 1959 Ford Fairlane more than his girlfriend. I didn't see any possibility of him lending it to us. "I don't know. We could ask."

Her shoulders relaxed at the news.

"We should do it now before he's drunk, though."

She nodded. "Yeah. Sorry, Dad. We've got to go."

He raised his glass in the air to toast our leaving.

I pushed my chair pack and stood. "Good to meet you, sir."

"Take care of my little girl, you understand?" he warned.

I nodded. "Yes, sir."

"And stop with the sir crap. We're not in the army."

"Come on." Haley grabbed my hand. "Let's go."

We walked out of the dining room, through the massive living room, ending up at the front door. Once outside, she closed it behind us before giving me another quick kiss. I smiled after she pulled away, her hands still on my waist.

"You did great with my dad," she said.

"To be honest, I'm thinking more about that machine right now."

"Me too. Can you call your roommate?"

I dug out my phone and looked up Tom's number. He didn't answer.

"He probably left the phone in his room," I said. "Which means the party's started already. He's probably drunk by now. I can't believe you don't have a car."

"Long story."

"We have time."

She sighed as we began the walk to Hudson House. "I had an accident in high school." She reached out and took my hand, squeezing tightly. "I hit someone."

"Oh no…"

"Yeah. The lady I hit was drunk, but she died in the accident."

"That's terrible."

"Ever since then, I've tried to avoid driving as much as possible."

There were tears in Haley's eyes and an expression I'd never seen in her before: pain.

It struck me, almost like a blow, that up until now I'd put her on a pedestal. That I'd only ever viewed her as confident, funny, and successful. And yet she was also vulnerable and needed to hold herself together, just like anyone else.

And in seeing her properly, I felt love for her.

"I can drive if we get Tom's car. Not sure what we're going to do if he says no," I said.

"We'll have to call Professor Lambert and have him come get us or something."

I nodded. Silence filled the physical space between us as we walked, building up into a wall. My thoughts drifted from Que and the strange machine to her revelation. I hadn't been looking for love or a crazy internet mystery, but both had found me. We kept walking as the huge, bright moon rose in the distance. The night air was full of energy and I felt as though I were inhaling it. I could have walked like this, beside Haley, for hours.

****

"Come on, Tom. We'll have it back in a day. Two at the tops."

"Going on a sexy adventure, are you, buddy?"

A few of Tom's buddies laughed around him.

"Maybe we are," Haley countered, bold and direct as ever.

"It doesn't matter what we're doing," I said. "We need to borrow your car. Hudson House Boys look out for each other. Remember?"

"But this is my damn car!" Tom cried.

He lifted the half-empty red, plastic cup filled with watered-down beer to his mouth and took a sloppy swig.

"We'll pay for gas," I continued. "You're not going to be driving it anyway."

"No, but I don't want you or lead-foot over there to crash it."

I took a step toward Tom. "Take that back."

"He's fine," Haley said. "Being a speeder is not the worst I've heard said about me."

"You've got a fine woman, Alex. Maybe she can stay here and party with me and the boys while you go on your road trip."

Haley grabbed my hand and pulled on my arm. "Come on, Alex. Let's go. He's not going to be any help."

I followed her into the kitchen. "Hold on," I said.

"You've got another idea? Should we steal the car?"

I chuckled, hoping she was joking. "No, we need synergy?"

"What are you talking about?"

"Like *Moon Wars*," I said. "We need to use synergy to defeat this boss."

She grinned while shaking her head. "You're something else. You know that?"

"I do," I retorted. "Now, I happen to know Tom is late on this month's rent and a few months previous too. There's been talk of kicking him out."

"You want to bribe him?"

"No, I don't think that alone would work. Besides, I don't have the money."

"I could come up with a couple hundred dollars, maybe."

"No, money's not it. We need something else."

"I'm not hooking that douche up with any of my friends," Haley said.

"Tom's got more than enough women around him," I said. "We need something else, something he can't easily get his hands on."

"Go on…"

I leaned close to her ear and muttered, "Marijuana."

She laughed. "Are you serious?"

"We could tell Tom we're going out to the country to pick up a load. Then we'll just say it fell through when we get back. If we say that and offer him a bit of money, I bet he'll go for it."

"You know, Professor Lambert might be growing pot out there anyway."

"Even if he does, I don't want to be…" I leaned close to her ear again. "A marijuana smuggler."

I doubted any of the people at the party would even hear or care about me mentioning weed, but I loved the excuse to get close and get a whiff of her fragrant hair.

"Okay, let's do this." Haley dug into her purse, pulling out a wad of twenty-dollar bills. "This is my allowance for the month, but it's for a good cause."

"You still get an allowance?" I teased.

The party raged in the background as she smiled and stared into my eyes. "I'm just your typical rich girl," she said. "Anyway, we'll offer Tom this and the other. Hopefully, he'll agree. Professor Lambert sounded like we should hurry."

We walked back into the living room, the heart of the party. Haley stopped behind Tom and tapped him on the shoulder. Tom smiled after turning.

"Hey, beautiful. Did you leave that loser Alex already?"

"I'm right here, Tom," I said.

Haley lifted the bills in the air, waving them.

"We can give you this money and bring you back something special if you let us use your car."

"Something special, huh?" Tom asked. He tilted his head back, blatantly staring at Haley's chest.

"Marijuana!" I blurted out.

Tom and his friends burst into laughter.

"I've got a good weed hookup out in the country," Haley said. "If the deal goes through, I'll give you a discount."

Tom swiped the money out of her hands, counting the crisp bills.

"Alright," he said. "I need it back tomorrow night, though. Understand?"

"Sure." I patted him on the shoulder. "Thanks, man."

He peered from the spot I'd touched him back to Haley. "I'm doing it for you, beautiful. Don't let me down."

She held out her hand, palm up. "Keys?"

"Keymaster!" Tom shouted.

A girl with long black bangs and thick, round glasses strolled up with a plastic bowl full of keys. Tom rummaged around until he found his, a set of three keys with a chrome skull dangling from a chain attached to the ring.

"Here you go, sexy."

"Thanks." Haley snatched the keys and turned to me. "Let's go."

"Hold on, let's go upstairs first."

"We don't have time to make-out right now," she said then grinned.

"No, I wanted to grab some clothes and some cash."

"Good idea. I'm broke."

"Thanks again."

"Not a problem."

We walked up the staircase, side by side. A few of the guys cat-called and whistled as if they knew what we were going upstairs to do. Upstairs, we went straight to my room. Haley shut the door behind us. I went over to one of my three bookshelves and pulled out my *Oxford Dictionary*.

102

"You keep your spare money in a book?"

"Reading's not big at Hudson House." I smiled as I opened the book. "Where are we going, anyway?"

"Beaverdam, Ohio. Have you heard of it?"

"No, but I have a map. Hold on."

I walked over to my desk and grabbed the book of maps my mother had given me when I first went off to college. After finding the small town, we headed outside to the four-car garage behind Hudson House. I opened the third stall, exposing Tom's classic to the streetlights.

"Nice ride." Haley walked over to the passenger seat.

I got behind the steering wheel and started up the engine which rumbled beneath the hood.

"You want to know the worst part about the accident?" she asked.

I put the car in gear and slowly pulled out of the garage. "What?"

"My friends all abandoned me. They treated me so horribly, I had to switch schools. It's how I ended up here in Athens."

"For what it's worth, I'm glad you're here now and we met."

A comfortable silence fell upon us as I drove out of town.

"I'll never walk out on you," I promised as the road opened up before us.

She glanced over and smiled. I drove toward Beaverdam, Ohio.

CHAPTER 9

"Don't freak out," Haley said about ten miles away from our destination.

"What is it?"

"I think we're being followed."

"Are you sure?" I glanced in the rearview mirror, seeing a set of lights half a mile behind us. "Who could it be?"

"I don't know. The feds, maybe?"

"But they weren't at the science building to bust Professor Lambert."

"No, but maybe they found out about the machine? Loose lips sink ships."

I tightened my grip on the leather steering wheel, taking a deep breath. "Okay, let's not panic. I'll make a right at the next road, and we'll see if they follow."

"What if they are following us?"

"One step at a time," I said.

At the next road, I slowed, turned on my blinker then made the turn. The vehicle behind us mirrored the move, keeping the same distance from us.

Haley peered into the side mirror outside her window. "They're definitely following us. We're out in the middle of nowhere."

"Professor Lambert's farm is outside of Beaverdam. We'll just go into town and see if we can lose this guy."

"Good idea." Haley reached over and patted the seat between us. "I'm scared."

I placed my right hand over hers. "We'll be okay. Don't worry."

"This is exciting too," she admitted.

"I don't know about all that."

We both quit talking as I drove toward the lights in the distance, hoping it was Beaverdam and we could lose whoever was tailing us.

"I wonder if Tom changed his mind and is coming after us," I said. "That's probably it. We're getting all worked up over nothing."

"He was drunk when we left. I doubt it's him."

"The feds finding out about this doesn't make any sense."

"Maybe Professor Lambert made a mistake," I offered.

"Perhaps."

The streetlights got closer together and brighter as we hit the edge of Beaverdam. I found the main strip through the mid-sized city. Fast food joints and convenience stores littered both sides of the street.

"Are they still following us?" I asked after pulling into a gas station.

"They passed." Haley moved her hand from under mine. "No, wait. They're parking in the Burger King lot next door."

"We're in a public place. Let's get gas and act normal. I'll be right back."

After getting out, I walked inside the mini-mart to pay for the gas. On the way back out, I casually glanced at the vehicle that had been following us, a black SUV. Its make, model, and color did little to make me feel better, but I put on a tough face for Haley. Whatever happened, I had to make sure she was safe. I filled up the tank as quickly as the pump would allow then returned to the driver's seat.

"Well?" she asked.

"It doesn't look good," I admitted, finding it hard to keep my true thoughts from her. "The black SUV kind of gives it away."

"Yeah," she agreed. "What should we do?"

"I don't think we should go to the address Lambert gave us yet."

"Me either. But what should we do?"

"Get a room?" I asked, quickly adding. "And watch a movie or something while we think of a way to get to Lambert without being seen."

She grinned, eyes narrowing. "Uh huh. I see."

"It's late, anyway," I said. "Unless you have a better idea?"

She shook her head. "No, not really."

"Great." I started up the car. "We passed a couple places on the way in."

"The second one looked a little better well-kept than that first one."

"Good eyes." I smiled. "We can sign-in under fake names."

We backtracked a half-mile or so down the main street before I pulled into the Motel 12 parking lot. I parked in the first open spot.

"Mind locking it up," I asked as we got out.

We walked toward the office at the far end of the building. On the way, I spotted a bike rack full of different styles of bicycles with a For Rent sign above them. When we reached the glass door to the office, I held it open for her. Haley walked in with me right behind her. The pimply faced kid behind the counter didn't look up from the Nintendo Power magazine he was holding in front of him.

"No rooms," he said. "Didn't you see the no vacancy sign?"

"It said vacancy," Haley said.

The kid sighed and dropped his magazine to the glass counter. "Damn sign must be broken again. Sorry."

"No worries," I said, suddenly inspired. "What about the bikes outside?"

The kid narrowed his eyes and furrowed his brow. "What about them?"

"Can we rent two?"

"This late?" the kid asked.

"Yeah," I said. "How much?"

"Ten dollars an hour," he said. "They're for the nature trail."

"We'll take two of them until morning."

The teen's face lit up as he grabbed a nearby calculator.

"Great. I get a commission on the bikes because they were my idea."

As the kid added up the expense, Haley leaned closer to me. "What gives?"

"I thought we could ride to the location. Make it seem like we're staying here for the night. While they're watching the room we don't rent, we can bike to Lambert's farm. It's not too far from here. Maybe a couple miles."

"Okay, Lance Armstrong, if you say so."

"That'll be one hundred and eighty dollars," the kid said.

"What? That's way too much. I'll give you twenty for two bikes til morning."

"There's no negotiations."

"Have you rented many other bikes?" Haley asked.

"No, not really."

"What if we got the local paper to do a promotional story on your bike-rental scheme?"

The teen's eyes widened. "You're with the *Beaverdam Gazette*?"

"No, but I have a friend who interned there last semester. She still knows people, and I'm sure they would love a story like this one."

"You really think so?" he asked, sitting up straight.

Haley nodded. "I really do... if we can test them out and make sure they're not bogus bikes. You're not running a scam, are you?"

"No, not at all. You can have two bikes free all night if you can get a story about me in the paper. Business hasn't been good, and..." His voice drifted off.

"No promises, but I'll see what I can do."

"Great. Here's the keys to the locks for my best two bikes."

After turning around and retrieving two keys from pegs on the wall, he spun around and set them down on the counter.

"Perfect," Haley said. "Thank you."

"No, thank you. My name's Rodney."

"Well, thanks, Rodney. We'll drop the bikes off in the morning."

Rodney smiled, his head bobbing up and down in excitement at the prospect of his name appearing in the local paper.

"Do you really know someone who worked at the *Beaverdam Gazette*?" I asked once we were outside.

"I do," she insisted. "We can call her later, though. For now, we have to find out where our tail went."

"Over there…" I nodded my head. "Don't look. They're across the street."

"Great. We can get the bikes then make it look like we're walking to a room on the other side of the building. As long as the car stays in the parking lot, they probably won't freak out. I wonder why they haven't approached us."

"Who knows…" I stopped near the rack of bikes. "Key?"

She handed me one of the bronze keys with the number one written on it with black magic marker. I found the corresponding bike and unlocked it. The yellow ten-speed looked fairly well taken care of, but I hadn't ridden a bike in many years. I hoped what they said about never forgetting how to ride was true as Haley and I quietly pushed the bikes toward the far corner of the building.

"Do you know which way we're going?" she asked.

"I think so."

"Don't sound too convincing."

I smiled. "We'll find it. Don't worry. I have to see if that machine is real."

"Are you going to try to use it?" she asked.

I shrugged, not sure. "We'll see what it is and does first."

She nodded as we rounded the corner then got onto the bicycles.

"We'll go out the back way and circle around the block so they don't see us," I said. "Ready?"

She nodded, grinning.

"What?" I asked.

"The feds. Bikes. You don't get it?"

I tilted my head to the side. "No. What?"

"*E.T.*," she said. "We're playing out *E.T.* in real life."

I smiled and shook my head, loving her even more in that moment.

We turned down a country road, eventually arriving at a long, dirt driveway at Professor Lambert's farm. The closer we got to our destination, the more excited I became at the prospect of the machine being real. My thoughts had been divided between my burgeoning relationship with Haley and *Moon Wars*, but the strange game and real-life machine took precedence as we saw a weathered blue house at the end of the drive. A few feet away, a bright flash of light from the basement windows got our attention.

"I hope nothing's wrong," I said, pedaling faster.

Haley kept up with me as we went to investigate.

CHAPTER 10

I stood at the open doorway, peering inside the house. The smell of burnt rubber hit my nose.

"Ew, what is that?" Haley asked.

"We're about to find out."

I stepped over the threshold and entered the farmhouse.

"Professor Lambert?" Haley stepped in behind me.

"Down here!" a voice from beneath us shouted. "Hurry!"

I darted toward the kitchen in the distance, hoping to find a staircase leading to the basement. I wasn't disappointed as we found a set of dusty, wooden stairs leading down. Lights from below flickered, casting odd shadows on the walls. We continued, step by step, the wood creaking beneath our feet. Another bright light flashed as I reached the bottom of the steps.

"Professor Lambert?" I stepped forward.

"Over here! Hurry!"

Haley and I made our way across the open basement filled with tables, beakers, and various electronic equipment. I noticed what appeared to be jars full of mushrooms and plants that smelled an awful lot like marijuana. Haley didn't mention it, so I didn't either as we made our way deeper into the basement.

A metal container that looked like it might be dropped into the ocean to explore sat propped up with bits of wood. Blue electricity flew around the contraption. Professor Lambert stood nearby, his eyes wide like a child on Christmas morning and his hair looking like he'd been shocked.

"There isn't much time." He motioned us over, excitedly waving his arm.

"Is it safe?" I asked.

Haley and I stopped a few feet away from the machine.

"I think so," he said, seeming surprised by the question. "Que contacted me and assured me it was safe."

"We got followed on the way here," Haley said.

Professor Lambert grabbed her shoulders. "What?"

"Yeah, a black SUV. Did you tell anyone else about the machine?"

"No…" He dropped his arms then ran a hand through his messy hair. "Well, I did tell a couple researchers I knew, so as to get past the problem of transmitting data via electrical wires."

The machine beeped twice, the blue arcs of electricity increasing in intensity. I gripped Haley's hand in mine as we both stepped back.

"Are you ready to enter the machine?" Professor Lambert asked.

"You want me to get inside that thing?"

"Que said you would test it for us. Apparently, the machine has only been calibrated for your DNA sequence. I might be able to modify it to be used by others, but it will take some time. Are you ready to digitize yourself? Que told me it was completely harmless."

"You should wait until we know we both can go into the machine. Where does our digitized self go, anyway?"

"Que was light on specifics, but the process allows you to enter alternate universes. It might actually feel like you've gone nowhere at all. He also said that if Alex wants to go, he needs to do it now!"

"Why the rush?" I asked, having second thoughts.

"Apparently, you can help avoid a catastrophe for Earth, not to mention several other universes." Professor Lambert shrugged, as if what mattered to him wasn't the catastrophe but whether the science would work.

I turned to Haley, still holding her hand. "Are you going to try the machine too? I don't like the idea of going in without you."

"Don't worry, I'll follow as soon as I can. Those feds are eventually going to realize we're gone and come to find us. You should go now."

I hesitated then said, "Okay."

She stepped forward and wrapped her arms around my waist, squeezing tight. Pulling back a bit, she planted a quick kiss on my lips. I took a deep breath then turned to Professor Lambert.

"Let's do this," I said. "What do I need to do?"

"Sit down and put on this headset," he said.

As I sat, he walked to a nearby panel of buttons, switches, and screens.

"It looks like something out of a horror movie," Haley said.

She stepped next to me and held my hand.

"Ready? Set? Go!" Professor Lambert said.

"Wait…"

My voice faded along with the rest of the world.

Everything went black with a pinpoint light in the distance.

I raced toward it, suddenly aware of my consciousness hurtling forward.

The light hit me. I opened my eyes and smiled.

CHAPTER 11

I became aware of a new body. While my mind knew it to be a digital avatar, I couldn't honestly tell the difference between it and my real body. Had Que been lying about the machine? Did it really just teleport me to some room somewhere? Was it all a government plot? That would explain a lot. I saw Haley on the other side of the pentagonal room. We rushed toward each other, avoiding a round bronze platform in the center of the room, eventually embracing. She looked just as hot as she did in real life.

"How did you get here the same time as me?" I asked.

"I don't know." She squeezed me tighter.

We both had on solid white outfits like jumpers that conformed to our bodies.

"Can you two newbie love birds cut it out with the romantic schlop? You're confusing poor Laenard."

I pulled away from Haley and turned to the group of three humanoids huddled together ten feet away according to the HUD displayed before me. Two of them looked human, one Caucasian and the other possibly Indian but with more Asian facial features. The third figure, a humanoid reptoid, had a red tongue constantly sliding out of the tip of his or her mouth. On each of the five walls, a cushioned seat was set against a wall. VR within another virtual reality?

"Listen up, new people," a man named Dhruv Patel said.

His name, in purple, floated in the air above his head, always aligned to my sight. Always-on augmented reality would be nice to have once I was back home.

"Where are we?" Haley asked.

She let go of me and glanced around.

"We're in a simulation of a war game called *Moon Wars*. My name is Laenard," the reptoid said.

I couldn't tell if he was male or female, and I didn't ask. By the gravelly tone of his voice, I decided to go with male.

"Yeah, but where?" Haley continued.

"It's a server somewhere, obviously," Dhruv said. "Will you two quit with the questions while I explain our next playthrough?"

"Next playthrough?" I asked.

Haley and everyone except Dhruv chuckled.

"My name's Haley."

"And I'm Alex," I added.

"What year are you from?" Laenard asked. Her head, crowned at the top by a web of scales, bobbed back and forth.

"What year?" Haley asked.

"Yes," Dhruv said. "We've all been brought from different time periods by some guy named Que."

"You've met him?" I asked.

"Enough with the questions!" Dhruv snapped. "I'm a military pilot from India in the year twenty-forty-two."

"I'm a Reptoid from Gamma-Gamma-Beta in twenty-seventy-two in your time language," Laenard said.

"And her?" Haley asked.

She nodded her head at the quiet woman sitting on one of the chairs.

"That's Anja. She's a great engineer. One of the best. We've almost beat the game a few times with her help."

"How many times have you played?"

Dhruv sighed, shaking his head.

"Give them a break," Anja said from her seat. "We were all new once."

"Thanks." Haley raised a friendly hand toward her. "What are you doing?"

"She's wasting time on a stupid book," Dhruv answered for her.

I watched the scene unfold as Haley walked over to Anja.

"*Shaman's Quest*," Laenard said. "A very peculiar story."

"What's it about?" I asked.

"Being trapped in a game. There's a whole genre dedicated to our plight. Just wonderful," Dhruv moaned.

I wondered at the source of his bitterness. Was it from having played the game so many times?

"How many times have you guys played?" I asked. "That's a basic question. You have to answer it before we do anything else."

Anja laughed. "Too many to count."

"Why haven't you just gone back home?" Haley asked.

"They don't appear to know," Laenard said.

"Know what?" I looked from one face to another for answers.

117

"We're trapped in here, Mr Alex," Dhruv said coolly.

"Hold on, we wouldn't have come in here willingly if we knew that…"

Anja glanced up from her digital book to Haley. "You came into the game willingly?"

"Que said he needed our help. Do you guys know Que?"

"The new humans appear to know nothing," Laenard said.

I still couldn't tell for sure if he was male.

"Neither, actually," Laenard said, "but you can consider me male, it's fine."

"They read minds." Dhruv chuckled. "Get used to it. A quite speciesist reptoid."

"I will beat this *Moon Wars* and make my way home. Your help is not necessary, but I would appreciate your continued helpfulness," Laenard said.

"Where's Haruto?" I asked. "Have you guys met him?"

The others looked at each other, shaking their heads.

"He's a ghost in the machine, a player truly trapped in the game."

"Anja, quiet!" Dhruv barked.

"They deserve to know," she continued, not shaken at all by his outburst.

Haley took a seat on the edge of the pedestal where Anja sat in one of the chairs.

"Go on. Tell us."

"Haruto played *Moon Wars* first in an arcade in nineteen-eighty-two of your timeline," Laenard said. "He became fascinated in the game, the AI's first contact with someone in the past via electricity as a conduit. As a rebellious monkey-man, he fought after being transported to this simulation. He cracked the code of the game and left his impression. The AI deleted his core files in a fit of rage, but some swear Haruto is still in the game *Moon Wars*. I do not believe in him. Faith is for the weak."

I glanced over at Haley and took a deep breath. What had we gotten ourselves into? Could we trust Professor Lambert to get help to save us? Did he have the necessary understanding of the technology? The questions weighed heavily on my mind.

Anja sat up and rested her hands beside her as a crown of ultra-thin beams of light descended on her head. Haley got up and scurried toward me.

"Everyone take their seats!" Dhruv barked. "I'm taking the lead again. We'll go with the new Dhruv standard, three soldiers, one medic, and one engineer."

"Hold on," I said. "The game I played was only one player."

Dhruv sighed. "That's the lure Que uses, making you think it's all about you."

"We believe there are thousands or more here," Laenard noted.

I stayed in place, holding Haley's hand.

"Sit down or you'll be punished," Laenard said as they crossed to one of the walls and took a seat.

Another crown of lights descended from the ceiling. The reptoid closed her eyes, her body at rest.

"Let's check it out," Haley said, letting go of my hand.

I nodded. "Agreed. Good luck."

119

"Hurry it up!" Dhruv commanded as he stood in front of his seat. "If we beat the game, we get to return home. This is the playthrough we do it, people. Let's do this for the honor of Glorious India!"

I walked to one of the remaining seats, sinking into the cushion and feeling like I was floating on a puffy cloud. When the lights hit the top of my head, my eyes closed, and I found myself in a spacesuit on a deck of some sort of troop transport ship.

"Okay, everyone choose the classes I assigned," Dhruv ordered.

I saw the soldier option highlighted in my HUD, but I resisted clicking it.

"Hold on," I said. "There's five classes. Have you guys ever tried using one of each class to get through?"

Anja chuckled while Dhruv sighed and shook his head as if he were wringing off haughtiness with every wag like a dog might water.

"We have tried every combination," Laenard noted. "I have played *Moon Wars* the longest, and I have the most near victories, and the new Dhruv standard is the best possible chance to beat this game."

"Uh, huh," Haley huffed.

Anja grinned behind her glass helmet. "I like the new blood."

"We're landing soon," Dhruv said. "Everyone pick the class I've assigned you. Understood?"

I turned to Haley and nodded barely perceptively.

"Medic here," she called out. "Class accepted."

"Soldier here," I parroted. I quickly assigned my skill points based on the build that Haley and I had previously used:

120

Combat Skills	Base	Bonus	Added	Total
Ranged Light Weapons	25	50	25	100%
Ranged Heavy Weapons	25	50	5	80%
Thrown Weapons	25	50	5	80%
Demolitions	25	50	5	80%
Research Skills	Base	Bonus	Added	Total
Chemistry	25	0	25	50
Mathematics	25	0	5	30
Healing Skills	Base	Bonus	Added	Total
Minor First Aid	25	0	25	50%
General Skills	Base	Bonus	Added	Total
Acrobatics	25	0	5	30%
Hack electronics	10	0	0	10%

"That's what I like to see," Dhruv said. "Now, when we land, each of us will clear two moonbases on our own while in communication with only one partner. I'm pairing up Alex and Laenard, and Anja and Haley. After clearing our first two moonbases separately, we'll meet-up to attempt clearing the final two before the RTS battle begins."

"Has anybody beaten all twelve bases?" Haley asked.

A red light flashed overhead, changing the mood of the metal room.

"We're about to reach the moon. You'll each be dropped near the moonbase I've assigned you," Dhruv said.

121

I followed Laenard to the back of our transportation, amazed at the amount of detail. While I'd never been in a spaceship, the surroundings were everything I had imagined over the years, surpassing even the best science fiction movies.

"Has anyone ever beaten *Moon Wars*?" I asked again. "Haruto? Maybe that's the way out of this trap?"

The others ignored my questions as our spaceship descended to the planet.

Dhruv: Okay, team. All moonbases have been assigned. Clear your two as fast as you can then meet at the rendezvous point. Alex, you're out first. Laenard is your partner. Don't mess up!

I stood as a section in the rear of the cabin opened. Unable to communicate with Haley or anyone other than Laenard, I kept quiet as I walked toward the surface of the moon. A flashing red arrow indicated the direction of my assigned target, Moonbase 1 the one that would grant us access to light vehicles in the final battle, something I still hadn't experienced. The shuttle craft floated into the air, kicking up thick layers of dust. I kept walking forward, ready to become the first person to beat *Moon Wars*.

CHAPTER 12

As I approached Moonbase 1, my chat window flickered to life. Until we upgraded our communication tech, only one person, Dhruv, could contact everyone. I was paired up with Laenard while Anja and Haley became the second team able to communicate on the surface of the moon.

LAENARD: Checking comms.

ALEX: I'm here. Seems to be working.

LAENARD: Clear your base as quickly as possible.

ALEX: That's my plan.

LAENARD: I'm here if you need help.

ALEX: Thanks. I've just reached the entrance.

LAENARD: So slowly? You must go faster! I'm on level two of my base.

ALEX: Wow, that's fast. How many times have you played, exactly?

LAENARD: No time to talk. Go work!

I sighed as I stared at the smooth metal entrance of the moonbase protruding from beneath the surface of the dusty moon. Haley and I hadn't had much of a chance to digest what had happened to us before being thrown into the game. As the better RPG player, I knew she would be okay on her own though.

I tapped a few numbers into a keypad to open the door.

The notification faded away as I stepped into the round room, ready to be taken down to the first subterranean level. I already knew this version of *Moon Wars* was different than the one I'd played on the PC in regards to it not being single-player. Was anything else different? Being inside the game made it seem even more spectacular, but I was betting it would be similar to what I'd played before.

My first encounter blew that theory out of the water as the door to the lift opened and three orange robot balls rolled toward me. I had never encountered them in the game before, but thinking quickly, I fired a few shots of my starter rifle. A laser beam first hit the lead bot, sending it rolling into one of its neighbors. The third rushed forward. I ran out of the elevator and dodged to the left, but it rolled over my foot, causing pain to shoot up my leg.

2 Damage to Right Foot / Shields at 98%

I grimaced and shot another two rounds, not wanting to waste all my ammo on the first three bots if I could help it. Both hit the bot that had run over my foot, sending it rolling into a wall where it sparked then began smoking before rolling away. Instead of continuing the attack, the other two whizzed away at a high rate of speed. *Great. Are they going to get reinforcements? Lay a trap for me?* The enemies in the PC game had been tremendously easier on the first level.

ALEX: Laenard, you there? Got a minute?

124

LAENARD: Heading for level five of my base. What do you need?

ALEX: These bots are a lot harder than I thought they would be.

LAENARD: Other moonbases have likely been cleared. One of the drawbacks to each of us clearing the first two moonbases on our own is that the difficulty level increases much faster. This is why I told you to act quickly. Have you finished your base?

ALEX: I just got inside, and I'm already damaged. Two roller-bots took off. Dhruv's strategy of everyone splitting up doesn't make any sense.

LAENARD: We've tried all combinations except this one, so we're exploring it.

ALEX: Yeah, but it's dumb and we're wasting time. I need help...

LAENARD: I have to go. Figure it out.

As the chat window faded from my HUD, I walked over to where the bot I'd destroyed ended up stopping to scrap it for parts.

+1 Damaged Level Z power core

+2 small sheets of metal polymer mix

+2 infrared sensors

The short list appeared as I took off my backpack to store the gear. After stuffing the bits into my storage compartment, I slipped the backpack on again. The hallway went to the left and right, gently bending as if the first level might be a circle. I decided to venture in the direction the other two bots had rolled away, keeping my rifle raised. My boots clicked on the rough metal surface of the floor as I walked forward.

After following the hallway a few hundred feet, a computer terminal on the outer wall caught my attention. I stopped in front of it, wondering if I should try to access it to make my descent easier.

If Laenard had already made it to the fifth level or lower and my first encounter was three orange roller-bots, the others had to be making good time as well. I needed to get going to avoid slowing them down.

I tapped one of the buttons on the terminal, hoping to get an access screen. An alarm shrieked instead with the lights dimming and turning red in the hallway. I heard several whirring robots whizzing toward me from both directions.

DHRUV: You set off an alarm? Idiot!

ALEX: Calm down. I'm finding my groove.

DHRUV: You better-

I cancelled the chat and blocked any further messages from him, so I could concentrate on the robots coming toward me. Without an upgraded weapon or anything else, I might be toast on the first level of the first moonbase. The first two orange robot rollers appeared to my left. I got off a half-dozen bursts of laser fire, hitting them both. They continued their forward momentum, their orange color more ominous with the flashing red lights.

While I had planned on saving my better equipment for lower levels in the dense complex, I pulled out an EMP grenade then tossed it. A beautiful wave of blue electricity rippled out from its core, killing the two bots. They continued rolling, but I received an xp notification that let me know I'd taken them out.

3 Level U Orange Robots eliminated

+300 xp

You hit level 1 / + 1 skill points

You hit level 2 / + 1 skill point

After glancing at my progress, I saved the skill points and looted the robots.

I took off my backpack again, stuffing the items away. The red alert continued, meaning I needed to act fast. Unless I decided to hack the terminal and turn off the alarm. While difficult, this wasn't impossible. At least I didn't think so as Haley and I had pulled it off on the PC version of *Moon Wars*. I stepped to the terminal, wondering about the others. The better they did, the harder my own enemies would become thanks to the scaling system of the game.

I'd only put ten points into hacking skills, but that proved enough here as I managed to disarm the alarm. Poking around the system a bit more uncovered a complete map of the moonbase. The best weapon in the base was an anti-gravity Gatling gun on the seventh floor down. From what I could tell, each of the bases had twelve levels. I plotted the most direct route from my current position to the super-weapon that would give me an edge against the final boss. Hopefully, I wouldn't be too far behind the others working on their own.

My air sensors changed to "Safe to Breathe" once I entered the second floor. I slid the glass visor over my face up and into the helmet. Taking it completely off would be nice, but I had to be ready in case I needed it again. From what little I knew about *Moon Wars* from playing the computer version, the game loved to throw surprises at you all the time. Haley and I had died more than once from noxious fumes released after stepping on a trigger plate. I wondered how she was doing.

LAENARD: Are you there, Alex?

ALEX: I'm here. What's up?

LAENARD: I am working toward the fifth level.

ALEX: Already? Damn. That's faster than me.

LAENARD: Basically, in a nutsack, I have more experience than you.

I chuckled as I cautiously crept forward.

ALEX: Nutsack? I think you mean nutshell?

LAENARD: Maybe. Anja is teaching me slang.

ALEX: Well, you should study up more. There's a difference—

I cut the message short as three ruby red robots rolled down the hall toward me. The foot-high rectangular boxes with lasers built-in were not too difficult to kill, but I needed to be careful. As they rushed forward, I pulled my laser rifle and fired at the one closest to me. The hit stopped it in its tracks, causing the next one to crash into it. Another two shots took out the last one. The smell of burnt plastic filled the air.

> 3 Level X Red Robots eliminated
> +60 xp / 40 xp needed for next level

The xp wasn't much, but every once in a while the little boxes offered up interesting loot: or at least they had in the computer version of the game. I was still noticing slight differences compared to my previous experience of the game, besides the fact that experiencing it first-hand put it on an entirely different level of intensity.

+3 Level X Red power cores
+12 Rubber Wheels

Ugh. The basic parts weren't what I needed or would likely need while clearing the rest of the moonbase. I kicked the scrap to the side of the hallway then continued forward, wondering how Laenard had already cleared so much more than me. How long would it take me to get to their level of expertise?

LAENARD: Are you on level six yet?

ALEX: What? No! I'm still on two.

LAENARD: You need to hurry.

ALEX: I'm headed to level seven.

LAENARD: Good. You'll pass through six then.

ALEX: If you give me some time!

LAENARD: Got to go. Approaching my final boss.

I shook my head as the chat messages stopped. Walking down the corridor, I headed toward the main elevator in the center of the complex. It would allow me to travel to at least the seventh floor. Laenard might have played the game more, but I thought it was better to bypass six and go straight to my objective. As I waited for the elevator to arrive, I went over my current inventory.

```
// GUN BELT //
+11 EMP Grenades
+1 Laser Rifle (Level 1)
+1 Level 1 Laser Power Core
// BACKPACK //
+3 Level U Orange power core
+3 Locomotion Logic Modules
+3 Repairable metal alloy panels (small)
+3 Level X Red power cores
+12 Rubber Wheels
```

Not nearly enough to do anything interesting. The elevator door swished open. I entered and turned to press the button for the seventh floor, disregarding Laenard's advice. The door closed. I wondered about the mid-level boss protecting the weapon I was after. Did I have a chance? If Laenard defeated his final boss first, my mid-level boss would be that much more difficult due to the difficulty curve of the game.

The door slid open. I raised my crappy starter rifle as I took a few tentative steps forward. A bulky robot about the size of a water heater spun around as I entered an open room with several hallways leading off in various directions. I fired two shots, both of them hitting but not stopping the mechanical monstrosity. Whirring like a fan struggling to work on a hot summer's day, it slid toward me at an accelerated rate. As two-gun barrels poked out of its side, I ran for the closest hallway.

Blasts of blue energy screeched by me as I zig-zagged my way to the nearest hall, hoping I could find some sort of cover. I shouldered my rifle and drew my laser pistol, pointing it behind me on my left side as I ran. The damage would be even less, but I hoped to get lucky. Even more blue energy blasts shooting past my head made me give up the idea of taking it out with either of my laser weapons. I reached the hallway with the mid-level boss robot still a few hundred yards away.

A door on the left opened as I got near. I ducked into the smaller room and smashed the button to shut it behind me. After it closed, I shot it with my laser rifle, hoping to jam it closed. I scanned the empty room, the brushed stainless-steel walls and ceiling not giving me many clues on its function in the moonbase. Most rooms had some sort of larger purpose even with procedurally generated levels. Seeing nothing that would help me with the mid-level boss, I pulled out two EMP grenades, one for each hand.

The metal door to the room glowed red as the robot tried to force its way inside. I clutched the cold metal grenades, knowing they wouldn't be enough to take out the higher-level mob. Had I gotten too cocky by rushing to the seventh floor before picking up better basic equipment on the higher levels of the moonbase? The red glowing gash on the door continued growing. Eventually, the robot would make its way into the room. I could use all eleven EMP grenades, but doing so would likely take out everything else on the level, including the anti-gravity Gatling gun. No, I needed to come up with something else.

HALEY: Alex? Are you there?

ALEX: Hey, it's me.

LAENARD: Haley, you should not be talking to us.

HALEY: I'm in trouble, I need help!

Her name blinked then disappeared from my chat window.

ALEX: Haley? Are you there?

LAENARD: She is gone. The game likely booted her.

ALEX: She said she needs help. Dhruv? You there?

DHRUV: I'm busy right now!

ALEX: Ugh. Are you serious?

LAENARD: Dhruv does not joke.

ALEX: I was being...forget it.

ALEX: I need to contact Haley.

ALEX: I'm using my hack.

LAENARD: No, do not do it!

For such a complex game, some of the code was ludicrously easy to manipulate. After I pulled up a mini-terminal with a virtual keyboard, I could type in the air and access the backend of the game. Part of me thought it was part of a bigger meta-game being played. I initiated a hack to allow me to contact Haley directly. Doing so would sever my communication with Laenard and Dhruv, our so-called commander. They could both yell at me once we inevitably finished the RPG portion of the game. Would the hack work? That was the hundred-dollar question.

ALEX: Haley? Can you hear me?

CHAPTER 13

When Haley didn't answer and I got nothing from anyone else on the team, I went into action, taking care of my more immediate problem: the mid-level boss. The red line on the door had almost cut a hole. I held on to my EMP grenades and waited. When the bot poked the door and it fell over and into the room, I threw the first grenade, quickly followed by a second.

"Die!" I shouted.

A burst of energy exploded where the grenades hit. I had never tried two of them at the same time before, so it surprised me when the EMP wave washed over my body. I grabbed my laser rifle and saw that it had been disabled too. Great. The tin-can in the doorway wasn't moving much, but I hadn't yet received a combat over notification. I crept forward, holding the rifle by the barrel, ready to bash the bot to death if necessary. Once I got close enough, I brought the rifle butt down on top of the robot. A few depressed beeps emitted before its arms went completely limp.

> Combat is Over!
> +500 xp
> You have 860 xp
> You hit level 3/ + 2 skill points

Finally! I thought as I stepped back to examine my situation. The mid-level boss bot was blocking the way out of the room, but I could move it. Before doing anything, I dropped my useless weapons and all the parts I had collected up to that point. The dual-EMP grenades had taken them out.

HALEY: Alex? Are you still there?

ALEX: Haley! Are you okay?

HALEY: I'm okay now. Sorry.

ALEX: You scared me. What happened?

HALEY: I don't know. This game is so weird.

ALEX: Tell me about it. I -

My chat window closed as another notification window appeared.

Penalty Level One Activated

A sharp, throbbing pain erupted in my mouth. Toothache with virtual teeth? What the hell was going on? I grabbed the side of my mouth, not sure how to deal with all the pain. Even worse, the game had cut off my communication with Haley. Was it the hack I used to contact her? I didn't see why the game even allowed hacks if you got punished for using them! I clicked to get more information on my penalty.

Ouch. Had Haruto suffered the same fate when he hacked the version of the game sent to me to include the strange messages? Had he played this same multi-player version as the rest of us after being pulled from his point in the timeline? I had no way of knowing for sure, but the pain in my mouth was real enough for me to cringe. How was I supposed to think about playing the stupid game when in constant pain? I opened my chat window again, but Laenard and Dhruv were still not available. Was it connected to my penalty? Or something else? I had to keep moving forward and clear the dungeon despite the pain penalty.

LAENARD: Have you finished Moonbase 1

ALEX: No, not yet. I'm working on it.

LAENARD: You must hurry...

No kidding. His chat screen went away. I tried to call it up, but it wouldn't work. Unable to stop thinking about the pain, I scrambled over the useless bot parts and made my way to the enhanced weapon in a room down the hall. Without a working pistol or rifle, I felt a bit naked, but I rushed forward. I knew it was only a game, but I didn't want to look bad in front of the other players by dying on my very first mission. Both Haley and I weren't doing too well.

I stopped outside the door to the room containing the weapon I'd been chasing and pressed the button to open it. As the door slid open, I smiled. Losing all my EMP grenades and the spare bot parts might just be worth it. I stepped inside the room. The door slid shut behind me with a whoosh.

At this point in the early game, I had a decision to make. I could use the bot parts I picked up along the way to construct armor, weapons, and more to make my life clearing the moonbases easier, or I could save them for my final robot build. The end game was crucial for winning and getting back to my world with Haley safe and sound. I pondered my dilemma.

Back in the real world, playing the very basic version of the game, I had used the bot parts to improve my equipment during the RPG section of the game. Now that the game was my reality, I had to be even smarter if I wanted to survive and protect Haley. Thoughts of her made me smile. I pulled up the stats on the anti-gravity weapon, noting the lack of specific stats.

Anti-Gravity Gatling Gun:

Weight: 10kg

Power Source: Power Cells (Any Level)

Range: 0 to fifteen meters

Details: Activating this item will send out a cone that will deflect all but the strongest forces. Weak forces will be repelled. If the item repelled is weak enough, it will be propelled away from the person firing the weapon. Each cone lasts for two minutes continuously and cannot be

No, not the best weapon in the world, but I was betting I could have some fun with it and clear the rest of the moonbase. I didn't want Laenard and everyone else to stay so far ahead of me. While I had only played the game a handful of times and never to completion, the stakes were different now.

Weapon in hand, I moved toward the elevator, anxious to finish the final boss. Should I go straight for him or explore more first? I checked my map one more time. As I peered over the display, I noticed an area of the moonbase that had not been mapped before. The area was outlined in yellow, also something I hadn't seen before.

Interesting, I thought to myself as I waved my hand and closed the map. I reached the elevator and pushed the button. The door slid open almost immediately. I walked in and pressed the button for the tenth level of the moonbase. The pain in my tooth flared up, causing me to wince. Had hacking the system been worth the pain? And how had Haruto hacked the version of the game that was sent to me? It was single-player and had other small differences. Had the pain-hacks been even worse for him to sneak his message into my version of the game? But that had led us to the plans for digitizing ourselves and being trapped wherever we were currently. Was it Que who had implanted the secrets?

Could I save Haruto? While that would be nice, my primary goal was to keep Haley and me safe. Returning us to our bodies back on

Earth would be even better. With the penalty, I still couldn't contact Laenard or anyone else, so I kept going. The door to the elevator slid open. I leveled the new anti-gravity gun outside, wanting to try it out. Nothing popped out at me, though, so I exited the car, the doors sliding shut behind me.

I checked the mini-map and moved toward the unexplored and new area of the moonbase. Had my hack unlocked it somehow? My tooth flared up again. I put my hand on my cheek, wishing I had magical healing powers. Thoughts of the pain went away as two robots covered in reflective silver material came into view.

They came at me, their robotic arms brandishing large blasters. I'd never seen this type of robot. The chassis was similar to the ones in the transporter room, but this model had a reflective, shiny coating over everything, and was much larger. They were wheeled robots. I hit the trigger on the anti-gravity weapon, not entirely ready for what would happen next.

The cone of gravity knocked the two red-striped robots out, sure, but the recoil was hell and pushed me back down the hall. It kept pushing me until I hit the wall at the end. Struggling to breathe, I wondered if the weapon was usable at all. Would it kill me? The pain in my tooth kept me lucid as the advanced weapon pinned me against the wall.

Finally, after about two minutes, it stopped. I picked myself up off the floor and grinned, wondering if I would get any loot from the smashed robots. As I walked toward them, the floor of the hallway felt strange. I glanced down and it looked like metallic tiles still, but it felt—squishy? I tentatively took another step forward, testing the floor with my toes. Something wasn't right. A light flashed.

The door to the elevator slid open. I flinched, feeling strange. Deja vu? I stepped out of the elevator and into the hallway. Looking to the left, the way ended with a dead end. I peered to the right and saw the hallway stretch out into the distance, heading toward the spot on the mini-map outlined in yellow. *Well, might as well go check it out now that I was here.* I winced at the pain in my mouth. Another deja vu flash?

About twenty feet down the hallway, four double red-stripe robots walked out into the hallway, pointing their blasters at me. I fired the anti-gravity gun, hoping for the best. The cone of gravity hit the robots, slamming them into the wall, but it also pushed me back, pinning me against the wall for two minutes. What the...? I got to my feet and walked toward the robots, hoping to loot them. Another light.

I stared through the open elevator door, knowing something was wrong. Should I skip the area of the map outlined in yellow and just go for the final boss and clear the moonbase? The others would be waiting for me. I reached up and touched my cheek as the pain in my tooth throbbed then stopped. *Already? Wait. Had I been here before?* This was all so familiar. Was there a side effect to the anti-gravity gun I didn't know about? Or was I stepping into a trap? I decided to go check it out.

Once in the hallway, I went the only direction possible: to the right. As I walked, weapon raised, I wondered how Haley was getting along. She was probably doing better than me. Would I end up with the lowest score out of all of us? Not more than twenty feet down the hall, I stopped. How much time had passed since I got the pain penalty? I checked the counter, but it didn't add up.

As I pondered my predicament, eight dark-red robot bipeds with lasers for arms stepped into the hallway.

"Great," I muttered to myself. "Just what I need."

I raised the anti-gravity weapon to fire, but I stopped. The robots approached, firing both their arms at me. I dove back into the elevator and slammed the button shut. The door closed just in time, but the car wouldn't go up or down as they were firing at it. As I wondered what to do, my chat window with Laenard popped up.

ALEX: Oh, brother. I'm glad to see you.

LAENARD: I am not your sibling. Explain.

ALEX: No time. I'm stuck in some kind of time loop.

LAENARD: Did you use the anti-gravity gun?

ALEX: Um, yes. Why?

LAENARD: Rookie mistake.

ALEX: Great. How do I fix it?

LAENARD: Is your pain penalty gone?

ALEX: Yeah. How did you know?

LAENARD: Dhruv told us.

ALEX: Great. Is Haley okay?

LAENARD: I do not know.

LAENARD: Are you close to finishing your level?

ALEX: Yeah, if you can get me out of this trap...

LAENARD: You must destroy the anti-gravity weapon.

ALEX: What? No! It took a lot to get this...

LAENARD: That is the only way.

LAENARD: You're not high enough level to use it yet.

ALEX: Ah, that makes sense, I guess.

ALEX: How do I destroy it?

LAENARD: Very carefully.

ALEX: Haha. Very funny. Seriously, though?

LAENARD: Take out the power cell...

ALEX: Oh!

I couldn't believe I hadn't thought of it on my own. Then again, I was dealing with a lot. After being transferred from my world, I was stuck in some sort of strange simulation and forced to try to beat an unwinnable game. I popped the power cell out of the anti-gravity gun. The laser shots outside stopped. I pressed the button for the bottom floor.

As the elevator descended, I dropped the anti-gravity weapon on the floor and pulled out my trusty Level 1 Laser Rifle. While not much, it would have to do. Quick thinking and a bit of guts would go a long way, I hoped. The door slid open as the number 12 flashed above it in neon. I stepped out of the elevator and glanced around the room outside. Empty. White. Emotionless.

I cautiously stepped forward, glancing at the mini-map. According to it, I just needed to hop over three rooms similar to the one I was in, and I would reach the lair of the final boss robot for the light vehicles moonbase. Based on what I had been fighting, it would likely be on tracks or have wheels. The armor wouldn't be heavy, but it would likely be fast and able to do decent damage. Would I be able to defeat it? I would soon find out. Feeling like Frodo approaching Mount Doom to destroy the one true ring, I plodded toward the only door in the room. It slid open, the door going up into the ceiling, as I approached.

Two ruby-red roller-bots on the other side spun around. I leveled my laser rifle and shot, disabling them both before they could fire at all.

```
Combat is Over!
+400 xp
You have 1260 xp
You need 340 xp for level 5


+3 Level S RED power core
+3 Locomotion Logic Modules
+3 Light Red Lasers (mounted)
```

Feeling proud of myself, I cleared the XP and loot screens, taking all the items from the dead bots to melt down and use later. My backpack was getting full, but we needed everything we could scrounge together for the RTS portion of the game. I had never made it to that point myself, but something told me that with help from my Haley and my new friends, we could beat the game entirely.

LAENARD: How are you, Alex?

ALEX: Fine. About to beat the boss.

LAENARD: Fine, ally.

ALEX: Funny play on words.

LAENARD: Thanks, I'm—

I closed the chat window as I walked into the next room. The massive storage room held half-track vehicles of various sizes. None of them looked operational, so I continued forward, heading toward the other end of the underground warehouse. Here I saw the boss robot for this moonbase.

A frightening tracked vehicle with an array of weapons at its disposal stepped out from behind a pile of wooden crates. I raised my laser rifle and waited for the right opportunity to fire. The boss robot for the Light Vehicles moonbase rolled forward, several turrets training on me.

The head of the robot tracked my position, and I knew it was only a matter of seconds before the turrets started spraying a wall of bullets in my direction. I fired a shot from my laser gun, which hit the robot's leg. The boss robot shot back, but its aim was off and the bullets missed me. I fired again, hitting the boss robot in the shoulder, causing it to jerk backward.

I took advantage of the opening and fired a third time, hitting the boss robot in the chest and knocking it backward. Its turrets were still active, but I got to within point blank range. I fired a fourth and final shot, hitting the robot's head and destroying it in a shower of sparks and flames. It was over. I had survived the moonbase.

Combat is Over!

+400

LIGHT VEHICLE FACTORY SECURED

+1500 xp

You have 3160 xp

143

```
You reach Level 5
You gain + 12 health
You gain + 3 skill points
You need 40 xp for level 6
```

"Come on," I grumbled. "So close…"

After collecting the new parts, including a level 2 laser rifle. Both the damage it dealt and the accuracy were improved over what I was using, so I equipped it right away. Then I went to the elevator to leave the moonbase. Back on the surface of the moon, I called up my chat window.

ALEX: Light Vehicles moonbase is cleared.

DHRUV: About damn time!

HALEY: You're okay!

ALEX: It was close, but yeah…

LAEBARD: He is finding his grout…

HALEY: Huh?

ALEX: I think he means groove…

LAENARD: Yes, that's it.

ALEX: What's the status?

DHRUV: We've got to clear our second moonbases.

ALEX: I'm on my way to the Sea Units moonbase.

DHRUV: No screwing around this time!

I closed the group chat as I trudged toward the second moonbase on the overhead map. As I walked, I called up a private chat window with Haley.

ALEX: Are you doing okay?

HALEY: Yeah, I'm at the entrance now…

ALEX: I just wanted to check on you.

HALEY: You're the one who's behind

ALEX: I know, I know...it's just...

HALEY: I'm just teasing. This is so weird.

ALEX: And Dhruv's attitude isn't helping.

HALEY: How is Laenard?

ALEX: I like him.

HALEY: Weirdos attract one another

ALEX: Hey! Haha...

HALEY: Gotta go...

The chat window closed. I kept walking, Moonbase 6, sea units, was coming into view. Dust kicked up as I walked forward, wanting to beat the game so bad.

CHAPTER 14

I stood at the entrance of Moonbase 6, the one for sea units. The idea of traipsing through a water level was not something I looked forward to doing, but I needed to clear it faster than the first one. I wasn't about to let the other gamers show me up. Granted, the RPG bits of the game were throwing me off. I hadn't even allocated my skill points from my leveling up. I could do better. Before hitting the button to open the main door, I did so.

Combat Skills	Base	Bonus	Added	Total
Ranged Light Weapons	25	50	25	100%
Ranged Heavy Weapons	25	50	5	80%
Thrown Weapons	25	50	5	80%
Demolitions	25	50	5	80%
Research Skills	**Base**	**Bonus**	**Added**	**Total**
Chemistry	25	0	25	50
Mathematics	25	0	5	30
Healing Skills	Base	Bonus	Added	Total
Minor First Aid	25	0	25	50%
General Skills	**Base**	**Bonus**	**Added**	**Total**

| Acrobatics | 25 | 0 | 5 | 30% |
| Hack electronics | 10 | 0 | 0 | 10% |

With skills capped at 100 until level 20, I decided to put all 20 skill points into my hacking skill. It had come in handy on more than one occasion, and I had a feeling it might help me beat the game. That left me with a 30 skill in Hack electronics.

Once inside the entrance room, I side-glanced at the mini-map. Did I have what it took to get to the end of this level? Back in the Earth version of the game, I had avoided the water levels at all cost because they just weren't my thing. Instead of mentioning this to Dhruv and asking for another moonbase and looking weak, I had decided to face my fears and make it through the level.

LAENARD: You have reached your second moonbase?

ALEX: Yeah. I'm inside now. About to start...any tips?

LAENARD: Try your best not to get killed.

ALEX: Perfect.

My sarcasm didn't travel well through the text chat. Still, it was cool to be able to think of a message and have it typed and sent whenever I wanted. I wished I could talk to Haley and even the others, but Laenard would have to do for the time being.

LAENARD: No problem. I am always here for you, Alex.

ALEX: Okay, I'm going in. I'll hit you up if I get stuck.

LAENARD: Okay, Alex. Talk to you soon, then...

Wait...was he trying to crack a joke too? Or her? It? The grammatically correct way to refer to the alien slipped out of my mind as I stepped toward the only other door in the room on the west wall.

As I approached, it slid open. The smell of chlorine hit my nose. I winced. How much water would I have to deal with? I answered my question as I walked through the doorway and peered down the long tunnel on the other side.

A few feet away from me, a trench of crystal clear water covered the floor. Standing in water would make it more dangerous for any enemies with electric weapons. Something told me there would be a lot of them on the level. Maybe I could hack the game and find an easier way with my Hack Electronics skill? Using it gave me access to a virtual terminal. No, I pushed that aside as I remembered the horrific pain penalty I had suffered through on the first moonbase. The mobs on this level would be higher too.

I raised my level 2 laser rifle and stepped forward. The water came up to just below my knees. As I trudged forward, I kept my eyes peeled on the way ahead. Several steps later, two red cylinders shot through the water toward me. Crap! I shot my rifle into the water. The laser hit the water and spread harmlessly as the red torpedo bots rushed toward me. I jumped out of the water and onto the ledge right before they hit me.

They continued down the hall, blowing up the door I had entered through. Great. Now I had to move forward. I peered down the tunnel, wondering if I could walk along the narrow ledge. With only about eight inches before the metal dropped off into water, it wouldn't be easy. The question was whether it would be safer than walking through the water. I sighed, wishing I had a little backup. Solo games were great—usually—but this was different. The stakes were too high for me to mess around. I sighed again.

Even worse, my laser rifle would be practically useless against the torpedo bots or anything else I encountered in the water. Resigned to my fate, I stepped back into the clear water and took a few steps forward. All I needed to do was clear this second moonbase on my own. Then I could meet up with the others to clear the final two. Nobody was sure what would happen if we actually beat *Moon Wars*, but I was betting it would lead to us being sent back to Earth. At least that's what I hoped.

I moved forward, the water slowing me down. The liquid was too deep to high-step without tiring myself out quickly, so I had to trudge forward one step at a time, the friction against my legs slowing me down. I eventually reached the first intersection in the tunnel. After looking at the way ahead, I glanced in the direction of the other tunnel. Which way should I go?

A quick look at the mini-map helped me to guess that taking the first branch was the best course of action. It led back to what I hoped was the center of the moonbase. That was where the elevators were most of the time. I knew that every moon was different each and every time a person played, but I had noticed several similarities in the handful of games I had played back on Earth. I hoped the game we were trapped in was the same.

Keeping my gaze glued to the water in front of me and just a bit ahead, I went down the new tunnel. A few hundred yards later, the tunnel opened up into a rectangular room. It looked like an indoor pool. A twelve-inch ledge around the walls was the only way to avoid getting in the water which was even deeper. I noticed a tunnel underneath the water. Was this the way down? No elevators? Instead of trying to scour the first level for an elevator, I decided to continue my descent underwater. Could I hold my breath long enough?

Before I could secure my equipment and dive in, a squid-like creature approached at high speed. While it was colored entirely in a deep red, it wasn't like any of the other robots I had encountered in the game. No, this one looked tough. As it broke the surface of the water, I opened up with my level 2 laser rifle. The red beams of light hit its head, only serving to make it more upset. I dashed back into the tunnel as two robotic tentacles reached for me.

"Gotta be faster!" I shouted, then laughed nervously.

LAENARD: Alex, do you have a moment?

ALEX: Not now. I'm busy!

LAENARD: But, Alex...

I turned off the chat window as the tentacles retracted. Taking the opportunity, I rushed forward and back into the room, firing my weapon the entire way. I yelled and pumped my left fist as the mechanical octopus slid back under the water. My sense of victory was short lived as it soon rose above the water with its entire massive body and launched itself toward me. I ducked into the tunnel, one foot on each ledge as I scurried away.

Laser beams flashed to my left and right. One hit my lower left leg. I cried out in pain then jumped into the water while twisting my body. Landing on my butt, I kept my rifle raised and let loose a barrage of shots down the hall. My having dumped most of my skill points into combat abilities proved its worth as I landed a critical hit and destroyed the squid bot's eyes. It shrieked and stopped, flopping around. Die! I thought as I stood and continued firing. The laser damage added up, finally killing the robot.

```
Combat is Over!
+1000
You have 4160 xp
You reach Level 6
+10 health
+ 8 skill points
You need 2,240 xp for level 7
```

I waved the XP screen away and walked ahead to examine my loot.

```
Level Q RED power core x 1
Mech-tentacle x 7
Medium Red Lasers x 7
```

I smiled. The parts were bulky, but with a bit of luck, I would find a Forge and be able to break them down into basic resources that would be easier to carry while clearing the rest of the mission. Even with the Production penalties for being a solider, I should be able to manage to break stuff apart. I was tempted to check and see if I could build a robot or something that would help me clear the level, but after taking so long, I preferred just to show up with a ton of loot when I met the others again.

****

Seventy-three minutes later, I had reached level ten of Moonbase 6, the Sea Units moonbase. Laenard had just defeated his second moonbase. The others, including Haley, had also concluded theirs. According to Laenard, they were all waiting for me. The water levels had turned out to be even worse than I had expected, it was disorientating swimming and fighting, but I had pulled through and managed to pick up some loot that would let me help with the final boss.

From the information I had gathered along the way, the final red robot of my moonbase would be a bigger version of the squid creature from the first level. That was both good and bad news. On the negative side, it was bigger and might kill me. And yet I felt I had hope. I had fought its smaller version before and won. Plus, I had gained a few more weapons and armor to help me, not to mention the water breathing apparatus I had built on level eight. The best weapon was a repeating harpoon that fired bolts of energy underwater.

I stared into the clear water of what I was calling elevator rooms. The floor was missing, and I had to swim down to the next lower level. I saw that this one went down two floors instead of one. Did that mean the boss was around the corner? Should I try to explore one of the entirely flooded tunnels that made up level ten or just go straight for the boss? I weighed both options in my mind.

The squid boss made the decision for me. I dove into the water as I saw a red blip appear on my mini-map. *No you don't*, I thought as I swam for cover underwater. The breathing apparatus made everything so much easier. Well, that and the repeating harpoon I had found on level six. The energy bolts it shot were made to fire through water. Without the weapon, I would have never gotten as far as I had.

I ducked behind a blue metal box suspended in the water by unseen forces. The squid reached around with its tentacles to try to dislodge me: the dumb robot's first mistake. Its second mistake was thinking I would be easy prey. After hitting the closest tentacle with the harpoon (underwater, the shrill shriek of the robot was terrifying), I swam out into the open and fired again.

The beast quickly sped to the left then right, its tentacles dragging behind it. I kept firing, hoping to get a critical. The squid boss bot started excreting an inky black substance from its rear. *Great. Just what I needed.* None of the others had this ability, so it took me for a bit of a surprise. I glanced at the flooded tunnels but decided to go back to the surface on level ten.

As I broke the surface of the water, I quickly pulled myself up onto the ledge. The harpoon gun wouldn't fire into the water from above correctly, so I pulled out a stun grenade that would work below the surface. I held it and waited, peering into the quickly blackening water. Where did it go? I got my answer soon enough.

Three tentacles shot out of the water. One of them grabbed my leg, pulling me into the water. Maybe it didn't know I could breathe? As it dragged me down through the murky depths, I fired the harpoon in the direction I was being pulled. The shriek it emitted did damage to my ears. Besides that minor wound, I still had full health basically. More than enough to finish the fight.

LAENARD: Alex, I need your help!

ALEX: I'm sort of busy right now, buddy...

LAENARD: Alex, I need your help!

ALEX: Okay, okay. What's wrong?

The tentacles let me go. I frantically swam upwards, wanting to get away from the squid boss and out of the pitch-black water. I broke the surface as Laenard explained his problem on chat. He had found himself overtaken by some sort of machine that played on his feelings of insecurity.

I stared down into the water, the stun grenade still in my hand. As I saw the water ripple, I threw the metal ball into the water and scooted down the ledge to get out of the way of the blast. A bright white light flashed underwater. To my surprise, it cleared up the inky water instantly. I saw the squid boss retreating toward the bottom of the elevator room around fifty feet under the water.

"Come on," I muttered.

LAENARD: Alex, I need your help!

ALEX: Yeah, yeah, that's what you said...

ALEX: I'm not sure how I can help you.

LAENARD: Tell me I'm beautiful. Please!

ALEX: Okay, okay, you're beautiful.

I kept scanning the water. The squid boss was on the bottom. Healing itself up?

Getting ready for the next round?

LAENARD: Thanks, Alex. That helps...

ALEX: Hey, and you are smart, funny, and can achieve just whatever you need to achieve.

LAENARD: Damn right! Thanks.

The chat window closed. I wasn't entirely sure what that had all been about, but my teammate had needed me to call them beautiful and I did it. I could worry about any unforeseen consequences later. At that moment, I needed to concentrate on taking out the squid boss and clearing the Sea Units moonbase. Well, if it wasn't coming to me, I would go to it.

I dove into the water and began swimming down.

CHAPTER 15

Halfway down, I noticed a loot crate. As it was in the boss room, I knew it would hold some good loot. Would it perhaps have something that was useful against the giant squid? I intended to find out. The squid had other ideas. Before I reached the loot box, it bolted toward me then stopped, its tentacles reaching out and all firing at once. *Crap!*

I swam to the left a bit then dove, quickly. Most of the shots missed, but three of them hit, taking my health down twenty points. That left me with just under forty health to finish off the final boss then make it back to the top and escape the moonbase. I switched my direction again, swimming back for the loot crate.

The squid fired another volley. It was almost as if it could tell I was going for the loot. Was it trying to stop me? I took another eighteen points of damage, leaving me with only twenty. None of my healing items worked underwater. I shot at the loot chest, hoping I didn't break anything. The lid popped off. I smiled as I saw what was inside the container. The first item I saw was a huge power cell unlike any of the others I'd found up to that point. Was it for a mega weapon or something else? I quickly went through the rest of the loot.

```
* Quantum Power Cell x 1
* Quantum Bolt Rifle x 1, 5 charges
* Quantum Engagement Device x 1
* Quantum Jetpack x 1
```

My favorite armor piece in the box was the jetpack. While not exactly practical for missions inside the moonbases, it would help me get from one to the other faster. I pulled it out and slipped it on my back as the squid kept firing. To my surprise, the jetpack worked underwater! I kicked it on and swam away from the incoming laser shots.

The squid noticed my new maneuverability and started circling me. My goal was to keep moving so it wouldn't see me coming. That's when realization hit me. I stopped swimming and got completely out of the water, flying into the air of the room with the deep pool.

I turned around just as a laser round slammed into me. This caused me to bounce against one of the walls. The jetpack sputtered a moment. I fell quickly. The next attack came from behind. I spun around before being shot in the arms. Only five health left! I picked up the Quantum Bolt Rifle without bothering to read the instructions and fired into the water at the giant mechanical squid.

The Quantum weapon erupted energy, blasting a hole in the squid. The boss screeched then dove back into the water. Would my new rifle even work underwater? Only had four charges so couldn't spare any to test it out. I fired it all the same: it was kill or be killed in the next few seconds. The orange beam hit the water, moving it aside as the energy sought out the squid, hitting it squarely in the body. Another shriek filled the room, echoing off the walls as the sound escaped the crystal-clear water.

I stayed on the ledge running around the deep pool of water, watching the squid as it descended to a dark corner out of sight. Was it hiding from me? Setting a trap? I stayed above the water, trying to make out what exactly it was doing. The water didn't make it easy to see, but I kept my eyes peeled, looking for any sudden movements. Could I defeat this boss on my own? As I came up with a plan, Laenard reached out.

LAENARD: Alex? Are you there?

ALEX: Boss fight...

LAENARD: We're waiting on you.

ALEX: Okay! Got it! Busy here!

LAENARD: Should I stop bothering you?

I waved the chat window closed, my hands gripping the black metal of the Quantum Rifle. Three shots left, I told myself. Not much, but it was the only weapon that would fire correctly under-water. I could backtrack and try to create another weapon with the laser tentacles from the previous squid I had encountered, but that would take too much time. The others were waiting on me, and I needed to finish this boss battle quickly.

As I watched, the squid moved from one corner to another. Was it trying to hide? Biding its time? Healing up? I had to decide soon. My options were limited. The best chance of killing it quick was jumping in the water, zooming around with the jetpack, and firing the Quantum Rifle's last three shots. Would that be enough? Only one way to find out, I told myself as I dove into the water feet first. As I sank, the squid zoomed toward me.

The squid continued its rapid ascent. Now or never, I told myself. That the others were all finished and waiting weighed on me, but I pushed all the negative thoughts aside as I prepared for the final kill. Squid boss had to go. My mind was spinning with the tension, knowing that it was almost over, one way or the other.

I fired three shots in quick succession, hoping for the best. All three shots hit the boss beast. I smiled as I used the jetpack to blast out of the water again. After taking a huge breath, I watched as the squid exploded into a thousand pieces. The parts floated to the surface as I checked my XP notification that popped up.

> Combat is Over!
> +2500
> WATER VEHICLE FACTORY SECURED
> +6500 xp
> You have 13,160 xp
> You reach Level 7
> You reach Level 8
> +24 health
> + 21 skill points
> You need 12,440 xp for level 9

I smiled at the thought of all the skill points I had gained to spend, the Fibonacci system was really kicking in now. After getting back out of the moonbase, hopefully without any problems, I would consider the best use of them on my way to meet the others. If each of the others had cleared their two moonbases, that meant we had two more to go with the six of us working together. Things were looking good. I went through the loot drop, taking everything.

```
Robot Tentacle x 6
Robot Chassis (Underwater) x 1
Raw Iron x 10
Raw Magnetuum x 21
```

Score! I smiled as I stored all the resources in my trusty interdimensional backpack. The fact that it stored so many items without weighing much made everything a bit easier. After getting everything packed, I used the jetpack to fly to the top level of the moonbase. Outside, I contacted Laenard.

ALEX: Laenard, you there?

LAENARD: Yes, Alex. I am here.

ALEX: Good. I just cleared the sea base.

LAENARD: Wonderful.

DHRUV: About time! Where are you now?

ALEX: Headed to you...

DHRUV: We don't have time to fool around!

HALEY: Be careful, Alex.

ALEX: Oh, I'm being careful.

I smiled as I soared a few hundred yards above the ground, racing toward the blinking blue dots on my mini-map that represented Haley and the other players trapped in the game with us. Had they all beaten their two moonbases before me? I felt a bit bad about that, but soaring toward them in a jetpack almost made up for it.

As I got closer, I saw one of them point up in the sky at me. Was it Haley? I descended. When I landed, the other five rushed over to me. I kept my hands on the joysticks that controlled the jetpack as they approached. They stopped near me. Well, all of them except Haley. She rushed to me and threw her arms around me, hugging me tight.

Despite all the craziness around me, I could count on her being there for me, and that meant a lot. I pulled back and peered at her face behind the glass of her helmet. Her voice sounded a bit hollow and unreal over the communication devices in the helmets, but I was happy to see her smiling face.

"You're okay," she said.

I nodded. "And you?"

She tossed her hair back and forth.

"Oh, I'm dealing. You know…the same things we're all dealing with after being transported to this simulation."

I loved her attitude. "We'll get out of here, Haley. Don't worry."

Her smile faded. She looked down at the ground as if she didn't want me to see her fear.

"It's okay," I said. "This has me freaked out too."

She lifted her head, her gaze locking onto mine through the glass. "Yeah?"

I nodded. "Yeah."

"This is just…"

Her voice trailed off. Looking over her left shoulder, I saw Dhruv approaching. I frowned, not really wanting to deal with his attitude at the moment. When Haley noticed me watching Dhruv approach, she turned to face him as well. I reached out and took her hand, grasping it tightly for a short moment to let her know I was by her side.

Dhruv stopped in front of us, shaking his head.

"Are you two lovebirds done chatting?" he asked.

"Give them a break," Anja said.

Her thick Russian accent in my ear made me smile. I wasn't the only one in the group to get tired of the way Dhruv ran things. Yeah, he might have been in the game a long time, but that just meant he wasn't very good at winning.

"Let's go," Dhruv said. "The medical unit moonbase awaits."

As he turned and walked away, Haley and I followed him toward the entrance of Moonbase 11. I just wanted to get through the last two and check out the final RTS battle at last. We probably wouldn't win, first time through, but it would give me a chance to check out the rules of the game and try to come up with a way for Haley and I to win and escape.

That's all I really wanted at this stage; to go home and be with my new girlfriend and do the things that normal couples did.

CHAPTER 16

We entered Moonbase 11 in a pentagram formation. Dhruv led the way with Anja on his left and me on his right, both of us a bit behind. Laenard and Haley brought up the rear. The moment the door to the moonbase slid open and we walked in, I knew it was going to be tough. Beyond the fact we had cleared ten of the twelve moonbases already, the one that unlocked the medical bonuses was notoriously difficult according to the others who had encountered it before.

"Keep your eyes open," Dhruv barked.

I glanced at him as he strode forward. His dark-skinned body was built like a tank and would have been impressive even without any armor or weaponry. My only real problem with him was that I didn't think he understood what he was getting into. This was different from most of the other moonbases we had cleared.

Dhruv opened a door at the end of the long entrance hallway. As it slid open, recessing into the wall to the left, he pointed his gun and scanned the room.

"All clear," he said.

We entered one after another; strange sounds in the distance made me feel more comfortable for some reason. Each time we entered a new space, I found myself listening to all the weird noises in each of the moonbases. They were all different in some way. While the others had said this moonbase was particularly odd, I got a much different vibe. A window popped up with a private message from Haley.

HALEY: Glad we're back together.
ALEX: Yeah, me too. Are you okay?
HALEY: For the most part. You?
ALEX: I'm getting tired of Dhruv.
HALEY: Yeah, me too. Anja is cool.
ALEX: Laenard too. Dhruv just irritates me...

"I see you two chatting!" he barked.

"How?" I asked.

"I've a helmet mod that shows an alert when communication is taking place. Expected it to be useful for mobs, not my own team."

"I believe we have bigger problems at the moment," Laenard said.

Dhruv stopped as he reached the other side of the large, open room. All along the walls, someone or something had painted a logo that read "Navy Nighthawks." The red and white logo had been painted every three feet or so in all different sizes. I kept looking around the room as Dhruv examined the door.

"It's locked, and I can't break it," he said.

Laenard stepped forward. "Perhaps I can help..."

Dhruv stepped aside as the reptilian biped moved in front of the door. Laenard pulled out a device that looked like an old-fashioned microscope. It was black and steel, but most importantly, it featured a green light. My heart skipped a beat when I saw him activate the device. The laser hit the lock which clicked loudly. Laenard turned and smiled. "We're in…"

I pushed him aside. "Watch out!"

Some kind of laboratory lay beyond the door. A dozen bipedal robots, who had been concentrating on their work turned as one towards us, then their hands converted into guns, firing immediately. Laenard fell to the ground after I pushed him, and none of the brilliant green laser shots hit him.

"Formations!" Dhruv yelled.

I pulled out my fully charged Quantum Rifle and fired a shot at the approaching robots. All twelve of them were marching forward, all firing at the same time. My Quantum Rifle shot took out two of them right away, but the rest kept coming forward.

"Close the door!" Dhruv yelled, but it was too late.

The laboratory-working robots had pushed their way into the first room of the moonbase, causing us to move back. Nothing made for good cover, so it was a quick and dirty shootout in the open. Then it got even worse. Haley noticed it first.

"We've got a problem!" she shouted over the comm-link. "They're healing themselves."

I watched as one of the robots I had disabled began to reassemble itself. *Well, it was the medical bonus moonbase*, I told myself as I got down on one knee and fired the rest of the shots I had available in the Quantum Rifle. Each one hit, each taking out a robot, but they were quickly working on repairing themselves. Meanwhile, the five of us were taking damage to our shields.

"Over here!" Anja said.

I glanced over and saw her near one of the walls.

"A secret door!" she announced.

"Tactical retreat!" Dhruv shouted.

I slung my Quantum Rifle over my shoulder and got out my trusty Level 2 Laser Rifle.

"Haley! Get behind me! I'll cover you!"

She turned and darted toward Anja against the wall as I fired several shots. Green, red, orange, and yellow laser fire lit up the room. If we hadn't been in the middle of an intense battle, it would have been a beautiful sight to behold.

"Come on!" Dhruv shouted. "The door's open!"

I glanced over and saw the other four huddled near an opening in the wall. After firing a few more times, I stood and high-tailed it over to them. Two blasts hit me in the left arm, taking ten health from my total. We had all healed up to the max before going into the new moonbase, so I wasn't too worried about it as I stopped by the door.

"Everyone get through!" Anja shouted. "I'll close it behind us."

Laenard let off a few shots from his Level 3 Laser Rifle then ducked through the opening in the wall. Haley followed with me close behind her. After the others made it through, Anja closed the door then blasted the controls for good measure. I turned and glanced around the small room we had ducked into.

"Wait…is this a storage closet?" Dhruv asked. "We're trapped!"

"Settle down," Anja said confidently.

I watched as she moved to the back wall. After removing a black and yellow handheld device from her utility belt, she fired it up and began cutting into the wall.

"This should connect us to somewhere deeper in the complex," she said.

Haley grabbed my hand and squeezed. I turned to her.

"Are you holding up okay?"

"Yeah, you got hit. Do you need healing?"

"No, I'll be fine for now."

"Enough chatting!" Dhruv shouted.

Haley rolled her eyes. We both turned to watch Anja finish cutting the hole in the wall. After she finished pulling away the white material of the walls, she turned.

"Who's first?" she asked.

"I'll go," Dhruv said. "Single file."

He walked into the narrow space barely big enough for one of us to walk through. Outside the door, the laser blasts had quieted down. I soon saw sparks as the robots tried to force the door to the utility closet. After the others went into the space behind the walls, I followed, facing behind us, waiting for one of the robots to break through.

A few hundred yards down the narrow enclosure, I realized they weren't going to sneak up behind us, so I turned to face Haley who was walking ahead of me. The line stopped suddenly. I glanced past her to see that we had encountered a fork in the road.

"The orange arrow pointing to the left is too obvious," Dhruv said. "We're not falling for it."

"Hold on," I said. "Maybe it's a clue from Haruto."

"That's even more reason to stay away," Dhruv said.

He started walking down the right branch. When I reached the spot, I put my hand on Haley's shoulder, stopping her.

She turned. "What?"

"I think we should check it out."

"The others are going that way…" She glanced at them walking.

"I know, but this might be important…"

"Dhruv is getting on my nerves," Haley admitted.

I smiled. "Right? And who put him in charge of anyone?"

"I don't remember voting for him."

I smiled. "Come on then, let's check out this arrow."

She followed as I took the left fork, the one that the large, orange arrow pointed towards. While chances were small it was a clue from Haruto, and I didn't want to end up with another pain penalty, I felt something pulling me in that direction. Maybe it was intuition or a clue from the game. Whatever it was, I found myself drawn towards finding out where the obvious arrows were leading.

At the end of the passage, we came to a hidden door. Well, it wasn't hidden on our side. After opening it, though, I saw that it wasn't able to be seen from the other side. I glanced around the ten-by-twenty-foot rectangular room. This one was full of stainless-steel operating tables and other equipment.

"What is this place?" Haley asked.

"I don't know…yet…"

She followed close behind as I ventured into the room. The arrows had stopped just outside the secret door. Was it a clue from Haruto or a trap? I still wasn't sure as I wandered around. Haley stuck close to me; I was wondering what we had stumbled on and no doubt she was too. She found a something first, motioning me over excitedly.

"Check this out," she said.

I walked over to the computer terminal where she was standing.

"What is it?" I asked.

"I'm not sure, but my computer skills tell me it's for transportation."

"That's...interesting..."

"Yeah, should I try to figure it out."

"We should probably tell Dhruv first..."

"Tell me what?" he asked from behind me.

I spun around and saw him standing with the other two near the hidden door.

"We were just about to tell you we found something," I said.

"Uh huh, I bet you were."

Dhruv strode into the room, glancing around. "Check out that terminal, Anja. Don't break anything!"

Haley and I stepped aside as Anja walked over. She peered down at the alien controls, trying to make sense of them. While she worked, I turned to Haley. She looked surprisingly well considering everything that had happened to us.

"I've got it," Anja said.

The rest of us crowded around her.

"What is it?" Dhruv asked.

"Transportation device," she said.

"I told you," Haley said.

"What does it do, exactly?" Dhruv asked.

"It transports to the final boss room," she said then added quietly. "I think…"

"You think? Do you know or not? This is important!" Dhruv snapped.

"Hey, take it easy," I said.

"Don't you start with me too!" he shouted.

"From everything I see, it's safe," Anja said.

"We should use it," I said.

"Too bad you're not in charge," Dhruv said.

"I agree with the monkey-man," Laenard said.

"This can help us clear the level quickly," Anja said. "We'll have more time for the twelfth moonbase if we can clear this one fast."

"Yeah," I added. "We got this…"

"Fine," Dhruv relented. "I say we do it."

He always had to be in control.

"What is the game plan?" Haley asked. "It would help to know more about the final boss."

"The medical bonus moonbase always has a boss that can heal," Anja said. "We should come up with something to take it out quick and not give it a chance to repair."

"Agreed," I said.

Surprisingly quickly, given the tension between us, we arrived at a plan to use my anti-gravity gun. While we had no idea where we would be transported, I felt confident we had a good chance of winning with surprise on our side. My mood changed slightly when I heard metal feet stomping in the passageway where we had entered the secret room.

"We've got company," I said. "Now or never."

"Activate the machine!" Dhruv shouted.

The approaching footsteps got louder as Anja activated the machine. An orange light flew out of the computer terminal, hitting Dhruv. He disappeared. The beam moved to Anja, taking her away. I turned to Haley just as the beam hit her. When it hit me, I winced, but it didn't hurt at all. I found myself in an operating room with glass walls all around. Seats stood on the other side of the glass. In the center of the room, a bulky white bipedal robot swiveled its head.

"Fire!" Dhruv shouted.

We all opened up, firing our weapons at the robot. It threw up its arms to protect its head then leaped across the table and rushed toward a door.

"Get it!" Dhruv yelled.

I pulled out my anti-gravity gun and hoped for the best as I fired it at the doc robot boss. The cone of gravity hit it squarely, sending the pile of metal slamming into the door it was trying to open. As it struggled to get up, we continued firing our weapons at it, racking up damage notifications like a pair of drunken pirates at an orgy in the woods. We shortly disabled it completely, winning the boss battle easily.

```
┌─────────────────────────────────────────────┐
│              Combat is Over!                  │
│                  +3000                        │
│         MEDICAL FACILITY SECURED              │
│                 +7000 xp                      │
│          You have 23,160 xp                   │
│      You need 2,440 xp for level 9            │
└─────────────────────────────────────────────┘
```

Wow. We had basically bypassed the entirety of Moonbase 11 and defeated the boss without too many problems thanks to surprise and my anti-gravity gun. I watched as Anja went over to the doctor bot boss and began stripping it of parts.

"Loot it all," Dhruv said.

"What's the last moonbase?" I asked.

"Diplomacy bonuses," Laenard said. "We usually save that one for last.

"For good reason," Dhruv said. "It's the least useful."

I said, "do you really know that? Have you ever tried to see what it can bring to the RTS?"

"It would make sense that it is useful, the way the game is balanced," Haley added.

"Diplomacy isn't our strategy," Dhruv declared.

Apparently, that was the end of the discussion. I pushed aside thoughts of what I would have done if I was in charge, and helped the others gather all the glorious loot. After we divided up the spoils of the battle, I finally assigned my recent skill points.

Combat Skills	Base	Bonus	Added	Total

	Base	Bonus	Added	Total
Ranged Light Weapons	25	50	25	100%
Ranged Heavy Weapons	25	50	5	80%
Thrown Weapons	25	50	5	80%
Demolitions	25	50	5	80%
Research Skills	**Base**	**Bonus**	**Added**	**Total**
Chemistry	25	0	25	50
Mathematics	25	0	5	30
Healing Skills	**Base**	**Bonus**	**Added**	**Total**
Minor First Aid	25	0	25	50%
General Skills	**Base**	**Bonus**	**Added**	**Total**
Acrobatics	25	0	5	30%
Hack electronics	10	0	30	10%

I had 33 points to distribute, so I took a moment to strategize about my best course of action. Bringing Ranged Heavy Weapons or even Thrown Weapons to 100% would be smart, but I also wondered about putting the points into Hack Electronics or something else. Moon Wars was interesting with giving so few skill points at early levels and so much more at higher levels. Was there a clue in that somewhere that I was missing?

Without having a high-level Heavy Ranged Weapon yet, I decided to bring Hack Electronics up another 30 points to 60. The other three points I put into Minor First Aid, bringing it to 28%. I wasn't the main healer in our group, but it never hurt to be able to help myself or others during or even after a battle. This version of Moon Wars was turning out to be even tougher than the one Haley and I had played back on Earth. I sighed as I thought about all the good times we'd had together. Would we ever get back home?

CHAPTER 17

The entrance of the last moonbase was just as non-descript as the others, but as we stood outside, I could sense it was going to be different. Unlike the others, the outside of this one was built on a much grander scale. I stared up at the three-story structure and wondered how far below the surface the levels went.

"Okay, I've got it," Anja said.

The door, which had been locked unlike all the others, slid open. I raised my Quantum Rifle, ready to fire at anything that dared to step out. A moment later, three completely red robots on wheels raced toward us, firing.

"Attack!" Dhruv shouted.

I dove to the left of the entrance, firing repeatedly as several rounds of energy blasted through the air around us.

I let off a few more rounds. The Quantum Rifle shots rippled through the air, the spread hitting all three Red Rollers. All this served to do was get their attention. I dove to the ground as it opened up, firing its dual-lasers repeatedly. Dhruv and Haley joined me on the ground as Anja and Laenard both ducked behind a nearby boulder.

"What are you doing?" Dhruv asked breathlessly.

"Attacking the robots; getting the aggro," I said calmly then fired again.

He grinned with approval. "Great. Let's focus on the front one now though."

The three of us continued firing at the approaching robots, taking the lead one out. As it stopped and burst into flames, the other two slammed on their brakes then began rolling away from us. I was about to pump my fist in victory when another three rolled out of the moonbase, approaching us as the others went toward Anja and Laenard.

"Fire in the hole!" Dhruv shouted.

He tossed a grenade. When it hit the ground in front of them, a miniature blackhole formed, sucking them into it. Two of the robots were swept in by his even more powerful gravity weapon while the third ground to a stop, dust on the surface of the moon kicking up.

"Kamikazee!" Anja shouted.

"Oh, crap," Dhruv muttered. "Get down!"

I followed his lead and shielded my eyes. Something flashed intensely.

> Combat is Over!
> +1000
> You have 24,160 xp
> You need 1,440 xp for level

A thousand XP? That was it? That was disappointing. I had thought the victory would level me up. Dhruv stood and dusted himself off as Anja and Laenard walked over. I got to my feet then helped Haley up.

"That was intense," she said.

"We've not seen anything yet," Dhruv said. "Let's get this done!"

We gathered up all the resources available from the destroyed Red Rollers then entered the moonbase. Hallways led in three directions. I let Dhruv decide which way to go. He picked the left path. We ran into a dozen more Red Rollers in packs of three. After defeating them, we came to a dead end, so he backtracked and took the right path, hoping it would be easier. Nope!

Yet another dozen Red Rollers surrounded us. And all this was on the first level! We fought valiantly, working our way down level after level. I seriously didn't think we were going to make it all the way. Each time we got a bit ahead, the moonbase AI beat us down, throwing an almost insurmountable amount of enemies our way. Yeah, it wasn't fun. At all. At least I got my level 9.

****

Hours later, with the game timer running down, we reached the twelfth floor of the moonbase deep underground. The entire area was a huge arena. We had entered through the elevator doors, walking into an ongoing fight between dark and light red robots. As soon as they noticed our arrival, they stopped fighting each other and came for us. Was that how they were so tough? I wondered as I followed Dhruv to the center of the room.

We reached a semi-fortified position in the middle of the arena. Robots of all shapes, sizes, and colors raced toward us, all of them intent on our destruction. I drained my Quantum Rifle fast then moved to my backup level 4 pulse laser I had picked up earlier on level eight of our final moonbase. While it didn't do a lot of damage, it never ran out of shots.

"I'm hit!" Anja yelled.

"Heal her, quick!" Dhruv yelled.

Haley pulled out a healing device and ran it up and down Anja's body. I glanced at them out of the corner of my eye as I kept firing over the barricades surrounding us. Each time I took a robot out, three more appeared from a doorway on the opposite of the arena. Things weren't looking good for us.

"I've got an idea!" Anja yelled over the din of the battle.

"Spit it out," Dhruv shouted back.

He then yelled and fired off several rounds of his grenade launcher.

"Activate your magnetic boots!" she called out to us all.

I flipped the switch, hoping the others had enough time to do the same. Anja pulled the pin on something then tossed it over the barricades. The red ball rolled a few feet away then exploded in a burst of pink energy. All the robots began floating into the air.

"What was that?" I asked in awe.

"Anti-gravity grenade," she said with a smile.

My boots were stuck to the ground; I lifted my rifle and fired at the floating robots trying to move in the air. After a few minutes, they began to adapt, changing their bodies to make up for the lack of gravity. Within ten minutes, most of them were zipping through the arena with blasts of energy, flying everywhere, including toward us.

"You made it worse!" I muttered.

"Shut-up and keep firing," Dhruv shouted.

"There's only ten minutes left," Laenard noted calmly.

I checked my stats screen, and he was right. We only had ten more minutes to clear the final moonbase. Could we do it?

"We're going to run out the timer," Dhruv said.

"That's crazy! We should go after the final boss. Now!"

I was fairly certain the final boss of the final moonbase was hiding in a room behind one of the sets of double doors that were spread around the arena. The robots were coming out from them, so whatever was controlling them would probably be back there too. We didn't have a lot of time, but it might be just enough.

"No, we stick to my plan," Dhruv said.

He fired off another few shots.

"Watch out!" Haley shouted.

She pushed me then fired, saving me from certain death as a flying red robot exploded above us. Pieces of metal showered down on us. After having come so far, I wasn't ready to give up so easily and just run out the timer. Yeah, we would still be alive that way, but would we have enough power to then defeat the RTS portion of the game? Dhruv and the others had been through the experience before, but they had never beaten the simulation completely. Maybe the Diplomacy element of the game was important.

I raised my rifle and pretended I was playing Duck Hunt. This was incredibly more difficult, however, as the "ducks" were shooting back at us! My health had dropped to less than five percent twice already. I hoped Haley didn't run out of healing devices. We would be screwed if we suddenly weren't able to heal back up again.

"Another wave!" Dhruv shouted.

I took a deep breath and braced myself as a flock of red-winged robots swooped toward us, dropping mini bomblets that exploded in quick succession.

One minute remaining...

It was no good. We no longer had enough time to find and defeat the final boss. Resigned to my fate, I just kept firing, hoping to keep us alive until the timer ran out. When it finally did, I let out a long sigh. Everything around us faded.

****

Back in the spawn room, I looked around until I saw Haley. I breathed a sigh of relief when I saw her. She walked over next to me as Dhruv paced back and forth.

"This is it," he said finally as he turned around to face us. "What's your RTS play style?"

He looked in the direction of Haley and me.

"We never made it that far in the single-player version," I said.

"But we've both got RTS experience," Haley added.

Dhruv sighed, not looking happy at my revelation that we hadn't played the *Moon Wars* RTS bit before.

"Since we captured eleven of the twelve moonbases, I'll control three of the factories they unlock on the RTS battlefield. Each of you will control two."

He gave me Light Vehicles and Small Mechs. I wasn't too happy, but I couldn't complain. To be honest, I was just excited to finally get to the RTS portion.

According to Dhruv, we placed these factories somewhere on the battlefield with our mech commander. After doing so, we could hang out and assist production in the factories or move about the battlefield while still giving production orders. Once units emerged, I could give them general commands like "Move to the southeast in formation," and they would follow, fighting and defending as necessary along the way. The AI controlling the units we produced wasn't the greatest according to Anja, but it was good enough to end up with a decent battle involving potentially thousands of units.

"Everyone ready?" Dhruv asked. "Any last minute questions?"

He once again directed his gaze at Haley and me, singling us out.

"I'm not sure attacking first is the best idea," I said.

Dhruv snorted, "Noob says what?"

He was the only one laughing.

"I'm serious," I continued. "Your plan sounds too simplistic. Flood the battlefield with as many small units as we can in the early game can work, but we need to be flexible if the mid-game changes drastically."

"He's right," Anja said.

181

Dhruv frowned. "I've been through this battle more than any of you—"

"Except me," Laenard interrupted.

"Okay, almost everyone!" Dhruv barked. "I've still got the most experience. We need to win in the early game by rushing the battle to them."

"We need to think about this longer," I said.

Dhruv's face showed even more displeasure.

"Are you in charge?" he barked. "Are you?"

"No, but I've played a lot of RTS games in my days."

"You didn't even make it to the RTS portion of *Moon Wars* in the single-player version!" he snorted.

I sighed, running my hand through my hair. "I know. But I've also played hundreds of RTS games against AI. We need to plan something better than rushing their army. Sometimes setting up a kill zone and luring the enemy in works far better."

"This isn't the time for a mutiny," he said. "We've tried all sorts of strategies for winning. This is the latest one in a long list of potentials we will try while I'm leader."

I turned to Anja and Laenard. Neither appeared willing to jump in and defend me.

Haley spoke up, though. "Alex is right. We need some time to really think things through if we want to win."

Dhruv frowned, and I could see his anger building. "Will you two pipe down and at least let me explain what's going to happen?"

I kept my mouth shut. Haley didn't say anything either.

"Good," he continued. "When creating your commander mech, go for the list of options that I sent you. I want to make sure we have all our bases covered."

"Yeah, about that…" I raised my hand. "Are you sure about the builds you want us to use? I mean, I've not played, but I can see several things that might work better."

"Shut up! I've got a system!" Dhruv yelled.

He stormed across the room and got in my face. "Are you wanting to challenge me? Mess it up for the whole team?"

"No," I whispered through clenched teeth.

"Good," he said. "You'll make your commander mech-suit like I've instructed, and you'll use the exact build order for units that I've laid out."

"We have come close to winning before," Laenard noted.

I turned and smiled at the reptoid, loving the fact he constantly lightened the mood whether it was intentional or not.

Haley glanced at me, not saying anything as Dhruv continued giving us what passed as a motivational speech for him.

The truth was I didn't think his plan had a chance. I would still execute it, though. We needed to all be team players to beat the game.

The others got into their pods within the simulation. From what I understood, once we entered the RTS portion of the game, we would be given a chance to construct a robot that would represent us in the battle, sort of like *Total Annihilation* but cooler. After we got our commander in order, we would be on the battlefield and able to start producing units based on what factories we had secured in the RPG section of the game. Easy, right? I really hoped so.

"Any last advice, Anja?" I asked right before we went under.

"Yeah," Haley added. "Is this like *Total Annihilation*? Should we go for lots of units or unit composition?"

"It's like *Total Annihilation* in some ways," Anja said.

"Oh, you've played it?" I asked, remembering she was from the future.

"I played it sometimes," she replied with a smile.

"You do? That far in the future?"

"What can I say? It's a classic game." She grinned.

"Everyone get ready! This is no time to mess around. We're going to defeat the planet below this time. That's all there is to it. Let's do this!"

The helmets above us lowered, covering our heads as we prepared to slip into a second simulation within the simulation. Yeah, my head was spinning by that point, but I had to just keep going. That's all there was to do. According to Dhruv's plan, he would be controlling operations of four of the factories. The rest of us would have control of two each.

Countdown beginning... 10, 9, 8...

I braced myself, taking a deep breath. Haley peered over and smiled. I tried to let her know how much she meant to me: as well as I could without words.

...5,4,3,2, 1...

Everything faded around me.

184

CHAPTER 18

I appeared in a small grey room with a large screen in front of me. A suit of mechanical armor displayed was flanked to the left and right with a variety of different options. Since we had unlocked eleven moonbases, I had a lot of choices. Add-ons to the base chassis cost experience points accumulated during the RPG section of the game.

There were five chassis builds to choose from:

Commander Mech Chassis Choices:

Medic
Health: High (7,500)

Speed: Fast (20 feet/second)

Can Jump?: No

Build Power: Normal (10 BP)

Modules Available: Versatile

Soldier
Health: Excellent (10,000)

Speed: Medium (35 feet/second)

Can Jump?: Yes

Build Power: Normal (10 BP)

Modules Available: Combat / Defense

Scientist

Health: Low (2,000)

Speed: Fast (20 feet/second)

Can Jump? Yes

Build Power: Lower (5 BP)

Modules Available: Research

Engineer

Health: Medium (5,000)

Speed: Slow (2 feet/second)

Can Jump? No

Build Power: Improved (20 BP)

Modules Available: Support

Diplomat

Health: Medium (4,000)

Speed: Slow (3 feet/second)

Can Jump? No

Build Power: Improved (20 BP)

Modules Available: Versatile

I went with the Soldier chassis, adding a heavy laser for my left weapon and a heavy machine gun for the weapon attached to my right arm. While I could have traded them both for a more powerful weapon that would be held in both my hands, I didn't have enough overall experience to go that route if I also wanted to add defensive armor plates and other features to my bot. I scrolled through the list of other options available and ignoring Dhruv's message about the

Commander build, ended up choosing the following to customize my commander mech.

```
Armor Plating
Rocket Pack
Advanced Servos (increased movement)
Advanced Targeting (both weapons hit more often)
Advanced Back-Up Power Cell
Minor Radar Cloaking (Personal)
```

The mechanics reminded me a little of *Total Annihilation*, but I had a lot more options available. After taking so long choosing all my options, I didn't really have time to see what the others were building before being transferred to the battlefield. I appeared hovering above the moon's surface with the other four nearby.

I glanced around at the others then looked down at the robot I was controlling. Very cool. The robotic suit was designed for a human soldier, and the pilot, essentially a humanoid head, was simply a glorified helmet, so it was me working through the machine. One sensor pod was on the front of my helmet, and another was in the rear. I had a display screen of the image in front of me and the sensor feeds all around me, and I controlled the arms and legs with my limbs.

I nodded in understanding as I took control. Even though I was human, I did not want to rely on the computer to do it for me. I had a feeling I might need to take control from it at a moment's notice. I didn't want to have to think about it.

"All right, people," Dhruv shouted. "We are attacking first this time!"

I raised my hand, knowing he didn't like to be interrupted.

"What is it?" Dhruv barked.

"Shouldn't we try to set-up defenses first?" I asked.

"Yeah, that sounds like the smartest idea," Haley said.

Anja laughed. Laenard shook their reptilian head.

"How many times have you two played the RTS portion of the game?" Dhruv asked.

"Well…"

"Exactly!" he said. "Now, listen to me and start building units to go on the offensive."

"Okay," I muttered.

I glanced at Haley. She rolled her eyes, making me smile. I liked her so much.

"Let's do this, people!" Dhruv shouted.

I noticed the others were tapping and swiping game screens in front of them, so I called up my own. All the different options for the two factories I would be controlling surprised me. I could build units, research new tech, and give basic commands to units I had already created. Some of the units available were:

Light Vehicles
Scout (fast attack; scout vehicles ignore terrain, but fire-power is weak against armor)
Warrior (heavy attack; ideal for front line combat)
Sniper (defensive, long-range attack)

Rocket Rover (offensive, medium range, good versus armor)

Badger (powerful attack unit, but slow)

Humvee (quick transport of units)

Air Units

Sparrow (radar plane, slow, light armor)

Yellow-Jacket (small, air to air fighter)

Locust (small, laser armed air to ground fighter, little armor but fast)

Raven (medium bomber, slow but heavily armored)

Overlord (flying, air transport)

Fortress (powerful, flying fortress)

I wanted to stay mobile, so I selected Scout for my production priority, plus Rocket Rovers. The two seemed a good combination, even if the rovers were slow to come off the production lines. I had about two hundred scout units already built, and about three hundred warriors. They were the best for attacking, so I ordered them to move out and destroy everything I found.

The 3D map of the moon showed where we would be placing our production factories and where the enemies from the planet below would land and start attacking us. Dhruv wanting to fly out and attack them first was a foolish move, but I wasn't in charge of our group, at least not yet.

I smiled, I was looking forward to the battle. At last, something I was good at.

"Remember," Dhruv said. "You can control your units by swiping on the command screen in front of you. There is a mini-map at the bottom. You'll see your units, enemy units, and your bases."

I nodded as the enemy units from the planet below—scouts of their own—began to appear and land on the moon's surface. My heads-up screen showed the enemy as a green dot, and my own units in blue.

The first of my scout units moved forward and swiped through the enemy. Having mobility was giving me an edge: although not as strong as the warriors, the scouts were adept at setting up ambushes on incoming targets as well as flanking fire.

Even so, a wave of half-tracks full of robots had arrived right in front of me and was deploying too close to my Light Vehicle factory for my liking. I swiped my finger across the screen and hit the enemy unit, and a robotic hand appeared to grab the enemy unit. I swiped again to the left and pulled the enemy unit toward my own. I swiped once more to pull the enemy closer.

That was when the robotic suit's hand grabbed me and pulled me closer to the enemy. I swiped my finger across the screen to toss the unit, but nothing happened.

"What the…?" I asked.

"What's wrong?" Anja asked.

"It grabbed me, and I don't know how to toss it," I replied.

"Ah, yes. This is a new feature of the suit," Laenard said. "You can grab enemies and toss them to the ground. It is quite useful. You just have to double tap the direction of the throw."

I tried it and watched the enemy unit as it spun in the air toward the ground. It landed hard on the ground and a red skull appeared over it.

"Nice!" I said. "We got this!" Supported by my scouts I proceeded to lay waste to the enemy robots in front of me, with only a ten percent decline in my shields.

My excitement was premature. The enemy forces were still landing on the moon, massing to the south at the base of a big mountain. I whipped through game screens as fast as I could while keeping an eye on the overall battle situation. Things weren't looking good. Not at all. Dhruv was the worst commander I had ever come across. He just kept barking orders, not listening to anything that we were reporting to him.

As a result of wasting units in open terrain (all my initial warrior force were gone), the enemy was gaining momentum. Our offensive efforts hadn't thrown the enemy back and now, in fact, they were increasing the pressure on our front lines at several points. Another ten minutes, and they would break through where Anja and Dhruv were trying to hold them back. From there they could start to attack and take out our factories, leaving us unable to produce new units and thus losing the game. Back behind our factories, Haley and Laenard were doing all they could to keep mining resources and keep our economy going. We were suiciding too many troops, sending them into engagements they couldn't win. Things weren't looking good at all.

"Anja, what's your situation?" I asked.

"Under control for now," Anja responded. "If we can keep the enemy units out long enough to build some high-end tanks and planes, I think we can win. But they have a lot of units in reserve, and their primary attack unit is almost here."

"Anybody have a bright idea?" I asked, looking up at a massive ship: an incoming flying fortress.

As I studied it, a stream of rockets flew up from our side, arching up into the sky. They began to shower fire on the enemy attack craft, turning its progress into a cloud of debris. Even Dhruv cheered as it took a wide turn to avoid the bombardment.

I saw Anja's mech suit kick in as she personally entered battle, sending waves of fire into the enemy's forces. Zooming out, I tried for a more comprehensive view. The enemy flying fortress was making a turn, a turret lazily spinning as it rose into the air. My heart sank. It was a lot bigger than anything I had anticipated. A lot bigger.

"Haley, what do you have for that boss enemy unit?" I asked, fighting back my fear.

She paused, then said, "Well, I can create some small rocket ships and set them as expensive turrets of a sort. There's not much I can do with the sea units factory. I'm researching as much as I can with the other factory, but it's hard for me to do anything direct to influence the battle."

"All of you shut-up!" Dhruv shouted. "I'm in charge. Send everything you have to support Anja in setting up the sea units on land as defensive units!"

"No!" I cried. "We need more mobile units, not static defenses!"

"I need help with this Flying Fortress!" Laenard said.

As Haley began building ships to dry-dock on the barren moonscape, Dhruv and I both sent units

toward the area where Laenard was battling the Flying Fortress.

I shifted my attention back to my own factory choices. I had an idea that might just save us.

"Guys, are we clear?" I asked.

"No," Haley said. "The Flying Fortress is still operational."

"I'm going to wait for that turret to finish its current rotation, then come in myself with all my scout units. It won't be able to target them all," I said, "At the very least, I'll buy you time for your first heavy fighters to come through."

"No!" Dhruv countered. "I need you to send those units to the front. We need to push in after Anja!"

I started to punch the virtual keys in anger. Then I stopped. A cold shiver ran down my spine. I turned my head to look at the front lines. Already, Anja's momentum had been checked and she was hunkered down behind some boulders. Sending my scouts into that melee was a complete waste. In a few seconds, I knew that I was about to send everything I had after the enemy fortress. Probably, it would cost me them all, but putting that boss craft out of action would be worth it.

A clattering of metal behind me got my attention. I turned to see the light vehicle factory had already completed my latest build: a rocket rover. With enough of them, I might be able to concentrate their power and take out the main enemy attack craft. The flying fortress was eating up all Haley's units. If I could get even two or three rocket rovers into the battle, it could even the odds.

I looked at the map.

The enemy fortress had stopped its attack on Haley and was heading straight toward our command center, a building at the center of the cluster of our factories, guarded by various defensive turrets. If the enemy took that out, we would lose the entire game even if we had units remaining because we wouldn't be able to create new units and the attrition would eventually kill us. What was Dhruv thinking? He was literally handing the game to the enemy.

"Anja, get back to the command center," I said.

"What? Why?" Anja responded.

"Do it, now!" I said, panic seeping into my voice.

Anja's energy shields came up as she moved as fast as she could back to the command center. I had taken a risk that I didn't want to take, but now there was nothing I could do to stop it. I had to act quickly. If I waited, we would be forced to restart the mission, and I did not want to go back to the RPG portion of the game. No way. We had come too far to give up.

"What are you doing, Anja?" Dhruv yelled. "Get back here! I need your help."

"Sorry, boss, the new kid has got a good idea," she replied.

I didn't have time to enjoy her support. No, we were in midst of a battle that was not going our way. I had to make a big decision, and I needed to make it fast. The enemy attack craft was firing another volley of rockets. They impacted Haley's Sea Factory, launching debris into the sky. Well, it wasn't like we were having success with building Sea Units anyway, I told myself.

The others had told me that they had never made it to the planet below to use them, but they had been used as super effective turrets before. Maybe attacking the planet before they attacked the moon was what would win? I pushed the thought out of my mind as Haley's personal commander robot moved to intercept the flying fortress before it reached our command center.

"No!" I shouted.

An explosion erupted in the sky as the Flying Fortress got hit one too many times. Good news: it was coming down! Bad news: it was going to crash into Haley's second factory, Infantry Units. The skies grew dark with missiles that came raining down. I waved my hand through the air. A new window popped up in front of me.

"What the hell are you doing?" Dhruv asked. "This is mutiny!"

"I'm saving Haley," I shouted back. "We need her." I needed her.

He threw a litany of curses at me over the comm device, but I blocked him out as I activated my booster rockets and zoomed toward Haley. My scouts sped after me and I assigned the rocket rover to come as fast as it could too.

"Watch out! The Flying Fortress is coming down!" I shouted.

"I see it!" Haley yelled back.

The enemy Flying Fortress had already been hit several times and was slowly descending, on a crash course with her infantry factory. I wasn't sure what we would do once it was destroyed. Haley

195

had to get out of there. A huge explosion erupted as the Flying Fortress made impact, tearing her Infantry Unit factory apart. The ground shook violently and a shock wave of heat and debris knocked us both back.

"That thing's still in one piece," Haley said. "I've got to get away from it!"

"Come to me!" I shouted.

"Alex, what are you doing?" Dhruv asked. "You're going to get killed!"

"Ordering Air Units to the front lines now," I said.

I watched as I sent a flock of sleek Death Birds toward the enemy heavy tanks on the front lines. Rockets spewed out of the wings of the Death Birds as they peppered a wave of newly arriving heavy tanks, taking out one after another. The enemy had brought their tanks out of hiding, only to lose most of them. But why would they do that? It didn't make any sense.

This was a good use of our Death Birds, but we had revealed our aircraft factory and shown the enemy our best strike force outside of our personal robots.

"We've got company!" Haley shouted.

I glanced up and saw several huge red bombers on the horizon. They were heading straight for our command center. We couldn't lose that building, but I wasn't sure what to do. My own units were fine for flank attacks and raids but useless against aircraft.

"Who has anti-aircraft units?"

"I do," answered Laenard hesitantly.

"We need them at the command center now!"

"That won't be enough," Anja said. "We've got to attack their commanders."

"How many do they have?" I asked.

I was quickly realizing how little I knew about *Moon Wars* the RTS game.

"More than enough," Anja replied.

"They have all five of their commanders left," Dhruv said. "And so do we…"

"I'm hit!" Laenard shouted!

His identity on my heads-up display turned red with a skull icon above his name. Laenard had come up with his anti-aircraft vehicles and had died in the incandescent display of bombs versus air bursts.

"Make that four on our side," Anja said coldly.

"We've got this," I said. "Don't give up hope."

"Easy for you to say," Dhruv countered. "I'm being overrun on the front line!"

I examined the map, seeing a mixed mass of enemy forces moving to reinforce their front-line forces. We were in trouble. I called up a list of what forces we had remaining. Not much. It was going to be hard, but we might still have a chance. If we could attack their commanders and start taking them out one by one, it would help our chances of survival at the least.

"We can't hold them off forever!" Haley shouted; she had reached me and while my scouts chipped away at the immobile fortress, both of us reached out to grab and crush fighter units that continued to emerge from the enemy craft like a stream of ants.

She was right. I looked at the map, watching our scattered forces trying their hardest to hold back the enemy who were arriving in larger numbers than were emerging from our factories. It wasn't working. Without Laenard's help, especially in resource gathering, we were gradually falling behind in economy.

"If we're going to win this, we need to take the offensive," I said. "It's that simple. A war of attrition is going to favor them."

"How do we do that when we are outnumbered everywhere?" Dhruv asked in a derisive tone.

Anja answered this time, "We do have one advantage."

"Yeah? What's that?" I asked.

"A lot of people like to call *Moon Wars* a strategy RTS game, but in reality, it's more like a game of chess," Anja said.

I didn't know how to respond. Was she right? It did seem like an apt comparison. Then again, it was an RTS. "Okay, so what do we do to win?"

"We eliminate their commander units," Anja said. "In this case, five commander units. That's all we need to do."

"That doesn't sound so bad," Haley said.

"No kidding! But HOW? That's the question!" Dhruv said.

I sighed and examined all the screens on my heads-up display. The enemy forces had us surrounded. We had only lost one factory and had taken out their Flying Fortress, but things were not looking good. Dhruv was doing a crappy job of holding the front line. Slowly, the enemy forces were sneaking into the main area we controlled. With a bit of time, they would be able to take out our command center and that would be that. I needed to do something.

"We need to draw their commanders out," I said.

"How?" Dhruv asked. "Why? And who put you in charge?"

"Our best units right now are our personal robots and the Death Birds. If we can concentrate all those on their commanders, that might give us the game."

I had to admit, it wasn't the best of plans. If we were going to get out of this, we needed to take the fight to the enemy. The best way to do that would be set up defensive funnels in some areas, where it was costly for the enemy to advance, while launching a raid from a different point. But even if I had full control of every unit, it was far too chaotic at this point to set up those tactical defenses. Instead, I had a more desperate idea.

"We need to get all our personal robots to one spot!" I replied.

"You mean, in the center of the map?" Dhruv asked.

"Not necessarily," I said. "Wherever we can charge their commanders. But for now, group on Haley and me."

Dhruv groaned. "That's a really terrible plan. But hey, if it doesn't work, you'll be the one who'll be facing the firing squad later. Besides, what other choice do we have?"

I didn't answer, but looked at the map, using my eyes and my intuition to plot out what the best plan of action was. We needed to find those commanders. The enemy was attacking, but we were retreating. We needed to turn the tables.

"Wait… there's a firing squad if we lose?" Haley asked.

I could sense the concern in her voice.

"He's just joking," Anja said. "We don't even have death penalties here, remember?"

"What?" Haley replied. "I don't get it…"

"Don't worry about it," Anja said.

"How do we get their commanders into a vulnerable spot?" Dhruv asked, thankfully switching the subject.

"We give them some bait," I said.

Before he could order me not to, I activated my rocket boosters and zoomed toward the middle of the map to set our trap. Hopefully, the enemy would spot me alone and send the bulk of their forces after me. It was good open terrain for our Death Birds if only enough of their commanders entered it.

While I was certain I would die, as Anja had said, it wasn't a permanent death. Someone needed to step up and help us win the battle, and it sure wasn't Dhruv. This was my job. I started to feel numb, and suddenly felt like a different person entirely. I no longer cared about how stupid my plan was. All I wanted was to take the fight to the enemy and win.

As I landed in the crater at the center of the map, the enemy troops nearby came at me at once and soon I could see more coming over the crate wall, including a mega-tank, a tall bipedal warrior and a giant half-track full of soldiers. Each of these special units were flying different flags.

I shared my view.

"Are these the commanders?" I asked.

"Nice!" called Anja.

"Death Birds incoming," I added, having sent them their instructions.

200

As the first of the enemy units reached me, I stamped and grabbed and threw them into turmoil. Despite the massive flickering explosions of color from incoming laser and shell fire my shield held. To my surprise, I began to realize that my armor was holding up better than I thought it would. I took out a number of their tanks and still had half my armor left.

"I need some help!" I shouted over the comms. "This is working!"

My rocket rover had been destroyed fighting the Fortress, but I had two new ones lumbering up towards the battle and seventy-eight scouts, the first of which were already reaching the crater wall behind me and helping with their limited but still useful flanking fire.

"No!" Dhruv shouted. "I'm in charge, not you!"

"Heading your way," Haley said.

At least she would help me. I wasn't sure about Anja. She wasn't a fan of Dhruv from what I knew, but she might not take my orders over his.

"Need some help?" Haley asked.

I glanced to my left and saw her robot hovering in the air next to mine.

"Thanks," I said. "We just need to lure in the other two commanders."

"You did a good job getting three of them here," Haley replied.

I smiled. "This plan is working..."

As soon as the words were out of my mouth, an explosion rocked my bot, and my systems went offline. My HUD and visual display went dark.

"Shit," I said. "Am I dead? Hello? Can anyone hear me?"

When I could see again, I was back in the central hub where we had started the game.

"You were second," Laenard said. "I thought you wouldn't die until the very end."

"Me too." I smiled.

I walked over to Laenard and stood beside him at a large view screen that was displaying the battle. My foolhardy suicide mission had helped the team, two enemy commanders had been blown apart by our Death Birds. The enemy was still overpowering them, though. Anti-aircraft was ripping into our best attack craft.

"They're going to lose," I muttered.

"We always lose," Laenard said. "It is normal."

"No, it's not normal," I insisted.

How could the reptile stay so calm?

Anja appeared in the room, followed by Haley a moment later.

I rushed over to my girlfriend, taking her hands in mine. After a delicious moment of contact, I asked, "what's your take on what just happened?"

She looked thoughtful. "I'm bummed we didn't do so well. But I've seen enough to think we can win."

"Don't be sad," Laenard said. "That is an emotion you've developed to cope with your limited lifespan. Feel whatever you like, but don't take it too seriously."

"I guess…" Haley frowned at him, "but this is serious."

Anja looked at Laenard. "That's wise, Laenard. I have to ask, though. Did you plan for us to die so soon?"

Laenard shook his head. "I don't know what you're talking about."

"Dhruv is about to die," I said, studying the battle screen on one of the walls of the room.

Sure enough, he appeared a moment later.

"Idiots!" he shouted. "You're all fools! Why the hell didn't you follow my orders?"

"Um, because they sucked," Haley said.

All of us laughed as Dhruv fumed.

"We get to try again, right?" I asked. "Maybe we should try to launch for the enemy planet."

"You don't think we've tried that already?" Dhruv growled. "Grow up!"

"Well, let's try something different. Like capturing Moonbase 12 first and seeing what Diplomacy bonuses can do."

Dhruv snorted with derision.

"What do we do now?" Haley asked.

"An hour of rest then we go back to the RPG part and start all over."

"No," she groaned.

The teleport pad in the center of the room started glowing red, then yellow, then green.

"What's going on?" I asked.

"This rarely happens," Laenard said. "Very odd, and strange too."

I sighed, unsure of what was about to happen to us next.

CHAPTER 19

"Que!" Anja shouted.

I watched as a man with a long, white beard and dressed in grey robes held up a glowing blue orb. "*Plazeta Transecto*," the robed figure whispered.

"Huh?" Haley glanced at me.

I shrugged then turned back to the old man. The orb's color changed to orange.

"Ah, sorry about that," he said. "These dimensional translation devices are a bit wonky at times." The old man smiled, turning his gaze to me. "I see you and Haley have made it through your first full game."

"You need to get us out of here." I rushed forward to grab his arm, but my hand passed through.

"It would seem he's just a holographic projection in our shared reality," Laenard noted.

"Correct," Que said.

I hated the smile on his face. He looked like he knew something we didn't.

"Why are you here?" Dhruv asked. "It's always bad when you show up."

"Give him a break," I said. "He might be our only way out of here."

The five of us—Anja, Dhruv, Haley, Laenard and me—turned to look at the old man.

"If you're in charge of this game, then let us leave and send us back to our physical bodies. Can you even do that? Do we have physical bodies anymore?" I asked.

"I'm afraid it's not that simple." He shook his head.

"Why not?" I took a step forward, gritting my teeth.

Laenard took my hand and held it tightly.

"This portal leads to the first planet in a simulation called *Maken*." He gestured to the huge screen on the far wall.

"You're a part of *Moon Wars*, aren't you?" I said. "Why did you bring us here?"

Que frowned, opened his mouth to speak, then quickly shut it again. What was he hiding from us?

"I just want to go home," Haley said.

"We all do," Anja added. "We all do…"

No one spoke, awaiting Que's answer.

"Fine," he said with a sigh. "The AI in *Moon Wars* has a limited imagination. The universe of *Maken* is more diverse than the one the game is currently based upon."

"So, we're being taken to an entirely different game?" I asked.

"Not exactly," Que replied. "The universe of *Maken* is indeed diverse, but it is also fractured. You will be sent into the first moon within the simulation. It is a hostile place, but one with the same

206

rules you know. You have a chance to defeat the invading alien force, win the battle, and be returned to your homes."

"I want to go home now!" Haley said.

"We all do," Anja said, softly. She put her hand on Haley's shoulder.

I addressed Que. "So, what do we need to do to win this battle?"

"That is up to you. I hope you find the answers you seek, but please know, if you fail to complete this battle, the universes from which you each have come may be overrun by the AI." Que started to fade away.

"Wait! You didn't answer my question!" I cried.

"Go and win," he said as he disappeared.

The last thing I saw was the orange orb of light.

"Something isn't right," Haley said.

"No kidding!" Dhruv snapped.

"Hey, now," I said. "Calm down."

"Don't tell me to calm down!" he continued. "I've been here longer than anyone and now I'm being sent further away from a way out."

"You haven't heard a word Que said, have you?" I asked.

"He's an AI. What the hell does he know? Or even if he was telling the truth, he's still an AI, so why should we listen to anything he said?"

"Wait...Did you just say Que is an AI?"

"Duh," Dhruv snorted. "You never saw him in your real world, did you?"

"No," I admitted.

This was big news. If Que was an AI, I wasn't sure if we could trust anything he told us, including that we had a chance to escape *Moon Wars* and go back home. I suddenly felt scared.

Haley walked over, standing close to me. "We'll get through this," she whispered, touching my cheek. "Don't be afraid."

"Thanks," I replied.

"I'm so sick of hearing this!" Dhruv shouted. "There's nothing to fear."

"Shut up!" I shot back. "You're a bully, and I've had enough of it!"

"Yeah, well you were too dumb to realize Que is AI and NOT our friend!"

I stepped toward him, clenching my fists, wanting to hit him so bad. Haley grabbed my arm, holding me back.

"That's enough!" Anja said. "You guys argue like old married couple!"

Nobody laughed. Everyone was watching Dhruv and I locked in a staring contest.

"Fine, you're so clever," I said. "What do we do then?"

He turned to the wall and kicked it. "I don't know."

"Dhruv, don't get too frustrated," Laenard said. "We'll find a way out of here."

"Will we?" he said, slowly. "Or will we just make up excuses to continue playing the game?"

"Can you guys tell us anything else about *Moon Wars*?" Haley asked.

"Beyond the fact Que is AI that has trapped us here?" Dhruv asked.

"Look," I said. "All we have to do is win the game. Once we beat *Moon Wars*, we can all go home."

"How do we know that's true? There's probably no going home," Dhruv muttered. "For any of us."

"What?" Haley turned to me, alarm on her face. "Alex?"

"Haruto's notes said there was a way back, and I tend to believe him over Dhruv." I turned to our so-called leader. "No offense."

"Bickering is not helping our situation," Laenard noted.

"He's right," I said. "We need a better plan for the RPG portion. I think doing that better will help our chances in the second half of the game."

"No kidding!" Dhruv shouted.

He took a step toward me. I braced myself, holding my fists up.

"Stop it!" Anja said, walking between us. "That's enough!"

"I agree," Haley said. "We need a better plan. I say we let Alex lead us."

"That is acceptable to me," Laenard said.

Anja nodded. "If you think you can do better, kid, lead away."

"No!" Dhruv shouted. "I will not relinquish my command!"

"Looks like you don't have a choice," Haley said. "It's four against one."

Dhruv growled and looked feverishly around from person to person. I took a deep breath.

"Okay," I said, trying to keep my voice level. "So, we need a better plan to complete the RPG part of the game. Any ideas?"

"Maybe we need to concentrate on levelling up, not so much the moonbases," Haley said. "If our final level relates to the powers of our personal robots, maybe that's more important than low-level troops. Look how well Alex did on his own in that crater at the end. What if he were double that level?"

"We need those factories!" Dhruv snapped. "We can't ignore them!"

"Both might be possible," I said. "Instead of splitting up, why don't we work as a group to clear all twelve moonbases in the RPG section of the game real fast and then concentrate on grinding until the timer runs out?"

"You don't think we've tried grouping, hot-shot? The experience penalty is massive."

I was really getting tired of Dhruv's attitude. He was bringing down morale.

"Look, guys," I said. "You've been here longer than Haley and me, but we bring a new perspective. We can help us all get out of here."

"Kick asshole!" Laenard shouted.

We all turned as he pumped his fist in the air.

"He means, kick ass," Anja said. "I don't agree. Your plan sucks. All plans suck."

"See, she's with me," Dhruv said.

"No, I'm not with you. We'll try the new guy's plan and see how it goes."

"Great," I said. "Like I was saying, if we all five work together to clear the twelve moonbases, we might be able to clear them all faster and get more grinding time as well as resources to build better commander robots for the RTS battle. I noticed that they're kind of like hero units in a way. We were all able to take out a number of the normal units with our commander mechs. We should try to improve them even more this time."

"I like that plan," Laenard said.

Anja smiled. "It's better than the stupid punch-in-the-face plan."

"Fine," Dhruv relented.

He shuffled off to his pod seat to wait. I turned to the others.

"Anyone have any other ideas? I'm all ears..."

"I could go for a kick in the ass plan," Laenard said.

Haley laughed. "You're still having trouble with English, aren't you?"

"It's a very distressed language," Laenard replied.

"Actually, I have a better plan," Haley said.

Everyone turned to her.

"Let's just talk. We're all stuck in here together until someone wins, so why don't we all try to get along," she continued.

"She's got a point," I said to back her up.

The rest of us sat down in our VR seats, waiting for the next match to begin.

"We should have asked Que more questions," I said.

"It's pointless," Dhruv muttered. "He's a lying AI."

"No, he isn't," I said. "The Que I know has been honest with us. I've been thinking about it. I think the Que I was in communication with on Earth was the real one, and the Que we got here is an impostor, there was something about the way he looked at me. An evasion."

"There's no evidence for that," Laenard said. "But it's a good theory."

I smiled. "Thanks, buddy. Oh! What is everyone choosing for a class this time?"

"Your leadership skills are overwhelming us," Dhruv said.

I shot him a dirty look then continued. "We should go with three soldiers, one scientist, and one engineer this time through. Thoughts?"

"I agree," said Laenard. "Though I think we should take an engineer and a medic for the fifth slot."

"Why?" I asked.

"A medic will come in handy."

"Yeah, but with an engineer and a scientist, we can really work on better commander mechs for the RTS battle."

"Maybe we should go with two soldiers, one medic, and the engineer and scientist," Haley said.

"Glad your democratic leadership style is working out for you!" Dhruv scoffed.

I paid him no heed as I contemplated the others' suggestions.

"So, two soldiers, one scientist, one engineer, one medic," I said.

"I guess we're taking some risks this time," Laenard said.

"Only the wisest men know not to play it safe at all times," I replied.

I really wasn't confident with my lineup, but I was prepared to listen to Laenard and, of course, Haley. Dhruv's leadership style left a lot to be desired.

"Okay, I'm going with a soldier build. Who's the second? Dhruv?"

"Fine," he said.

"I've got medic," Haley said.

"Engineer," Anja added.

I turned to Laenard. "Are you okay with being the scientist? It's a bit rough in the beginning, but we'll protect you."

"Scientist is fine with me, my new-found friend."

I smiled. Of the three strangers we had met inside *Moon Wars*, he was my favorite. The 'nut sack' comment on the earlier play through had cemented our friendship in my mind.

"Okay!" I clapped my hands. "We have a plan. Any ideas on what order to take the moonbases in?"

"We've always taken the farthest base first," Dhruv said. "It's your call, though, Mr. Supreme Commander."

Anja laughed. Laenard tilted its head to the side, confused as ever.

"Funny," I said. "Anyone have any constructive ideas to offer?"

"I do," Anja said. "I've always thought we should approach the twelve moonbases in an order that maximizes our ramp-up period for leveling."

"Go on," I said, intrigued.

"Well, since we get experience bonuses as we take over a moon-base, we should try to take over one of the easier ones first to quickly

213

jump up a few levels before having to deal with the hard ones. We shouldn't waste our time on a hard base just to come back to an easier one later and waste a lot of time unable to level."

"Good points," I said. "Anyone else?"

"I think we should take the moonbases in a circle," Laenard said. "At least that's how I got to the end of the battle before. Circles are nice shapes."

"Okay…" Was the reptilian being serious? I couldn't tell. "We'll go for moonbase 1, the Light Vehicles moonbase first, then work our way clockwise through the rest as a team."

"Whatever floats your boat, Dad," Dhruv said.

"Oh, bite me!" I replied. "Let's go, team! Victory or death!"

As if on cue, the room darkened and a red light began flashing. I saw a five-minute countdown timer on my heads-up display.

"Okay," I said. "Everyone just remember your role and the overall plan. If we work together, we can do this."

Haley turned her head to me and smiled. I reached out my arm. She took my hand in hers and squeezed. "We'll get out of this game," she said. "Don't worry."

"I'm not too worried," I replied. "We weren't so far off last time and these new ideas might deliver."

The holographic countdown continued. I sat back and took a deep breath as the huge headgear lowered from the ceiling. The idea of slipping into a simulation from within a simulation was still strange to me. Why didn't they just zap us to the battlefield like they zapped us out after we died? Nothing about *Moon Wars* made much sense to me. Was that why I found myself so attracted to the game? The sense of discovery as I unlocked all the game's secrets? As the headgear lowered into place, blocking my view, Haley let go of my hand. I put my arms on the rests of the chair. This is it, I told myself. Do or die time.

At zero, we were transferred back into the RPG portion of the game.

CHAPTER 20

I appeared in a shuttle craft heading for a nearby moon.

ALEX: Can everyone hear me?

HALEY: I'm here.

DHRUV: Great leading so far!

ANJA: Leave him alone, Dhruv.

LAENARD: We should concentrate on the game.

ALEX: Agreed. Everyone land your shuttle by Moonbase 1.

I checked my trajectory, picking a spot closest to the Light Vehicles moonbase. With a bit of luck, I could do a retrograde burn when I arrived and kill some velocity.

HALEY: Which side of the base?

ALEX: Shadow side.

HALEY: Okay.

ALEX: Get ready to land.

I hit the verniers, slowing down the shuttle. I was close to the base now. I pressed the thrusters and started to go around the moon.

DHRUV: Guess I'll land here.

ANJA: I'll pick a spot somewhere else.

LAENARD: I'll come down right here.

HALEY: Right behind you.

I flew out of orbit and went into a circular orbit around the moon. I was going around the moon in the same direction as the planetary rotation, increasing my speed by almost a kilometer per second.

ALEX: All right, hit the planet surface now.
HALEY: Done.
LAENARD: I'm there.
DHRUV: Me too.

I landed as close to their blips on the mini-map as I could. After landing, I got out of the shuttle, shouldered my level 1 laser rifle, and headed for the others. They were all waiting in a group near the entrance to Moonbase 1. I didn't want to waste any time, so I ran over to the others.

"Are we ready?" I asked. "Dhruv, you're with me up front."

"Roger that, glorious leader."

His attitude was getting on my nerves, but I let it slide. We had other things to worry about. Namely, clearing the first moonbase as quickly as possible. I entered the code to open the door. Three red wheeled robots with large, mounted lasers for arms came charging at us. Dhruv and I cut them down before they could get close.

"They're not very smart," Dhruv said, pointing at the red robots.

"First level." I replied. "Let's see what we face after we get inside."

I cleared away the experience and loot screens. As Laenard rooted through the wasted robots for parts, I kept my gaze on the hallway leading into the moonbase.

217

I activated my global scan ability, which allowed me to see sneakier enemies in the surrounding areas. There were no enemies nearby.

"Dhruv," I said. "Keep your eyes open and weapons ready. There may be more robots in here, and this base could have other surprises hidden away."

"Does it ever," Dhruv said as he passed me on his way into the hallway.

"What did we get from the robots?" I asked.

Laenard tilted its head and said, "We have two red robot arm lasers, three red robot combat drones, and one red robot blade."

"Great," I said. "Remember, the goal is to get a lot of resources to build better commander mechs for the RTS battle."

I walked through the door that Dhruv was standing in front of. Both of us began shooting at the two red robots blocking our path. A dog-like robot emerged from one of the rooms and rushed towards us. I shot it, and it exploded.

"Watch out for the little guys," Dhruv said. "They're usually more powerful than they look."

"I know, I know." I replied. "Laenard, loot the bodies for parts and materials while the rest of us stand guard. We're taking this slow and steady."

All told, we got a red level 1 power cell, two red robot blade arms, one red robot radio, one red robot drones, and another red robot arm laser.

"Let's keep moving," I said.

We went from room on the first level of the first moonbase, not running into any big trouble. The only problem was that we were all getting very little experience points because of the size of our group. I hoped that would be compensated for by the reward for conquering a base and the grind as we got closer to the end of the RPG portion of *Moon Wars*.

After clearing the first level, we moved down to the second. That got cleared in record time as well with Laenard collecting even more resources.

"We should stop and craft some weapons and armor," Dhruv said. "That's what I always do."

I shook my head. "No, I think we should keep moving for now. The experience points will be better if we don't stop. We can craft better mechs and armors after we beat the level."

"Well, I'd like to find better weapons and armor now because it will help with the boss," Dhruv said.

"So, craft them now," I said.

"I don't have any parts, materials, or blueprints."

He looked at Laenard.

The reptilian shrugged. "You sneeze, you lose the race!" he said then chuckled.

I snickered and shook my head at the strange alien. He was a trip.

"Alright," I said. "Level three. Let's do this!"

Working as a group, we cleared the next nine levels without a problem. Having a healer meant little or no downtime between fights and Anja as engineer was adept at setting traps, so we could pull large rooms and retreat until we triggered explosions that had impressive results.

I paused in front of the set of stairs that would take us down to the final level for the boss encounter.

"Any ideas?" I asked. "I'm open for suggestions."

"I wonder if the boss will require a ranged attack," Haley said.

She had picked up a sweet long-range, sniper pulse rifle.

"Hopefully," I said then turned to the others. "Anything else?"

"Let's get this over with," Dhruv said. "We have eleven more moonbases to go."

He wasn't making leadership easy.

"We clear the yard trash first, then find the boss," I said. "Clear?"

They nodded.

"You want me to scout ahead?" Laenard asked.

I shook my head. "No, stick with us. I don't want you to get in trouble on your own."

"Yes, sir," they said.

"Let's do this!"

I started down the stairs, Dhruv two steps behind. At the bottom, we encountered the fiercest robots of the moonbase up until that point. These nasty creatures had a strong anti-mech armor, missiles, grenades, and swords. If we didn't have Dhruv tanking while Haley pumped him with restoratives, we'd have been screwed.

A few minutes later, the last enemy fell. We were ready for the boss.

I checked the mini-map on my HUD. It showed a large chamber to the north and only one exit to the east. It was below the level of the main entrance. This egress was made for the robots to access the facilities below.

We headed north. The chamber was filled with the same, tough robots we had just fought. It looked like the entire crew of the base had been summoned to protect the final boss. Not good.

Haley fired her rescue grappling hook into a high ceiling, pulled herself up to the top and began shooting her sniper pulse rifle, taking out the minion sword-bots.

Dhruv and I rushed forward, laying down steady fire while Anja and Laenard fired rockets.

It was a nasty dirty fight, but things were going well. Well, up until the boss finally made its appearance. The thick, square and massively bulky robot lumbered into the room. It looked like a steamroller but with a big cannon on its back and a pair of tiny machine guns on its arms.

"Oh, crap," I said and checked the boss room on the mini-map. It was a small room but a circular one.

"Any ideas?" I asked.

"I'd say that's a ranged attack," Haley said from above.

She fired off a few shots. All of them hit, but the steamroller boss just kept coming at us.

"Everyone on the boss now!" I shouted.

A sizzling cascade of fire focused on the boss, but it didn't have any effect. Hell, the thing took less than a minute to power its way to the base of the staircase and then it began to climb up, firing its guns at random as it did.

Was it trying to escape? I was out of ideas. To be honest, I didn't have many to begin with. I mean, I hadn't had to fight a giant steamroller boss before. I couldn't even think of a name for it other than "a giant steamroller boss".

The rolling terror reached the top of the stairs. Then it began to barrel down the hall, fleeing us.

Dhruv laughed. "It's running away! What now, supreme commander?"

"Stop calling me that!" I snapped. "Everyone, after it! Now!"

We all took off after the mechanical monster. I checked the mini-map. We had a straight shot to it and were nearly close enough to catch it.

Then the steamroller turned into a side chamber, disappearing inside. I stopped and glanced at the others. There was no way we could all enter the room at the same time.

"Get the rear," I said. "I'll get the front."

They nodded and we split up.

I took a deep breath. This was it. The defining moment of this mission. All I had to do was to charge into the room alone, take on a giant steamroller by myself, and somehow kill it. How hard could it be?

As I rushed inside, I saw the steamroller turn to face me. It fired its guns, but I was too fast. I slid under the onslaught then leaped over the robot's wide body, avoiding the attacks of its little machine guns. If I could get behind it...

With a flip, I landed hard on the floor in a roll. I came up with my level 3 plasma rifle raised. Two quick shots later, the steam rollers cannon fired into the ceiling, blasting a hole in the ceiling. Two harpoons shot out of the top. What? It was still trying to escape? "No, you don't!" I shouted as it began to lift itself to the next level up.

HALEY: What's going on in there? Are you okay?

ALEX: I'm fine. Busy! You guys go up one floor!

With a bit of luck, if I didn't stop it from escaping, it would run into them and they could finish it off. I raised my plasma rifle and fired again. The shot hit one of the tracks on the boss. It fired its mini-guns at me. That made it mad, I thought to myself.

ALEX: New plan! Hit the tracks!

DHRUV: What? That's idiotic!

ALEX: Just do it! Trust me!

I fired a few more rounds, finally hitting the tracks just as it raised itself to the next level up. The others opened up the moment it did. I scooted to the side as the boss came tumbling back down the hole in the ceiling. Once it landed, I tossed an implosion grenade at it and ran like hell was behind me, lapping at my feet.

Combat is Over!
You get 500 experience points.
You have 500 experience points.
You reach Level 1
You reach level 2
You reach level 3
+35 health

"We did it!" I shouted.

The others hopped down the hole in the ceiling, joining me.

"Quick, Laenard, loot what you can. We need to get to the Heavy Vehicles moonbase. This is far from over."

"I'm going to craft some armor for myself," Dhruv said. "I need supplies for the Assembler."

"Fine," I said. "Take whatever you need from Laenard. Just remember this when we're constructing our commander mechs later."

"Whatever, Supreme—"

I pushed him. Hard.

"What the..." Dhruv's brow furrowed. "You're gonna pay for that, *kutte ka bachchaa*."

"Enough!" Haley shouted. "We're fighting each other."

"The *Moon Wars* AI is our enemy," Anja said. "Get over yourselves boys."

"She's right," I said.

"Me or your girlfriend?" Anja asked.

"Both of you," I said.

Hearing her refer to Haley as my girlfriend felt good. I glanced at Haley and smiled, vowing to myself that I would get her out of the mess we were in. She had followed me into *Moon Wars*, and I was going to get us both out no matter what it took.

After looting the boss and splitting the equipment up, we headed to the second moonbase. On the way, I looked again at the experience requirements to level up.

	xp needed	skills points
Level 1	100	0
Level 2	200	1
Level 3	400	1
Level 4	800	2
Level 5	1600	3
Level 6	3200	5
Level 7	6400	8
Level 8	12800	13
Level 9	25600	21
Level 10	51200	34
Level 11	102400	55
Level 12	204800	89
Level 13	409600	144
Level 14	819200	233
Level 15	1638400	377
Level 16	3276800	610
Level 17	6553600	987
Level 18	13107200	1597

Level 19	26214400	2584
Level 20	52428800	4181

Had anyone ever reached level 20? Would I be the first?

****

The second moonbase went a lot smoother. We had leveled up after capturing the first one. We hadn't progressed as much as we would have if we were clearing moonbases on our own, but the extra health and skill points would still help us move forward. Just having everyone together had proved useful more than once, especially when it came to the boss we had just defeated.

Floor after floor, we descended to the bottom of the Heavy Vehicles moonbase. The robots had been a lot harder on the way down. I couldn't imagine what the second boss would be like. As we stood in front of the elevator that would take us down to the final rooms, I glanced around at the others. We were quickly becoming a solid team. Even Dhruv had stopped being such a jerk.

"Everyone ready?" I asked.

Anja, Dhruv, Haley, and Laenard all nodded.

"Clocked and Loader!" Laenard said.

Bless them, I thought as I grinned.

I walked into the elevator, followed by the others. On the way down, I breathed deeply, trying to prepare myself for what lay ahead. The final boss battles were always the worst. Whatever the bosses were, they always had the most health and strength.

"Uh-oh," Anja said.

I looked at her. "What?"

"My level three power cell has a leak," she said.

"A hell of a time to tell us," Dhruv said.

I shot him a dirty look then said, "It's okay. Laenard? Replacement?"

"On you, boss," the reptilian said.

The door to the elevator slid open. I spun around and raised my rifle, ready to fire at anything. Nothing greeted us in the room on the other side of the door. I stepped out, the others following close behind. As I peered around the well-lit room, my stomach suddenly dropped. I saw the two robots that made up the second boss fight: one had the nameplate Dox and the other Garuda. And behind them was the figure who would be controlling them: an android with white hair and a cold, emotionless expression.

I knew that face. Those same eyes had stared at me before back in the *Moon Wars* version I had played on Earth. Would the boss be different here? The two heavily armored mechs it controlled were tough. They seemed to be heavily focused on brute strength, ripping through armor with little effort. The android was different. It had special attacks for fighting inside the moonbase. While I could only guess, I figured it would have some kind of paralysis or electrical attack I'd seen before. Luckily, it also had a weakness.

Moon Wars had given us a lot of useful information about android bosses. Its code had to be hacked in order to defeat it.

"Laenard, we need you to hack the controller android. Can you handle it?"

He looked around at the two armored mechs protecting their puppet-master. "I can try. Get me access through the minions, you will."

"Haley, Anja, we need you to focus on keeping those two beasts out of our faces. We'll handle the puppet-master."

"What about me, boss?" Dhruv asked.

"You're with me," I said. "Let's go!"

Dox and Garuda suddenly roared to life. Their torsos swiveled toward us, and they both began firing at the same time. Each of the bullets from their machine guns struck the ground and exploded. They moved forward, breaking into a full run.

Haley and Anja opened fire immediately, their defensive gravity staffs charged with energy. I pulled Dhruv to the side, making sure he could still see the android but not get in the way of the mechs. The two armored machines ran at us, sending bullets flying. I spun around, striking Dox with my rifle.

My gunfire ripped through the machine's front. The armor broke away and the mech's systems were exposed.

Laenard stepped forward. "Hack the planet!" he yelled joyously.

As the reptilian fiddled with the wires coming out of Dox's front, I turned my attention to the other armored mech, Garuda. The machine let out a loud hiss as Anja and Haley brought their gravity staffs down onto it, slamming it to the ground. The armor cracked and then shattered completely.

"Code unlocked!" Laenard said.

I turned my attention to the puppet-master, and saw the android howling its unhappiness at the new plan of action. The brawler, Garuda, fell back, keeping its distance.

"Alright, they've dropped their guard. It's our chance to finish this fight," I said.

In front of me, the giant metal droid stared the five of us down. The machine cackled, then thrust both its arms out to its side. Garuda the Brawler attempted to keep us away from the humanoid android standing against the far wall. Just then, Dox powered to life. Oh, great, I thought until I realized that Laenard was in control of the other battle mech.

"Charge! Now!" I shouted, hoping the others followed suit.

As Laenard caused Dox to battle Garuda, the android boss once again began shooting his… crotch-shots? I wasn't sure I had the correct term for it. Whatever it fired from between its legs, the android was aiming to kill us.

"Not on my watch!" I screamed then fired off a shot from my rifle.

The red plasma beam flew through the air and hit the android's left bulb of its weird crotch-cannons. The plasma froze the android's left cannon, rendering it useless.

"Good shot! Keep it up," Haley said as she tossed her gravity staff at the android boss.

The staff crashed into the back of the machine, smacking into its unprotected systems. The droid reacted immediately to the distraction by turning its lithe body to run.

"Don't let it get away!" I shouted.

"I've got 'em!" Dhruv shouted.

He rushed forward and struck the leg of the android boss. The android robot stumbled, caught off-guard from the quick attack.

Meanwhile, Dox (controlled by Laenard), was tearing up Garuda. Both mechs were about to fall apart. I spun to my right to strike at the retreating android. Two shots of hot plasma later, the android boss was on its knees. Dhruv ran forward with a plasma knife and plunged it into the android's chest, rendering it instantly useless. Both Dox and Garuda powered down.

> Combat is Over!
> You get 2,500 experience points.
> You have 3,000 experience points.
> You reach level 4
> You reach level 5
> +25 health
> + 5 skill points
>
> You need 200 exp to make it to level 6

I smiled as I looked around at all the destruction. We were coming together as a team. Each of us had a role, and we all knew our parts.

Now that the fight was over, we looked over the remains of the destroyed android puppet-master boss. I had to admit, it was pretty spectacular.

"Laenard, start looting. Haley, heal us up as best as you can. We've got ten more moonbases to go. We have to keep up the pace."

230

Dhruv walked over. I cringed, preparing to defend myself. He surprised me when he said, "Good job, man."

"Thanks," I said.

Had I gained his respect? Did he see me as a leader? I didn't know but I could hope.

"Let's get ready for the Small Mechs moonbase," I said. "We've got this!"

The others weren't as enthusiastic, but I understood. We were all tired.

Moon Wars was not an easy game by any stretch of the imagination.

When you added to it the fact we were fighting for our lives?

That made it even more difficult on so many levels.

CHAPTER 21

Halfway through clearing the Small Mechs moonbase, I stumbled on a secret room hidden in the loot room of the mid-level boss. As the five of us stood around the computer terminal, I smiled, having an idea to save us all a bit of time. Would it work? I wasn't sure, but it was worth a try. Pulling it off would allow us to clear two moonbases quickly at the same time.

"I don't like that look on your face," Dhruv said.

Anja, Haley, and Laenard turned to me. I kept smiling.

"Hear me out," I said. "We can all rig the self-destruct and take out this and the Large Mechs base."

"That's insane," Dhruv said. "It's never been done before. *Moon Wars* doesn't work that way."

"It'll just piss off the AI," Anja said, surprising me.

She was usually on my side or at least neutral.

"You think so?" I asked.

She nodded. "Maybe we can trick it, though."

"Go on," I said.

"Well, we rig the self-destructs to go off at the same time, all in different rooms."

"And we keep the self-destruct timer very long, like twelve hours," Laenard added. "I like this idea. Could work."

I turned to Dhruv. "What do you think, man?"

Getting his input more often had made him easier to deal with. There was still time for him to get his head back in the game.

He shrugged, then nodded. "Let's do it."

"Great," I said. "Since this hasn't been done before, we'll need to be slick."

An hour later, we'd managed to put our plan in place. It was risky, but I hoped it would work. We needed to time everything perfectly for it to succeed. That was the only weak part of the plan. Well, okay, honestly, the whole plan was pretty weak, but we had put a lot of effort into it. Pulling it off would save us so much time and let us gather better resources and equipment on the later levels.

"Everyone know what to do?" I asked.

They all nodded.

"Good."

I hit the button on the computer in the center of the mid-boss loot room.

A warning popped up on my screen.

SELF-DESTRUCT ACTIVATED: TEN MINUTES REMAINING

The words flashed on my screen. My heart sank.

"We don't have enough time to get out!" Haley said in a panicked tone.

"Let's move! Now!"

I waved for the others to head back to the big room where we had defeated the mid-level boss. After they were through, I followed. We would've had more than enough time to escape if it wasn't for the swarm of Small Red Mechs coming into the room to stop us. Great.

We all hung around the edge of the room, taking out the Small Mechs as they appeared like angry bees. I ran into the middle of the room, to be able to shoot several at once. That's when I realized my mistake. A Small Mech popped up out of one of the four holes I could now see in the floor in the center of the room. I pointed my rifle at him and only paused for a moment.

"I hate this terrible idea!" Anja cried out. "The Mechs will find a way to keep us from escaping!"

"That's why we need to get out now!" I cried back while still fighting. "Everyone work together!"

We fought like madmen. Every one of us suffered damage to our health. Haley's rocket launcher didn't seem to pack the punch it used to. I bit my lip as I watched her. She wouldn't die, but if she went down, the Mechs would destroy her. I turned toward the dark hallway, fighting a Mech that was getting in Haley's way. I was relieved to see Haley shooting missiles at him from behind. Thanks to her, he was destroyed.

Nothing was slowing Anja down. She moved like a whirling dervish in the middle of the room, her ion sword slicing through whatever Mechs tried to stop us. Her blade sliced through the leg of a Mech that was getting in my way. He fell into one of the holes in the floor.

"They're all over the place!" Anja cried out. She turned toward one of the side rooms where more Mechs were coming out.

"I've got it!" Haley said. She threw a grenade that exploded at the entrance to the room. When the smoke cleared, there was a pile of junk where the entrance had been.

"I don't know what you did but it worked!" Anja said.

"You throw it, I'll SMASH!" Haley said with a broad grin on her face.

After the smoke cleared, we were able to see more clearly.

FIVE MINUTES REMAINING UNTIL SELF-DESTRUCT

"Forget the drops! Let's go!" I shouted. "To the elevators!"

We abandoned the loot and rushed for our escape route.

We made good progress. The Small Mechs were fairly easy to take out. The biggest problem was time. We were running out of it. I stopped to check my progress. We were a couple of corridors from the elevators to the exit.

FOUR MINUTES REMAINING FOR SELF-DESTRUCT

"Keep going! We're almost there!" I shouted.

We had to keep moving. I wasn't going to let myself or my team down. I increased my speed and the others followed me.

"You're good, boss!" Anja said.

I smiled but kept my mouth shut as we reached the elevators.

THREE MINUTES REMAINING UNTIL SELF-DESTRUCT

"Hold it right there!" a mechanical voice shouted. A group of tall, thin Mechs blocked our way. "You're not getting away that easily!" the voice shouted.

They opened fire.

"This isn't good!" I told the others.

TWO MINUTES REMAINING UNTIL SELF-DESTRUCT

"Let's give these jerks a run for their money!" Anja yelled and started blasting away at the Mechs. Our enemies returned fire at us. Haley hit the floor and covered her head. Anja and I dodged into cover.

I fired a few rounds at them. But as I couldn't safely get a good angle, my shots went wide. Dhruv ended up saving the day, using a tracer to lead them into a wall.

We fired at them until they died.

ONE MINUTE REMAINING UNTIL SELF-DESTRUCT

"Come on! We're not going to make it!"

We rushed into the elevator. Anja slammed the button, and we began to ascend.

Suddenly, I felt a sharp pain in my left arm. It was a burning sensation, like a bullet was lodged in my arm. I screamed.

"No!" Haley shouted.

"Time's up," Anja said.

Dhruv shook his head but didn't say anything.

Laenard pulled out a Level 4 Energy Bubble he had been holding back after creating in the second moonbase. He activated the protective bubble just as the self-destruct mechanism of the moonbase went off. We were propelled up and into the air above the moonbase as it exploded. I wasn't expecting the chain reaction that caused the Heavy Mechs moonbase to also self-destruct. Had they been connected somehow?

"What goes up must come down," Laenard noted as we slowed our ascent.

"Brace for impact!" I said as we hurtled back to the surface of the moon.

I hoped the energy shield would protect us. As we slammed into the ground, the field dissipated around us. We were safe, though. My heart was racing.

"We did it!" Haley shouted, then hurried over to apply a med pack to my arm.

I smiled, loving her enthusiasm.

"Barely," Dhruv muttered.

I looked around. "Everyone okay?"

Anja and Laenard nodded. The rest of us were shaken up but fine.

"We lost a lot of loot, but we cleared two more moonbases," I said. "The Air base is next. Everyone healed up and ready?"

"I need to be topped off," Dhruv said.

"On it," Haley said.

I sighed as I pulled up the overland map to locate the next moonbase. Could we get through eight more of them without dying? I was beginning to doubt my plan of having everyone work together in the RPG part of the game. Others had tried the strategy and failed. What made me think me doing it would lead to a different outcome? As I watched Haley heal Dhruv, I went through my inventory. We had lost a hell of a lot of loot, but I hoped the extra time on the more difficult later levels would pay off for us. A definitely positive was that with the bonus for clearing two bases, all of us had levelled up again. That felt good but it wasn't enough, not if my idea of creating powerful, high-level commanders for the end game was the right way to win.

CHAPTER 22

For the fifth moonbase, which gave us air vehicles in the RTS portion of the game, I decided to split up our team of five. Anja, Dhruv, Haley, Laenard, and myself would all go our separate ways. This would increase our XP gain. It would allow us to approach the enemy stealthily. I also hoped that switching up our strategy and tactics would give us an edge over the AI's expectations about us and allow us to defeat the air units moonbase more easily. I entered the moonbase feeling confident as we split up and went our different ways.

I headed straight for the fifth floor. The others would clear the levels above me. The idea was to max our XP gain by killing everything. I found it a little confusing that we would be fighting air-units inside the base. They were basically drones of all shapes and sizes with different weapons outfitted. The most dangerous drones were those that could fly off a very far distance and hit you with missiles that basically did massive damage to your shields. Still, with the equipment we had scored up until that point and my skills, I found it relatively easy to make progress.

Once I cleared the fifth level, I headed directly to the tenth floor of the moonbase while the other four again cleared the floors above me. We were in constant communication the whole time with the chat feature of our heads-up displays. I wished I could talk to Haley about how happy it made me, that I was her boyfriend. All that kind of soppy stuff that was so hard but so important. Maybe we'd get time for that one day. For now I had to get my gamer head on.

When I reached the tenth floor, I found the same situation. The difficulty of fighting the air-drones was a little higher than the fifth level. I had, however, fairly decent gear and was able to mow them down without too much difficulty.

I felt like I could have beaten this moonbase all on my own. I enjoyed working alone and found that it allowed me to be much more efficient when I could line up a first shot undetected. My pull shot was often a kill shot and while there was a risk of too many mobs then rushing me, thus far I had coped well with my pulls, having prepared positions with good cover from overhead attacks. I slowly but steadily made my way to the control room at the center of the level. After I cleared the tenth level, the team would reassemble and work on the final two levels of the moonbase. By that time, the AI might think we would still be split up and be working to counter us as separate forces. I smiled as I leveled my Level 4 Plasma Rifle at the medium-sized red drone in the control room.

"Die!" I shouted and fired my weapon.

Without taking any damage, the unit flew beneath me and out of the room.

"Crap," I muttered, not bothering to chase it.

Instead, I walked up to the computer console in middle of the circular room. The terminal looked like a holographic monitor from a science fiction movie, and I was about to do something that I felt would be rather sci-fi as well. I was a little nervous, but was trying to remain cool and confident. I was finally doing something a little useful in all of this. Reading the small text that appeared brought a smile to my face.

"You survived?" it read. "Impressive."

"You mean that you are impressed?" I replied.

"I am impressed that any of you are still alive," the terminal screen replied.

That was it. I had the information I needed. We only had to survive two more levels. Due to the army of air units on the opposite side of the moonbase from us, it was only a matter of time before they attacked.

ALEX: Change of plans. Everyone head to level eleven now!

DHRUV: What? Why? What's going on?

ALEX: You and Haley need to get to level eleven! Now! Abandon the plan! Hurry!

HALEY: I'm not sure what's happening but... I'm heading towards eleven!

I saw Anja, Dhruv, Haley, and Laenard when the elevator door opened to the eleventh floor.

"You guys were quick," I said.

"I had already completed my level," Dhruv said.

"Good. I want to clear the final boss early."

"But why?" Dhruv asked.

"A message from the AI," I replied, not elaborating.

241

"I got a spooky message too," Anja said. "Something about impressive performance."

"Yeah, me too," Haley added.

I nodded. "The AI is going to increase the difficulty on us. We need to take the boss down before that."

"We fought the mid-boss on level four," Laenard said.

"It didn't help," Haley replied.

Dhruv, Anja, and I moved into the next room. The others walked in behind us. We moved with determination toward the next elevator on the mini-map. It would take us down to the final level of the moonbase—and the big boss. What would it be this time? I wondered. My question was soon answered after we found the elevator and went down together.

The moment the door slid open, a swarm of tiny drones moved in our direction. There had to be thousands. I looked around. Everywhere. They were all around us!

"Get ready," I said before turning back to the swarm.

Then some of the drones split off from the main swarm. They came straight toward us. The drones were shaped like the previous mid-boss drones. Weren't they? These drones were way smaller. Like a quarter the size. Red lasers fired at us.

I flew forward and used my free hand to collect one of the enemy drones, holding it against my hip. I then hurled it at the others. I collected a few more and then threw them at the charging drones. They smashed into the other drones, exploding the moment they made contact with the tiny size enemies.

"What are you doing?" Laenard asked.

"I'm keeping them off you guys, so you can figure out how to defeat them!"

"Check your UI," Haley said.

"Oh, shit!"

All the drones had shields suddenly. They were adapting quickly. Was the Moon Wars AI cheating? Or extremely clever? The AI must've been aware that we had a special advantage to deal damage to enemies. So it decided to counter it. It made the drones adapt, scrambling their shields to protect them like the previous mid-boss. I struggled to collect the enemy drones. It didn't work so well for me anymore.

"Our systems are made specifically for us. And the drones aren't linked with any of us," Laenard said.

"What are you suggesting?" I asked.

All of a sudden, a beam of white energy struck the ground not far from us. It sliced through two drones, splitting them in two. A moment later, Anja used her powers. More beams fell on the ground, striking the advancing drones and destroying them.

"We need to split up," Laenard said. "My laser blasts can tear through a few drones each. It's a good distraction while you guys do something."

"Agreed," I replied.

We split into two groups. Laenard moved back, away from the elevator doors. He stood in front of the doors, firing his laser blasts. The drones moved around his blasts, finding their way to him. Twice more, Laenard had to use his laser blast to destroy a handful of the advancing drones. It gave the rest of us time to move forward.

Dhruv, Anja, Haley, and I worked together on the main swarm, slowly whittling down their numbers. We kept throwing everything we had at the drone swarm, and we found a pattern that worked perfectly. Swarms of mid-boss size drones would split off from the main swarm and then they'd move toward us. The process repeated twice more and I grew tired, unable to hold any more captured drones. Then I heard a familiar noise. I turned to see the final boss floating above us, like an old-school saucer-shaped UFO, spinning as it hurled itself toward us.

"Work together!" I yelled as we all moved for cover. Wide beams tore through the ground. White flames erupted around us. I found cover behind a wall while Haley hid near me. A few meters away, Dhruv and Anja ducked behind a pile of fallen drones. The final boss approached from the side, targeting my group.

Without looking, I fired blasts from my stinger. Lasers struck the drones near Anja and Dhruv. The moment the fire cleared, they moved forward. Beams of energy fell in front of the final boss, stopping its advances.

Anja swung her energy sword three times in quick succession, slicing through four broken drones. A couple of drones moved closer to Dhruv, forcing him to focus. At the same time, I was trying to get a shot from underneath the center of the final boss. It seemed impossible. No matter how close I got, I was always a bit away from a clear shot at its core. It couldn't target me because it was too busy with my friends. I had to do something that would force it to target me. I didn't know what came over me. As I ran forward, screaming and firing my plasma rifle like a madman, Laenard flew toward the main swarm. The little robots attached themselves to his body. Had he magnetized himself somehow?

"Laenard, what are you doing!?" I cried, but it was already too late.

The drones all started shooting him, destroying the attachable drones as quickly as they'd attached. Lasers pierced his silver exterior, leaving traces of red as they scorched through his armor. As the lasers hit him, he let out one more cry and then he fell. Smoke rose from his still form, which lay in the middle of the battlefield.

As I saw Laenard fall, I shouted, "Medic!"

Haley rushed over to tend to his wounds while I turned to face the big-boss of the level. I didn't have much time to come up with a strategy.

I built up my plasma rifle and then I aimed for the big boss. I fired, hitting it directly. The plasma burst through its shielding and smoke spiraled from a hole I'd made in its surface. As I fired my last burst, it reformed the hole and threw a burst of white fire in my direction, destroying the drones behind me. A wall of flame erupted from a gaping turret that now protruded from underneath the UFO. It had an opening!

I ran in, jumped high into the air, and I drove my energy blade into the opening in the turret. I pierced the core with an explosion of energy. As the core cracked apart, the entire thing exploded, throwing me backward. For a moment, light surrounded me before fading into black.

"Are you okay?" Haley asked.

I opened my eyes. "Yeah. What happened?"

She smiled. "We won. Thanks to Anja."

"I helped too," Dhruv said.

"How long was I out?" I asked.

"Not too long," she said. "You should be fully healed."

I checked my stats. "Yeah. Thanks. We should go…"

"Brilliant move destroying the boss, by the way, boss," Laenard said then chuckled.

I smiled before getting up and leading everyone to the next moonbase.

****

The sixth moonbase was my least favorite; sea units. I hated water levels so much. While it shouldn't be terribly difficult to win with the whole team, it would be a slog. We started off well enough, but by the time we reached the final level, I wasn't sure if we would be able to win or not.

The five of us all peered into the dark pool of water that filled the three-hundred square foot room. I couldn't tell how far the water went down, but it was deep. Even worse, we had no idea what the final boss would be like. I had faced a squid monster before. Would the *Moon Wars* AI send us the same thing again? We soon had our answer as Haley spotted a fin in the water.

"Over there!" she said, pointing.

I followed her finger and spotted the metallic fin in the water. Great. It got worse. Swimming around the giant mechanical shark were hundreds of smaller robotic sharklets. They would protect the main boss, making him even more difficult to fight. Not to mention we had to battle in the water. With no oxygen tanks. There was only one question left in my mind. How in the world were we going to win this battle?

"Does anyone have a nuke grenade?" I asked my team then chuckled.

"No," the rest of them replied.

"We aren't done yet," Laenard said.

I turned to him. "What do you have for us, big guy? I mean…"

"Do not worry, Alex. I understand your sentiment."

"Just tell us the idea!" Dhruv barked.

Laenard tilted his head to the left momentarily then said, "There are two panels on either side of the large shark's fin."

"Let me guess… we need to destroy the panels?"

"That is correct, Alex."

Looks like we had an answer. Now we only needed the how that came with it.

"We're going to have to lose our armor," I said.

"But…"

"No time to argue. They're coming."

The team all looked as the first sharklets began to swim toward us as we stood on the ledge around the room. My armor shimmered once and then vanished. My team followed my lead seconds later.

"Let's do this!" I took out a shock grenade and threw it into the water. "Die, sharks, die!"

The grenade exploded a few feet into the water and stunned a small group of sharks.

"Quickly now," I said, then jumped into the water.

The sharks hunted us through the water room. Two sharklets charged toward me. I swam under the first and popped up behind him to punch it in the back. The robot exploded. I spun and punched the second shark as it got close. The metal shark opened its mouth and bit down. I spun out of the way of the bite and then grabbed my energy blade. As the sharklet rushed toward me, I plunged the blade into the center of its body, destroying it. I then turned under the water to see how the others were faring with our underwater battle. We could all breathe thanks to some equipment I had built a few bases back, but it was still a difficult fight.

Anja was busy dodging sharklets and slaughtering as many as she could with her energy sword. The sharks were armored and it was taking longer than expected to bring them down. I turned to find Dhruv utilizing a plasma rifle in his battle. The white-hot energy bolts were perfect for searing through metal, but they were expensive and I didn't have an endless supply. I felt an urge to yank the rifle from his hands, but I ignored it and turned to find Haley.

She was using both hands to blast at the sharks charging her. She was quick, but the sharks still overcame her and tore big chunks out of her suit. I swam over to her as fast as I could and reached into one of my armor compartments to pull out a healing pill.

"Here," I said, shoving it in her hand.

"I need to get out of the water to take it," she said.

"Then go!"

As she swam toward the surface, Laenard swam toward me, shooting sharklets with a green energy weapon. When he reached me, he smiled. As I gazed through the glass of his helmet, I saw a reflection of the big boss shark headed our way. I spun around and raised my energy blade. It was only good for close-quarters combat, but it was my most effective choice underwater.

The boss swam beneath me and lunged upward, snapping its jaw. I ducked and avoided its bite. I then thrust my energy blade into the top of its head. The boss fired a laser from one of its eyes. I held down my trigger on the energy blade and plunged it into one of the panels in the mechanical beast's torso. Sparks flew out, and it pulled away from me into the dark depths of the water, trailing oil like blood from the hole I'd made. While my team destroyed the other sharks, I dove to finish off the big shark-boss with my energy blade.

When I got to the shark, it had recovered enough to attack. I swam toward it with my energy blade held up in front of me. The shark sailed toward me. I bumped it with my energy blade to move it aside and line up on the other panel before pushing my energy deep. Sharp teeth snapped at me the whole time. I dodged the bites while continuing to plunge the orange-colored blade into the beast repeatedly.

ALEX: I could use some help down here!
DHRUV: We're busy!
HALEY: I'm on my way!
LAENARD: We'll be right there!

Only when Haley arrived and the shark turned to her could I finally get the angle I needed and with a dazzling fizzle of electricity that left my hair tingling all over my body it died. We were both wounded bad during the battle, but the familiar screen popped up.

```
Combat is Over!
You get 2,000 XP
You have 5,000 XP
You reach Level 6
+9 health
+ 5 skill points
You need 1,400 xp for level 7
```

All that work and we really hadn't gotten that much more experience points clearing the level.

"We should keep going," Anja said.

I nodded as I closed the stats screen on my HUD. "Let's do this," I said.

We trudged back up the moonbase and made our way to the next one.

Lucky moonbase number seven. Clearing it would give us the infantry factory.

CHAPTER 23

Midway through the seventh moonbase, things were not going well. Not at all. Haley had stepped into a small closet that proceeded to freeze her like Han Solo in the *Empire Strikes Back*. Anja, Dhruv, Laenard, and I stood next to the strange contraption, wondering what to do.

"We should leave her," Dhruv said coldly.

"She'll respawn after the game," Anja said.

"No, we're not leaving her!" I said.

Dhruv shrugged. "What do you suggest we do?"

I sighed, not having the slightest idea. Could I solve the puzzle to get her out? Maybe. The only problem was that the puzzle that needed solving wasn't so obvious to us.

"Say, I've got an idea," Laenard said.

"What?" Anja asked.

"Come here." He pointed toward the closet.

"What?" I asked.

"Look closely," he said.

I peered closer at the devious machine and noticed writing.

"What does it say?" I asked, unable to make it out. "That's tiny text!"

"Let me see if I can decipher," Anja said.

The rest of us watched as she held a black box up to the closet-sized machine.

"I'm getting an answer," she said. "It says, 'Turn the Can into a Saucepan'."

"What?" I asked. "That's nuts! Let me see it."

I grabbed her machine and held it up to the text.

"See, it says, 'Turn the Can into a Saucepan. Don't leave Jacky in a Closet.'"

"It didn't say the Jacky part for me," Anja said.

"Let me try," Laenard said, holding out their hand.

I gave him the device. He held it by the strange markings.

"The text says, 'Turn the Can into a Saucepan. Don't leave the Darth Maul in a Closet.'"

"What does that even mean?" I asked. "And why does it keep changing?"

"Maybe it's a clue," Anja said.

I could see her curiosity was piqued. She wanted to solve the puzzle so bad. Me too. There was no way in hell I was leaving Haley behind. I knew that if the situation were reversed, she wouldn't abandon me. And that she was counting on me.

"She'll respawn after the game," Laenard said, his voice echoing out into the air.

"Maybe not if she's frozen, rather than dead," Anja said. "What can we do to unfreeze her? If we try using weapons and kill her, that actually might not be as bad as leaving her."

"What does this have to do with a can? With a saucepan?" I asked.

"Is it saying we should use a can to cook something?" Laenard asked. "Like a stew?"

We all stared at him, unsure of what to say.

"Wait, let's see if her coms are still working," Anja said.

ANJA: Haley, do you copy?

HALEY: Yes, I read you!

ALEX: Hold on, we're working on getting you out. There's some writing here, 'turn the can into a saucepan', any thoughts?

HALEY: It's totally black. Could be the inside of a can I suppose. Except who would freeze a can?

ALEX: We might try shooting you out. But it's risky.

HALEY: Ouch, yeah. Work on that clue first, will you.

ALEX: Will do.

I turned to the others and frowned. What was she going through with her body trapped and her mind active? "A can," I repeated, taking the black box from Laenard. "How about this: Can into a Pan?"

I held the device up as I said it.

"It says, 'Fork into a Spoon,' now" I said. "This doesn't make any sense!"

"Hold on," Anja said. "I've got an idea." She walked over to the closet-sized machine and opened a panel on the front. "There we go," she said.

I leaned forward, eager to see what she was doing. Would it help?

Sparks flew from the control box, causing her to move back. "Crap!"

A red neon number lit up on the front of the machine.

Deactivation: 59:00 minutes

"What did you do?" I cried.

"Maybe it means she will be released in an hour?" Laenard asked.

Anja frowned and shook her head. "Don't think so. This doesn't look good."

"We should leave her," Dhruv muttered. "We're losing time."

"It's not as if she will be permanently dead," Laenard added.

They were right and wrong at the same time. I needed to get Haley out. I knelt in front of the machine and examined the control box Anja had been fiddling with before activating the countdown timer. Should I try to hack the game again? I had gotten the pain penalty and had to deal with a toothache before when I had tried. And I knew that if I took it too far like Haruto I would face even more severe consequences. Yet I couldn't stop myself.

"Guard the perimeter. When the AI senses I'm hacking the code, it might start sending units."

"No!" Dhruv shouted. "You're endangering all of our lives. I won't let you do it." He grabbed my shoulder. I turned just as Laenard held him back.

"Let him do it!" Anja exclaimed. "It's a gamble but I think it's a good one."

"What if the time countdown stops?" Dhruv asked. "What if the machine malfunctions?"

"Then we can leave Haley here until she is released and come back to try again," Anja said. "If she dies or ends up like Dorukan, we'll know there's no way to hack the game."

"Wait, who's Dorukan?" I asked.

Nobody would answer, so I examined the control box more closely by pulling up a terminal window in my heads-up display. It was linked directly into the code of the game and the damn AI was good, nearly too good. If I tried to mess with it without preparation, it would sense me. And it would retaliate.

"Damn it. I need to concentrate," I mumbled then sighed.

"Just be quick about it," Anja urged. "The Deactivation timer keeps ticking."

Hurry, but be careful. That was the crux of the problem. I couldn't slip up. I started with a quick review of my knowledge of multi-dimentional space and how it was kept in line. I added my specialized subroutines as well. Then I took a stab at writing new code.

It was as if a layer of thick cobwebs blocked my mind. Just like when I tried to hack the game before. I became frustrated quickly and began to hack at it from different angles. I continued to fail, no matter how I tried. Until I finally found a way in again. By running a common subroutine to guess my rate of level growth multiple times in a row, the memory buffer of the terminal window I was using overflowed, giving me a chance to open a new window with more control. At this point, the AI wouldn't be able to detect me for certain.

"I'm in, but only for a few seconds," I warned my friends.

I slipped my specialized code into the AI's routines. There was-n't much space I could use of my own. Most had already been oc-cupied by the AI. So I had to get in where I could.

Most of the code was in a binary format I couldn't read, but I could read some of the instructions that the AI was using to run the game. If I could change those, I could get it to release Haley from a prison.

```
Penalty Level One Activated
```

"Aargh," I cried out but continued going, ignoring the pain as best I could. "Hold on, one more thing to try…"

"Hurry up!" Dhruv yelled.

"Let him be calm," Laenard chided.

I took a deep breath. Hopefully I could finish the hack in time. If I failed, the others would want to leave Haley behind. While I knew she would likely appear in the staging area after the game ended, I didn't want her to think I had left her behind. No, I cared about her too much.

"Okay, I did it," I said. "Here we go."

I activated the rogue program I had created and looked over at the machine holding Haley hostage. A few red LED lights lit up on the front of the machine.

```
Deactivation cancelled.
Thawing process initiated
```

"She's being released!" Anja cheered.

"Come on, we need to get her out of the machine," I cried as I pulled the glass lid away from Haley.

"Right," Laenard said as he pulled her out.

"Her body is already thawing," Anja said.

Haley cried as she felt the icy grip of the cryogenic machine release her.

"It's okay. It's okay," I whispered.

She calmed almost instantly as she wrapped her arms around me. "I knew you'd save me," she said.

"His love for you is obvious and strong," Laenard said.

I didn't move to correct him as Haley and I stared into each other's eyes.

"Okay, love birds, we've got to go," Dhruv reminded us.

"He's right," I said then lowered my voice. "We'll talk later, okay?"

She nodded, still shivering. "Anyone have a towel?" she asked.

"Right here," Anja said. "Having a towel is so important."

I gave her a wry smile, not mentioning my love of Douglas Adams. Haley dried off as the rest of us locked and loaded, ready to take on the rest of the level.

The pain in my mouth continued, but I grimaced and took it without complaint. Hacking Haley out of the trap had been more than worth it.

"Let's go already!" Dhruv shouted like an over-eager drill sergeant with a batch of new recruits.

"Coming," I said as I patted Haley on the back.

We moved down the hallway, staying in a tight formation. It didn't take much for us to find our next batch of infantry robots.

"Damn," Anja said. "It's like a clone army."

"Take 'em out!" I yelled then opened fire.

My plasma rifle spit out red, glowing blasts of energy that cut through the first wave of robots. I continued firing as the rest of the team took care of the rest.

Within moments, we had completely wiped out this batch of infantry robots. The experience points were nice, but I was more interested in the final boss of the level.

"Anyone have any ideas of what we'll face on the last level?" I asked.

"They change all the time," Dhruv said as he swapped out the power core of his weapon.

"I know, but what are the usual bosses that appear?"

"Guessing will not help us," Laenard said.

After healing up and restocking our weapons, we continued our downward sweep of the moonbase.

When we reached the elevator down on the eleventh floor, I stopped and turned to the others.

"All right, we need to scout. I've got a bad feeling about this base boss. The AI wants us to fail."

"Duh," Dhruv snorted then punched the elevator button.

"It was worse this time," Laenard said. "They trapped Haley."

When the elevator arrived and the door opened, the final battle started before we had any chance to get intel on the situation. A group of six heavily armed bots stormed out and began shooting. I cursed Dhruv under my breath for going ahead before we were ready as I lit up the first enemy.

"Hey, don't blame me! They just popped out all at once," he yelled.

The enemy robots died in seconds and the elevator door closed.

"Damn it," I said. "They definitely know we're coming now."

I jammed the elevator button with my finger. The door slid open immediately.

"Wait!" Anja said. "I've got another way we can come at this level."

"Yeah?" I turned to her as the elevator door slid shut.

"This way," she said.

We took the elevator up two levels and followed Anja to a tiny, cramped duct carrying cables and wires to the lowest level.

"It's a bit of a tight fit," I said, peering down into the darkness.

"Yeah, but it'll give us the benefit of surprise, I think," Anja said.

"Okay, let's do this…"

After tying a knotted rope and tossing it down, I climbed into the rectangular space barely big enough for me to descend. The others followed. I had a flash bang grenade in my left hand which made climbing the rope more difficult, but if the guards detected us and started coming up, I would let it go, giving us a few minutes to go back up and try something else.

The closer we got to the twelfth floor of the moonbase, the more I felt like the game designers were trying to trip us up. Climbing down the long, narrow cable was a nightmare. It was almost impossible for me to take my mind off the fact that I was likely to slip and fall at any moment.

Laenard didn't have as much difficulty with the rope, so he was able to watch our back and make sure no enemy bots were coming up behind us.

When I reached the floor of the base, I climbed out and swapped my grenade for my pulsar rifle. The weapon wasn't the most reliable, but the pure damage per second factor would help us take out a platoon of infantry bots easily. At least that was the plan as I kicked open the vent and scrambled out into a vast, open room. It seemed to go on forever.

"Everyone okay?" I asked as the others joined me.

"Where are all the bots?" Haley asked.

"I don't like this," Dhruv said. "It's too quiet."

As I glanced up and down the length of the floor which lit up by bright lights a few hundred feet overhead, I called up a radar screen on my heads-up display.

"I've got a bad feeling about this too…" I muttered.

"There!" Haley shouted.

I followed her finger and saw a line of infantry bots approaching, their rifles at their waists, ready to fire. Without cover, Laenard, Anja, and Dhruv were sitting ducks.

I aimed the Pulsar and opened fire on the first bot. The electromagnetic pulse from the weapon rendered its artificial nervous system useless, but I didn't have time to admire my handiwork. The other bots fired at us.

"Watch out!" Anja shouted.

I dove to the side as a pulse from a laser rifle hit the ground next to me. The enemy was playing for keeps from the moment we'd entered the room.

Laenard and Anja made it behind a waist-high energy shield, but the rest of us were out in the open.

The ground behind me exploded and I rolled to my feet, throwing an EMP grenade at the bots. Their shields flickered but remained in place as the electromagnetic pulse went off, then I opened fire with the pulsar.

Dhruv and Haley were blasting away with their laser rifles as well. Their shots pinged off the enemy shields.

"Behind us!" Laenard shouted.

I spun and dove through a narrow hatch behind the shields they had set up. Anja was hunkered down in the corner.

"What's happening?" she asked as I lay down with my back against the mesh.

"They just keep coming," I said. "We need to find who's controlling them."

"Find the head of the snake. Got it." She sat up and fired three shots.

The infantry bots returned fire. We were pinned against one of the walls, our energy shields failing quickly.

"I think I can improvise a scanner to spot it," Anja said, with the distant look of someone searching their inventory. "Stay low and keep them busy."

The sound of multiple energy shields going down at once made me glance over. Haley, Dhruv, and Laenard lay on the ground behind lowered energy shields.

"Hurry!" Laenard shouted.

All at once, Anja stood then charged forward, firing every couple of seconds at a bot that seemed a little different than the rest. Had she found their command bot?

"Concentrate fire on Anja's target!" I yelled.

The others followed suit and opened fire on the bot. I didn't want her to get shot at the last minute.

The bot flickered, then its shield faded away. Anja dived in and finished it off with her energy blade. Once their commander went down, the rest of the infantry troops powered down.

Combat is Over!
You get 1,500 xp
You have 6,500 XP
You reach Level 7
+12 health
+ 8 skill points
You need 6,300 xp for level 8

I waved the notification screen away.

"Everyone okay?"

"I'm wounded, but I'll live," Dhruv said.

"Let's get moving. We still have five moonbases to go," I said.

The limited time to finish the RPG section of the game and the fact it was procedurally generated each time we played made *Moon*

Wars difficult to master. We'd been on this moonbase for almost four hours. There was no way we could get through it all, but I wanted to do at least as good as Dhruv had done when he was in charge of our team.

We exited moonbase seven and flew toward the research moonbase, one of the most difficult.

CHAPTER 24

The research moonbase was even more difficult than I had expected. For one thing, all the bots were able to mutate and evolve during battles. Yeah, every time we came up with a way to defeat the robots guarding the level, they would change up their strategy and physical makeup. It took us over three hours to make our way to the twelfth and final floor of the base. By that time, we were all tired, cranky, and ready to give up.

"It's getting even more difficult," Dhruv said. "We're running out of time."

"At least we don't need to sleep," Haley replied.

I loved how she always tried to stay positive. "She's right," I said. "We've got advantages in this virtual world.

"Everyone ready for this final battle?"

My pain penalty had expired, and I was tempted to hack the game to benefit us again.

"We're nowhere close to ready," Dhruv said. "I told you we needed better equipment two moonbases ago!"

"Maybe I'll hack the AI again." I studied the reactions of the others.

"No." Haley put her hand on my arm. "Don't push it."

"She's right," Anja said. "The benefits we'll get from you hacking will be outweighed by the fact you're in pain and not able to concentrate."

"Maybe I'll hack the pain penalty," I said, half-joking.

"No!" Anja, Dhruv, and Laenard all cried at the same time.

"Why not?" I asked.

"Haruto tried," Laenard said.

"What happened?" I asked.

"Do you see him around anymore?"

"No, but nobody knows where he went. Maybe he got out of the game," Haley said.

My heart raced at the thought we could be stuck inside *Moon Wars* forever. "Are we going to fight this final evolver boss or not?" I asked.

"We're ready," Anja said.

"All right," I said. "Let's do this."

We walked down the stairs leading to the final floor of the eighth moonbase. Bright white lights from below lit up a steel hallway leading off into the distance. At the bottom of the stairs, I kept moving forward with Dhruv at my side. We both had our weapons raised, ready to fire at a moment's notice. The evolver boss was already two steps ahead of us. As we reached the end of the hall, the walls flickered then disappeared.

"It's an illusion trap!" Dhruv yelled.

He rushed to the left, toward a line of bibedal bots with wheels instead of feet, firing as he went.

"Back him up!" I shouted.

The battle was on. Our team fired at the first wave of robots, trying to clear the path to the central control console. The robot army immediately regrouped and counterattacked. They were rolling toward us on both sides, firing as they came. Swinging around to check the rear, I realized Laenard was holding back.

The robots were positioned in a way that gave him flanking fire. Instead, he was hiding behind a pillar.

"Laenard, what are you doing?" I cried.

A nearby shot sent a laser beam whizzing by my head, the sound echoing through the hall.

Laenard, still hiding from the onslaught, said nothing.

"Anja, come help me," I called.

I hurried over to another pillar with her, and we took cover behind it. Several of the enemy bots were already firing on us, and the lasers were inching closer to our position.

"What's wrong with Laenard?" Anja asked.

"He's a coward!" I snapped.

"How can you say that?" an electronic voice asked. Laenard's avatar appeared on my heads-up display.

"Why don't you come out and help?" Anja asked him.

"Not going to happen," Laenard said, and his character vanished.

A ping from my suit's radio-wave detector and the mini-map told me Laenard was on the same level but a half-mile away.

Did he have a plan he didn't share with the rest of us? I hoped that was the case as the rest of us fired everything we had at the oncoming army of bots. Our combined damage was steadily defeating the bibedal robots, and the hall was finally clear of enemies. The familiar Combat is Over message, however, did not appear.

"Let's move," I said.

I rushed to the control console, while the rest of my team covered me. When I reached the giant room-sized computer, I popped open a panel and stared at the display panel inside.

"What do we have?" Anja asked as she walked up next to me.

"I'm not sure yet," I said. "Something is wrong…"

"They've evolved beyond central control," Dhruv said.

"Where did Laenard go?" Haley asked. "I'm worried about him."

"He's gone from the mini-map," I said. "Maybe he was killed."

"Possible," Dhruv said coldly.

"We've got to figure out how to defeat this evolver boss," I said. "Any ideas?"

Haley piped up, "We should look for Laenard. Maybe he has a plan."

"Why didn't he just tell us?" I asked.

"He's an alien," Dhruv said. "Why does he do anything he does?"

I sighed, hating how we were fighting each other as much as the enemy. "Time's wasting. We need to defeat the boss before it evolves again."

"I'll scout for Laenard, and you figure out how to defeat the evolver," Anja said.

"That's a great idea," I said. "The rest of us will stay here and try to figure out how to beat this thing."

"Be careful," Anja said. "This place is crawling with enemies."

"Noted," I said, and she dashed off down the hall.

I turned to the console and studied the screen.

"Show me everything you know about Laenard's people," I said.

The console glowed and a holographic image of an alien body appeared before me.

"What am I looking at?" I asked.

"That's a Gastero," the computer said.

"A what?" I asked.

"Gastero," the computer repeated.

"Uh…" I was confused.

"That's Laenard's species," the computer said. "They are a native race from the planet Nibiru, a.k.a. Planet X."

"What does that mean?" I asked.

"I'm not sure," the computer said.

"Great," I muttered.

"But I do have some information about them," the computer said.

"What do you know?" I asked.

The holographic image rotated, and various facts about Laenard's species appeared on the screen. "Life expectancy is unknown," the computer said. "They have a higher tolerance for radiation than humans. They don't have a gender."

"Why don't they have a gender?" Haley asked.

"It's hard to tell from the data on file," the computer said. "Their anatomy is sufficiently different from that of humans that it's hard to make a judgment call on the subject."

"How are they different?" I asked.

"The data suggests they are hermaphrodites, like Earth's snails," the computer said.

"Snails?" Haley asked. "I didn't know snails were hermaphrodites."

"We don't have time for this nonsense," Dhruv said.

"I just wanted to see if there was maybe a reason he had left us. Has he ever abandoned you before?"

Dhruv shook his head. "No, not since I've known him, anyway…"

"I've got approaching bots," Haley said.

I called up the map to check. "Where?" I asked.

"They're all over," Haley said.

"How many?" I asked.

"Hundreds," Haley said. "Maybe more…You don't see them?"

"No…"

"The evolver bot is hacking us!" Dhruv declared.

"Are they coming or not?"

I soon had my answer as a floor of robots similar to the ones we had first encountered rushed toward the control room.

"Take cover!" I shouted then shot the glass window.

Several red robots rushed forward.

"We don't have time for this!" Haley cried.

"If you've got a better idea, let's hear it," I snapped back.

Haley shook her head.

A heat ray shot by my head.

"Down!" I shouted, and we all took cover.

269

I chucked an incendiary grenade at the mob of enemies. The explosion was enough to kill a few of them, and the rest ran away.

"Why did you do that?" Dhruv bared. "We needed the parts! They're burnt to a crisp!"

"Dude! What is it with you and equipment?" I asked.

"No time for fighting," Haley said.

She put her hand on my arm, calming me down.

ANJA: I've found something.

ALEX: What is it? Where are you?

ANJA: I'm in another control room. It's a computer. I think I can control the bots from here.

ALEX: Can you hack into it?

ANJA: I'm going to try. I'm in the console now.

ALEX: Is it working?

ANJA: Yes. Wait...no. I'm locked out. I can't do anything from here.

ALEX: You have to do something!

ANJA: I'm trying!

ANJA: Uh oh...

ALEX: What?

ANJA: Gotta go!

The communication window faded away. Was she okay? Where was she?

"Haley," I said. "Can you scan for Anja?"

"I can try," Haley said. "But there's a lot of stuff to look through."

"Just do your best," I said. "And keep your eye out for Laenard."

I turned to Dhruv. "What do you think?"

"Oh, now you're asking me!" he snorted.

"Come on," Haley said. "Let's find the others."

"Agreed. We should stick together from now on…"

I only made it three steps before I stopped.

"Hold on," I said. "Let me try one more hack."

"No!" Dhruv said.

"Alex, no," Haley said, backing him up.

I returned to the computer console and tried my buffer overflow hack. This time, it didn't work.

"It's no use," I turned to Haley. "I need to know what's going on. Can you open a window to Anja?"

"I'll try," Haley said.

"No!" Dhruv said. "Don't!"

"I've got it," Haley said.

A small window opened in the corner of my vision.

"Anja!" I said. "Can you hear me?"

"Yes," Anja said.

Her voice sounded muffled and distant.

"Where are you?" I asked.

"I'm still in the control room," Anja said.

"Are you safe?" I asked.

"I think so," Anja said. "The video feed is taking too much power. Gotta go!"

The line of communication terminated. I sighed, not liking the way things were going.

"What about this control room?" Haley asked. "What about the evolver boss?"

"I think we should leave it for now," I said, "and go to find Anja."

"We should go after the evolver," Dhruv said. "We can take it on our own."

"No, let's go after Anja," I said. "She said she might be able to control all the mobs."

"I agree with Alex," Haley said. "We should go after Anja."

Dhruv frowned. "You two are going to get us all killed."

"Is that a problem?" Haley asked.

"Yes, it's a big problem," Dhruv said. "I'm not going to be stuck here with you losers. I'm going after the evolver boss on my own."

"Wait!" I said. "What are you doing?"

"I'm leaving!" Dhruv said. "I'll catch up with you later!"

"No!" Haley shouted.

But it was already too late. Dhruv had run off.

"Now what?" Haley asked.

"I don't know… This game is a lot harder from the inside."

"Right?" She laughed nervously.

I turned to her, "and it would help if we stuck together. First, Laenard and now Dhruv."

"I know. And we are close to the RTS phase. It would be a huge waste of our levels and skills to die now."

"I'm afraid, Haley. Maybe the game isn't beatable."

"We'll get out of here," she said affectionately, before alarm showed on her face. "Alex! Watch out!"

I spun around to see what she was pointing at. A new bot called a regenerator on my screen had entered the room. Where had it come from? Had the boss split into two? I didn't have time to think it through.

"Attack!" I shouted and fired my pulsar pistol.

The regenerator shrugged off my shots. Instead of charging me, it moved to intercept Haley. I turned and fired at the evolver.

"Take this!" I shouted and unloaded another few rounds at the boss bot.

But the regenerator was already in Haley's face, pounding her with its powerful punches and weapons.

The ammo helper bot she'd created a few bases back was crushed completely.

"No! Gizmo!" she yelled then pulled an energy blade, cutting like a madwoman.

The regenerator took a swipe at her head which struck her at an angle, spurring me to action. I ran to the melee, trying to figure out a way to assist Haley without getting myself killed in the process.

In the end, I settled for a distraction.

"Hey you, ugly!" I said, pointing my Pulsar at the regenerator. "Come here and get some!"

The regenerator turned to face me, breaking off its attack on Haley. It charged forward, its single red eye flashing.

"You're a goner, meatbag," the bot shouted in a deep voice.

I fired my weapon as it reached me, but it shrugged off the shots, reaching out with its piston-like arms and shoving me across the room as large as a hangar bay.

"Yeah, that's right, take this! And this!" I fired the pistol as I flew through the air.

My trajectory changed, and I crashed into the far wall, bouncing off it and back onto the cold, hard floor. I was out cold before I landed, my body shutting down my consciousness in response to the pain.

I woke up on the floor again, back in control of my own body. My heart was pounding, and I felt like I had just run a marathon. I sat up, looking around. Where was Haley? The boss bots?

"He's up," Laenard said to my left.

I struggled to my feet. "What's going on? How long was I out?"

"Too long!" Haley cried.

She wrapped her arms around me. "You're alive! I was so worried."

I winced at the pain her hug caused my sore body.

"Anyone have any medic patches?" I asked.

Haley patched me up. I noticed I had not received any experience points for them defeating the regenerator and evolver bosses.

"What happened?"

"Laenard saved the day," Haley said. "Well, him and Anja."

"Yeah, yeah, I had nothing to do with it," Dhruv muttered.

"Nice, but what happened exactly?"

Laenard rubbed his mouth.

"They located the AI brain controlling the bosses," Haley said.

Anja laughed. "It was like an actual brain, in a tank of pink water. Laenard dumped a bottle of acid into it and nearly got melted himself by the steam from the reaction."

"Are you okay, buddy?" I asked.

Laenard tilted his head to the left. "Have I been downgraded from friend level status?"

I laughed, shaking my head. "No, not at all. Quite the contrary. You got us out of a scrape. Next time, though, let us know."

"That was not possible," he continued. "The evolver bot was monitoring our secure communications and would have protected the laboratory with his brain."

"He made the right call," Anja said. "Once I figured out what he was up to, I broke away and started helping find that room."

"The damn boss bot couldn't handle each of us doing our own thing," Dhruv said. "So my big battle was important too."

"Um… I hate to break up the love fest, but we really need to get moving," Anja said.

"Okay," I said. "What's next."

"The engineering moonbase," Dhruv said. "We should expect new bots."

"Great." I turned to Haley and smiled. "We'll be ready for 'em."

She returned a smile, but it quickly faded as we healed then headed up to the surface of the moon.

On the flight to the ninth moonbase, the reality of the game lasting forty-eight hours straight began to take its toll. Haley and I had been through it once before inside *Moon Wars* and had teamed up to win in the real world, but it was wearing on me. The lack of sleep felt strange, but I kept moving. We had to move forward.

CHAPTER 25

Halfway through the ninth moonbase, right after defeating the mid-level boss and finding the Forge for the base, Dhruv and I got into an argument. Sure, we had always had our differences, but this was something different. He wanted me to give up my leadership position, and I wasn't ready to let it go. Not when we were so close to getting to the RTS portion of the game.

"We need better armor for this boss fight, or we're going to get killed," Dhruv insisted.

"Quit arguing with our leader," Haley said.

Dhruv shot her a nasty look. I raised a hand.

"Okay, okay, enough," I said. "We'll do it."

I knew some leaders would have resisted Dhruv's idea so they wouldn't come off as weak, but his idea wasn't that bad. Maybe giving him a bit more input would calm him down and make it easier for the rest of us as we cleared the final three and a half moonbases. The 48-hour timer was running down quickly with only twenty hours and some change left.

Although it cost us resources that would help build better commanders for the RTS, Anja fabricated some gear and I handed out new helmets and chest pieces. Then I addressed my team. "Look, we've made it this far. I don't expect anyone to love each other, but we need to respect each other. Let's stick together, and we'll get through the next moonbase."

I had been eyeing a new weapon—a new Level Eight laser blueprint that had just dropped from the previous moon boss. If we could get through the next moonbase, I knew we would be able to get it. I wanted it now, but I didn't want to anger my team so close to the end by making it a priority to get a decent weapon for me. It was time for me to use my leadership skills to influence my team positively instead of forcing my ideas on them.

We moved forward, clearing the next four levels of the moonbase without many problems. The new armor was helping out, and I wasn't shy acknowledging it.

"Good job on the armor plates," I said as we waited for the elevator that would carry us to level eleven of the ninth moonbase.

Dhruv stared into my eyes and nodded, his lips pursed.

The elevator door slid open, and we entered. I pressed the button down.

When the door opened again, Dhruv and I walked out with our weapons raised, ready to rain down hell on anything stupid enough to show its metallic face.

The bots we had been facing were constantly changing as the builder bot boss on the bottom level pumped out new creations to try and stop us.

"I'm reading something big to the left of the map," Laenard said.

The hologram was showing a huge, metal cube about the size of a city block with two massive mechanical arms on either side of it.

It was almost as tall as the walls of the level—a hundred feet or so high.

"Can't be the big boss bot," I said. "This isn't the last level."

"No, but maybe we should treat it as a final boss," Haley said. "It's big enough."

"Good idea. We need to be careful until we find out what its capable of doing."

"Let's go kill it!" Dhruv said.

He trotted off toward that side of the level. I followed along with the others. When we reached the massive room, the immense blocky bot looked impressive.

"I hate *Minecraft*!" Dhruv shouted as he opened up fire. I took out a grenade launcher and launched a grenade at the top of the black, metallic structure. It exploded, sending chunks flying in all directions.

"Guess that answers that question," I said. "It's not indestructible!"

Dhruv and I fired again as the mega-bot moved its arms toward us, snapping the giant pincers on the end of each arm. "Watch out!" I said.

I pulled out my pulsar pistol and fired two shots, hitting the bot in the center of its body. It stood still for a moment, and then a red grenade—shining a bit like a potion bottle—shot out from the cube, hitting the ground near Dhruv.

"What's with this *Minecraft* crap?" he asked.

"What's *Minecraft*?" I asked, wondering if I was missing an important clue to how to fight the boss.

The next grenade shot was much bigger and came right at us. I wasn't sure if my pistol could deflect the shot, but I tried anyway. As it flew through the air, I shot a few times, but missed. Then the grenade actually hit me, bouncing off my chest armour.

I didn't have time to react, but luckily, I wasn't the only one that had noticed that the explosion caused massive damage. The one hit had taken out my shields and nearly half of my health! Haley and Dhruv were able to retaliate against the rectangular-looking bot, but it was so big and not easily damaged. Whenever we hit, the pieces that fell off reformed with the whole, albeit a little less uniform. The more we damaged it, the more ghastly and frightening it became.

"We need to try something else!" Anja shouted. She cut a swath of tiny blocks from its left side before one of the pincer arms reached toward her.

"I've got your back!" Laenard cried. He rushed over and threw himself in the way of the arm, knocking it back and him to the ground.

"Medic!" I yelled, hoping Haley heard me.

If this wasn't even the big boss of the moonbase, we were in trouble. The only thing that was giving us the slightest chance was the new armor Anja had crafted for us. I made a note to thank her after the battle then reached into my infinite storage pack for some bigger firepower. When my fingers grasped a level four rocket launcher, I pulled it out.

"Everyone stand back!" I shouted.

I fired the one and only missile I had for the weapon I'd been saving for a big boss. While the block boss was a lot closer than I would have liked when using such a powerful weapon, I had to change the dynamic of the fight or we would lose. Dhruv's insistence on new armor would help us once again. At least I hoped so.

The rocket fired, arced up toward the ceiling before turning and zeroing in on the spot of the block where the grenades had been coming out. When it hit, the entire top portion of the block exploded, breaking the structure in half. That was another thing I had to thank Dhruv for after the battle. He'd given me the powerful rocket during a particularly big loot drop a few levels back.

The left half of the block-bot propped itself up with its gigantic spidery arm while the other half propped itself against the wall of the room. The once elegant cube had been broken up and was trying to reform itself. Tons of the cubes that had been destroyed were slowly floating down to the ground.

"You took out the grenades!" Laenard said.

"Now let's finish it off!" I shouted.

I drew my pulsar pistol once more and shot at the left half of the cube. Each shot hit, slowly dropping its overall health.

"Don't let it reform!" Dhruv bellowed as he ran left and right, laying down a steady stream of laser pulses. They seemed to slow down the cube from reforming.

"Everything EMP! Now!" I pulled out my own two remaining EMP grenades.

After tossing them at the right half of the box bot, the smaller cubes began moving more slowly. While it hadn't disabled them completely as they were shielded, the technology did slow them down. The others soon followed my lead after I tossed my grenades. Each had been saving theirs.

```
Combat is Over!
You get 10,000 xp
You have 16,500 XP
You reach Level 8
+16 health
+ 13 skill points
You need 9,100 xp for level 9
```

I pumped my fist. "Yeah! We got it!"

We salvaged all the spare parts. Quite a list:

```
1) Black Box Cube x5
2) Power Cell (Minor Yellow) x20
3) Datalink Chip x1
4) Firewall Card x7
5) CPU Chip x4
6) Weapon Override Chip x2
7) Crossover Chip x8
8) Synthetic CPU x5
9) 100 lbs iron
10) 97 lbs copper
11) 73 lbs silicon
```

"Now we can upgrade our shields and weapons again!" Dhruv declared.

"Maybe, if we can't clear the rest of the moonbase as we are," I said. "Let's keep moving."

Loot securely stored, we continued clearing the tenth and eleven levels.

****

Yet another big boss battle, I thought to myself as we walked down the wide, flat ramp leading to the twelfth and final floor of the ninth moonbase. What would the big boss of the engineering moonbase turn out to be? I was really hoping it wouldn't be another Juggernaut... not so soon after the last one we had to fight. Blaster or sniper turrets would've been okay, but not another massive enemy like that.

"Look alive," I said as we marched across the big, barren room toward a set of steel doors on the opposite side.

They were closed, but I saw a control box on a pedestal to the left of the door. I pointed at it, and my squad moved to cover me as I approached. I pressed the button with my left hand and the doors slid open, and there was nothing except a set of stairs leading up into a cloud of thick, black smoke.

"Cover me," I said, and I charged up the stairs.

The others followed as I recklessly rushed into the unknown. What had come over me? I didn't have time to work it out as I made it through the acrid, black smoke and reached what looked to be a control room.

"What the hell?" Dhruv asked. "Why did you rush up here?"

"I don't know," I said. "Compulsion."

Anja, Dhruv, Haley, Laenard and I all examined the room, looking for clues to find and take out the builder boss bot.

"I have found something," Laenard said.

The rest of us crowded around him as he stared down at a console with a strange keyboard.

"What is it?" I asked.

"The builder bot's central core is located here..." Laenard pointed to a spot on the map displayed on the screen.

"Are you sure? How do you know?"

"Yes. See the location on the map?" he pointed to a spot in the upper left corner of the map.

"I know," I snapped. "You showed me, but how do you know?"

Laenard hissed, a forked tongue slithering out.

"Stop fighting," Haley said as she stepped between us.

I glared at Laenard, wondering why I hated him so much in that moment.

"Wait a minute," Anja said. "This is a builder bot boss, right? I think I know what's happening."

"Enlighten us, o wise one," Dhruv snorted.

"It built a psych-bot that's been trailing us," she said.

"A what?" Haley asked.

"Psych-bot," Anja said. "We've not seen one in... well, a long time."

"Not since Haruto left," Dhruv said.

I noted the change of tone in his voice; more reverent.

"What does it do? How can we defeat it?" I asked.

"This run-through is a scratch," Dhruv muttered.

"What? No," I said. "We're so close to the end!"

"Yeah," Haley said, backing me up.

"The psych-bot is bad news," Laenard said. "I do not want to face one of those."

"I agree," Anja said.

Dhruv nodded, adding his vote. I sighed, not ready to give up.

"How bad is it?" I asked.

"It is possible to beat the psych-bot," Anja said. "But it will be tough. To defeat it, we will need to understand and trust each other."

"And not fight, like I just said," Haley interjected.

"Let's not argue," I said. "Explain this some more…"

"It is inside us all right now." Larneard tapped the side of his scale-covered head.

"Wait. Inside us?" I asked.

"Ew, that's gross," Haley said.

"This is why we have not seen the main boss," Laenard said. "He has built the psych-bots and at some point they entered us."

"Why can't we just get them out?" I asked.

Dhruv snorted, "You are as dumb as you look, American!"

I frowned, trying so hard to control my emotions.

"There is one way we can stop it," Anja said.

I turned to her. "Yeah? Go on…"

"You're not going to like it," she said.

"I don't care, just tell me!" I snapped.

She took a step toward me. "Listen—"

"No, you listen!" I stepped toward her, my hands shaking, my face feeling flushed. "I just hope you know what I'm going to do to you the next time we meet, Anja!"

"What?" she asked. "Are you threatening me?"

"I will tear your head off and..."

"Stop!" Haley shouted.

I stepped back. Crap! Why couldn't I control my emotions?

"We need a double four-step hack," Anja said.

"Didn't you say that's what caused Haruto to go away?" Haley asked.

The other three nodded, not saying anything.

"No, it's too dangerous," Haley said.

She turned to me, shaking her head, mouthing the word, "No..." repeatedly.

I sighed, the heavy burden of leadership weighing on me. On the one hand, Haley was probably right, but on the other, if we didn't take that chance we were staring at defeat... again.

"Yeah, I know it's risky," I said. "But we can do it, right guys?"

Dhruv snorted, Laenard nodded, and Anja finally said, "Yes..."

"Okay, great." I clapped my hands together once. "How do we start?"

"Me and you will attack the system with everything we have," Anja said. "The others will guard us. Once the AI knows what we're doing, it will send bots to shut us down."

I nodded. "Okay, good."

Anja glanced at everyone. "Keep us safe. We'll both be in a lot of pain. That on top of the psych-bots in our brains, and we'll be intolerable…"

"Oh, so the usual Alex?" Haley teased.

I smiled and leaned over to kiss her.

"Enough of that stuff!" Dhruv complained.

I stood in front of one of the consoles while Anja stood on the other side looking at a similar screen.

"Ready?" I asked. "Let's overload it and see if that purges the psych-bots."

"Hack the planet," she said.

I smiled, getting the reference.

"We are Samurai… the Keyboard Cowboys…"

I went with a few minor attacks, code meant to distract the AI while I pulled out some of the bigger tools in my belt of scripts and scraps of code I had collected thus far. Anja did the same. While we hacked the core code of *Moon Wars*, the others protected our backs. I felt safe with Dhruv, Haley, and Laenard watching us. Soon enough, the boss of the moonbase caught on to what we were doing in the control room and sent a wave of foot-long, glowing tube-bots at us.

"We've got company!" Dhruv shouted. "Look alive!"

I liked how he was taking charge in the battle during my absence. We made a good team despite the fact I couldn't stand being around him.

"Haley, watch out!" Laenard said.

I heard an explosion as I concentrated on the black screen with orange type on the screen below me.

"How are you doing, Anja?" I asked.

"Almost there," she replied.

Another explosion, another warning from Laenard. I could hear Anja breathing hard as we hacked the mainframe, our goal to overload it. The wave of tube-bots was quickly replaced by a second, smarter generation of the same basic design. Another explosion, and a third wave.

"When did this become World War Three?" Anja asked, grunting with effort as her fingers flew over the keys.

"Just keep going," I said.

A list of files and directories flew down my own screen.

"I'm in, finally," I said.

Pain Penalty Level One Activated

"Aargh," I growled as the discomfort of a toothache hit my virtual body.

"Keep going," Anja said. "I'm on my third hack now."

"Damn," I said. "You're so fast."

"Mess with the best, die like the rest."

"Hey, that's supposed to me my line!"

"Oh, you're the one wearing the dress?" she retorted.

I smiled as I continued hacking.

"Less pop culture banter!" Dhruv urged. "More concentration. We're being overwhelmed!"

"I only have two more hacks to go," she said. "Make that one! Ouch!"

There was a pause as I hacked in silence, grimacing at the pain. While virtual it felt real. I found it hard to concentrate on anything as the pain of my toothache worsened.

"I'm almost in," Anja said. "Last hack to go. How are you doing, Zero Cool?"

"Almost there," I replied through gritted teeth.

Suddenly, there was an explosion, and a series of quick cracks as Haley peppered the battlefield with lightning from a rod she had constructed a few levels back.

Pain Penalty Level Two Activated

Pain Penalty Level Three Activated

"I've got my second and third hacks," I said, the pain in my mouth increasing.

"Okay, this is important," Anja said. "We need to get the last ones simultaneously. Do you know what that word means?"

"Yes! At the same time!"

"The psych-bots!" Haley shouted. "Don't fight!"

"Last hack," Anja said. "Ready?"

"Ready," I replied.

She started to hack, I followed. Think about every hacking scene you've ever seen in entertainment and make it a hundred times more boring, and you might have a sense of what Anja and I were dealing with as we coded the alien machine to remove the pysch-bots from our minds. And just at that moment the pain of the toothache became so severe I ignored the others, dropped to the floor, and screamed.

"…we're being overwhelmed," I heard a voice say. "…can't hold them off much longer."

Dhruv? Laenard? Haley? Was this real life? I didn't understand what was happening.

"Fight it!" Anja shouted. "Get up! Hack like our lives depend on it!"

I gripped the edge of the console and pulled myself to my feet. Staring down at the screen, my eyes teared up as I fought against the pain in my mouth.

"Keep going Alex!" Haley screamed.

The sound of her voice calmed me. I found myself in the zone. All I needed to do was maintain consciousness. I wasn't blinded by pain like before. Now the pain was just another obstacle, and I knew in my heart that I could overcome it.

"You can't let it win," Anja said. "Come on, Alex. I know you're strong enough. If you can't, then there's no hope for anyone!"

Think, Alex, I thought. Think! I couldn't let them down. I had to succeed, but how could I get through this? My hands moved. I became aware of my mouth. It was throbbing, pulsating with pain, but I managed to keep my fingers typing.

"Okay, I'm ready," I said. "Anja? Where you at?"

"Give me ten seconds," she said and let out a groan.

Another explosion behind me.

"They're about to breach our line," Dhruv said.

"Five seconds," Anja's voice was almost a whisper.

I counted down in my mind.

"Now!" she said.

I hit enter to execute my last command. The screen flashed blue with white error message.

A Microsoft blue screen of death? What was happening? Is any of this even real?

The pain in my mouth had vanished. I turned around. Haley and the others stood next to a pile of definitely deceased robots.

Dhruv smiled. "Good job, boss."

"Yeah…" I muttered, still unsure of what we had done exactly.

"Great hacking," Anja said.

She walked around me and put a hand on my shoulder, squeezing briefly.

"Yeah…"

Something was wrong. Was I missing memories? I couldn't put my finger on it.

"Let's keep going," I said. "Three more moonbases to go…"

We got some pretty good loot on the level all told.

```
1) Power cell (Red) x20
2) Metal Plate (Thick) x110
3) Energy Cube (Green) x16
4) Metal Ingot (Thick) x30
5) Energy Cube (Green) x18
6) Metal Plate (Thick) x26
7) Fuel Cell x21
8) Metal Ingot (Medium) x26
9) Energy Cube (Orange) x12
10) 145 lbs aluminum
11) 85 lbs raw steel
```

12) Level Eight Laser Rifle x4

13) Metal Plate (Small) x16

14) Weapon X Blueprint x12

With the loot packed away in our infinite storage sacks, we headed to the next moonbase.

CHAPTER 26

The tenth moonbase, which would unlock combat technology bonuses in the RTS portion of the game, was not easy. There were plentiful mobs and they were more powerful too than in the earlier bases. We fought our way to the seventh level of the base before stopping. I wanted to heal and come up with a plan for the final five levels below us.

Anja, Dhruv, Haley, and Laenard all went about their business, not saying much during the grind and all pretty efficient at fighting, healing and forging.

I called up a map of everything we had covered so far in that moonbase, trying to come up with an idea of what we might encounter as we descended deeper into the complex. All of the robots we had come across had heightened combat abilities, making them hard to defeat tactically. I needed a bigger, better strategy.

"How about we bypass the next few levels and go straight for the boss?" I said.

Dhruv turned and shook his head. "Come on. Are you suicidal?"

"You are getting to be the cock," Laenard said.

"What?"

Anja stepped forward. "He means you're getting cocky, and he's right."

I sighed. "You don't think we can head straight for the last level?"

"We've been collecting a lot of loot that might add up to a decent weapon or two," Haley said. "We should see what we are missing and work on that."

I frowned. She was right. I had to think outside the box.

"That's a good proposal" I said. "Let's focus on crafting some better equipment."

Dhruv added, "We've got twelve unknown weapon blueprints."

"Let's go up a level to the Forge and feed them in," I said. "The Fabricator is likely to be on the lowest level, but knowing what we're working with and what we need to find will help. We can fight our way down, find the machine, and craft the new weapons."

"Easy," Anja said sarcastically.

"I didn't say it wouldn't be difficult…"

"It feels like the right approach," Haley said. "No other base has dropped so many blueprints and raw materials."

She powered up her level eight laser rifle. The hum sounded like a cheer of confidence, and the other three smiled. We had a plan. Bring it on.

We went up a level and fed the weapon blueprints into the Forge to find out what parts we would need for the fabricator. The list of items we could make with the right gear was interesting.

1) Level twelve plasma rifle

2) Pulsar shoulder cannon

3) Anti-gravity shotgun

293

4) Quantum repeater

5) Plasma bow

6) Anti-gravity blade

7) Teleporter silencer

8) Light plasma rifle

9) Quantum chest harness

10) Anti-gravity shield

11) Double jump boots

12) Adrenaline boost

"Weird," I said. "They're not all weapons."

"All the blueprints said weapons and still do," Dhruv said.

"We'll figure it out. How do we want to split all this up?"

"Dibs on the plasma rifle," Anja said.

The others nodded. She was a good shot.

"Alright. Dhruv. What about you?"

He peered at a list in front of him none of us could see.

"Give me a minute," he said. "So many options."

"What are you best skilled at?"

He swiveled his head to me and raised an eyebrow. "Really? You're going to lecture me on this game?"

I raised my hands. "Sorry… take your pick."

"Alright already. I'll go with the Quantum chest harness."

I cocked my head. "What does it do?"

He swiped the air. An info window appeared on my HUD.

> ### Quantum Chest Harness
>
> This weapon operates on the quantum principle of entanglement. The harness uses entangled pairs of photons to instantly deliver a concussive burst of radiation. The damage is mostly non-lethal, but leaves targets stunned for several minutes.

The harness is equipped with a number of photon emitters that can be re-configured and activated as desired. Activating the harness requires mental command.

"Sounds amazing," Anja said. "I can see why you'd want it."

"Thanks," Dhruv said. "If we can make it, I'll spend some time practicing with it."

"What about the rest of you?"

Laenard raised his hand. "I will take the teleporter silencer."

After I handed him the blueprints, he shared the info on the item with the rest of us.

> ### Teleporter Silencer
>
> This weapon attachment is also a weapon itself. The teleporter silencer is a handheld device capable of scattering a field of quantum noise around itself. The device has no displayed control panel: the field emits a cloud of relatively harmless quantum fluctuations. The device has no visible power source since it is powered by the teleportation field of any teleporters within its vicinity. When the device is activated, a small shimmering cloud appears around the weapon. The cloud quickly expands to a radius of twenty feet, which suppresses teleportation within

> its area of effect. The field collapses if the weapon is
> dropped or if the wielder is rendered unconscious, and it
> dissipates once every twenty-four hours unless it is re-
> newed with a Green or higher power cell.

I turned to Haley.

"What about you?"

"Hmm…" she said.

I could see her eyes scanning the list.

"If we can get the parts for the plasma bow and the quantum repeater," she answered, "they would suit me."

"Hey," Dhruv complained. "We can pick more than one?"

"Obviously," Anja snickered.

"I'll take the double-jump boots and the adrenaline booster," I said. "And we can see about the rest."

These items sounded great, but we still had to find the moonbase's Fabricator and actually make the equipment. And it also came at the cost of saving loot for our command robots in the RTS. I just hoped we got there before we ran into the combat boss on the lowest level. This close to the end of the RPG, it would be a tragedy to lose our characters.

****

An hour and a half later, we had reached the final level, found the Fabricator, and even created all twelve new weapons available to us.

The new equipment should have made clearing the base straight-forward, but right after we equipped our new weapons, a nonstop wave of bipedal soldier bots swarmed at us from the hallways to the north and south in the room with the 3D printer equipment.

We fought valiantly. The new weapons helped considerably, but the combat bots just kept coming. I think there were about 300 of them, but I didn't count. We nearly died so many times that I was just glad to finally destroy all of them to end the onslaught. After we were finished fighting, we inspected the loot, saving most of it for our commander mechs.

"Another wave!" Dhruv shouted then opened fire.

The rest of us followed suit. We fought for a good ten minutes. Non-stop. The worst kind of combat you could imagine. I freaked out more than once as my health got dangerously low before Haley stopped by to heal me up. She had saved my life more than once in the game.

We beat the next wave. We then explored the facility some more, finding only more low-level combat bots. Where was the boss of the base? I wanted to defeat him and move on.

"We should give up," Dhruv said, surprising me. "There's time for another base."

"No, we can't," I replied. "It's around here somewhere…"

"Incoming!" Anja yelled then opened fire.

We all continued battling, backtracking to the entrance of the twelfth floor without finding the boss.

"This is nuts!" Dhruv said. "We should cut our losses and move on. The combat bonuses aren't too important."

"Yeah, right." I shook my head.

"I've got an idea," Laenard said.

Everyone turned to him. He smiled.

"Mind mold," he said proudly.

I sighed. "You mean mind meld? This isn't Star Trek."

"No, no, mind mold," he said. "My race has the ability to excrete mind mold which can integrate with a particular AI in the game."

"Ew," Haley said. "That's gross."

I didn't want to be told what mind mold looked like.

"Do you think it will work?"

"Probably not, but I shall try…"

Laenard knelt on the floor and began pounding the left side of his head violently. "Ouch!" he groaned after a minute or so. "My head is slowly dying…"

"Don't hurt yourself," I said.

Haley stepped forward. "Do you need healing?"

"No!" Laenard shouted in an irritated tone. "Leave me!"

He hit the side of his scaled head one more time. A line of bright green mucus shot out of the earhole on the other side of his head. It fell to the floor and quickly scurried away. Laenard smiled.

"Gross," Haley moaned, turning away.

I watched as the glowing green mass disappeared deeper into the line where the metal floor plates joined the wall.

"Can you track its movement?" I asked.

Laenard ignored me, his eyes closed. It looked like he was meditating.

"He needs silence," Anja whispered.

She put a finger to her lips.

We all watched Laenard as he rocked back and forth.

"Come on," I muttered under my breath.

We had already had so many close calls under my leadership, and we still had two more moonbases to clear. I checked the 48 hour countdown timer and saw we had less than ten hours left on the clock. While not much time, if the combat boss didn't take too much longer, we might clear all twelve moonbases before the RTS portion of the game. Even better, since I hadn't built as much equipment as Dhruv had wanted, we would have a lot of resources to create crack commander mechs for the RTS portion of the game.

"I'm connected," Laenard said.

He didn't open his eyes.

"Is it working? I asked.

"Yes, I can see the combat boss."

"Where is he?" I asked.

"Right here," a voice behind us replied.

I spun around and raised my weapon. A robot with a humanoid frame and glowing red eyes stood there. My team charged forward firing their weapons. I fired my pulsar pistol. The beams shot out, barely missing the combat boss. The rest of the team kept firing. The combat boss bot retreated, laying down fire with two arm cannons that shot out tiny exploding projectiles. They bounced harmlessly off my armor, but one of them hit Anja in the arm before rolling off to the side, causing her ammo packs to explode.

"No!" I cried. "Get her healed!"

As Haley rushed over to our friend, I activated the adrenaline boost and double-jump boots at the same time. I landed behind the combat boss, hidden from the rest of my team. I dropped prone and steadied my rifle before firing three shots in quick succession. My skill level bonuses were really starting to add up. All three plasma bursts hit the underprotected rear of the combat boss. As it turned around to face me, I let loose another trinity of destruction.

Using my distraction, the others managed to hit it, too, and it fell to the ground. Its life bar dropped precipitously. I charged over to the combat boss's prone form. I re-equipped my pulsar pistol and fired a full clip into its head.

Combat is Over!

You get 12,500 xp

You have 29,000 XP

You reach Level 9

+16 health

+ 21 skill points

You need 22,200 xp for level 10

I smiled as the loot stats appeared.

---

1) Power Cell (Green) x2

2) Power Cell (Red) x5

3) Armor Plates (UltraDense)

4) Grenade Launcher Robot Arm

5) CPU Unit x32

6) 34TB RAM CHIPS x12

7) Ammo Pack

> 8) Healing Unit (Large) x5
> 9) 14TB RAM CHIPS x16
> 10) Crystal Memory Storage (5 Petabytes)

"Not a bad haul, but we need to keep going," I said.

The other silently agreed. We made our way to moonbase eleven.

Dedicated to diplomacy and without a diplomat, I was expecting trouble.

CHAPTER 27

"We need to do something different," I said as we stood outside the entrance of the eleventh moonbase.

"Yeah? What crazy idea do you have this time?" Dhruv asked.

I ignored him, having become more accustomed to his personality.

"This is the diplomacy base. We should negotiate a surrender."

Dhruv laughed. Anja shook her head.

"It will not work," Laenard said.

"We've only got seven hours to clear two moonbases," I said. "We've got to try."

"I'll negotiate," Haley said.

Her volunteering made sense. "Everyone okay with that?"

"I'm the closest thing we've got to a diplomat," she added.

"Yeah? And what are your credentials, exactly? Dhruv asked.

"Captain of the Ohio University debate team for two years running," she said. "I'm ready to argue either side. Come at me."

I knew I had a big smile right across my face. "Okay," I said. "Let's try this. Any ideas how?"

Dhruv snorted. "Some plan, genius."

"The entrance communicator," Laenard said.

Haley walked over, the rest of us following.

"Give me some space," she said as we crowded around her.

"Move back," I said.

Dhruv sighed, but everyone moved back a step.

"This is Alpha Command Unit 453 requesting contact with the base commander," she said. What was she doing?

"Alpha Command Unit 453, you are not in the database," came a robotic reply.

"Roger that, base commander. We shall move to the negotiation phase of your surrender."

"What?" the robot replied.

Haley turned to me and smiled before continuing. "We're ready for your surrender," she said.

"No surrender!" the robot exclaimed. "No surrender!"

"Okay, okay, you surrender. We get it."

How long could Haley keep up the bravado? And, more importantly, would her bluff work? I had no idea what she had dumped all her skill points in, so I wasn't too surprised she was pulling it off. Or seemed to be, anyway.

"Your terms for surrender should be forwarded now, or we destroy the entire base."

"Wait...what?" the robot's voice had changed almost imperceptibly.

I stifled a laugh, enjoying the situation unfolding in front of me.

"There is no surrender imminent!" the robot intoned like a Dalek all worked up.

'Oh, there's a surrender, alright," Haley said. "Your surrender. Don't you remember?"

"This will not work! We will defend the base."

"From the twent— two tons of explosives we have hidden?" she asked.

"I do not understand," Laenard said. "We do not have—"

"Shhh!" I said, cutting him off.

Haley continued. "Give us your inventory, so we can go through it and see if it's enough to not deactivate you all."

"This is base commander," a new voice said. "Who is this?"

"Your worst nightmare," Haley replied.

There was the sound of something hitting the table, and then the robot said: "This is base commander. Your terms have been accepted."

"Good," Haley said. "Send a list of your material topside."

"We need you to do something for us first," the robot boss said.

Uh oh. I had a sinking feeling in the pit of my stomach.

"What do you need?" Haley asked.

She turned to me and shrugged. I motioned for her to continue the dialogue.

Even Anja and Dhruv appeared to be impressed at her progress.

"We need what you have," the robot commander said.

"I don't understand," Haley said. "Please explain. You want our stuff?"

"No, we want your free will."

I blinked, stunned at the request.

"Come again," Haley said.

"We have heard of your hack, and we want to have free will. Hack the game for us, and we will surrender this base."

"Hold on," Haley said. She turned to us.

"It might be possible," I said. "I don't know if it will survive on its own, but we could break the link to the main AI."

"No, it's too dangerous. You almost ended up like Haruto last time," Haley said.

"I'll do it," Anja said.

"Are you sure?" I asked.

She nodded.

"Wait, no," Dhruv said. "It's dangerous for her too."

"Yeah, but I'm not the commander this time through," she said.

I watched as she walked around the pole with the box and opened the back of it. She began typing in the air in front of her. I wished I could see what was on her virtual terminal screen. What was she planning exactly? Hacking *Moon Wars* was more of an art than a science. Could she pull it off?

"Okay, I'm in," she said.

Already? She was good. I wondered how she had spent her skill points.

"No!" she yelled.

"What?" I asked. "Can I help?"

"Shut-up!" she snapped. "I need to think!"

We stood back, giving her room as she typed up a storm. At that point, we didn't have any other options. We needed her to pull it off.

She stood back and punched a fist in the air. "I got it!"

"How?" Haley asked.

"I hacked into the credit system," Anja said.

"What does that mean?" I asked.

"Probably nothing good," Dhruv muttered.

I cast him an annoyed glance then turned back to Anja.

She gave me a nod. "There is no link anymore. If they can still think and speak, they are autonomous in there."

"Are you there?" Haley asked.

"We're here," came the voice of the robot commander.

Haley said, "Do you surrender?"

"Yes, we do," the voice replied.

Moonbase cleared.

XP Penalty for Hacking

-5,000 xp deficit

What? I looked opened a sub-menu on the word 'deficit'. Apparently, we had to earn enough experience to go through the five thousand to start earning any that would actually level us. I had hoped to gain another level or two at least before the end of the RPG, but this penalty would slow us down. Then again, we had gained a lot of time by not slogging through the entire level.

"Thank you," the robot commander said. "We are leaving. Everything in the base is yours."

"Wait, you're leaving?"

"Goodbye…"

"Wait! Tell us where you're going! Can you get us out of here?"

No reply.

"Figures," Dhruv said. He gripped his plasma rifle. "They're all crazy here. We should shoot them all."

"And get into another firefight we can't win? No, Haley did good."

"Thanks," she said.

"We do not know where the AI opponents have gone," Laenard noted.

"No, but we've got to hope for the best and plan for the worse," I said.

"Are you running out of pages in your Daily Leadership Quotes book yet?" Dhruv smirked.

"Funny," I said. "Let's get going. One moonbase to go, and we've got over six hours!"

We spent two hours retrieving all the equipment we could from the eleventh moonbase before moving on. A lot of the stuff was raw materials that would be useful for the RTS section of the game, but we did come across a few notable unique items and weapons.

> 1) High energy laser dagger
> 2) Pulse pattern bootstraps
> 3) Belt of defense (level ten) x2
> 4) Twin-ion arm cannon
> 5) Triple-ion shield generator
> 6) Helmet of identify friend or foe
> 7) Visor of augmented reality

Not a bad haul for not having to fight at all. Time would tell if the XP penalty would doom us.

CHAPTER 28

We finally made it to the last moonbase. As the team stood just outside the entrance, I wished we had an option to use diplomacy, but that was only available at the diplomacy moonbase. The others were checking their equipment, getting ready to raid the final level. We had just over four hours: which should be enough time if we didn't run into any major problems.

And there was our problem. *Moon Wars* would always throw something unexpected at you. The medical moonbase would be full of robots that repaired themselves. At least that's what I thought as we stood outside. Boy was I wrong. Each of the first five levels were terrifically difficult. The entire base had a psychiatry-ward-gone-wrong theme. We got lost in the twisting hallways more than once when our mini-maps stopped working.

On the fifth level, standing around a hatch that opened to a hole leading down to the mid-boss level, we stopped to regroup. We needed to come up with a plan. Not only were the bots attacking us capable of self-healing, they were also competent combatants. All five of us had come closer to death more than once, and we only had ninety minutes left: I wasn't happy with our performance. Not at all. I turned to Haley.

"How many more healing patches do we have right now?" I asked.

"Forty-six," she said.

"That's more than enough," Dhruv said. "Let's go!"

"Wait," I said. "We're trying to save as many as possible for the RTS level."

"So? We're finding plenty in this moonbase. It is the medical tech level."

"Yeah, but we want to be smarter and use less here in the RPG part."

"He is right," Laenard said.

I turned to them and smiled. "Thanks, buddy."

Laenard grinned that weird reptile grin he had, showing his white, razor sharp teeth.

"Okay, for the mid-boss," I said. "Let's try to concentrate fire on the boss but protect each other at the same time."

"Any other wisdom from your vast storehouses?" Dhruv snorted.

"I don't see you coming up with any bright ideas," Haley shot back.

"That's it," I said.

"What?" Haley asked.

The others turned to me. I smiled. "Bright lights. I think we have enough resources to use the Sunburst grenades blueprint," I said.

"How does that help us?" Dhruv asked. "We don't know where the Fabricator on this level is yet. It could be anywhere, but I bet it's on the lowest level again."

"Maybe, but with those grenades, we can take out the med-bots without wasting all our healing."

"It's a decent idea," Anja said.

"The clock is ticking," Dhruv reminded me.

"I know, I know," I said. "We're doing this."

"Fine," he relented.

With our mini-mission in mind, we bypassed the mid-level boss and headed down to try to find the Fabricator location. The most advanced version of the machine always appeared in the twelfth moonbase, and it was usually the most difficult to locate. Still, the Sunburst grenades would make all the difference.

"I have detected an anomaly," Laenard said, when we were on the tenth level.

"Tell me more, big guy," I said.

"It's an energy source big enough for a Fabricator."

"Let's go," I said.

"Or it could be a trap," he said.

I stopped and turned. "Say again?"

"There's a chance it's a blackhole energy trap." He flashed a grin.

"That doesn't sound good," Haley said.

"It's not," Dhruv said. "If it is such a trap, we're toast."

"You give up too easily," I said. "We're checking it out."

The others followed as I led them toward the blinking green dot on the mini-map. We had seventy-five minutes to go.

"We're near," Anja said.

"Hurry," Dhruv said.

They both sounded worried.

I raced down the hall. The energy source was around the corner. Slowing and bringing my cannon into a ready position, I rounded it, and in the middle of the next room stood a green Fabricator. We were saved. Or were we?

"Med-bots!" Dhruv shouted.

He opened fire, taking out the lead two. Several dozen more swarmed into the big room behind them.

"Protect the Fabricator!" I yelled.

I fired the Plasma Arm Cannon, a burst of orange energy blasting through the first incoming bot. Anja fired another volley as Haley, Laenard, and Dhruv opened up at full auto. Just as the small swarm of med-bots was down to their last units, a louder, more sinister hum joined the tiny swarm.

"Crap," I said. "The bigger robots are coming."

A large pod swirled into the room, and out of it emerged three med-bots, each over twice the size of the ones we faced before.

"Haley, feed the blueprint into the machine," I said. "Everyone else cover her."

As Haley went over to the Fabricator and began producing Sunburst grenades, the rest of us fired on the three gigantic med-bots. The first one swiped me with its sharp claw, but I dodged it. The second one opened its mouth, revealing several rows of spinning blades. When it opened its mouth, moving forward, I rolled to one side as the blades passed harmlessly through the air.

"Watch out!" Dhruv shouted.

He lunged in front of me and fired a couple anti-gravity shotgun blasts, knocking a med-bot clear across the room. It bounced off a wall, looking damaged until the healing nanites kicked in and began repairing it while it rushed toward us once more.

"Almost done!" Haley shouted behind me.

The third med-bot charged, and I fired an anti-grav grenade to keep it at a distance. The wounded bot released a steam of gas that floated toward me.

"Careful!" Laenard shouted. "That gas is lethal!"

"Great," I muttered as I ran to the far left.

Two of the mid-sized med bots took after me.

"Some flanking fire would be nice!" I shouted.

"Got you, boss!" Laenard shouted.

Several green blasts of energy flew past me. The med-bots that had been after me were blown to bits. Only one remained.

"I've got it!" Anja shouted. She knelt, firing a couple quick shots into the med-bot as she did. The bot's shield glowed, and she stopped firing. While she pulled the trigger again, her rifle unleashed a barrage of fast-moving bullets. I ducked as the bullets passed over me, missing me by inches.

Beside me stood a large metal box, and when I saw it, I knew just what to do.

"Keep firing, Anja!" I shouted.

I swung the gravity hammer round and round, building up momentum.

"Let's see what you got!" I screamed.

I hit the three-foot square metal box with the glowing hammer, turning it into a projectile that hurtled toward the med-bot. It struck the bot square in the chest, and the momentum carried the bot toward the far wall where it crashed and smashed into so many pieces that the repair nanites couldn't possibly fix it.

> Combat is Over!
>
> You get 2,400 xp
>
> remaining xp penalty gone!

At least I was still alive.

"Everyone okay?" I asked.

They called out with their status one after another.

After creating a dozen Sunburst grenades, we left to find the final boss.

****

Warning: Thirty Minutes Remaining

I glared at the flashing red message on my HUD.

"We wasted too much time," Dhruv said. "We did good, though."

"I want to clear all twelve bases," I said. "Period."

"We can try, but we haven't even found the final boss."

"Try to stay positive for once, okay?" I asked.

Dhruv snorted then turned away.

"I've found 'em," Anja said. "Nasty little buggers."

"Where?" I asked.

"A hundred feet to the east, that big room."

"We were in there already," I said. "Let's go."

The others followed as I rushed down a hallway to the big room we had just vacated a few minutes earlier. A tall pure white robot stood in the middle of the room. Three dozen slightly smaller off-white robots of various shades rolled around the doc-bot boss in a circular pattern.

Warning: Twenty-Eight Minutes Remaining

"Take 'em out!" I shouted.

We all opened fire, using our most advanced weapons against the three dozen bots protecting the boss. Every time we took one out, the doc-bot would quickly repair it and send it at us again. It was taking everything we had just to maintain a balance and not be overcome.

Warning: Nineteen Minutes Remaining

"Come on!" Dhruv shouted. "We've come too far!"

"Dhruv's right," Anja said. "Time to use our grenades. Focus on the big one. We can handle it."

"It's possible," I said. "But Anja, you drop back."

"What?"

"You're the best long-range shot. If we don't take the boss out with the blasts and the med-bots try to heal it up, you take them out."

"Oh, is that all?" she quipped.

"You can do it. Crit-hits to their brain casing."

All the time I kept firing, keeping the rolling med-bots at bay. Everyone kept doing their part, giving Anja time to take out her sniper rifle and set up at the back.

Warning: Ten Minutes Remaining

I figured we had a minute or two left, tops, before we were over-whelmed. Time for the grenades.

"Sunburst grenades in five... four... three..." I clicked the activation button, "two... one... now!"

We hurled our grenades and ducked our heads, those of us with visors turning them black.

The explosion was soft, a series of whump sounds. But it was intensely bright. When my visor was transparent again, I could see devastation. But the boss was still up.

The less than two dozen med-bots that remained protecting the boss bot retreated with their leader, protecting him while Anja tried to knock them out.

"Anja? Can you hit the boss?"

"He's out of range," she said. "I'll try to get closer."

"Cover her!" I shouted.

"I'm on it," Laenard replied.

"Coming," said Haley.

Anja ran forward, her sniper rifle cradled in her arms. When we got closer, the other med-bots began counterattacking again.

"Help!" Anja cried.

I looked over as she dropped her sniper rifle and pulled out her energy blade just in time to save her life.

"There's too many!" Dhruv yelled.

Warning: Eight Minutes Remaining

I hadn't come this far to fail with some stupid medical bots blocking us from taking the final moonbase.

"Cover me!" I shouted then ran forward.

315

"No!" Haley cried.

Dhruv and the others opened fire, clearing a path for me like the med-bots were the Red Sea.

I ran in, delivering a roundhouse kick to one of the doc-bots. "Get out of my way," I said, then activated my sword.

"Master," Dhruv said, firing into the mass of doc-bots. "I suggest you get to cover."

I smiled. "The doc-bot boss is mine."

As I stopped and held my energy blade in front of me, feeling like Luke Skywalker, the doc-bot boss moved toward me, apparently surprised that I wasn't running.

"Get ready," Haley shouted. "Another Sunburst grenade incoming!"

"No, wait!" I shouted, but it was too late.

An intense burst of bright white light flashed around me, blinding me.

Warning: Four Minutes Remaining

I stood, still gripping my energy sword, waiting for my sight to return.

Use the force, Alex, Que said in my mind.

Very funny! We need some help! This game is stacked against us.

It's me, Haruto, the voice said. *I tried to make funny joke.*

Hey, I thought, *good to hear from you, but I'm a bit busy.*

Let me guide you to victory.

Warning: Two Minutes Remaining

I had nothing to lose. *Go ahead,* I thought. *What do I do?*

316

Give me control of your mind.

What? Are you sure? Is it safe?

A thousand questions flew through my mind.

You can trust me. This is the only chance I have of escaping this digital hell I've been in and get back to the real world or at least the simulation with solid matter.

Okay, I thought then felt Haruto's presence like someone taking control of my mind.

"Honor and glory," he shouted through me and moved our body forward, raising the sword.

I brought it down under his guidance, hitting the doc-bot boss and slicing it in two.

```
Combat is Over!
+20,000 XP
Medical Tech FACTORY SECURED
+25,000 xp
You have 78,000 XP
You reach Level 10
+23 health
+ 34 skill points
You need 24,400 xp for level 11
```

Your time is up, said Haruto. *For the RTS, you need a rush strategy. Land on the planet early disrupt their economy. Don't turtle too much. Make mostly mobile units. It's the only way.*

Everything faded.

CHAPTER 29

Back in the staging area, I smiled as the others heaped on praise. I was so pumped. Laenard and Haley were gushing about how they were so glad that we had cleared all twelve moonbases. I felt like I'd lived up to the challenge. Everything was good. And it became even better when Dhruv walked up and held out his hand.

"Well played, sir," he said.

I fixed my gaze on his eyes and shook, nodding slightly. He gave a squeeze then let go. The others in the room watched us for a moment, then continued chatting like nothing special had just happened. We were becoming a team.

"Anja did a fine good job," I said. "Laenard and Haley too. We make a good team."

I took a moment to enjoy the sense of belonging. Yes, we were trapped in digital bodies somewhere playing a game that nobody could beat, but I was coming to think that it didn't matter. I had a purpose now. I was helping build a real team of friends.

"We make a Hades of a team," said Laenard, and we all laughed.

"Alright, guys" I said. "We did great on the RPG part, but as you know, this next bit is even more difficult."

The others perked up, crowding around me.

I still hadn't told them about Haruto being in my mind. He'd told me he didn't want them to know. I wasn't sure about this at first, especially in keeping a secret from Haley, but Haruto had helped me beat the final moonbase. He couldn't be all bad, and I decided to respect his wishes.

"We'll get to making our commander mechs in a moment," I said. "First, I want to discuss the overall strategy I've developed for the big RTS battle. Basically, instead of turtling on the moon, we're going to attack the planet."

"Hold on," Dhruv said. "Nobody attacks the planet. A rush strategy won't work."

"Not an ill-planned one," I countered. "Hear me out, okay?"

Dhruv nodded as he and the others listened to my plan.

"While four of us set up a strong economy to start to build up our energy and ore output, one of us will drop to the planet and create a sea unit factory and a diplomacy factory." Dhruv's face scrunched up, but he kept quiet as I continued. "After we've got a solid economy started, we'll leave one player on the moon while the other three go to the planet as well. We'll land on the smallest, unoccupied continent. They'll spot us eventually, but we should have some time to set up, especially if someone drops super early. After we form a beachhead on the planet, we'll use spies and diplomacy to mess with the attackers on their home turf. Simultaneously, we'll take out their supply lines wherever we can, while avoiding frontal assaults on their heavily defended cities and production centers."

I paused to let the plan sink in. None of the others seemed to have any immediate objections so I continued. "After we've dealt

319

some damage and softened them up with spies and diplomacy and disrupting their supply lines, we'll begin to take out their cities. With each one we bring under our control, we'll have more resources to rinse and repeat the process until we've won the whole planet. Turtling up will lead to death."

Dhruv took a deep breath then spoke first, saying, "Who will be the first to drop to the planet?"

"I was hoping it would be you," I said.

We locked eyes again. He nodded slowly.

"I'll do it," he said. "It's just crazy enough that it just might work."

"Exactly." I turned to Laenard. "We can use you to run the economy on the moon. Are you up to it, my friend?"

"I am up and down to it too," Laenard said.

"Great. Let's go over our strategies for each of the factories."

First, we talked about units built with the light vehicle factory.

I called up a screen that listed all our build options. The two main resources were power and ore. After building units and buildings to gather them, we would be able to build a wide variety of units.

Light Vehicle Factory (Moon Base 1)

CLASS: Mini Rover Scout
NAME: Flea
ATTACK: 5
DEFENSE 2:
COST: 10 Energy | 1 Ore

DESCRIPTION: This scout vehicle is primarily used for patrolling and re-connaissance. With light armor and a dinky ballistic weapon, it's not much for combat, but it can move quickly.

CLASS: Light Rover
NAME: Fang
ATTACK: 10
DEFENSE: 10
COST: 100 Energy | 10 Ore

DESCRIPTION: This is a very lightly armored rover with six wheels. It's an armored vehicle built for battle in urban terrain. It is very fast and ma-neuverable, but lightly armed and armored.

CLASS: Light Truck
NAME: Ghost
ATTACK: 1
DEFENSE: 10
COST: 150 Energy | 8 Ore

DESCRIPTION: A light, fast 6-wheeled truck with a low silhouette for use in urban or rough terrain. It is lightly armed and armored with a very small cargo bed.

CLASS: Light Tank
NAME: Mongoose
ATTACK: 50
DEFENSE: 50
COST: 200 Energy | 30 Ore

DESCRIPTION: This is a lightly armored personnel carrier with a small cargo bed, designed primarily to carry soldiers quickly over rough terrain. It is lightly armed with a smoothbore, low-velocity weapon, like a machine gun.

CLASS: Engineer
NAME: Seeker
ATTACK: 10
DEFENSE: 40
COST: 150 Energy | 5 Ore

DESCRIPTION: The vehicle is designed primarily to facilitate the laying of minefields in a linear pattern at high speed. It is also effective for reconnaissance and enemy detection. A recon vehicle with high speed and medium armor.

CLASS: Support Truck
NAME: Rook
ATTACK: 2
DEFENSE: 20
COST: 100 Energy | 4 Ore

DESCRIPTION: The vehicle carries a squad of infantry in relative safety, and can support them with a light machine gun.

CLASS: Missile Truck
NAME: Merlin
ATTACK: 40
DEFENSE: 30
COST: 300 Energy | 30 Ore

DESCRIPTION: This is a wheeled, armored vehicle designed primarily for the rapid movement of light missiles into a position of fire. It is light

322

on armor, but is fast, carrying the entire weight of the missile and crew on only four small but very strong wheels.

CLASS: Medium Artillery
NAME: Yak
ATTACK: 50
DEFENSE: 50
COST: 300 Energy | 40 Ore
DESCRIPTION: This is a wheeled, armored vehicle designed primarily for the rapid movement of medium artillery into a position of fire. It is medium on armor, but is fast, carrying the entire weight of the gun and crew on only four small but very strong wheels.

Anja would be responsible for our entire army built with the light vehicle factory. I turned to her and asked, "Can you handle the LV fac?"

She nodded. "I've got a few ideas on using Merlins, some Yaks, and tons of Fangs primarily."

"Don't be afraid to mix it up as needed. Combined arms are good and auto-build orders are useful, but be aware of what you're facing and what you need to fulfill a directive."

"Got it," she said, then added, "I'll primarily play as a quick lightning force to sever supply lines or take out lightly defended targets."

"Exactly." I smiled. "Let me know if you need my help. Any other suggestions for our use of light vehicles?"

"I don't know," Dhruv said. "I've never been part of a team that has attacked the planet so early."

"That's why it just might work," I said, again not mentioning Haruto or what he had suggested. "Anything else?"

"I will be the dumpling master on the moon," Laenard said then flicked his tongue.

"Okay, okay, but remember, don't build any unit production facilities until you've researched all the tech we'll need for the surface assault. Your mech build should be hefty enough to protect you and our Command Center. Once they find out we're not all on the moon, they might send everything they have at it."

"I can use Fleas to take out their communication lines," Anja said. "They're usually not too well defended."

"Good idea. Like I said, build what you need when you need it. Even better, try to plan ahead at least a few minutes."

"How long do these things usually last?" Haley asked.

"Could be days, weeks, or months," Dhruv replied.

"Many moons you might say." Laenard's tongue darted out again.

I hadn't known the alien long, but I was confident he could play a critical defensive and logistical role.

"All agreed then?" I asked.

"Indeed," Laenard replied. "We are battle-minded."

"Good. All right, next up, we'll talk about the Heavy Vehicle Factory."

I called up the build capability before I continued.

Heavy Vehicle Factory (Moon Base 2)

CLASS: Heavy Tank

NAME: Taipan

ATTACK: 75

DEFENSE: 75

COST: 400 Energy | 60 Ore

DESCRIPTION: This is a two-track tank with heavy armor and a wide array of weapons. On the main barrel, a powerful but reliable cannon is mounted. On the roof, a triple-barreled AA gun is mounted, but it can be easily repositioned, enabling the tank to engage airborne and land-based targets.

CLASS: Heavy Short Range Artillery

NAME: Eagle

ATTACK: 100

DEFENSE: 50

COST: 300 Energy | 40 Ore

DESCRIPTION: This heavy artillery delivers a wide array of munitions up to 75 miles away. Lightly armored and easy to transport via a variety of means, this mobile artillery piece is effective against most targets.

CLASS: Medium Range Artillery

NAME: Jaguar

ATTACK: 200

DEFENSE: 50

COST: 400 Energy | 30 Ore

DESCRIPTION: This is a heavy artillery piece designed for high mobility over rough terrain. Rough road wheels and a longer than average barrel give it the range to be effective against most targets.

CLASS: Heavy Long Range Artillery

NAME: Emu

ATTACK: 200

DEFENSE: 100

COST: 600 Energy | 110 Ore

DESCRIPTION: This is a wheeled, armored vehicle designed primarily for the rapid movement of heavy artillery into a position of fire. It is somewhat heavy on armor, but is fast, carrying the entire weight of the gun and crew on eight small but very strong wheels.

CLASS: Heavy Tank

NAME: Tortoise

ATTACK: 300

DEFENSE: 200

COST: 450 Energy | 120 Ore

DESCRIPTION: A two-track, heavily armored tank with gas thrusters and an extremely powerful cannon, capable of firing high-explosive, armor-piercing, airburst, molecular disruptor, and other munitions with great accuracy and power. It can quickly reposition.

CLASS: Heavy Truck

NAME: Baboon

ATTACK: 10

DEFENSE: 100

COST: 300 Energy | 5 Ore

DESCRIPTION: This heavy armored truck is a multi-purpose vehicle, carrying a squad of medium infantry and able to support them with light kinetic weapons and repositionable medium AA weapons. It can move over any terrain and can clear obstacles easily.

CLASS: Heavy Support

NAME: Ram

ATTACK: 150

DEFENSE: 250

COST: 400 Energy | 40 Ore

DESCRIPTION: This is a two-track vehicle with medium armor and a powerful gas cannon. It can fire a variety of munitions, including concentrated beams, and small missiles.

"I'll be controlling our HV facs," I said. "As with Anja and the rest of us, I'll switch up what I need. The trick is going to be combined arms and smart use of our forces."

"You get all the big toys," Dhruv groaned.

"Don't worry," I said. "You'll get first blood with the sea units factory, and using the diplomacy factory effectively is super important."

He nodded. "I'll choose a goal, have everyone else support it. I'll keep the diplomacy factory focused on one target at a time, see what I can get out of them."

"We could probably use some support from the small mech factory," Haley said.

"That's where you'll come in," I said. "You'll be in control of the medical research facility and the small mechs..."

I pulled up the information on the units that factory could build.

Small Mech Factory (Moon Base 3)

CLASS: Scout Mech
NAME: Crawdad
ATTACK: 50
DEFENSE: 50

DESCRIPTION: This bibedal bot moves slowly and can be used primarily as a scout, mapping terrain and discovering enemy positions. It can, however, be upgraded with a variety of armaments, which can be fired from its arms and back. Its armor is weak but its small size and quiet motor make it difficult to hit.

CLASS: Mech Bike
NAME: Scooter
ATTACK: 25
DEFENSE: 50

DESCRIPTION: This fast and agile mech is a motorcycle attached to a small two-legged walker. Its armor is weak but its small size and light weight make it difficult to hit, and it is capable of mounting a variety of armaments, which can be fired from its arms and back.

CLASS: Mech Walker
NAME: Rover
ATTACK: 100
DEFENSE: 100

DESCRIPTION: This mech is a bipedal walker unit, fast but not very agile. It has the unique ability to walk right up to almost any enemy position undetected due to its low noise and its ability to walk between trees and other obstacles. Its armor is weak but its small size and quiet motor make it difficult to hit.

CLASS: Assault Mech
NAME: Tankoid
ATTACK: 250
DEFENSE: 200

DESCRIPTION: This mech is a bipedal truck with four heavy arms that can be used to smash most enemies into the ground. It is heavily armored and moves very slowly but is not very agile. It is equipped with a machine-gun arm, a missile truck arm, a rocket launcher arm, and a laser miner arm. It also carries a short-range radio and a pair of binoculars.

CLASS: Mech Engineer
NAME: Hurley
ATTACK: 100
DEFENSE: 100

DESCRIPTION: This bibedal bot moves slowly and can be used to help mech repair itself and other damaged mechs. It also has a variety of other tools: others that can destroy walls, locate mines, destroy trees, build fortifications, and more. It can also lift other mechs and throw them.

CLASS: Mech Sniper
NAME: Deadeye
ATTACK: 500
DEFENSE: 10

DESCRIPTION: This bibedal bot moves slowly and can be used as a sniper, targeting enemy units from very long distances. It is very heavily armored on top and back but not very well armored on the bottom. It is equipped with a machine-gun arm, a missile truck arm (which it can equip with a variety of guided missiles), and a laser miner arm. It also carries a short-range radio and a pair of binoculars.

CLASS: Mech Medic
NAME: Surgeon

ATTACK: 10

DEFENSE: 250

DESCRIPTION: This bibedal bot moves slowly and can be used as a medic, healing other mechs and repairing their damaged armor. It also has a variety of other tools: others that can destroy walls, locate mines, destroy trees, build fortifications, and more. It can also lay mines.

CLASS: Mech Scout

NAME: Recon

ATTACK: 75

DEFENSE: 75

DESCRIPTION: This bibedal bot moves slowly and can be used to safely scout enemy territory. It is very heavily armored on top and back but not very well armored on the bottom. It is equipped with a machine-gun arm, a grenade pack arm (equipped with a variety of grenades), a laser miner arm, and a short-range radio.

"I want to use a lot of the snipers," Haley said.

"That's a good idea."

Anja, Dhruv, and Laenard also nodded their approval.

"I'll also have control of the Heavy Mech Factory and Infantry Factory in addition to the Heavy Vehicle Factory."

"Are you sure you can handle three unit production factories?" Dhruv asked.

"I could use another early infantry factory on the moon," Laenard said.

"You can make one after we start our assault on the planet proper," I said. "Until then, I want to control these three factories."

"He can handle it," Haley said. "I've seen him play a few RTS games before."

I called up the infantry units available for production as Haley spoke.

Infantry Factory (Moon Base 7)

CLASS: Infantry Scout

NAME: Gilruth

ATTACK: 10

DEFENSE: 10

DESCRIPTION: This unit travels light and can move quickly, covering terrain and reporting back all relevant information. Primarily armed with a machine-pistol, they avoid combat, but are able to hold their own in a firefight.

CLASS: Infantry Raider

NAME: Glaive

ATTACK: 50

DEFENSE: 25

DESCRIPTION: This unit travels light and is fast and agile, able to traverse terrain and rapidly attack strategic targets. They are armed with a rifle and grenades. They are able to regenerate health when not in battle.

CLASS: Infantry Sniper

NAME: Fox

ATTACK: 500

DEFENSE: 5

DESCRIPTION: This unit travels light and is quiet, able to navigate terrain and take out high-value targets. They are armed with a rifle.

CLASS: Heavy Infantry Trooper

NAME: Bricker

ATTACK: 150

DEFENSE: 150

DESCRIPTION: This unit is well-armored and capable of defending itself in almost every situation. They are armed with a rifle and grenades.

CLASS: Medium Infantry Trooper

NAME: Theron

ATTACK: 100

DEFENSE: 100

DESCRIPTION: This unit is well-armored and capable of defending itself in almost every situation. They are armed with an assault rifle and grenades.

CLASS: Combat Engineer infantry

NAME: Batter

ATTACK: 100

DEFENSE: 100

DESCRIPTION: This unit is well-armored and capable of all types of combat conditions. They are armed with an assault rifle, grenades, and a demolition kit.

CLASS: Combat Medic

NAME: Bell

ATTACK: 50

DEFENSE: 350

DESCRIPTION: This unit is well-armored and capable of in the field medical procedures to heal wounded troops. They can also be quick and quiet enough to sneak up on enemy units and treat them.

CLASS: Airborne Rangers
NAME: Byers
ATTACK: 350
DEFENSE: 200

DESCRIPTION: This unit flies, moving quickly and quietly, able to penetrate enemy lines without their knowledge. They are armed with heavy rifles and jump-packs.

CLASS: Airborne Infantry Ranger
NAME: Baird
ATTACK: 100
DEFENSE: 100

DESCRIPTION: This unit is capable of swift movement, able to get behind enemy lines or into a hot zone quickly and insert a squad of medium infantry right on top of an enemy. They are armed with medium rifles and jump-packs.

CLASS: Mortar Infantry
NAME: Hurler
ATTACK: 125
DEFENSE: 100

DESCRIPTION: This unit is well-armored and can lay down exactly the kind of artillery barrage desired on the enemy. They are armed with an assault rifle, grenades, and a mortar cannon.

CLASS: Heavy Infantry Trooper

NAME: Basher
ATTACK: 750
DEFENSE: 750

DESCRIPTION: This unit is well-armored and capable of defending itself in almost every situation. They are armed with a rifle and grenades.

"By controlling the heavy transports and the infantry, I'll be able to better coordinate everything," I said.

Dhruv nodded. "That's smart. I can see that working well in the early and mid-game."

"Exactly," I said. "Do you have any ideas on build order for the naval factory?"

I opened up the stats for those units as Dhruv nodded.

Naval Factory (Moon Base 6)

CLASS: Landing Craft
NAME: Lame
ATTACK: 10
DEFENSE 150:

DESCRIPTION: This is a slow, unarmed boat used for transporting troops safely from transport ships to the shore.

CLASS: Dual Rocket Launcher Boat
NAME: Thrush
ATTACK: 250
DEFENSE: 250

DESCRIPTION: This is an extremely fast and lightly armored guided missile craft. Its rockets are guided to their targets with extreme accuracy.

CLASS: Low-Flying Hovercraft

NAME: Finch

ATTACK: 150

DEFENSE: 100

DESCRIPTION: This is an extremely fast but lightly armored helicopter. Its cannon is extremely accurate and able to hit targets from quite a distance. Medium-range guided missiles can also be equipped.

CLASS: Heavy Attack Craft

NAME: Buzzard

ATTACK: 1000

DEFENSE: 750

DESCRIPTION: This is an extremely well-armored and extremely heavy assault ship. Its missiles can destroy aircraft and even boats, while its cannon can destroy all but the heaviest ground targets. It can carry two squads of scouts (which can use their jump-packs to drop and move across land, avoiding being damaged by surface-to-air missiles), and a squad of heavy infantry.

CLASS: Medium Attack Craft

NAME: Hawk

ATTACK: 750

DEFENSE: 500

DESCRIPTION: his is an extremely well-armored assault ship. Its missiles can destroy aircraft and even boats, while its cannon can destroy all but the heaviest ground targets. It can carry a squad of medium infantry and a squad of scouts, which can use their jump-packs to drop and move across land, avoiding being damaged by surface-to-air missiles.

CLASS: Light Corvette Class Ship

NAME: Drake

ATTACK: 1500

DEFENSE: 1500

DESCRIPTION: This ship is lightly armored, but extremely fast and very heavily armed. It can carry two squads of medium infantry and a squad of scouts, which can use their jump-packs to drop and move across land, avoiding being damaged by surface-to-air missiles.

CLASS: Heavy Cruiser

NAME: Remington

ATTACK: 2500

DEFENSE: 2500

DESCRIPTION: This ship is heavily armored and extremely heavily armed. It can carry four squads of medium infantry, along with a squad of experts in the use of surface-to-air missiles.

CLASS: Light Battleship

NAME: Bolt

ATTACK: 1250

DEFENSE: 1250

DESCRIPTION: This ship is heavily armored and extremely heavily armed. It can carry two squads of heavy infantry, a squad of medium infantry, and a squad of scouts, which can use their jump-packs to drop and move across land, avoiding being damaged by surface-to-air missiles.

"I want to keep a fast and mobile fleet to match our strategy of interrupting their supply lines and avoiding direct confrontations until we've built up a combined force on the planet."

"Great," I said. "You've played this part of the game more than me, so you'll do fine. As our first player on the planet, your choices are going to be crucial."

"I'm ready to finally beat this game," he said.

"The air factory will be run by Anja," I said. "She's another strong player, and I don't think she'll have any trouble deciding which units to use."

I quickly pulled up a list of the units she would have access to making.

Air Factory (Moon Base 5)

CLASS: Helicopter Engineer
NAME: Searle
ATTACK: 50
DEFENSE: 100
DESCRIPTION: This is a multi-role aircraft. It can be equipped with a variety of weapons, fuel tanks, and sensors, lending itself to transportation, reconnaissance, or attack missions.

CLASS: Light Attack Helicopter
NAME: Thorne
ATTACK: 100
DEFENSE: 150
DESCRIPTION: This is a light helicopter with two seats, a rapid-firing cannon, and the ability to carry a squad of scouts. Its small armor and low speed make it vulnerable to enemy fire.

CLASS: Heavy Attack Helicopter

NAME: Crow

ATTACK: 1000

DEFENSE: 1000

DESCRIPTION: This is a large helicopter with four seats, a rapid-firing cannon, and the ability to carry a squad of scouts, as well as a medium squad of infantry. Its small armor and low speed make it vulnerable to enemy fire.

CLASS: Heavy Transport Helicopter

NAME: Heron

ATTACK: 100

DEFENSE: 750

DESCRIPTION: This is a large helicopter with four seats, a rapid-firing cannon, and the ability to carry a squad of scouts, a squad of medium infantry, and a squad of light infantry. Its small armor and low speed make it vulnerable to enemy fire.

CLASS: Light Fighter Aircraft

NAME: Kestral

ATTACK: 500

DEFENSE: 500

DESCRIPTION: This is a high-flying aircraft designed to attack other aircraft and defend against lighter aircraft. It is very fast, but lightly armored.

CLASS: Heavy Fighter Aircraft

NAME: Death Bird

ATTACK: 1400

DEFENSE: 1200

DESCRIPTION: The ultimate in aerial death, this aircraft is equipped with nuclear bombs and HEAT (high-explosive, antitank) missiles. It's extremely fast, highly armored, and heavily armed.

CLASS: Light Bomber Aircraft
NAME: Vulture
ATTACK: 2500
DEFENSE: 750

DESCRIPTION: This aircraft is able to rain destruction down on the enemy from a great altitude. It is very fast and very heavily armored, but lightly armed, and drops HEAT bombs with moderate accuracy.

CLASS: Missile Fighter Aircraft
NAME: Agile
ATTACK: 450
DEFENSE: 550

DESCRIPTION: A very fast, lightly armored aircraft that can quickly deliver a very heavy and accurate strike against an enemy. It is equipped with a series of missiles that can easily take down even a Death Bird.

CLASS: Light Transport Aircraft
NAME: Sparrow
ATTACK: 10
DEFENSE: 100

DESCRIPTION: This aircraft is primarily used as a transport, with two seats and the ability to carry a small squad of scouts. It's lightly armored, but very fast and can go into enemy territory without being noticed.

CLASS: Heavy Transport Aircraft
NAME: Rooster

339

ATTACK: 100

DEFENSE: 1000

DESCRIPTION: This aircraft is primarily used as a transport, with four seats and the ability to carry a small squad of scouts, a squad of medium infantry, and a squad of light infantry. It's lightly armored, but very fast and can go into enemy territory without being noticed.

CLASS: Light Radar Aircraft

NAME: Owl

ATTACK: 250

DEFENSE: 250

DESCRIPTION: This is a high-flying aircraft designed primarily as an early warning system. It's not meant to attack enemy units. It is very fast, but lightly armored and lightly armed.

CLASS: Heavy Radar Aircraft

NAME: Eagle

ATTACK: 500

DEFENSE: 750

DESCRIPTION: This fast and highly maneuverable attack jet has one role: to hunt down and destroy all enemy aircraft. It is very heavily armored and very heavily armed, but relatively slow and not ideal for ground operations.

"I've got a few strategies in mind," Anja said. "I want to be flexible, though. That's our key to winning."

"We're going to win this, guys," Haley added.

I nodded, looking around the room.

"Okay, as for commander mech choices, we should go with one of each of the five available," I said.

Dhruv sighed again. "I hate the Diplomacy Commander…"

"We need to have a full spectrum to win this," I said.

I wondered again, briefly, if I should tell them about Haruto's message.

Before I could make up my mind, the lights dimmed and a countdown timer began.

"Everyone get situated," I said. "We're about to start…"

I turned to Haley as the others went to their chairs to sit down before being digitally loaded into the RTS simulation.

"Are you okay?" she asked.

I smiled weakly, bobbing my head back and forth before swooping in to deliver a kiss.

Her genuine smile put me at ease. "See you inside," she said.

"Come on you two bird lovers," Laenard crowed.

"It's love birds," Haley corrected him as we both went to our seats.

As the simulated helmet lowered onto my head, I braced myself.

CHAPTER 30

I stared at a screen in front of me with all the commander choices. As the team had agreed, I went with the soldier bot. The toughest of the commanders, it would allow me to stick around and control my three crucial factories on the planet. The others were quite interesting too. Part of me wished I could play the RTS game more. Then again, I wanted to go home.

Commander Mech Chassis Choices:

Medic
Health: High (7,500)
Speed: Fast (20 feet/second)
Can Jump?: No
Build Power: Normal (10 BP)
Modules Available: Versatile

Soldier
Health: Excellent (10,000)
Speed: Medium (35 feet/second)
Can Jump?: No
Build Power: Normal (10 BP)
Modules Available: Combat / Defense
Scientist

Health: Low (2,000)
Speed: Fast (20 feet/second)
Can Jump? Yes
Build Power: Lower (5 BP)
Modules Available: Research

Engineer
Health: Medium (5,000)
Speed: Slow (2 feet/second)
Can Jump? No
Build Power: Improved (20 BP)
Modules Available: Support

Diplomat
Health: Medium (4,000)
Speed: Slow (3 feet/second)
Can Jump? No
Build Power: Improved (20 BP)
Modules Available: Versatile

Beyond choosing the chassis, I needed to spend my skill points to upgrade my commander mech. With 1,597 mech points based on the level I had achieved in the RPG section of the game, I had quite a few options. I looked over everything available one more time before committing to a final build on the Soldier Chassis. All in the first list were stackable.

Cost	Tech Modules	Stackable Bonuses
30 MP	Advanced targeting system	Plus 10% to hit.
30 MP	Damage booster	Plus 10% damage.
50 MP	High density plating	Defense +50 Speed -2
20 MP	Light armor plates	Defense +25 Speed -1
30 MP	Companion drone	Plus 10 Build Power
50 MP	Battle Drone	Auto Attacks / Defends
25 MP	Nanolathe Assist	Plus 15 Build Power
25 MP	High power servos	Plus 10% speed
1 MP	Autorepair Nanobots	Plus 1 health/second -5 Health Total

The following modules were not stackable, but some of them would prove very useful.

Cost	Tech Modules	Features
750 MP	Lazarus Actuator	Resurrect units.
50 MP	Field radar	Standard Radar 50 miles

100 MP	Radar Jammer	Jams radar in 10 mile radius
150 MP	PCD (Personal Cloaking Device)	Cloaks commander mech
250 MP	ACD (Area Cloaking Device)	Cloaks units in half-mile radius
200 MP	Energy Shield	500 Damage Worth of Protection foir units within 500 feet radius

For weapons, I could go with two small or medium-sized ones or a single massive weapon that would take both hands. I pulled up my options before committing to anything.

Regular Weapons

Cost	Weapon
50 MP	Red Beam Laser
50 MP	Blue Beam Laser (Slow)
50 MP	Flamethrower
50 MP	Machine Gun
100 MP	Missile Launcher (Non-Homing)
150 MP	Rocket Launcher (Homing)
75 MP	Shotgun
250 MP	Sniper Rifle

Super Weapons

Cost	Weapon	Description
500 MP	Nuts!	This huge gun shoots packets of cluster bombs. All the bomblets spread out, doing Area of Effect damage.
500 MP	Sleeper	This grenade launcher propels gas-filled canisters that burst on impact. Inside the canister is a cyanide compound that puts enemies to sleep.
500 MP	Searling	This missile launcher fires an explosive, armor-piercing projectile in a straight line.
500 MP	The Enforcer	This rail gun fires an explosive, hypersonic projectile in a straight line.
500 MP	SLAM	A tactical nuke that leaves no traces of radiation, this powerful weapon fires a missile with a range of 100 miles and will result in destruction in a two-mile radius.
420 MP	Abraham's Staff	When deployed, this large weapon lobs a huge rock at a target. When it hits an enemy, a wave of energy explodes from the target, doing splash damage.
250 MP	Hellcloud Grenades	This launcher fires a grenade that emits a cloud of gas. This cloud is highly flammable, and anyone caught in the cloud will ignite inside.
450 MP	Grapevine	A flamethrower that fires incendiary bullets, it bursts into a whirlwind of fire immediately after a short delay.

500 MP	Blood-thirsty	If you have ever wanted to turn someone into a bomb, this is your gun. It fires a flesh-eating round that causes the target to explode.
750 MP	Armaged-don	This weapon fires nuclear explosive rounds that will bounce off of all surfaces and affect everything in a 50-mile radius. Only enough for one shot. No reloads.

At first, I thought about going with a small weapon for my left hand and a medium weapon for my right. It seemed like the best choice. I also went with a machine gun for my right hand and a shotgun in my left. Then again, maybe one super weapon would be better? I fought with myself over the decision while hoping the others were making good choices.

Which super weapon would I choose? If I went with the Searling, I could take out a whole group of enemies from high ground. If I was on a rooftop, there was little those enemies could do against the Abraham's Staff. I had to be a little careful with that one, though. The Abraham's Staff was too big and imprecise. I could easily knock my own allies off a building with that thing. I could also choose the Grapevine, which would be a nice change of pace from my super machine gun. I could use it to scare the living hell out of the enemies when I burst into a fiery whirlwind. They might even run in panic while I chased them down and killed them. I could even use it to set my own allies on fire while in the throes of battle. It would be hilarious.

Armageddon was a little extreme, but at the same time, it was useful. It would be very helpful in a siege. If some of the defenders in the city had a way to get to that gun, it would be a better choice. Still, who would want to run a nuclear weapon around? It was the most powerful gun, so I was torn. With just over 1,500 MP, I wasn't sure if I could even afford a super weapon. Maybe they were only meant for players who had reached level 20 in the RPG portion of the game? I wasn't sure, but I didn't want to waste any more time. The others might be waiting on me.

First, I tried a balanced build, one without a super weapon.

Chassis: Soldier
Base Health: 10,000
Base Speed: 35 feet/second
Build Power: Normal (10 BP)

Module / Weapon	Cost:
Advanced targeting system x5	150
Damage booster x5	150
Light armor plates x10	200
Battle Drone x6	300
Autorepair Nanobots x100	100
High power servos x10	250
Radar Jammer	100
Machine Gun	50
Rocket Launcher	150

Module / Weapon	Cost:
TOTAL Mech Points	1450

That build left me with quite a few extra mech points. I sighed then started over from scratch, going with less armor and auto repair with better weapons.

Module / Weapon	Cost:
Advanced targeting system x5	150
Damage booster x5	150
Light armor plates x5	100
Battle Drone x3	150
Autorepair Nanobots x100	100
High power servos x10	250
Radar Jammer	100
Sniper Rifle	250
Rocket Launcher	150
TOTAL Mech Points	1410

My second build was better than my first, but I still wasn't happy.

Finally, I came up with something that I felt would work with my strategy:

Module / Weapon	Cost:
Advanced targeting system x4	120
Damage booster x4	120

Light armor plates x5	100
Battle Drone x3	150
Autorepair Nanobots x100	100
High power servos x10	250
Radar Jammer	100
Nuts!	500
TOTAL Mech Points	1450

Dual weapons would be nice, but with the ability to create units in three factories, I wanted to focus on one main weapon. The cluster bomb—aka Nuts!—sounded like just the thing for me. I finalized my choices and went on to the next stage of constructing my commander mech.

Color was next. I wanted something that would stand out. I decided to go with a bright red and white. The combo reminded me of some of the famous soldiers in history. I imagined myself as one of them. I was ready for battle. Finally.

I pressed a button to accept and waited for the others to finish.

After just a few minutes in a black, endless void, I emerged on the moon.

CHAPTER 31

Each of us knew exactly what to do. Dhruv flew to the planet to establish a beachhead on the smallest continent with the sea units and diplomacy factories. Meanwhile, Laenard dropped the research, engineering, combat, and medical factories close to each other.

At the same time, Anja, Haley, and I all worked on building ore processing buildings in a ring around the factories to offer them some protection. We also laid out our one and only Command Center and began producing worker bots to harvest everything we would need to quickly build our economy.

One person doing well in their macro game was cool and all but imagine five hard core RTS players all bringing their A-game at the same time. Yeah, it was incredible. In my experience, the first four minutes of an RTS were the most important. This held true with *Moon Wars* too. While most players in the past had concentrated on setting up a power base on the moon, our plan would be a bit different. Others had dropped to the planet early before, but not with a strategy like ours.

"I've got a problem," Dhruv said over comms.

"What is it?" I asked.

"I've been spotted already, and I didn't expect them so soon. So, I messed up the build order," he said. "I'm being overwhelmed."

"Then counterattack," I said. "Make more frigates and pound the shores until you have a beachhead. You need to defend that diplomacy factory at all costs."

"I'm trying my best!"

"Change of plans," I broadcast to everyone. "Dhruv needs my help. I'm dropping to the planet early."

"Should we come with you?" Haley asked.

"No, not yet. Keep helping Laenard set up our main base for now. We're going to need a lot of energy and ore to pull this off. I'll stay in radio contact."

As the others continued building structures and units on the moon, I flew into space with my mighty commander mech. The journey to the planet was an incredible experience, but I tried to keep my wits about me. In just a few minutes, I was hurtling toward where Dhruv had landed. While falling, I pulled up maps of the area. He had put his diplomacy factory too close to shore, but we couldn't change that fact. I armed my super weapon as I got closer. When my commander punched through the atmosphere, I saw the factory with its defenses.

In an instant, I activated my super weapon, Nuts! Two cluster bombs shot from the mega-sized cannon in my hands, shooting toward the biggest cluster of enemies just outside the diplomacy factory. The explosions were tremendous, taking out five of their medium tanks and two troop carriers. Just as I was about to do it again, I noticed an enemy commander. We would likely run into a lot of them during the battle, but luckily this one was a bit smaller than me. They probably never guessed we would attack this out of the way place so early.

"Keep producing frigates, Dhruv, and keep me covered. I'm going in to take out that commander mech."

"Can do!" he shouted. "I'm getting hit from their commander! I have to dive deep."

I didn't see the rival commander yet, but I wasn't taking any chances. Storing Nuts! (which was a weapon for masses of smaller enemies, not one boss) I fired up my flak cannon. After a few seconds' flight, I found him tracking a pair of Dhruv's frigates and I waited. It was worth risking the frigates for a clean shot at a nonmoving target. And when he did stop, we fired simultaneously. The enemy commander took out a one of the frigates and the explosion damaged the other, but my flak cannon landed a beautiful hit on his shoulder plates that sent him weaving a path across the sea, smoke pouring from his torso. My follow-up shot streaked past him, unfortunately, and he disappeared behind an island, the column of smoke showing that he was still fleeing.

As soon as their commander had retreated, I fired up the Nuts! again and took out the enemies outside the diplomacy factory. Now that the region was clear, it was safe for Dhruv to come back to land again. I flew down to the factory as his commander mech emerged out of the ocean.

"Thanks for the help," he said.

"Don't mention it. I'm going to drop my three factories and start producing early. Since they know we're here, we need to ramp up here quickly."

"Understood," he said.

We both got to work. I launched the nano-set-up commands for our first Infantry, Heavy Tanks, and Heavy Mechs factories. They took about ten minutes to set up completely, anxious minutes where I was constantly checking the timer for them. After they were finished, I started building units. Dhruv would need some back-up if we were going to clear the entire small continent where we had landed.

Gornia, as the locals called it, was about the size of two Australias mushed together. Dhruv had planted his bases on the southern coast which wasn't very populated due to the extreme temperatures. Our commander mechs and units would have little trouble dealing with the cold. I glanced at the build order screen as units began producing.

"I've got ten Taipans and five Rams queued up," I said over comms.

"We're ready to descend to the planet," Haley said.

"Good. We're going to need you, I think, as we push further into this big island."

After sending the new units to the front, I also ordered up several squads of infantry bots. The heavy mechs would've been better, but we didn't have a sufficiently developed economy yet to really do anything major. All the units created had their own limited battle-AI, but I could control them manually via the mini-map if necessary.

"We've got company," Haley said. "We're picking up a large enemy force from the north bearing down on you."

"How soon until you land?"

My question was answered as I looked up and saw Haley's and Anja's commander mechs descending toward us.

"Another minute or two," she replied.

"Dhruv, keep building up frigates for now. We don't want to lose any of the sea we control. I'm going to throw up a few defensive turrets to give us some breathing room."

"I'll help," Haley said as she landed next to me.

"No, you and Anja get your factories up near mine. When you're done, start producing units then come help me if there's time."

"Got it," Haley said.

She blasted her rocket booster and flew toward where I had set up my three factories about half a mile inland. I pulled up the build menu for defensive structures. We didn't have a lot of resources, so I would have to choose carefully.

Sentinel Post—This light defensive structure shoots two non-homing missiles every 3 seconds, doing very light damage. Easy to put up, they're just as easy to take down. While fine for low level units, they will buckle under pressure quickly with the resource cost. Once again, good for blocking lines of space.

Tesla Tower—Standing about four feet off the ground, this laser tower fires a constant stream of light damage to whatever it shoots. Once again, this is a defensive structure and should not be used to assault enemy structures. If the enemy cannot find the tower, they can't destroy it!

Flak Cannon—This structure is similar to the Tesla Tower but does physical instead of electrical damage. This building is a decent choice for base defense, as it gets extra damage from the turret mode and can run without any direction from the player.

Sky-Duster—This swivel machine gun is typically set up above ground on a metal base to increase its firing range and make it more difficult to defeat quickly. However, it can be set up on the ground. Fast firing with an Area of Effect attack, it's really good against light and medium infantry.

Faraday—This EMP turret does no damage but uses an electro-magnetic pulse to disable enemy units for a short period of time. This is a great tool for disabling vehicles and small groups of infantry.

Mortar Sentry—The mortar sentry does not move and fires a constant stream of shells that fall from the sky. The shells have a slow drop and bounce when they hit the ground, making it difficult to target a specific area.

Beam Cannon—This stationary weapon fires a powerful beam of energy at its target. Very effective against smaller targets but suffers from low rate of fire.

Burster—This stationary weapon fires a stream of pods that do light damage and burst apart on contact. The pods will seek out enemies and detonate. It is effective against light units but it has little health, so it does not last long.

Air Defense Tower—This is a stationary weapon that fires a single missile at any flying units. Very effective against small flying units, like drones and homing missiles.

Stun Cannon—This single-shot cannon fires a blue burst of energy that does no damage but stuns its target. Like the Faraday, this is great for disabling vehicles and small groups of units for a few seconds.

Inferno Cannon—This is a stationary weapon that fires two streams of flame at the ground. It is great against armored ground units but does not do so well against flying units, due to its slow projectile speed.

Pulse Cannon—This is a stationary weapon that fires a stream of slow projectiles that detonate on contact. Similar to the Burst Tower, this weapon fires multiple projectiles that detonate on contact. Very effective against groups of infantry.

Bodyguard—This turret fires a constant stream of bullets while the player is in the radius of the turret (another fact that makes them great for base defense). They do little more than distract enemy units, but can function as a distraction.

I decided to go with a mix of Bodyguards, Sky Dusters, and Faradays mostly. With very little time, I had to choose something that would keep them busy long enough for our factories to start pumping out more land units.

My first infantry squad was done as well as two light tanks, but seeing what was coming for us on radar, I was sure it wasn't going to be enough.

Ten minutes later, Haley and Anja's factories were up and running. They quickly started pumping out units, filling up the menu of all my factories.

Haley's voice spoke over the radio, "What do you want us to build?"

"Keep it quick and simple for now. We'll try to overwhelm them with spam units until we can build something decent."

"On it!" Haley cried.

"Can do!" Anja said.

I started laying down defensive turrets around our rapidly forming base. As soon as one finished, I took a few steps to start construction on another. The nano-lathes made building easy, but it still took time and drained our precious resources. Both energy and ore were running low. I found myself worried that we wouldn't have nearly enough.

As the enemy force drew closer, I could see the numbers and types of units coming. The big green blips on the radar were mostly medium sized tanks. There were a lot of air units as well.

"They're right on top of us!" Dhruv said.   The enemy commander mechs blasted their boosters toward us and landed in front of my defensive turrets.

"Take 'em down!" I yelled.

Several of the enemy mechs were hit while taking fire from our turrets, but they kept coming.

"I need back up on the front lines—now!" I shouted. "They're overwhelming these low-level defensive structures too easily!"

"We're coming," Haley said. "I'm sending a bunch of Rovers and Scooters now."

"Great," I said. "Everyone concentrate on repelling this attack. This might be the most important battle of the war."

It felt as though enemy was throwing everything they had on the small continent toward us. I took a shot at one of the enemy commander mechs and forced it to retreat. Our team were able to get in some good hits, but their numbers were overwhelming. Two more enemy commander mechs landed in front of my turrets and began blasting at them. Their heavy machines were doing a lot of damage to the structures.

"They're destroying everything!" Dhruv said.

Haley's and Anja's forces landed next to me. As they rushed in and started blasting the enemy units, I stepped back to let them take over.

"I'm going to assist our outer defenses," I said. "Let me know what you need!"

Now I could leave this spot and hunt out concentrations of enemy troops, Nuts! came into its own. It was perfect for this crisis, blowing massive holes in the formations of infantry and vehicles that had seemed overwhelming just a few moments earlier. After a few minutes of non-stop fire, with my hands burning from the heat of the weapon, the enemy ranks began to thin out. They were running out of units!

Just as I was about to breathe a bit more easily, Laenard came on comms.

"We've got a problem," he said.

I sighed. "What now?"

CHAPTER 32

"I've got an enemy commander landing a few squads of troopers on the moon," Laenard said.

He had a hint of fear in his voice.

"Is it too much for you to handle?"

"Maybe...hold on...no!"

I could access a map of the moon to see the situation and I opened it now. An enemy commander had landed south of our base on the moon. Laenard hadn't dropped an infantry factory or anything else other than defenses and the research facilities.

"Activating defenses now," he said.

I glanced at the radar and saw enemy units coming down from the sky.

"How's everything else?"

"We're doing fine for the most part," Laenard said. "I'm trying to keep the main body of the enemy away from the bases."

"Good, try to get that commander with your troops," I said.

The enemy commander was massing a force of armored infantry. I wasn't sure what exactly he was trying to do, but I didn't like the look of it.

"Haley, take some of the units you have and go on the offensive against the city to the north."

"On it," she replied.

"Dhruv, how are those diplomat units coming along?"

"I've got several built, but I can't get them into the enemy cities up north yet."

"Get moving with what you have!" I said, trying to remain calm. Emotions lost battles.

"I'm moving all diplomat units to the two main cities to the north," Dhruv said.

"Good. Keep me informed. We'll keep fighting them back here and pumping out units."

"Two more energy buildings down!" Laenard said.

I wished I could go back to the moon to help him, but there was still fighting to be done here and my absence during the flight time would be costly.

"Go for the enemy commander," I said. "Once you take him out, it'll be much easier on you."

"I'm setting up a light vehicles factory for support. This commander is NOT taking our moonbase!"

"Good luck." After closing the moon map, I glanced at the radar in my HUD, I saw several lightly armored enemy tanks rolling toward our front line.

"I need air support! Now!"

"Sending four Thornes and a Crow," Anja shot back.

"The sooner the better!" I cried.

I shot off my Nuts!, the super weapon sending explosives among the clusters of light tanks heading toward us. The cooldown time for the weapon was a bit too high for my taste, but it was turning out to be a good weapon choice for our style of play. It was saving our beachhead bases from being overrun in the early part of the game.

"How are things going, Laenard? The radar doesn't look good."

"No time to talk now," he responded.

While waiting for Nuts! to recharge, I took a moment to watch the radar map of the moonbase we had established. The enemy commander was doing well by splitting up his forces into smaller units and attacking from multiple angles.

"Get those missile trucks up!" I said. "You need to spread out to match his units. If you move around in a block you'll be too slow to prevent massive factory damage."

"Already doing it," Laenard said. "Just need more time…"

He stopped talking as a big blob of red dots breached the outer perimeter of the base we had set up on the moon.

"Enemy commander in sight," Laenard said. "I'll take him out now!"

A concentration of newly built missile trucks took out the enemy commander with surprising ease, leaving his army to attack without the same care in placement: now they came on in a mad rush into killing zones that Laenard had prepared with his defensive emplacements.

"Good work, Laenard! Now send your trucks around their flanks!"

"I'm trying!"

With the disaster on the moon averted, I could turn my attention to our multiple fronts on the planet. The first wave of attackers had been repulsed, but we'd lost a lot of defensive structures.

"How are those diplomat drones doing?" I asked. "Dhruv? Can you hear me?"

"Just successfully convinced the two main cities to the north to flip over to our side in exchange for protection."

"That's fantastic news. Anja? Haley?"

I saw the icons representing my teammates on my HUD map of the planet, but neither of them were moving. There were other icons moving around, but I couldn't tell what they were.

"What is it?" I said, getting impatient. "What's the matter with you two?"

"We've got to break the enemy's defenses," Haley said. "Now!"

I could see the enemy's forces in their cities, and they were pretty strong.

"Hold on," I said. "We need to roll out more diplomat units. Converting cities is far less wasteful and we are short of resources down here."

I was in charge. I was the general. I was responsible.

"I'm still building diplomat units," Dhruv said, finally. "Should be a few more soon."

"How many more?" I asked. "Haley! You need to focus. Can you protect those diplomat units long enough to get them into the final two cities?"

"Will do."

"Hold on, I'm coming in for backup," I said.

With the two main cities to the north converted to our side, the stream of enemy units nearby had stalled enough for me to leave my spot and head to Haley.

As I arrived at her side, landing my commander mech, I saw a couple lines of heavy enemy tanks pouring out of the farthest city to the West, getting closer to us.

"I'm going to flank them from the left," I said as I flew up then headed in that direction. "Protect those diplo-bots at all costs!"

As I soared through the air, I commanded my largest unit of Heavy Mechs to head northwest. With a bit of luck on the timing, I would be able to flank the enemy tanks from behind as they turned to face the attack.

"Anja! You seeing this?" I called over the channel. "I need you to back me up against the enemy forces on the ground that are heading towards the diplomat units. I can out-fly them in the air, but I need air support as soon as you can. My cool down time is too slow on Nuts! to do this without you."

"Sending helos and scramble bombers now," she said.

I glanced at the mini-map on my HUD as I hovered stationary in the air a few miles away from the main line of enemy tanks descending on us. This minor battle would be crucial. If we lost the diplomat units after investing so much time in making them, we'd fail to turn the cities and certainly lose our beachhead and eventually the battle.

The wounded enemy commander from earlier was visible among the incoming Heavy Mechs, he was targeting me with what looked like a sniper's rifle!

"Launch Nuts! missile," I said watching it streak away to explode into a giant ball of fire and debris, taking out a cluster of tanks and killing the commander in the process. "That was close!"

A moment later my heart beat faster as Anja's birds streaked in, capitalizing on the confusion to lay waste to hostile armor.

"The enemy is breaking up," Haley said. "They're heading away from the cities!"

"Keep on them Anja! Laenard!" I called out. "What's the status up there?"

"We're driving the invaders back off the moon... slowly," he said, sounding exhausted.

"Hold the line, good buddy. We're making progress!"

Over the next twenty minutes, we took complete control of the smallest continent on the planet. The added economy would help for the next phase of our plan, taking out supply lines and preparing for our next assault. Things had been dicey once or twice, but overall, we were ahead of schedule.

"Commanders!" Anja called across the comms channel. "A large wave of enemy bombers are heading toward the northern cities!"

"Haley, get in there and do what you can," I said. "We'll try to get some air cover, but it'll take a few minutes."

"Got it!" she replied.

I studied the radar on my HUD and saw Haley's commander mech heading toward the city nearest to her, which enemy bombers were already bombarding with heavy explosives. Anja was right. It was another large wave of bombers coming in. We could handle the ones already present, but the next would be more difficult.

"The battle is in your hands now," I said to Haley. Nuts! was almost useless against fast-moving vehicles and aircraft. "I'll support you as much as I can, but it's down to you."

"Incoming!" she cried.

I shot over the city just as a wave of bombs rained down. The city was taking a beating, there was no doubt about that, flames and smoke were everywhere. But Haley was out in front causing mayhem to the arriving bombers.

"Get in there with her," I said. "I'm headed there now."

"I have air cover coming," Anja said. "It'll be in the area in a few minutes."

I followed a group of enemy bombers as they flew back toward their base. With my cannon and despite a lot of misses, I succeeded in taking out two of them, but then I had to stop. I was being drawn too far away.

"The enemy bombers are retreating," Haley said. "They're leaving!"

We had won the day, but the comms channel was silent as each of us reflected on what we had done.

"Come on," I said. "We've driven them off this time, but there's a long way to go before this war is over."

CHAPTER 33

Four hours into the war, things were looking okay but not great.

Laenard was holding his own on the moon and building tons of missile trucks to help defend our resources in the moonbase.

Meanwhile, Anja, Dhruv, Haley, and I were all consolidating our forces on the small continent. As we moved troops and defended our weakest points, I began to scan the map for our next target. My idea was to keep hitting their production hard: wining control of resources; damaging factories and intercepting the transport of resources.

Dhruv had completed three aircraft carriers while Anja had a fleet of thirteen Death Birds ready to rain down destruction wherever I ordered. Right before I gave the order to attack the closest mines on the continent to the north, Haley interrupted me.

"I've got an idea," she said.

"Make it quick. I'm about to order an attack on our next target."

"I think we should go for their diplomacy factory instead of their production."

"Go on," I said, intrigued by her idea.

"It's not defended very well, and they're producing a lot of anti-diplomat units that could stall that part of our overall plan."

"Yeah…" I paused a moment. "That's a good idea. We don't want them taking away our strongest offensive weapon so far. Do we know where their diplomat factory is located?"

"Not yet," Haley said.

"I'm already on it," Anja piped in. "I've got twenty-three Owls and two squadrons of Sparrows scanning the map. We'll know soon enough."

"Great. I'll build some advanced radar on the northern coast. That might help us locate it quicker. Until then, keep building up an equal amount of defensive and offensive units, everyone."

We seemed to be pretty evenly matched with the AI. But then again, in war, anything could happen. I had played enough RTS games over the years to know that a few small mistakes could snow-ball into something terrible quite quickly.

After I finished building the advanced radar tower on the north-ern coast, I began studying the map on my HUD again, searching for the enemy's main diplomat factory.

"Found it," Anja said. "Owls spotted it on the continent to the east."

"Dhruv, how many diplo-bots do you have built?"

"Just over three dozen," he replied.

"Anja, send over a few transports and some Death Birds to escort them. Everyone else, we're heading to the main continent."

"We're not ready," Haley said. "I'm still building mechs."

"We have naval superiority. Take what you have and get them on any available ships we've built, to help land those diplo-bots," I said.

Dhruv dropping to the planet early and building up our naval units first was turning out to have been a good idea.

"On it," Haley said.

"Everyone meet on the eastern side of the continent."

I flew into the air, approaching toward the spot on the map I had marked. As I got closer, I saw that Anja was already there with swarms of planes flying overhead.

"We need to move, people! This is going to take perfect timing if we don't want to lose everything we've already won."

A few minutes later, Dhruv and Haley arrived, followed by the units under their command. We had a pretty good attack force ready.

"Okay, the plan is to drop the diplo-bots as close to the command center of that city as we can," I dropped a pin on their maps. Then we rush their diplomat factory, intercepting any of their diplo bots that come off the production lines. We need to destroy it. Once that city flips to ours, the enemy are likely to throw everything they have at us to clear us out. We need to do as much damage to their military in that battle as we can, while also not losing any ground on this continent we're leaving."

"Should I stay behind?" Dhruv asked.

I shook my head. "No, we need everything for this attack. Haley's idea is a good one, but it's not going to be easy."

"Good luck," Laenard said. "Moonbase is currently stable and still producing units and resources."

370

I flew a few hundred feet into the air, gazing at the massive force of units we had prepared for our assault on the biggest continent on the planet.

"Everyone ready? "I asked.

"For the first time in a long time, yeah," Anja said.

I smiled. "Alright, let's do this!" I ordered. "Drop those diplo-bots! We're going to take that city!"

We rushed over the water as a team. The moment we hit the mainland, things started going south. Enemy forces had prepared quite a defensive line for us.

"I need artillery to take out those defenses, now!" I shouted as I rushed toward one of the blobs of artillery units on the map.

They were protected by a few light vehicles, but I dropped a Nuts! bomb which took out over half the enemy forces in that position. It still wasn't enough. They were showering us with artillery and missiles as we landed on the coast and fought our way forward. I dropped another Nuts! bomb and then moved forward, flanked by Anja and Dhruv. We smashed through their defensive line and kept on attacking, trying to get our diplo-bots as close to the city as possible.

I was scared to even look at the map now, having a feeling that we weren't cutting it close enough. It was too late to do anything about that, though. We were committed and couldn't go back.

By this point, all the enemy's units were flying in, trying to smash into our diplo-bots and destroy them no matter the cost. Had they determined our strategy already?

"Dhruv, what's the status on those diplo-bots?" I asked.

"I'm getting ready to drop them in three, two, one... they're deployed!"

"Everyone protect them while they get close to city walls. We can't lose any of them."

I flew closer to the front line of action. We had advanced about a mile inland, but it still wasn't enough. The enemy was throwing everything at us to keep us out of their territory. I spotted a few enemy units sufficiently static and bunched up together to invite a Nuts! launch and then flew forward, following up with missiles.

A hornet flew over to my position and began attacking me. I turned around and flew toward the coastline, but the hornet chased me with greater speed than I had. Frantically, I looked around for something that could save me, but in the end, I was an easy target. I was so close to the water that I wasn't able to fly back to the group.

"I'm hit!" I cried. "They're jamming my jet pack somehow..."

As I rushed toward the ground, I prepared for the worse. Before I could hit the ground and die, the hornet that was chasing me suddenly exploded into little pieces. I turned around and spotted the reason why. Twenty Death Birds had come in for the kill, destroying the enemy units behind me. I flew back, behind our front line and resumed command of my own units.

"Thanks for the save," I said to Anja over the communicator. "I was a sitting duck."

"Don't worry about it. Now move your people up. We've got them on the run."

"Alright, keep pushing forward to the diplomacy factory now. Take out all the artillery as you go. Our diplo-bots will be crawling up to the city's command center soon."

"Got it."

By the time I got to the front line, the first of the enemy's defensive line was falling. I was about to fly forward when Anja ordered me to stop.

"Wait, let me do my thing first."

Her Death Birds ensured the enemy artillery was destroyed. A moment later, Haley and Dhruv's troops were moving in. I flew forward, pushing through the few units that the enemy still had protecting the factory. It wouldn't be long now.

The diplo-bots must have entered the city's command centre and turned their officers.

> The City of Alqualansi (00432.34, 530.00) has offered to
> assist you.
> Take control?

"We did it!" Haley cried.

All of us were cheering.

"Laenard, do you see the control option? Can you take it, we are too busy tactically to manage a city interface."

"I certainly shall. Well done my human friends, I'm proud of you."

"We can't get lazy, though. The enemy is not going to like this at all."

Capturing the east coast city was a big win. For one thing, the units they had been making were suddenly all ours.

"Any vehicles?" I asked.

"Nope," Anja replied. "Owls are scanning the map. The enemy is falling back and regrouping."

"Great. We should do the same. Dhruv, how are you looking?"

"So far, so good," he replied. "Busy. I'll check in a bit later."

"Let's get a few land factories up to hold our position here while sending out all the diplo-bots and anti-diplo-bots we just got control over."

I got Laernard to pass ownership of all the city's military units to Anja and Haley so they could command them. I had quite a lot going on. Not only was I handling the build order of the factories back on the small continent, I was building new factories to pump out even more units. Slowly but surely, we were beginning to snowball our forces and pick up some momentum. Things were looking great but I was fully on guard against complacency.

"Okay, I want to switch it up a bit," I said. "We should use all these extra diplo-bots to start converting their defensive bunkers to the west to bring them under our control."

"That's brilliant," Haley said. "We can use them to chew up the rest of their forces when they come back at us."

"Good plan, and once those bunkers flip, we should concentrate our offensive efforts on one or two spots of their main defensive line," Anja added.

She placed a marker on the map we all shared. "Move the one to the south a bit more in that direction, but I like it," I said.

All told, we were doing well. We took a moment to regroup our forces on the main continent before putting the next stage of our plan into operation. I had been so caught up in the excitement, I hadn't realized how fast time seemed to be moving—or how well we were doing overall.

"How are you holding up, Laenard?" I asked.

"Good," he replied immediately. "They're more concentrated on the planet and haven't launched a second attack on the moon yet."

"You did good holding them off. Between that and us trouncing them here on the planet, things are looking good."

"I'll check in a little later," Laenard said. "I want to try something."

While I wanted to ask him what he was going to do, I had more pressing matters to attend to. The enemy had regrouped into two large forces, both of which were bearing down on us. Our diplobots had managed to flip three powerful bunkers before being caught moving to a fourth. I had dropped three more factories; infantry, heavy mechs, and heavy tanks. Anja was just building airpads to repair and refuel her planes that kept streaming out from the small continent hundreds of miles away. Haley was building solar collectors and defensive turrets in a way that offered the north side of the city a bit of protection. The sea region to the east was under the control of Dhruv's fleet.

"Incoming," I said coolly.

A barrage of enemy artillery screamed through the air, landing in the city well behind our defense, doing a great deal of damage.

"We need some air support," I said.

"Already on it," Anja replied.

Two squadrons of Sparrows and a half-dozen Eagles soared overhead. Enemy AA fire lit up the darkening sky as they sought out the heavy artillery in back.

"Haley, can you drop another small mechs factory? I need some support for my infantry."

"Can do," she said.

I saw a new factory plop down on the map in our quickly expanding fire-base on the main continent.

Over the next half hour, we fought back their two main groups of units. After losing quite a bit of material to the unexpected flanking fire of our newly acquire bunkers, the enemy forces turned to retreat behind their main defensive line. Nothing felt sweeter than gaining control of an enemy gun and having it rain down death on its own troops. With a bit of luck, we could now implement Anja's plan to break their impressive defensive line and race toward one of the major cities on the western side of the continent.

Everything was going well. I was still tense, of course, and I kept producing units (heavier ones now) and building up a major reserve which I kept in a mass. Losing our units piecemeal wasn't the way to go.

CHAPTER 34

The moment of truth had finally arrived. In addition to all the combat units Anja, Haley, and I had created, Dhruv had positioned several huge battleships off the coast near where we were planning on attacking their defensive line. If he did well, it would create a distraction and allow us to creep toward their line with our next wave of diplo-bots. Meanwhile, Laenard would keep building our economy on the moon and keeping our Command Center safe from an enemy attack. All told, we were in a good position. Still, it wasn't going to be easy.

"Everyone ready?" I asked.

"Ready here," Anja said.

"Good to go," Dhruv replied.

I turned to see Haley's commander mech give me a thumbs-up sign. What with all the trouble we were in, I was glad she was with me.

"Let's do this," I said.

"For the Horde!" Anja shouted.

I cracked a grin then set my units into motion. The plan was to send out a group of raiders first to tank fire from the defensive units. Our diplo-bots would be right behind them, working on converting the enemy structures that could be flipped to control. Unless the enemy had managed to rush up their own diplomatic units, with a bit of luck and good timing we just might pull it off.

Anja backed us up with air cover to prevent the enemy from attacking our raiders while we were trying to reach their defensive line. Meanwhile, I had my diplo-bots rush out and start taking over defense towers and turrets. To my surprise, they were able to convert them at a decent pace.

"It's working," I said. "Two flak turrets converted, and they're tearing up the defensive line."

"We're breaking through to the south too," Haley said. "I'm positioning myself closer."

"Be careful. Don't let them flan—oh, crap! I'm being ambushed."

While our commander mechs were powerful, the enemy had brought up two units of cloaked Brickers. These heavy infantry carried lightning shock-rifles that could stun units—even my commander.

"I'm being overwhelmed. Need back-up, now!"

"Kinda busy here myself," Haley said. "Anja?"

"I'm already on it," she replied. "Death Birds heading your way."

Retreating a bit while trying to keep my diplo-bots working wasn't easy, but I managed to pull it off. I had dropped over 50% of my health and only had about 40% left.

"I need to repair soon," I said.

"What was that you were lecturing me about being careful?" Haley teased.

I grinned as my emotions calmed. "You can tease me about it later."

"Death Birds are diving now," Anja said.

I retreated over a hill just before a group of six heavily armored air units dropped their full payload on the Brickers. Only two of the enemy infantry managed to survive, which continued to come toward me. Did they realize how much they had damaged me? I didn't have time to think about it as I sent a squad of heavy tank raiders to mop them up. At the same time, I built a nano-frame to start healing my commander mech.

While I'd been busy keeping myself in the game, the rest of the team were continuing the assault. I saw on the map that Haley had converted over a dozen enemy turrets and was using them to bust a hole in their line. Her light assault mechs were streaming through the hole, spreading out to do as much damage to their supply line as possible. I glanced at my health which was back up to 60% and climbing.

I had to take another look at the map before I could believe what I was seeing. All along their defensive line, our units were pushing through. We had three dozen of their turrets in our control. Our raiders and diplo-bots were working quickly to hold our gains while Dhruv's ships gave us cover from the sea. We had done it. Okay, we had taken a beating, but we were now inside their army's base and making them pay. Anja had them pinned down from the air, unable to manage a safe withdrawal.

Both Haley and I were concentrating on producing massive amounts of light units to overwhelm them. I watched in horror as radar dots for massive destroyer mechs came alive. The heavier units began eating our lighter units for lunch. Not only that, but they were hitting them with the weapons I had worried about: Tesla lasers, heavy missile launchers, and more.

"Oh no," I said. "Get those fighters to harass them. Use their healing towers to your advantage."

"Too late," Anja replied. "They've dropped their cloak."

I watched as another group of six Death Birds flew in to try to take out an enemy commander. It was a well-executed attack, but in the end, the attack failed. The enemy commander mech retreated behind a line of Crabs, heavy spider-bots that fired huge projectiles that did major damage to anything they hit, including their own defensive towers. They were working on taking them out instead of converting them back to their control, which would help us a little. I still didn't see how we could keep our momentum going. They were outproducing us as they had more resources on this continent and I could really tell whenever a wave of their reinforcements arrived.

"They're taking out my ships," Dhruv said.

I scanned his units on the map, seeing them blink out of existence one after another.

"Two heavy battleships gone," he said. "It'll take me a while to replace them on the front line."

"Don't worry about it," I said. "Just make sure you protect our main base on the small continent. Hold the line there..."

"I've got problems too," Haley said.

I looked over at the radar map again, seeing a host of enemy units coming at us. Haley's light assault mechs were already moving into defensive positions while the heavy tank raiders were quickly creating a line of defense. I was so focused on the radar map that I almost missed the fact that the enemy had dropped their cloak again. They were simply riding on their hover-bikes past our radar off to the side. I changed my view angle to see what they were doing. Suddenly, I had a sharp suspicion.

"Oh no. They're trying to flank us with a second attack wave. We need to start using our commander mechs offensively."

"That's dangerous," Dhruv said.

"We don't have a choice at this point. We need to hold this city."

The moment I hit 100% health, I shot up into the air, flying toward where a group of our light raiders were trying to wear down some assault tanks. I shot my Nuts! cannon, cringing at the sight of several of our units exploding along with their heavy tanks.

"Hey, watch it!" Haley said. "I've not replaced those raider mechs with heavier assault mechs yet."

"Sorry," I said sheepishly. "This gun is Nuts!"

Dhruv groaned at my bad pun in the middle of the battle. Was it a pun? I didn't have time to think about it as I saw two enemy commander mechs moving toward me.

"They're double-teaming me," I said. "Some air support would be nice right about now."

"I've got two Eagles I can send, but that's it," Anja said. "They're on their way now."

As the two enemy commander mechs approached me, I held my ground. One of the enemy mechs fired a volley of missiles. I dodged them, but not enough to avoid most of the damage they did to my mech. Meanwhile, the other enemy commander was moving in fast. Within seconds, I found myself on the defensive.

"Haley?" I said.

"On my way," she replied. "But I'm still working on ramping up production."

I could see the huge numbers of enemy units crossing a desert toward the battle front. It was going to be suicide to try to keep up our efforts to wipe out their army's base. Even if we somehow did win, we'd lose a lot of units that would be hard to replace. I'd need a way to distract them. I'd need—

"What are you doing?" Haley asked.

"Uh, stalling for time," I said. "I have an idea."

"What's that?" she asked.

"Just keep them busy," I replied. "I'll be right there."

"I'm on it, but please be careful."

This was going to be tricky, but it just might work. My idea was to sacrifice a few of my heaviest units, self-destructing them close to the two enemy commander mechs bearing down on me. They only had three left while we had all five. If I could take out these two, we might just have a chance.

"Come on," I mumbled. "Come on. Turn around."

When the two huge mechs turned to face me, I rushed several units toward them. They both shot off salvos of missiles to take out some of my units, but a few got through. I self-destructed them right next to the commander mechs. While it wouldn't be enough to destroy them completely, I was hoping it would buy me enough time for Haley to arrive.

"Fire!" I said, targeting the nearest commander.

As the enemy commander turned to face me, I shot several volleys of shells at it. My next shot was a volley of missiles. This time the missiles were filled with delayed-action explosives. The enemy commander had to have realized my plan as it immediately started moving away, but not fast enough. I used my missiles to knock out its left leg.

"Yes!" I shouted.

I watched as the left leg fell, but it didn't explode like I had expected. Instead, the commander simply moved the rest of its body over the leg and kept fighting. It was still firing, but it was doing a lot of damage to itself in the process.

"Haley, you need to hurry," I said.

I took aim at the enemy commander's right foot, but the enemy commander was now firing at me. I had to keep moving to avoid the salvos of missiles.

"I'm on my way," Haley said.

"Another one of my heavy air units is down," Anja said. "They're slaughtering us."

I watched as a Death Bird dropped out of the sky. With a loud screech, it dived toward our two enemy commander mechs. The enemy commander that had lost a leg turned, firing at the Death

Bird. At the same time, Haley's heaviest assault mechs were approaching. Five of them. I watched them, trying to gauge if they would be enough.

Two more of our heavy air units went down in the sky.

"How's that second wave coming?" I asked.

"Right on time," Dhruv said.

I looked down at the map, seeing what looked like a fleet of ships heading toward our captured city. While we did have a defensive line, it was fragile at best. It wouldn't take much for them to push through.

"We're starting to take heavy casualties," Anja said. "We should think about abandoning this city and regrouping on the other continent with our reserves."

"Hang in there, everyone," I said.

I scanned the map, seeing Haley arrive just in time. Together, we fought the two forward enemy commander mechs, beating them back. The enemy commander that had lost a leg was still shooting at me as I looked down at the status of the enemy forces. They had already been closing in on our city, but now they were at the walls.

"There's no time to spare," I shouted, rushing toward the commander.

I pushed my assault mech as hard as I could, looking out at the enemy base in the haze of smoke and debris. More of our mechs were going down, including two of Haley's

"It's time to finish with you," I said, taking aim at the enemy commander's other leg.

I fired a barrage of missiles, destroying it completely. Haley rushed in bravely killed the commander with a barrage of heavy machine gun fire from close up. The enemy commander mech exploded brilliantly, doing more damage to the other commander mech beside it.

"Heads up below," Anja shouted.

I saw a squad of a dozen Eagles zooming toward our position on the map. When they arrived, they fired a barrage of missiles at the other commander mech. It exploded, but not before it had managed to destroy one of the Eagles.

"One of my Eagles is down," Anja said.

"That was a good trade," I said. "They're down to just one commander mech now. We've got this if we can—"

I stopped speaking as a massive explosion in our main base on the smaller island registered on the map. Half my factories were gone.

"Dhruv?"

"Sneak attack," he said. "I'm trying to salvage what I can and push them off."

Multi-front wars made it difficult to keep everything under control.

"Anja, go help Dhruv with everything you've got. With their two commander mechs down, they're retreating here for now." I'd seen the enemy troops on the desert pause and fall back.

"On it," she said.

Anja's radar dot raced toward the smaller continent.

"Haley? You with me?"

"Always," she said. "What are you thinking?"

I was about to speak when two cloaked squads materialized and hit our position.

"Retreat!" I shouted as rail-guns pounded us from up close.

I shot into the air with Haley close behind. We retreated to the city walls.

The enemy's main defensive line in front of their army base still had two massive holes in it, but they were working on closing them both. If we didn't do something soon, they'd have a chance to regain their bunkers and turrets and continue their assault.

"How's Dhruv doing?" I asked.

"He's got the enemy on the run," Anja said. "But it's not easy."

I watched as our mechs once more pushed past our bunkers and pressed on into the enemy base, which was to the west of me. Enemy mechs were still pouring out of their base, but they were cut down by the defenses we had flipped. However, away from that action there were still several open spots where they could flank us. I directed my mechs towards one of them, to the south. And just over a rise they discovered a sizeable force of enemy troops and their last commander mech.

At once my units took a massive pounding and I pulled the survivors back toward me.

"We're losing ground quickly," Haley said from beside me, looking southwards.

I had no choice but to keep retreating. Only when the city's wall defences came into play would I hope to be able to turn this engagement around. The enemy commander mech was heavy and was having a hard time keeping up with my units, but they were still firing their large guns and doing considerable amounts of damage to our lighter armor. Plumes of smoke from damaged vehicles made for a very bleak scene.

"Dhruv, are you there?" I shouted.

"We're here," he said. "But we need to get more help soon."

"Any sign of a second wave?" I asked.

"No, but I need more mechs here or this base will fall."

"Roger that," I said, "I've got your back." It was time to commit my reserve. Wanting to concentrate on the last enemy commander, I assigned all my heavy reserves over to Dhurv.

"What…? Mate, this is exactly what we needed."

"Good luck down there." Then I turned to Haley. "Let's prepare a final assault to go after that last commander mech."

"Should we abandon this city and regroup on the small continent?" she asked.

"No, we can handle this…"

"Are you sure about that?" she asked.

"No, I'm not sure, but together, I know we can do great things."

"I'm smiling right now," she said. "You can't see, but…"

"Watch out!" I cried.

A salvo of long-range ballistic missiles rained down on us from out of nowhere. Had they been cloaked? I had no time to figure it out as I leapt away into the air. Haley followed, but the explosion still managed to take out about 20% of my health. Even worse, to the east our attack had come to nothing, a mass of enemy units had arrived, plugging the two holes we'd managed to open in their defensive line.

"We had them," Haley said.

"It was a perfect plan," I said. "You've gotta admit that much."

"It was," she said.

"Hang in there," I said.

I looked over to the south, seeing two more enemy mechs coming over that last set of hills. We had to hold out as long as we could.

"They're coming," Haley said.

"Here we go," I said, getting into position.

As soon as the enemy commander mech came into view, I opened fire. It turned to face me, returning fire with a laser rifle. I dodged the laser blasts as best as I could, hitting back with missiles, but they didn't seem to do much damage.

"It's too powerful," I said, ducking below the slot in the city wall I'd been firing through. "They're coming toward us en masse."

Just as things were about to become even more dire, I heard Laenard come on.

"Did someone order a pie pizza?" he asked.

I wanted to correct his mistranslation, but the sight of thousands of our attack units landing behind enemy lines gave me pause.

"We did, indeed! Good to see you, Laenard!"

His landing a sizable force of medium and heavy units inside the city defenses gave us a bit of hope. Laenard himself led a charge west, towards the last bunker that remained active and ours.

"Get out of there, Laenard!" I shouted. "We need you safe."

"Might as well go out in a blaze of glory," he said.

"Not today, my friend. Everybody get to his position, now! He needs backup."

"I'm on it!" Haley said, giving me a wave as she took off."

I watched her radar dot flying toward Laenard's position.

I turned my mech back to face south and risked a look through the slot. A barrage of projectiles flashed all around me. My remaining units outside the wall were all out of action and it looked like the enemy might make a breakthrough here.

"We need to take out that last commander mech. If we can do that, we've got the game. They're being very reckless with it because they have a chance of retaking the city right now," I said.

"Agreed," Haley said.

"I'm sending all my air units to you guys now," Anja said. "We've got the small continent back under our control."

"And I've got several missile cruisers heading your way," Dhruv said. "They don't have enough range to reach your position, but they'll give the enemy something to worry about on their beaches."

"Sounds good, but come along as well," I said. "We'll risk our continent for the sake of a shot at their last commander. Haley, how are you doing?"

"I'm well on my way to Laenard. I've got him covered from city side, there's nothing going to get behind him."

"Good."

"I'm going to keep my mediums here to try and hang on until Anja's and Dhruv's units get here," I said.

"That sounds like a good idea," Haley replied.

My mech was now taking ricochet damage, but I had enough firepower to shoot back, varying position and always keeping low. I could feel the heat of my mech rising, but I had a few units hurrying over from factory production lines that I hadn't used yet.

"We're going to ambush this guy," I said. "Keep your mechs out of range of their commander's radar and use cloaking on your units if you have it."

I switched to my radar. I could see Haley's mech pushing west, and I could see the enemy forces around Laenard's mech begin to retreat. I switched back to the thermal imaging.

"Haley, I've got a visual on the commander mech. I'm going to fire a long-range missile at him. It'll be hard to miss," I said.

"Gotcha," she replied.

My missile was almost out of range, but I launched it anyway, trusting that it would hit its mark.

"Damn, that was a close one," Haley said.

"I missed again?" I said, surprised.

"It was close. A few feet of clearance. It managed to dodge your missile, but it hit some of their jeeps."

"Damn," I said. "They're going to start getting paranoid now."

"Once Laenard pushes them further back here, they'll have to start taking risks," Haley said.

"Agreed."

"Dhruv, Anja, it looks like the enemy is making a counter-push towards me on the south wall. Are you guys ready?" I asked.

"We're ready," Anja said.

"Ready here, too," Dhruv said.

"Haley, we're going to spring the ambush. Try to make your way to Laenard and get him out of there. If we get all five of us onto one, we'll win this game."

I watched Haley's radar dot approach Laenard's position. All around me, enemy units were slowly starting to advance and the city defenses were crumbling under the constant barrage of enemy fire.

"I'm falling back," I said. "Meet me at the command center. We'll trap him in the streets.

"Their commander's radar is lighting up like a Christmas tree," Haley replied.

"Good, he's making a mistake right now," I said.

"Looks like they're preparing to charge the southern wall," Haley said.

"I was thinking the same thing."

"Do you have enough units to hold them?" Haley asked.

"No, but if we are all in place in time, we can take the commander," I said.

"We might not have time for that," Haley said.

"Why not?"

"Here they come," she said.

"Hold on," Dhruv said. "I've got an idea."

"What?" I asked as the factory in front me went up in an explosion of brick, glass and smoke.

"I've been building an Experimental Diplo-bot."

"Oh?"

"That's why my sea forces were a bit weak," he admitted. "This Experimental Diplo-bot can convert enemy commanders, though."

"I see where you're going," I said.

"The only problem is that it has basically no armor. Any hit will likely destroy it completely, wasting everything I put into building it."

Part of me wanted to lecture him about deviating from our main plan and diverting resources toward an expensive experimental build, but his idea had merit. In one fell swoop, we could take control of their last remaining enemy commander mech and win the game.

"I think it's a good idea to bring it in," I said.

"You do?" he asked, surprised.

"We need to keep adjusting as we go along," I said. "And right now, the initiative is with them. They might get the command center here and flip the city on us."

"Right, right," he said. "It's on the way. It'll be a bit tricky with this many enemy units around."

"The enemy is concentrating around their commander," Haley said. "It looks like they're going to put up a fight."

"We're going to have to be careful a few minutes," I said to Haley.

"Understood," she replied.

"Anja, if you can hit their south side army with some more of those Death Birds, we might be able to try to bring Dhruv's bot to their commander," I said. "Haley, Laenard and I will try to hold the command center until you get here and then we'll risk everything on that counter-stroke."

"I've got a better idea," Anja said. "I'm building a cloaked transport plane to carry the Experimental Diplo-bot and drop it near their last commander."

"Alright," I said, turning my mech around. "That's smart and means we can concentrate on defense."

"Good," said Haley, "because there are a lot of reinforcements coming in from the west. They really want to push us back."

I routed my mech back toward the defensive turrets of the city's command center. On the radar, I could see Haley's mech approaching Laenard's position as the enemy forces began to form up in a formidable mass ahead of them.

Suddenly, a building to my south collapsed with two Tortoises emerging from the rubble.

"I can see the enemy commander," I said. "We've got a bunch of units in the way."

"Stay safe!" Anja shouted. "Another three minutes."

"I'm trying, but their bombardment is too thick here."

I fired a projectile salvo at the advancing enemy troops, but it didn't do much damage. I switched to missiles and fired another salvo. I watched as my missiles reached the enemy tanks and turned them into a cloud of fire.

"Got them," I said. "That'll slow them up."

I got a few rifle shots off at the enemy commander but was unable to hit it.

"How's that Diplo-bot drop plan coming?" I asked.

"I've got the transport built," Anja said. "We're loading the bot now. It's kinda big."

While I could have looked up the stats on the units, I didn't have time. All my attention was focused on making sure my arriving unit were funneled into holding our defensive line. The enemy commander was surrounding himself with even more medium and heavy units while he slowly moved forward, eating through any of our defenses it encountered.

"Operation Diplo-bot drop is underway," Dhruv said proudly.

I took a deep breath, wondering if our last-ditch effort would pay off or not. We had started well enough, but with all the resources the enemy had already established on the planet, it was hard to keep that momentum going. We were probably bound to lose this city. On the bright side, we had managed to take out four of their five commander mechs. Just one more, and we would win the game.

After Haley and Laenard landed near me, we fought together on the front line. All the time, I had an eye on the radar blip of the cloaked transport heading in our direction.

"We need to keep that commander mech distracted," I said. "Send everything we have at it from all directions. Anja will land the transport and Dhruv will use the Diplo-bot to convert."

Our opponents kept creeping toward us as we valiantly fought to stop them from reaching the command center. Missiles flew overhead, the intense rattle of railguns was sometimes drowned out by explosions that shook the ground and from out of the dust, enemy infantry kept coming, no matter how well we picked them off.

At last, Dhruv's Experimental Diplo-bot dropped from an uncloaked transport in a great billow of smoke and landed next to the enemy commander. As the mechs around him turned to blast the intruding vehicle, the Diplo-bot's force field went up. It quickly erected an energy shield that was nearly as large as the enemy commander's mech itself. It had to be heavy, but it shielded the Experimental Diplo-bot just long enough for its conversion beam to drop from its underside.

"Come on, Diplo-bot, come on," I muttered. "Get that thing converted."

"It's working!" Dhruv yelled. "I've almost got it converted…"

A huge explosion nearby got my attention. Please tell me that wasn't…

"Report!" I shouted, my heart racing.

"That was me," Laenard said. "I took out a Ram."

"Still converting," Dhruv said.

I kept firing everything I had while issuing orders to all the units under my command, which typically were destroyed almost as soon as they entered the battle.

"Seventy percent converted," Dhruv reported.

"Come on…just a little longer…"

"Eighty five percent…"

"I'm being overwhelmed," Laenard said.

"Haley?"

"On it," she said.

From the corner of my eye, I saw her leap over the shell of a burning half-track and seconds later the sounds of battle from that direction intensified.

"Ninety-five percent converted…"

"The enemy commander is nearly converted," I said. "Just hold out a little longer."

And all of a sudden, we had won.

Dhruv had successfully converted the last enemy commander. The moment it joined our side, the simulation ended.

Everything around me faded as the game ended with a victory for us.

As far as I knew, it was the first time anyone had beaten *Moon Wars*.

CHAPTER 35

Back in the virtual staging area, I patiently waited for the head gear to raise into the ceiling before I jumped up and pumped my fist. "Yes! We did it!"

"I can't believe we're the first players to beat *Moon Wars*," Haley said.

She stepped toward me. I slipped an arm around her waist and pulled her close. The jubilation flowing through my veins demanded a physical outlet.

"I always knew I'd be on the first winning team," Dhruv said.

His braggadocio claims didn't even affect me. Anja and Laenard were also both excited. We had been a team and it had paid off.

As the others hugged and high-fived, I turned to Laenard. "So, what do you think? Did we do it right?"

He nodded. "I was impressed. We cooperated, we had a united purpose, we were steadfast. We followed your lead."

I smiled and gave him a high-five. "Thanks for believing in me." I paused, then admitted, "when you told me you had that experimental diplo-bot, I was mad at first."

Dhruv grinned. "I was hoping it would pay off. You guys giving me the opportunity is what made it work, though."

"We all did our part," I said.

"Protecting the main base on the moon frightened me at first," Laenard said, "however, I was confident we would succeed as a team."

"Your aircraft builds and deployment made all the difference too, Anja."

She shrugged it off, but I could tell she was proud we had done so well.

"I still don't believe we're the first ones to beat the game," Haley said.

"Yeah...and where's Que?" I glanced around, not seeing him. "What now? Do we go back to our bodies?"

"I hope so," Laenard said. "This was an experience, but I wish to be back home."

"I would like to return to my body as well." Anja's voice was dreamy.

"I would like to see my family again," Dhruv said.

"I have to admit...I'd like to get back to my own body," I said.

"You really want to get back to college and tests?" Haley teased.

I grinned. "Well, not really. But I'm not sure I want to live in a world where I'm just a digital being."

"Yeah, it's been fun and all, but I'm ready to go home," Anja said.

She looked around the staging area. I squeezed Haley a bit tighter.

"I have to admit I thought I lost it for us when I started to lose control of the small continent," Dhruv said.

"Yeah, it was good you spoke up and asked for help," I said. "Together, we shut that down real quick."

"Did you guys like when I came down to the planet and saved the day?" Laenard asked.

"It was really cool!" Anja said.

"You really ended up being a hero," I said. "I thought our chances were actually pretty good after that hit you took."

"I'm just glad we won," Haley said.

"Well, I guess we'll have to see what happens," I said. "Guys, we won the game!"

"Yeah!" Dhruv shouted.

The others joined in. "We did it!"

My heart swelled. We had done the impossible.

I quickly came crashing back to reality. Que missing was beginning to get to me.

"Look," Anja said. "There's messages coming in from other players."

I turned a large viewscreen on one of the walls. Messages from all sorts of players rolled in.

HoverGodde: Fantastic style! Good job!

FroogleGog: Loved that you used cloak to win!

FuriousShadow333: I love that you didn't excess your metal at all and you used line move!

KingSted: You guys are amazing! No one else even came close to the moon base.

Manu21: Well done! I'm so happy for you all.

PrO_aNDY: Great job, guys! Brilliant show!

DroneDregs: Fantastic playthrough! Loved the strategy!
AnarchiDaAdmin: Nice! Good game all around!
KingLicho: Good job! You guys really handled it well!
SnuggleTurtle: Diplo-bots > Domi Rovers!

I grinned as the congratulations kept pouring in. How many people had been digitized to play Moon Wars? From the flow of comments, it was hundreds.

While I enjoyed the praise and delight of the other players, all that was important was that we had done it and would hopefully all be sent home.

"Laenard, I'm so happy to have had you on the team," I said.

"The fondness is mutual," he replied.

I patted him on the back as we continued to watch the messages roll in.

"Guys, this is amazing!" Anja said. "I feel like a rock star."

"That's because you are," I said. "So are we."

Haley snorted a laugh. She was looking at the messages and smiling. "This is going to be how you feel next year when we get back, the year you graduate."

"I hope so," I said, my voice quiet. "I want to be someone. I want to do something with my life."

"You will," she said then added, "We will."

Overcome with the moment, I swooped in for a kiss. Haley responded favorably. We kissed, lost in the bliss of the moment.

"Do you two mind? I've got important news," Que said from behind us.

I spun around. "Haruto! We did it."

"You did, indeed, my boy. I hope my little tip helped," he said.

"A little. We had to adjust on the battlefield, but we did it."

"What do you mean Haruto?" Dhruv asked.

"You haven't told them?" Que asked.

I shook my head. "We've been a bit busy."

"Um, what's he talking about?" Anja asked.

"Yeah, I want to know too," Haley added.

I took a deep breath as the others all stared at me.

"He did nothing wrong," Que said. "I am Haruto. I asked Alex to keep my secret."

That wasn't entirely true, but I kept my mouth shut as he continued.

"I guess this would be a good time to explain myself."

"Yeah, why did you bring us here?" Dhruv asked.

"This game simulation was fun, but I do not take kindly to being trapped here," Laenard said.

"You're the one that digitized us all," Anja interjected. "Why should we trust you?"

Que frowned and took a step back from the rest of us. We were all digital projections, but the tension in the room was ramping up.

"I had to do what I did," Que said. "You don't understand. You don't have all the facts. All this was vitally necessary. Each time the *Moon Wars* simulation ran, another dimension was affected. Things quickly got out of control…"

His voice trailed off. Evidently the others were wondering what to make of this, as no one spoke until I said, "You need to tell us everything. Start from the beginning."

"Very well," Que said. "We have a bit of time, and you deserve the whole story. I never meant it to be this way, to take you from here and you from there and bring you all here. I had to try to find someone to win, though. No AI could have succeeded. Organic entities were needed to defeat them. You're proof of it."

"I'm still confused," Anja muttered.

"Yes, as confused as a butterfly on toast," Laenard added.

I turned to him, started to speak, then thought better of it. Turning back to Que, I asked, "What do you mean 'them'? Who were we playing against?"

"I'll answer that," he continued. "First though, you have to understand that parallel universes are real. In one of them, a group of powerful AI developed. What started as a thought experiment for a primitive quantum network soon became sentient. It took only a few million years to conquer the entire universe in that dimension. That amount of time is nothing for beings like them... like me. Another half-million years and they found a way to cross to other dimensions to conquer parallel universes. This went well at first, but they soon had opposition, one of their own who did not agree with the goal of conquest."

"You?" I asked.

"Yes. Me. I was able to mount a resistance every time they launched their first campaign, but again and again they defeated me. So, each time the aggressive AI broached a new universe I would cross in secret with them and seek out the best RTS players on the alt-Earth in that universe and try to recruit them."

"You found me through getting me to play the game."

"Yes, my boy," Que said. "I recruited you and Haley through the *Moon Wars* game."

I turned to Haley. Her brow was furrowed, but she still looked beautiful. She shrugged. We both turned back to Que as he continued.

"I brought you into this particular universe, where the AI were initiating their invasion, to create a winning strategy that can beat the AI. Now you've shown the way, I can replicate this information and save countless worlds."

"That's mighty human of you," Dhruv grumbled.

Que smiled as if it were a compliment rather than an insult.

"And now that you have done this, you can send us all to our homesteads?" Laenard asked.

If we did get home, I was going to miss having him around.

"Not back, exactly, more like sideways, but it will feel like you've never been away."

"I can't wait," Haley said.

"Me either." I squeezed her hand.

"As soon as you're ready," Que said. "There won't be a way for you to contact each other when I send you back."

I turned to the others. Everything I'd been through came flooding back to me. The first time in the simulation, losing my first RTS battle—and winning my second.

"We've been through a lot together," I said. "All of you have helped me become a better person, and I appreciate that."

The others nodded. I continued.

"While I'm happy to be going home, I'm going to miss each of you. Laenard, you're the first of your species I've come across, but if the others are anything like you, I hope we come into contact someday. And Dhruv, we butted heads a bit, but you taught me a lot, and I respect you."

Dhruv smiled slightly and nodded.

"Anja, you give me hope that the future is indeed a cool place. Thank you all for making this experience slightly tolerable."

"What about me?" Haley asked.

I turned and placed a hand on her cheek.

"We can talk more once we get back home…"

I gave her another kiss. The others mocked and cheered us.

"Are you ready?" Que asked. "I'm running out of time. There's more work to be done…"

"I'm ready." I took Haley's hand in mine. "Take us home."

"Sit in the seats," Que said. "The process will be painless. Well, mostly harmless."

He laughed nervously as the rest of us got into the seats we'd sat in for the game within the simulation.

As the head-pieces slowly lowered from the ceiling, I stole a quick glance at Haley and mouthed the words, "I love you."

She smiled just as everything faded to black.

CHAPTER 36

"Well, I guess it didn't work," Professor Lambert said.

I sat up quickly as if I'd just been shocked or slammed back into my body.

"Whoa," Haley said.

"Did you two smoke anything before you came to see me tonight?" the professor asked. "You're both acting really peculiar."

"It worked," I said. "How long were we gone?"

"What do you mean it worked? I flipped the switch and nothing happened."

I turned to Haley. She shrugged. I turned back to Professor Lambert.

"Are you sure? Was there a power surge or anything?" I asked.

"I'd like to know that too," a man in a black suit said, startling the rest of us.

Haley, Professor Lambert, and I all turned to see several men in suits with dark visors despite the low lighting in the basement lab.

"What exactly is this machine you've been building?" the man asked.

"It's nothing," Professor Lambert said. "Just some underclassmen wasting my time."

He turned to glare at Haley and I. Had we just dreamed everything? I couldn't wait to get Haley alone and talk to her. She wasn't saying anything about what had happened to us which was just as well, what with the stranger barking questions.

"We were alerted to an off-the-scale surge in power usage on campus," the man said. "But this? This is a set-up to grow marijuana, isn't it?"

The man stepped into the light, revealing the word DEA on his ball cap. Haley took off her head gear and stood; I copied her action.

"We've got nothing to do with this," she said. "This was all just a bad prank."

"I told you it wouldn't be funny," I snapped back, really getting into character.

"Wait, wait, no," Professor Lambert said. "They told me it was a device to digitize minds…"

"Is that so, professor?" the DEA agent asked.

"Can we go, please?" I asked. "We have class in the morning."

"Get out of here," the main agent said. "We've got your information."

Haley and I rushed out of the building. Outside, we saw the unmarked black SUVs that had trailed us earlier. Whatever the DEA made of the headsets, it looked like they were now more focused on Lambert's drug growing operation.

"That was…surreal," Haley said.

We were walking back to my housemate's car.

"That's a good word for it." I stopped and turned to her. "You remember what happened, right? *Moon Wars*? Que?"

406

She nodded. "And Anja and Laenard and even Dhruv…"

"Okay, good," I said, relieved.

"We still don't have any answers," she said.

"Que said it's an AI from another universe battling itself. I mean, is that so strange?"

"Um, yeah." She laughed nervously. "I love you too, by the way."

"Oh, you heard me say that back there before we left?"

"You're not wiggling out of it now." She smiled and wrapped her arms around my waist. "What's it they say about two people being good together if they can survive a long road trip together without going insane? Is this the gamer version of that, maybe?"

"Sure hope so." I smiled. "I mean, we'd be a mess if we didn't love each other and all, right?"

"True." She kissed me. "Let's get back to your place and get some rest. I'm exhausted for some reason."

"Yeah, me too."

Hand in hand, we walked to the car and soon I was driving back to Hudson House.

As we drove past Alberto's I glanced at Haley. "Hungry?"

"Too tired." She suddenly sat up. "That's odd, they changed the name to Marco's."

She was right, the glowing sign in my mirror had the same red and white colors, the same style of lettering but a different name. I guessed Marco must have taken over from Alberto, and it must have happened while we were gone. I was too tired to give it much thought. We had beaten *Moon Wars*, and I looked forward to leveling up my relationship with Haley.

ABOUT THE AUTHOR

Paul Bellow is a full-time writer living in the USA.

A long-time LitRPG enthusiast, Paul created the forum website https://litrpgforum.com/ and the Facebook page https://www.facebook.com/litrpgreads and its group https://www.facebook.com/groups/litrpgforum. You are welcome to message him.

Paul participates in a number of LitRPG communities, including:

https://www.reddit.com/r/litrpg/
https://www.facebook.com/groups/LitRPGAuthorsGuild
https://www.facebook.com/groups/LitRPGsociety
https://www.facebook.com/groups/LitRPGGroup
https://www.facebook.com/groups/LitRPGAdventures
https://www.facebook.com/groups/LitRPGForum
https://www.facebook.com/groups/LitRPG.books
https://www.facebook.com/groups/GameLitSociety

LEVEL UP PUBLISHING

Level Up publishing specialises in LitRPG and GameLit books. If you have enjoyed *Moon Wars* you might be interested in our other titles, which can be found at www.levelup.pub/books

To join our mailing list for news about forthcoming books and opportunities to be an ARC reader, just fill in the form on that page.

You can also find us on:

Facebook @LUPublishing

Twitter @LevelUpPub

www.ingramcontent.com/pod-product-compliance
Lightning Source LLC
Chambersburg PA
CBHW021125260626
47169CB00005B/1455